CLASSIC ROBERT B. PARKER

Promised Land

Looking for Rachel Wallace

Robert B. Parker

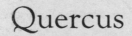

First published in Great Britain in 2011 by

Quercus
21 Bloomsbury Square
London
WC1A 2NS

Promised Land first published in 1976 by Delacorte Press/Seymour Lawrence
Copyright © 1976 by Robert B. Parker

Looking for Rachel Wallace first published in 1980
by Delacorte Press/Seymour Lawrence
Copyright © 1980 by Robert B. Parker

Copyright © 2011 by the Estate of Robert B. Parker

A CIP catalogue record for this book is available
from the British Library

ISBN 978 1 84916 289 0

10 9 8 7 6 5 4 3 2 1

Printed and bound in Great Britain by Clays Ltd, St Ives plc

Contents

Promised Land   1

Looking for Rachel Wallace   247

PROMISED LAND

For Joan, David and Daniel

1

I had been urban-renewed right out of my office and had to move uptown. My new place was on the second floor of a two-storey round turret that stuck out over the corner of Mass Ave and Boylston Street above a cigar store. The previous tenant had been a fortuneteller and I was standing in the window scraping her patchy gilt lettering off the pane with a razor blade when I saw him. He had on a pale-green leisure suit and a yellow shirt with long pointed collar, open at the neck and spilling onto the lapels of the suit. He was checking the address on a scrap of paper and looking unhappily at the building.

'I've either got my first client in the new office,' I said, 'or the last of Madam Sosostris'.'

Behind me Susan Silverman, in cut-off jeans and a blue-and-white-striped tank top, was working on the frosted glass of the office door with Windex and a paper towel. She stepped to the window and looked down.

'He doesn't look happy with the neighborhood,' she said.

'If I were in a neighborhood that would make him happy, he couldn't afford me.'

The man disappeared into the small door beside the

tobacco store and a minute later I heard his footsteps on the stairs. He paused, then a knock. Susan opened the door. He looked uncertainly in. There were files on the floor in cardboard boxes that said FALSTAFF on them, the walls still smelled of rubber-based paint and brushes and cans of paint clustered on newspaper to the left of the door. It was hot in the office and I was wearing only a pair of paint-stained jeans and worse sneakers.

'I'm looking for a man named Spenser,' he said.

'Me,' I said. 'Come on in.' I laid the razor blade on the windowsill and came around the desk to shake his hand. I needed a client. I bet Philo Vance never painted his own office.

'This is Mrs Silverman,' I said. 'She's helping me to move in. The city knocked down my old office.' I was conscious of the trickle of sweat that was running down my chest as I talked. Susan smiled and said hello.

'My name is Shepard,' he said. 'Harvey Shepard. I need to talk.'

Susan said, 'I'll go out and get a sandwich. It's close to lunchtime. Want me to bring you back something?'

I shook my head. 'Just grab a Coke or something. When Mr Shepard and I are finished I'll take you to lunch somewhere good.'

'We'll see,' she said. 'Nice to have met you, Mr Shepard.'

When she was gone, Shepard said, 'Your secretary?'

'No,' I said. 'Just a friend.'

'Hey, I wish I had a friend like that.'

'Guy with your kind of threads,' I said, 'shouldn't have any trouble.'

'Yeah, well, I'm married. And I work all the time.'

There was silence. He had a high-colored square face with crisp black hair. He was a little soft around the jowls and his features seemed a bit blurred, but he was a good-looking guy. Black Irish. He seemed like a guy who was used to talking and his failure to do so now was making him uncomfortable. I primed the pump.

'Who sent you to me, Mr Shepard?'

'Harv,' he said. 'Call me Harv, everyone does.'

I nodded.

'I know a reporter on the New Bedford *Standard Times*. He got your name for me.'

'You from New Bedford, Harv?'

'No, Hyannis.'

'You're gonna run for President and you want me for an advance man.'

'No.' He did a weak uncertain smile. 'Oh, I get it, Hyannis, hah.'

'Okay,' I said, 'you're not going to run for President. You don't want me as an advance man. What is your plan?'

'I want you to find my wife.'

'Okay.'

'She's run away, I think.'

'They do that sometimes.'

'I want her back.'

'That I can't guarantee. I'll find her. But I don't do kidnaping. If she comes back is between you and her.'

'She just left. Me and three kids. Just walked out on us.'

'You been to the cops?'

5

He nodded.

'They don't suspect, if you'll pardon the expression, foul play?'

He shook his head. 'No, she packed up her things in a suitcase and left. I know Deke Slade personally and he is convinced she's run off.'

'Slade a cop?'

'Yes, Barnstable police.'

'Okay. A hundred a day and expenses. The expenses are going to include a motel room and a lot of meals. I don't want to commute back and forth from Boston every day.'

'Whatever it costs, I'll pay. You want something up front?'

'Harv, if you do run for President I will be your advance man.'

He smiled his weak smile again. I wasn't taking his mind off his troubles.

'How much you want?'

'Five hundred.'

He took a long wallet from his inside coat pocket and took five hundred-dollar bills out of it and gave them to me. I couldn't see how much was left in the wallet. I folded them up and stuck them in my pants pocket and tried to look like they were joining others.

'I'll come down in the morning. You be home?'

'Yeah. I'm on Ocean Street, 18 Ocean Street. When do you think you'll get there? I got just a ton of work to do. Jesus, what a time for her to walk out on us.'

'I'll be there at nine o'clock. If you got pictures of her,

6

get them ready, I'll have copies made. If you have any letters, phone bills, charge-card receipts, that sort of thing, dig them out, I'll want to see them. Check stubs? List of friends or family she might go to? How about another man?'

'Pam? Naw. She's not interested much in sex.'

'She might be interested in love.'

'I give her that, Spenser. All she could ever use.'

'Well, whatever. How about the kids? Can I talk in front of them?'

'Yeah, we don't hide things. They know she took off. They're old enough anyway, the youngest is twelve.'

'They have any thoughts on their mother's whereabouts?'

'I don't think so. They say they don't.'

'But you're not certain?'

'It's just, I'm not sure they'd tell me. I mean, I haven't talked with them much lately as much as I should. I don't know for sure that they're leveling with me. Especially the girls.'

'I have that feeling all the time about everybody. Don't feel bad.'

'Easy for you.'

'Yeah, you're right. You have anything else to tell me?'

He shook his head.

'Okay, I'll see you tomorrow at nine.'

We shook hands.

'You know how to get there?'

'Yes,' I said. 'I know Hyannis pretty well. I'll find you.'

'Will you find her, Spenser?'

'Yep.'

2

When Susan Silverman came back from her Coke I was sitting at the desk with the five one-hundred-dollar bills spread out in front of me.

'Whose picture is on a one-hundred-dollar bill?' I said.

'Nelson Rockefeller.'

'Wrong.'

'David Rockefeller?'

'Never mind.'

'Laurance Rockefeller?'

'Where would you like to go to lunch?'

'You shouldn't have shown me the money. I was ready to settle for Ugi's steak and onion subs. Now I'm thinking about Pier 4.'

'Pier 4 it is. Think I'll have to change?'

'At least wipe the sweat off your chest.'

'Come on, we'll go back to my place and suit up.'

'When you get a client,' Susan said, 'you really galvanize into action, don't you?'

'Yes, ma'am. I move immediately for the nearest restaurant.'

I clipped my gun on my right hip, put on my shirt and

left the shirt-tail out to hide the gun and we left. It was a ten-minute walk to my apartment, most of it down the mall on Commonwealth Ave. When we got there, Susan took the first shower and I had a bottle of Amstel while I called for reservations. In fact I had three.

Pier 4 looms up on the waterfront like a kind of Colonial Stonehenge. Used brick, old beams and a Hudson River excursion boat docked alongside for cocktails. A monument to the expense account, a temple of business lunches. One of the costumed kids at the door parked my convertible with an embarrassed look. Most of the cars in the lot were newer and almost none that I could see had as much gray tape patching the upholstery.

'That young man seemed disdainful of your car,' Susan said.

'One of the troubles with the culture,' I said. 'No respect for age.'

There'd be a wait for our table. Would we care for a cocktail in the lounge? We would. We walked across the enclosed gangplank to the excursion boat and sat and looked at Boston Harbor. Susan had a margarita, I had some Heinekens. Nobody has Amstel. Not even Pier 4.

'What does your client want you to do?'

'Find his wife.'

'Does it sound difficult?'

'No. Sounds like she's simply run off. If she has she'll be easy to find. Most wives who run off don't run very far. The majority of them, in fact, want to be found and want to come home.'

'That doesn't sound particularly liberated.'

'It isn't particularly liberated but it's the way it is. For the first time the number of runaway wives exceeds the number of runaway husbands. They read two issues of *Ms* magazine, see Marlo Thomas on a talk show and decide they can't go on. So they take off. Then they find out that they have no marketable skills. That ten or fifteen years of housewifing has prepared them for nothing else and they end up washing dishes or waiting table or pushing a mop and they want out. Also lots of them get lonesome.'

'And they can't just go home,' Susan said, 'because they are embarrassed and they can't just go crawling back.'

'Right. So they hang around and hope someone looks for them.'

'And if someone does look for them it's a kind of communicative act. That is, the husband cared enough about them to try to find them. It's a gesture, in its odd way, of affection.'

'Right again. But the guilt, particularly if they have kids, the guilt is killing them. And when they get home things are usually worse than they were when they left.'

Susan sipped at her margarita . 'The husband has a new club to beat her with.'

I nodded. 'Yep. And partly he's right. Partly he's saying, hey, you son of a bitch. You ducked out on us. You left me and the kids in the goddamned lurch and you ran. That's no reason for pride, sweetheart. You owe us.'

'But,' Susan said.

'Of course, but. Always but. But she's lived her life in

terms of them and she needs a chance to live it in terms of her. Natch.' I shrugged and drank the rest of my beer.

'You make it sound so routine.'

'It is routine in a way,' I said. 'I've seen it enough. In the sixties I spent most of my time looking for runaway kids. Now I spend it looking for runaway mommas. The mommas don't vary the story too much.'

'You also make it sound, oh I don't know, trivial. Or, commonplace. As if you didn't care. As if they were only items in your work. Things to look for.'

'I don't see much point to talking with a tremor in my voice. I care enough about them to look for them. I do it for the money too, but money's not hard to make. The thing, in my line of work at least, is not to get too wrapped up in caring. It tends to be bad for you.' I gestured to the waitress for another beer. I looked at Susan's drink. She shook her head.

Across the harbor a 747 lifted improbably off the runway at Logan and swung slowly upward in a lumbering circle before heading west. LA? San Francisco?

'Suze,' I said. 'You and I ought to be on that.'

'On what?'

'The plane, heading west. Loosing the surly bonds of earth.'

'I don't like flying.'

'Whoops!' I said, 'I have trod on a toe.'

'Why do you think so?'

'Tone, babe, tone of voice. Length of sentence, attitude of head. I am, remember, a trained investigator. Clues are my game. What are you mad at?'

'I don't know.'

'That's a start.'

'Don't make fun of me, Spenser. I don't exactly know. I'm mad at you, or at least in that area. Maybe I've read *Ms* magazine, maybe I spend too much time seeing Marlo Thomas on talk shows. I was married and divorced and maybe I know better than you do what this man's wife might be going through.'

'Maybe you do,' I said. The maître d' had our table and we were silent as we followed him to it. The menus were large and done in a stylish typeface. The price of lobster was discreetly omitted.

'But say you do,' I picked up. 'Say you understand her problem better than I do. What's making you mad?'

She looked at her menu. 'Smug,' she said. 'That's the word I was looking for, a kind of smugness about that woman's silly little fling.'

The waitress appeared. I looked at Susan. 'Escargots,' she said to the waitress. 'And the cold crab.' I ordered assorted hot hors d'oeuvres and a steak. The waitress went away.

'I don't buy smug,' I said. 'Flip, maybe, but not smug.'

'Condescending,' Susan said.

'No,' I said. 'Annoyed, maybe, if you push me. But not at her, at all the silliness in the world. I'm sick of movements. I'm sick of people who think that a new system will take care of everything. I'm sick of people who put the cause ahead of the person. And I am sick of people, whatever sex, who dump the kids and run off: to work, to booze, to sex, to success. It's irresponsible.'

The waitress reappeared with our first course. My platter of hot hors d'oeuvres included a clam casino, an oyster Rockefeller, a fried shrimp, a soused shrimp and a stuffed mushroom cap.

'I'll trade you a mushroom cap for a snail,' I said to Susan.

She picked a snail up in the tongs and put it on my plate. 'I don't want the mushroom,' she said.

'No need for a hunger strike, Suze, just because you're mad.' I poked the snail out of its shell and ate it. 'Last chance for the mushroom.'

She shook her head. I ate the mushroom.

Susan said, 'You don't know why she ran off.'

'Neither of us does.'

'But you assumed a feminist reason.'

'I should not have. You are right.'

'I'll take that soused shrimp,' Susan said. I put it on her plate with my fork.

I said, 'You know they're my favorite.'

She said, 'And I know you don't care that much for the mushroom caps.'

'Bitch.'

Susan smiled. 'The way to a man's remorse,' she said, 'is through his stomach.'

The smile did it, it always did it. Susan's smile was Technicolor, Cinemascope and stereophonic sound. I felt my stomach muscles tighten, like they always did when she smiled, like they always did when I really looked at her.

'Where in hell were you,' I said, 'twenty years ago?'

'Marrying the wrong guy,' she said. She put her right hand out and ran her forefinger over the knuckles on my left hand as it lay on the tabletop. The smile stayed but it was a serious smile now. 'Better late than never,' she said.

The waitress came with the salad.

3

I was up early and on my way to Hyannis before the heavy rush-hour traffic started in Boston. Route 3 to the Cape is superhighway to the Sagamore Bridge. Twenty years ago there was no superhighway and you went to the Cape along Route 28 through the small southern Mass towns like Randolph. It was slow but it was interesting, and you could look at people and front yards and brown mongrel dogs, and stop at diners and eat hamburgers that were cooked before your very eyes. Driving down Route 3 that morning the only person I saw outside a car was a guy changing a tire near a sign that said PLYMOUTH.

As I arched up over the Cape Cod Canal at the Sagamore Bridge, Route 3 became Route 6, the Mid-Cape Highway. In the center strip and along each roadside was scrub white pine, and some taller, an occasional maple tree and some small oak trees. At high points on the road you could see ocean on both sides, Buzzards Bay to the south, Cape Cod Bay to the north. In fact the whole Cape echoed with a sense of the ocean, not necessarily its sight and not always its scent or sound. Sometimes just the sense of vast space on each side of you. Of open brightness stretching a long way under the sun.

Route 132 took me into Hyannis center. The soothing excitements of scrub pine and wide sea gave way to McDonald's and Holiday Inn and prefab fence companies, shopping malls and Sheraton Motor Inns, and a host of less likely places where you could sleep and eat and drink in surroundings indistinguishable from the ones you'd left at home. Except there'd be a fishnet on the wall. If Bartholomew Gosnold had approached the Cape from this direction he'd have kept on going.

At the airport circle, I headed east on Main Street. Hyannis is surprisingly congested and citylike as you drive into it. Main Street is lined with stores, many of them branches of Boston and New York stores. The motel I wanted was at the east end of town, a big handsome resort motel with a health club and a good restaurant of Victorian décor. A big green sign out front said DUNFEY'S. I had stayed there two months ago with Brenda Loring and had a nice time.

I was in my room and unpacked by nine thirty. I called Shepard. He was home and waiting for me. Ocean Street is five minutes from the motel, an extension of Sea Street, profuse with weathered shingles and blue shutters. Shepard's house was no exception. A big Colonial with white cedar shingles weathered silver, and blue shutters at all the windows. It was on a slight rise of ground on the ocean side of Ocean Street. A white Caddie convertible with the top down was parked in front. A curving brick path ran up to the front door and small evergreens clustered along the foundation. The front door was blue. I rang the bell and heard it go bing-bong inside. To the left of the house was a beach, where the street curved. To the right was a high hedge concealing the neighbors' house next door. A blond teenage girl in a very small lime-green bikini answered the door. She looked maybe seventeen. I carefully did not leer at her when I said, 'My name's Spenser to see Mr Shepard.'

The girl said, 'Come in.'

I stepped into the front hallway and she left me standing while she went to get her father. I closed the door behind me. The front hall was floored in flagstone and the walls appeared to be cedar paneling. There were doors on both sides and in the rear, and a stairway leading up. The ceilings were white and evenly rough, the kind of plaster ceiling that is sprayed on and shows no mark of human hand.

Shepard's daughter came back. I eyed her surreptitiously behind my sunglasses. Surreptitious is not leering. She might be too young, but it was hard to tell.

'My dad's got company right now; he says can you wait a minute?'

'Sure.'

She walked off and left me standing in the hall. I didn't insist on port in the drawing room, but standing in the hall seemed a bit cool. Maybe she was distraught by her mother's disappearance. She didn't look distraught. She looked sullen. Probably mad at having to answer the door. Probably going to paint her toenails when I'd interrupted. Terrific-looking thighs though. For a little kid.

Shepard appeared from the door past the stairs. With him was a tall black man with a bald head and high cheekbones. He had on a powder-blue leisure suit and a pink silk shirt with a big collar. The shirt was unbuttoned to the waist and the chest and stomach that showed were as hard and unadorned as ebony. He took a pair of wraparound sunglasses from the breast pocket of the jacket and as he put them on, he stared at me over their rims until very slowly the lenses covered his eyes and he stared at me through them.

I looked back. 'Hawk,' I said.

'Spenser.'

Shepard said, 'You know each other?'

Hawk nodded.

I said, 'Yeah.'

Shepard said to Hawk, 'I've asked Spenser here to see if he can find my wife, Pam.'

Hawk said, 'I'll bet he can. He's a real firecracker for finding things. He'll find the ass off of a thing. Ain't that right, Spenser?'

'You always been one of my heroes too, Hawk. Where you staying?'

'Ah'm over amongst de ofays at de Holiday Inn, Marse Spensah.'

'We don't say ofays anymore, Hawk. We say honkies. And you don't do that Kingfish dialect any better than you used to.'

'Maybe not, but you should hear me sing "Shortnin' Bread," babe.'

'Yeah, I'll bet,' I said.

Hawk turned toward Shepard. 'I'll be in touch, Mr Shepard,' he said. They shook hands and Hawk left. Shepard and I watched him from the front door as he walked down toward the Caddie. His walk was graceful and easy, yet there was about him an aura of taut muscle, of tight-coiled potential, that made it seem as if he were about to leap.

He looked at my '68 Chevy, and looked back at me with a big grin. 'Still first cabin all the way, huh, baby?'

I let that pass and Hawk slid into his Cadillac and drove away. Ostentatious.

Shepard said, 'How do you know him?'

'We used to fight on the same card twenty years ago. Worked out in some of the same gyms.'

'Isn't that amazing, and twenty years later you run into him here.'

'Oh, I've seen him since then. Our work brings us into occasional contact.'

'Really?'

'Yeah.'

'You know, I could sense that you knew each other pretty well. Salesman's instinct at sizing people up, I guess. Come on in. Have a cup of coffee or something? It's pretty early for a drink, I guess.'

We went into the kitchen. Shepard said, 'Instant okay?'

I said, 'Sure,' and Shepard set water to boiling in a red porcelain teakettle.

The kitchen was long with a divider separating the cooking area from the dining area. In the dining area was a big rough-hewn picnic table with benches on all four sides. The table was stained a driftwood color and contrasted very nicely with the blue floor and counter tops.

'So you used to be a fighter, huh?'

I nodded.

'That how your nose got broken?'

'Yep.'

'And the scar under your eye, too, I'll bet.'

'Yep.'

'Geez, you look in good shape, bet you could still go a few rounds today, right?'

'Depends on who I went them with.'

'You fight heavyweight?'

I nodded again. The coffee water boiled. Shepard spooned some Taster's Choice from a big jar into each cup. 'Cream and sugar?'

'No thank you,' I said.

He brought the coffee to the table and sat down across from me. I'd been hoping maybe for a doughnut or a muffin. I wondered if Hawk had gotten one.

'Cheers,' Shepard said, and raised his cup at me.

'Harv,' I said, 'you got more troubles than a missing wife.'

'What do you mean by that?'

'I mean I know Hawk, I know what he does. He's an enforcer, what the kids on my corner used to call a legbreaker. He freelances and these days he freelances most often for King Powers.'

'Now wait a minute. I hired you to find my wife.

20

Whatever business I'm in with Hawk is my business. Not yours. I'm not paying you to nose around in my business.'

'That's true,' I said. 'But if you are dealing with Hawk, you are dealing with pain. Hawk's a hurter. You owe Powers money?'

'I don't know a goddamned thing about Powers. Don't worry about Powers or Hawk or anybody else. I want you looking for my wife, not peeking into my books, you know?'

'Yeah, I know. But I've spent a lot of years doing my business with people like Hawk. I know how it goes. This time Hawk came and talked to you, pleasantly enough, spelled out how much you owed and how far behind you were on the vig and when you had to pay it by.'

'How the hell do you know what we were talking about?'

'And at the end he told you, with a friendly enough smile, what would happen if you didn't pay. And then I came and he said goodbye politely and he left.'

'Spenser, are you going to talk about this anymore or are you going to get to work on what I hired you for?'

'Harv. Hawk means it. Hawk is a bad man. But he keeps his word. If you owe money, pay it. If you haven't the money, tell me now, and we can work on the problem. But don't bullshit me, and don't bullshit yourself. If you're dealing with Hawk you are in way, way, far way, over your head.'

'There's nothing to talk about. Now that's it. There's no more to say about it.'

'You may even be in over mine,' I said.

4

I had a sense, call it a hunch, that Shepard didn't want to talk about his dealings with Hawk, or King Powers or anybody else. He wanted to talk about his wife.

'Your wife's name is Pam, right?'

'Right.'

'Maiden name?'

'What difference does that make?'

'She might start using it when she took off.'

'Pam Neal.' He spelled it.

'Folks living?'

'No.'

'Siblings?'

He looked blank.

'Brothers or sisters,' I said.

'No. She's an only child.'

'Where'd she grow up?'

'Belfast, Maine. On the coast, near Searsport.'

'I know where it is. She have friends up there she might visit?'

'No. She left there after college. Then her folks died. She hasn't been back in fifteen years, I'd bet.'

'Where'd she go to college?'

'Colby.'

'In Waterville?'

'Yeah.'

'What year she graduate?'

'1954, both of us. College sweethearts.'

'How about college friends?'

'Oh, hell, I don't know. I mean we still see a lot of people we went to school with. You think she might be visiting someone?'

'Well, if she ran off, she had to run somewhere. She ever work?'

He shook his head strongly. 'No way. We got married right after graduation. I've supported her since her father stopped.'

'She ever travel without you, separate vacations, that sort of thing?'

'No, Christ, she gets lost in a phone booth. I mean she's scared to travel. Anywhere we've ever gone, I've taken her.'

'So if you were her, no work experience, no travel skills, no family other than this one, and you ran off, where would you go?'

He shrugged.

'She take money?' I said.

'Not much. I gave her the food money and her house money on Monday and she took off Thursday, and she'd already done the food shopping. She couldn't a had more than twenty bucks.'

'Okay, so we're back to where could she go. She needed

help. There's not a lot you can do on twenty bucks. What friends could she have gone to?'

'Well, I mean most of her friends were my friends too, you know. I mean I know the husband and she knows the wife. I don't think she could be hiding out anywhere like that. One of the guys would tell me.'

'Unmarried friend?'

'Hey, that's a problem. I don't think I know anybody who isn't married.'

'Does your wife?'

'Not that I know. But, hell, I don't keep track of her every move. I mean she had some friends from college I don't think ever married. Some of them weren't bad either.'

'Could you give me their names, last known address, that sort of thing?'

'Jesus, I don't know. I'll try, but you gotta give me a little time. I don't really know too much about what she did during the day. I mean maybe she wrote to some of them, I don't know.'

'Any who live around here?'

'I just don't know, Spenser. Maybe Millie might know.'

'Your daughter?'

'Yeah, she's sixteen. That's old enough for them to have girl talk and stuff, I imagine. Maybe she's got something you could use. Want me to get her?'

'Yeah, and old phone bills, letters, that kind of thing, might be able to give us a clue as to where she'd go. And I'll need a picture.'

'Yeah, okay. I'll get Millie first, and I'll look for that stuff while you're talking with her.' He hadn't come right home and done it like I told him. Maybe I lacked leadership qualities.

Millie didn't look happy to talk with me. She sat at the table and turned her father's empty coffee cup in a continuous circle in front of her. Shepard went off to collect the phone bills and letters. Millie didn't speak.

'Any thoughts on where your mother might be, Millie?'

She shook her head.

'Does that mean you don't know or you won't say.'

She shrugged and continued to turn the coffee cup carefully.

'You want her back?'

She shrugged again. When I turn on the charm they melt like butter.

'Why do you think she ran off?'

'I don't know,' she said, staring at the cup. Already she was starting to pour out her heart to me.

'If you were she,' I said, 'would you run off?'

'I wouldn't leave my children,' she said, and there was some emphasis on the *my*.

'Would you leave your husband?'

'I'd leave him,' she said, and jerked her head toward the door her father had gone through.

'Why?'

'He's a jerk.'

'What's jerky about him?'

She shrugged.

'Work too hard? Spend too much time away from the family?'

She shrugged again.

'Honey,' I said. 'On the corner I hang out, when you call someone a jerk you're supposed to say why, especially if it's family.'

'Big deal,' she said.

'It's one of the things that separate adults from children,' I said.

'Who wants to be an adult?'

'I been both and adult is better than kid.'

'Sure,' she said.

'Who's your mother's best friend?' I said.

She shrugged again. I thought about getting up and throwing her through the window. It made me feel good for a minute, but people would probably call me a bully.

'You love your mother?'

She rolled her eyes at the ceiling and gave a sigh.

'Course,' she said, and looked back at the circles she was making with the coffee cup. Perhaps I could throw it through the window instead.

'How do you know she's not in trouble?'

'I don't know.'

'How do you know she's not kidnaped?'

'I don't know.'

'Or sick someplace with no one to help her.' Ah, the fertility of my imagination. Maybe she was the captive of a dark mysterious count in a castle on the English moors. Should I mention to the kid a fate worse than death?

'I don't know. I mean my father just said she ran away. Isn't he supposed to know?'

'He doesn't know. He's guessing. And he's trying to spare you in his jerky way from worse worry.'

'Well, why doesn't he find out?'

'Ahhh, oh giant of brain, come the light. What the hell do you think he's hired me for?'

'Well, why don't you find out.' She had stopped turning the coffee cup.

'That's what I'm trying to do. Why don't you help? So far your contribution to her rescue is four I-don't-knows and six shrugs. Plus telling me your old man's a jerk but you don't know why.'

'What if she really did run away and doesn't want to come back?'

'Then she doesn't come back. I almost never use my leg irons on women anymore.'

'I don't know where she is.'

'Why do you suppose she left?'

'You already asked me that.'

'You didn't answer.'

'My father got on her nerves.'

'Like how?'

'Like, I don't know. He was always grabbing at her, you know. Patting her ass, or saying gimme a kiss when she was trying to vacuum. That kind of stuff. She didn't like it.'

'They ever talk about it?'

'Not in front of me.'

'What did they talk about in front of you?'

'Money. That is, my old man did. My old lady just kind of listened. My old man talks about money and business all the time. Keeps talking about making it big. Jerk.'

'Your father ever mistreat your mother?'

'You mean hit her or something?'

'Whatever.'

'No. He treated her like a goddamned queen, actually. That's what was driving her crazy. I mean he was all over her. It was gross. He was sucking after her all the time. You know?'

'Did she have any friends that weren't friends of your father's?'

She frowned a little bit, and shook her head. 'I don't think so. I don't know any.'

'She ever go out with other men?'

'My mother?'

'It happens.'

'Not my mother. No way.'

'Is there anything you can think of, Millie, that would help me find your mother?'

'No, nothing. Don't you think I'd like her back. I have to do all the cooking and look out for my brother and sister and make sure the cleaning lady comes and a lot of other stuff.'

'Where's your brother and sister?'

'At the beach club, the lucky stiffs. I have to stay home for you.'

'For me?'

'Yeah, my father says I have to be the hostess and stuff

till my mother comes home. I'm missing the races and everything.'

'Life's hard sometimes,' I said. She made a sulky gesture with her mouth. We were silent for a minute.

'The races go on all week,' she said. 'Everybody's there. All the summer kids and everybody.'

'And you're missing them,' I said. 'That's a bitch.'

'Well, it is. All my friends are there. It's the biggest time of the summer.'

So young to have developed her tragic sense so highly.

Shepard came back in the room with a cardboard carton filled with letters and bills. On top was an 8 $^1/_2$ × 11 studio photo in a gold filigree frame. 'Here you go, Spenser. This is everything I could find.'

'You sort through any of it?' I asked.

'Nope. That's what I hired you for. I'm a salesman, not a detective. I believe in a man doing what he does best. Right, Mill?'

Millie didn't answer. She was probably thinking about the races.

'A man's gotta believe in something,' I said. 'You know where I'm staying if anything comes up.'

'Dunfey's, right? Hey, mention my name to the maître d' in The Last Hurrah, get you a nice table.'

I said I would. Shepard walked me to the door. Millie didn't. 'You remember that. You mention my name to Paul over there. He'll really treat you good.'

As I drove away I wondered what races they were running down at the beach club.

5

I asked at the town hall for directions to the police station. The lady at the counter in the clerk's office told me in an English accent that it was on Elm Street off Barnstable Road. She also gave me the wrong directions to Barnstable Road, but what can you expect from a foreigner? A guy in a Sunoco station straightened me out on the directions and I pulled into the parking lot across the street from the station a little before noon.

It was a square brick building with a hip roof and two small A dormers in front. There were four or five police cruisers in the lot beside the station: dark blue with white tops and white front fenders. On the side was printed BARNSTABLE POLICE. Hyannis is part of Barnstable Township. I know that but I never did know what a township was and I never found anyone else who knew.

I entered a small front room. To the left behind a low rail sat the duty officer with switchboard and radio equipment. To the right a long bench where the plaintiffs and felons and penitents could sit in discomfort while waiting for the captain. All police stations had a captain you waited for when you came in. Didn't matter what it was.

'Deke Slade in?' I asked the cop behind the rail.

'Captain's busy right now. Can I help you?'

'Nope, I'd like to see him.' I gave the cop my business card. He looked at it with no visible excitement.

'Have a seat,' he said, nodding at the bench. 'Captain'll be with you when he's free.' It's a phrase they learn in the police academy. I sat and looked at the color prints of game birds on the walls on my side of the office.

I was very sick of looking at them when, about one-ten, a gray-haired man stuck his head through the door on my side of the railing and said, 'Spenser?'

I said, 'Yeah.'

He jerked his head and said, 'In here.' The head jerk is another one they learn in the police academy. I followed the head jerk into a square shabby office. One window looked out onto the lot where the cruisers parked. And beyond that a ragged growth of lilacs. There was a green metal filing cabinet and a gray metal desk with matching swivel chair. The desk was littered with requisitions and flyers and such. A sign on one corner said CAPTAIN SLADE.

Slade nodded at the gray metal straight chair on my side of the desk. 'Sit,' he said. Slade matched his office. Square, uncluttered and gray. His hair was short and curly, the face square as a child's block, outdoors tan, with a gray-blue sheen of heavy beard kept close shave. He was short, maybe five-eight, and blocky, like an offensive guard from a small college. The kind of guy that should be running to fat when he got forty, but wasn't. 'What'll you have?' he said.

'Harv Shepard hired me to look for his wife. I figured you might be able to point me in the right direction.'

'License?'

I took out my wallet, slipped out the plasticized photostat of my license and put it in front of him on the desk. His uniform blouse had short sleeves and his bare arms were folded across his chest. He looked at the license without unfolding his arms, then at me and back at the license again.

'Okay,' he said.

I picked up the license, slipped it back in my wallet.

'Got a gun permit?'

I nodded, slipped that out of the wallet and laid it in front of him. He gave it the same treatment and said, 'Okay.'

I put that away, put the wallet away and settled back in the chair.

Slade said, 'Far as I can tell she ran off. Voluntary. No foul play. Can't find any evidence that she went with someone. Took an Almeida bus to New Bedford and that's as far as we've gone. New Bedford cops got her description and all, but they got things more pressing. My guess is she'll be back in a week or so dragging her ass.'

'How about another man?'

'She probably spent the night prior to her disappearance with a guy down the Silver Seas Motel. But when she got on the bus she appeared to be alone.'

'What's the guy's name she was with?'

'We don't know.' Slade rocked back in his chair.

'And you haven't been busting your tail looking to find out either.'

'Nope. No need to. There's no crime here. If I looked into every episode of extramarital fornication around here I'd have the whole force out on condom patrol. Some babe gets sick of her husband, starts screwing around a little, then takes off. You know how often that happens?' Slade's arms were still folded.

'Yeah.'

'Guy's got money, he hires somebody like you to look. The guy he hires fusses around for a week or so, runs up a big bill at the motel and the wife comes back on her own because she doesn't know what else to do. You get a week on the Cape and a nice tan, the husband gets a tax deduction, the broad starts sleeping around locally again.'

'You do much marriage counseling?'

He shook his head. 'Nope, I try to catch people that did crimes and put them in jail. You ever been a cop? I mean a real one, not a private license?'

'I used to be on the States,' I said. 'Worked out of the Suffolk County DA's office.'

'Why'd you quit?'

'I wanted to do more than you do.'

'Social work,' he said. He was disgusted.

'Any regular boyfriends you know of?'

He shrugged. 'I know she slept around a little, but I don't think anybody steady.'

'She been sleeping around long or has this developed lately?'

'Don't know.'

I shook my head.

Slade said, 'Spenser, you want to see my duty roster? You know how many bodies I got to work with here. You know what a summer weekend is like when the weather's good and the Kennedys are all out going to Mass on Sunday.'

'You got any suggestions who I might talk to in town that could get my wheels turning?' I said.

'Go down the Silver Seas, talk with the bartender, Rudy. Tell him I sent you. He pays a lot of attention and the Silver Seas is where a lot of spit gets swapped. Pam Shepard hung out down there.'

I got up. 'Thank you, captain.'

'You got questions I can answer, lemme know.'

'I don't want to take up too much of your time.'

'Don't be a smart-ass, Spenser, I'll do what I can. But I got a lot of things to look at and Pam Shepard's just one of them. You need help, gimme a call. If I can, I'll give you some.'

'Yeah,' I said. 'Okay.' We shook hands and I left.

It was two fifteen when I pulled into the lot in front of the Silver Seas Motel. I was hungry and thirsty. While I took care of that I could talk to Rudy, start running up that big bar bill. Slade was probably right, but I'd give Shepard his money's-worth before she showed up. If she was going to.

There's something about a bar on the Cape in the daytime. The brightness of lowland surrounded by ocean maybe makes the air-conditioned dimness of the bar more striking. Maybe there's more people there and they are vacationers rather than the unemployed. Whatever it is, the bar at the Silver Seas Motel had it. And I liked it.

On the outside, the Silver Seas Motel was two-storied, weathered shingles, with a verandah across both stories in front. It was tucked into the seaward side of Main Street in the middle of town between a hardware store and a store that sold scallop-shell ashtrays and blue pennants that said CAPE COD on them. The bar was on the right, off the lobby, at one end of the dining room. A lot of people were eating lunch and several were just drinking. Most of the people looked like college kids, cut-offs and T-shirts, sandals and halter tops. The décor in the place was surfwood and fishnet. Two oars crossed on one wall, a harpoon that was probably made in Hong Kong hung above the mirror behind the bar. The bartender was middle-aged and big-bellied. His straight black hair was streaked here and there with gray and hung shoulder length. He wore a white shirt with a black string bow tie like a riverboat gambler. The cuffs were turned neatly back in two careful folds. His hands were thick, with long tapering fingers that looked manicured.

'Draft beer?' I asked.

'Schlitz,' he said. He had a flat nose and dark coppery skin. American Indian? Maybe.

'I'll have one.' He drew it in a tall straight glass. Very good. No steins, or schooners or tulip shapes. Just a tall glass the way the hops god had intended. He put down a paper coaster and put the beer on it, fed the check into the register, rang up the sale and put the check on the bar near me.

'What have you got for lunch?' I said.

He took a menu out from under the bar and put it in front of me. I sipped the beer and read the menu. I was working on sipping. Susan Silverman had lately taken to reprimanding me for my tendency to empty the glass in two swallows and order another. The menu said linguica on a crusty roll. My heart beat faster. I'd forgotten about linguica since I'd been down here last. I ordered two. And another beer. Sip. Sip.

The jukebox was playing something by Elton John. At least the box wasn't loud. They'd probably never heard of Johnny Hartman here. Rudy brought the sandwiches and looked at my half-sipped glass. I finished it – simple politeness, otherwise he'd have had to wait while I sipped – and he refilled the glass.

'You ever hear of Johnny Hartman?' I said.

'Yeah. Great singer. Never copped out and started singing this shit.' He nodded at the jukebox.

'You Rudy?' I said.

'Yeah.'

'Deke Slade told me to come talk with you.' I gave him a card. 'I'm looking for a woman named Pam Shepard.'

'I heard she was gone.'

'Any idea where?' I took a large bite of the linguica sandwich. Excellent. The linguica had been split and fried and in each sandwich someone had put a fresh green pepper ring.

'How should I know?'

'You knew Johnny Hartman, and you add green peppers to your linguica sandwich.'

'Yeah, well, I don't know where she went. And the cook does the sandwiches. I don't like green pepper in mine.'

'Okay, so you got good taste in music and bad taste in food. Mrs Shepard come in here much?'

'Lately, yeah. She's been in regular.'

'With anyone?'

'With everyone.'

'Anyone special?'

'Mostly young guys. In a dim light you might have a shot.'

'Why?'

'You're too old, but you got the build. She went for the jocks and the muscle men.'

'Was she in here with someone before she took off? That would have been a week ago Monday.' I started on my second linguica sandwich.

'I don't keep that close a count. But it was about then. She was in here with a guy named Eddie Taylor. Shovel operator.'

'They spend the night upstairs?'

'Don't know. I don't handle the desk. Just tend bar. I'd guess they did, the way she was climbing on him.' A customer signaled Rudy for another stinger on the rocks. Rudy stepped down the bar, mixed the drink, poured it, rang up the price and came back to me. I finished my second sandwich while he did that. When he came back my beer glass was empty and he filled that without being asked. Well, I couldn't very well refuse, could I? Three with lunch was about right anyway.

'Where can I find Eddie Taylor?' I said.

'He's working on a job in Cotuit these days. But he normally gets off work at four and is in here by four thirty to rinse out his mouth.'

I looked at the clock behind the bar: 3:35. I could wait and sip my beer slowly. I had nothing better to do anyway.

'I'll wait,' I said.

'Fine with me,' Rudy said. 'One thing though, Eddie's sorta hard to handle. He's big and strong and thinks he's tough. And he's too young to know better yet.'

'I'm big-city fuzz, Rudy. I'll dazzle him with wit and sophistication.'

'Yeah, you probably will. But don't mention it was me that sicked you onto him. I don't want to have to dazzle him too.'

6

It was four twenty when Rudy said, 'Hi, Eddie' to a big blond kid who came in. He was wearing work shoes and cut-off jeans and a blue tank top with red trim. He was a weightlifter: lots of tricep definition and overdeveloped pectoral muscles. And he carried himself as if he were wearing a medal. I'd have been more impressed with him if he weren't carrying a twenty-pound roll around his middle. He said to Rudy, 'Hey, Kemo Sabe, howsa kid?'

Rudy nodded and without being asked put a shot of rye and a glass of draft beer on the bar in front of Eddie. Eddie popped down the shot and sipped at the beer.

'Heap good, red man,' he said. 'Paleface workem ass off today.' He talked loudly, aware of an audience, assuming his Lone Ranger Indian dialect was funny. He turned around on the barstool, hooked his elbows over the bar and surveyed the room. 'How's the quiff situation, Rudy?' he said.

'Same as always, Eddie. You don't usually seem to have any trouble.' Eddie was staring across the room at two college-age girls drinking Tom Collinses. I got up and walked down the bar and slipped onto the stool beside him. I said, 'You Eddie Taylor?'

'Who wants to know?' he said, still staring at the girls.

'There's a fresh line,' I said.

He turned to look at me now. 'Who the hell are you?'

I took a card out of my jacket pocket, handed it to him. 'I'm looking for Pam Shepard,' I said.

'Where'd she go?' he said.

'If I knew I'd go there and look for her. I was wondering if you could help me.'

'Buzz off,' he said, and turned his stare back to the girls.

'I understand you spent the night with her just before she disappeared.'

'Who says?'

'Me, I just said it.'

'What if I did? I wouldn't be the first guy. What's it to you?'

'Poetry,' I said. 'Pure poetry when you talk.'

'I told you once, buzz off. You hear me. You don't want to get hurt, you buzz off.'

'She good in bed?'

'Yeah, she was all right. What's it to you?'

'I figure you had a lot of experience down here, and I'm new on the scene, you know? Just asking.'

'Yeah, I've tagged a few around the Cape. She was all right. I mean for an old broad she had a nice tight body, you know. And, man, she was eager. I thought I was gonna have to nail her right here in the bar. Ask Rudy. Huh, Rudy? Wasn't that Shepard broad all over me the other night?'

'You say so, Eddie.' Rudy was cleaning his thumbnail

with a matchbook cover. 'I never notice what the customers do.'

'So you did spend the night with her?' I said.

'Yeah. Christ, if I hadn't she'd have dropped her pants right here in the bar.'

'You already said that.'

'Well, it's goddamned so, Jack, you better believe it.'

Eddie dropped another shot of bar whiskey and sipped at a second beer chaser that Rudy had brought without being asked.

'Did you know her before she picked you up?'

'Hell, I didn't pick her up, she picked me up. I was just sitting here looking over the field and she came right over and sat down and started talking to me.'

'Well, then, did you know her before she picked you up?'

Eddie shrugged, and gestured his shot glass at Rudy. 'I'd seen her around. I didn't really know her, but I knew she was around, you know, that she was easy tail if you were looking.' Eddie drank his shot as soon as Rudy poured it, and when he put the glass back on the bar Rudy filled it again.

'She been on the market long?' I said. Me and Eddie were really rapping now, just a couple of good old boys, talking shop. Eddie drained his beer chaser, burped loudly, laughed at his burp. Maybe I wouldn't be able to dazzle him with my sophistication.

'On the market? Oh, you mean, yeah, I get you. No, not so long. I don't think I noticed her or heard much about her before this year. Maybe after Christmas, guy I know banged her. That's about the first I heard.' His tongue was getting a little thick and his S's were getting slushy.

'Was your parting friendly?' I said.

'Huh?'

'What was it like in the morning when you woke up and said goodbye to each other?'

'You're a nosy bastard,' he said and looked away, staring at the two college girls across the room.

'People have said that.'

'Well, I'm saying it.'

'Yes, you are. And beautifully.'

Eddie turned his stare at me. 'What are you, a wise guy?'

'People have said that too.'

'Well, I don't like wise guys.'

'I sort of figured you wouldn't.'

'So get lost or I'll knock you on your ass.'

'And I sort of figured you'd put it just that way.'

'You looking for trouble, Jack, I'm just the man to give it to you.'

'I got all the trouble I need,' I said. 'What I'm looking for is information. What kind of mood was Pam Shepard in the morning after she'd been all over you?'

Eddie got off the barstool and stood in front of me. 'I'm telling you for the last time. Get lost or get hurt.' Rudy started drifting toward the phone. I checked the amount of room in front of the bar. Maybe ten feet. Enough. I said to Rudy, 'It's okay. No one will get hurt. I'm just going to show him something.'

I stood up. 'Tubbo,' I said to Eddie, 'if you make me, I can put you in the hospital, and I will. But you probably don't believe me, so I'll have to prove it. Go ahead. Take your shot.'

He took it, a right-hand punch that missed my head when I moved. He followed up with a left that missed by about the same margin when I moved the other way.

'You'll last about two minutes doing that,' I said. He rushed at me and I rolled around him. 'Meanwhile,' I said, 'if I wanted to I could be hitting you here.' I tapped him open-handed on the right cheek very fast three times. He swung again and I stepped a little inside the punch and caught it on my left forearm. I caught the second one on my right. 'Or here,' I said, and patted him rat-a-tat with both hands on each cheek. The way a grandma pats a child. I stepped back away from him. He was already starting to breathe hard. 'Some shape you're in, kid. In another minute you won't be able to get your arms up.'

'Back off, Eddie,' Rudy said from behind the bar. 'He's a pro, for crissake, he'll kill you if you keep shoving him.'

'I'll shove the son of a bitch,' Eddie said, and made a grab at me. I moved a step to my right and put a left hook into his stomach. Hard. His breath came out in a hoarse grunt and he sat down suddenly. His face blank, the wind knocked out of him, fighting to get his breath. 'Or there,' I said.

Eddie got his breath partially back and climbed to his feet. Without looking at anyone he headed, wobbly-legged, for the men's room. Rudy said to me, 'You got some good punch there.'

'It's because my heart is pure,' I said.

'I hope he don't puke all over the floor in there,' Rudy said.

The other people in the room, quiet while the trouble had flared, began to talk again. The two college girls got up and left, their drinks unfinished, their mothers' parting fears confirmed. Eddie came back from the men's room, his face pale and wet where he'd probably splashed it with water.

'The boilermakers will do it to you,' I said. 'Slow you down and tear up your stomach.'

'I know guys could take you,' Eddie said. There was no starch in his voice when he said it and he didn't look at me.

'I do too,' I said. 'And I know guys who can take them. After a while counting doesn't make much sense. You just got into something I know more about than you do.'

Eddie hiccupped.

'Tell me about how you left each other in the morning,' I said. We were sitting at the bar again.

'What if I don't?' Eddie was looking at the small area of bar top encircled by his forearms.

'Then you don't. I don't plan to keep punching you in the stomach.'

'We woke up in the morning and I wanted to go one more time, you know, sort of a farewell pop, and she wouldn't let me touch her. Called me a pig. Said if I touched her she'd kill me. Said I made her sick. That wasn't what she said before. We were screwing our brains out half the night and next morning she calls me a pig. Well, I don't need that shit, you know? So I belted her and walked out. Last I seen her she was lying on her back on the bed crying loud as a bastard. Just staring up at the ceiling and screaming crying.' He shook his head. 'What a weird bitch,' he said. 'I mean five hours before she was screwing her brains out for me.'

I said, 'Thanks, Eddie.' I took a twenty-dollar bill out of my wallet and put it on the bar. 'Take his out too, Rudy, and keep what's left.'

When I left, Eddie was still looking at the bar top inside his forearms.

7

I had lamb stew and a bottle of Burgundy for supper and then headed into my room to start on the box of bills and letters Shepard had given me. I went through the personal mail first and found it sparse and unenlightening. Most people throw away personal mail that would be enlightening, I'd found. I got all the phone bills together and made a list of the phone numbers and charted them for frequency. Then I cross-charted them for locations. A real sleuth, sitting on the motel bed in my shorts shuffling names and numbers. There were three calls in the past month to a number in New Bedford, the rest were local. I assembled all the gasoline credit-card receipts. She had bought gasoline twice that month in New Bedford. The rest were around home. I catalogued the other credit-card receipts. There were three charges from a New Bedford restaurant. All for more than thirty dollars. The other charges were local. It was almost midnight when I got through all of the papers. I made a note of the phone number called in New Bedford, of the New Bedford restaurant and the name of the gas station in New Bedford, then I stuffed all the paper back in the carton, put the

46

carton in the closet and went to bed. I spent most of the night dreaming about phone bills and charge receipts and woke up in the morning feeling like Bartleby the Scrivener.

I had room service bring me coffee and corn muffins and at 9:05 put in a call to the telephone business office in New Bedford. A service rep answered.

'Hi,' I said. 'Ed MacIntyre at the Back Bay business office in Boston. I need a listing for telephone number 555–3688, please.'

'Yes, Mr MacIntyre, one moment please . . . that listing is Alexander, Rose. Three Centre Street, in New Bedford.'

I complimented her on the speed with which she found the listing, implied perhaps a word dropped to the district manager down there, said goodbye with smily pleasant overtones in my voice and hung up. Flawless.

I showered and shaved and got dressed. Six hours of paper shuffling had led me to a surmise that the Hyannis cops had begun by checking the bus terminal. She was in New Bedford. But I had an address, maybe not for her, but for someone. It pays to do business with your local gumshoe. Personalized service.

The drive to New Bedford up Route 6 was forty-five miles and took about an hour through small towns like Wareham and Onset, Marion and Mattapoisett. Over the bridge from Fairhaven across the interflow of the harbor and the Acushnet River, New Bedford rose steeply from the docks. Or what was left of it. The hillside from the bridge to the crest looked like newsreel footage of the Warsaw ghetto. Much of the center of the city had been demolished and urban renewal was in full cry. Purchase Street, one of the main streets the last time I'd been in New Bedford, was now a pedestrian mall. I drove around aimlessly in the bulldozed wasteland for perhaps ten minutes before I pulled off into a rutted parking area and stopped. I got out, opened the trunk of my car and got out a street directory for Massachusetts.

Centre Street was down back of the Whaling Museum. I knew the hill and turned left past the public library. Out front they still had the heroic statue of the harpooner in the whaleboat. A dead whale or a stove boat. The choices then were simple, if drastic. I turned left down the hill toward the water, then onto Johnny Cake Hill and parked near the Whaling Museum, in front of the Seaman's Bethel.

I checked my street map again and walked around the Whaling Museum to the street behind it and looked and there was Centre Street. It was a short street, no more than four or five buildings long, and it ran from North Water Street, behind the museum, to Front Street, which paralleled the water. It was an old street, weedy and dank. Number three was a narrow two-storey building with siding of gray asbestos shingles and a crumbly looking red brick chimney in the center of the roof. The roof shingles were old and dappled in various shades as though someone had patched it periodically with what he had at hand. It needed more patching. There was worn green paint on the trim here and there, and the front door on the right side of the building face was painted red. It had the quality of an old whore wearing lipstick.

I hoped she wasn't in there. I wanted to find her but I hated to think of her coming from the big sunny house in Hyannis to burrow in rat's alley. What to do now? No one knew me, neither Rose Alexander or Pam Shepard, nor, as far as I knew, anyone in New Bedford. In fact the number of places where I could go and remain anonymous continually amazed me. I could enter on any pretext and look around. Or I could knock on the door and ask for Pam Shepard. The safest thing was to stand around and watch. I liked to know as much as I could before I went in where I hadn't been before. That would take time, but I wouldn't run the risk of scaring anyone off. I looked at my watch: 12:15. I went back up toward what was left of the business district and found a restaurant. I had fried clams and coleslaw and two bottles of beer. Then I strolled back down to Centre Street and took up station about five past one. On North Water Street a municipal crew was at work with a backhoe and some jackhammers, while several guys with shirts and ties and yellow hard hats walked around with clipboards and conferred. Nobody came down Centre Street, or up it. Nobody had anything to do with Centre Street. No evidence of life appeared at number three. I had picked up a copy of the New Bedford *Standard Times* on my way back from lunch and I read it while I leaned on a telephone pole on the corner of North Water and Centre. I read everything, glancing regularly over the rim of the paper to check the house. I read about a bean supper at the Congregational church in Mattapoisett, about a father–son baseball game at the junior high school field in Rochester, about a local debutante's ball at the Wamsutta Club. I read the horoscope, the obituaries, the editorial, which took a strong stand against the incursion of Russian trawlers into local waters. I read 'Dondi' and hated it. When I finished the paper, I folded it up, walked the short length of Centre Street and leaned against the doorway of an apparently empty warehouse on the corner of Centre and Front streets.

At three o'clock a wino in a gray suit, a khaki shirt and an orange flowered tie stumbled into my doorway and urinated in the other corner. When he got through I offered to brush him off and hand him a towel, but he paid me no attention and stumbled off. What is your occupation, sir? I'm an outdoor men's room attendant. I wondered if anyone had ever whizzed on Allan Pinkerton's shoe.

At four fifteen Pam Shepard came out of the shabby house with another woman. Pam was slim and Radcliffy-looking with a good tan and her brown hair back in a tight French twist. She was wearing a chino pantsuit that displayed a fine-looking backside. I'd have to get closer but she looked worth finding. The woman she was with was smaller and sturdier-looking. Short black hair, tan corduroy jeans and a pink muslin shirt like Indira Gandhi. They headed up the street toward the museum and turned left on the Purchase Street pedestrian mall. The mall had been created by curbing across the intersection streets and had a homemade look to it. Pam Shepard and her friend went into a supermarket and I stood under the awning of a pawnshop across the street and watched them through the plate-glass window. They bought some groceries, consulting a shopping list as they went, and in about a half-hour they were back out on the street, each with a large brown paper sack in her arms. I followed them back to the house on Centre Street and watched them disappear inside. Well, at least I knew where she was. I resumed my telephone pole. The warehouse door had lost some of its appeal.

It got dark and nothing else happened; I was beginning to hope for the wino again. I was also hungry enough to eat at a Hot Shoppe. I had some thinking it over to do, and while I always did that better eating, the fried clams had not sold me on New Bedford cuisine, and I would probably have to sleep sometime later on anyway. So I went back and got my car and headed back for Hyannis. There was a parking ticket under the wiper but it blew off somewhere near a bowling alley in Mattapoisett.

During the ride back to Hyannis I decided that the best move would be to go back to New Bedford in the morning and talk with Pam Shepard. In a sense I'd done what I hired on for. That is, I had her located and could report that she was alive and under no duress. It should be up to Shepard to go and get her. But it didn't go down right, giving him the address and going back to Boston. I kept thinking of Eddie Taylor's final look at her, lying on the bed on her back screaming at the ceiling. There had been a pathetic overdressed quality to her as she came out of the shabby two-storey on Centre Street. She'd had on pendant earrings.

It was nine thirty when I got back to the motel. The dining room was still open so I went in and had six oysters and a half bottle of Chablis and a one-pound steak with Béarnaise sauce and a liter of beer. The salad had an excellent house dressing and the whole procedure was a great deal more pleasant than hanging around in a doorway with an incontinent wino. After dinner I went back to my room and caught the last three innings of the Sox game on channel six.

8

In the morning I was up and away to New Bedford before eight. I stopped at a Dunkin' Donuts shop for a training-table breakfast to go, and ate my doughnuts and drank my coffee as I headed up the Cape with the sun at my back. I hit New Bedford at commuter time, and while it wasn't that big a city its street system was so confused that the traffic jam backed up across the bridge into Fairhaven. It was nine forty when I got out of the car and headed for the incongruous front door at 3 Centre Street. There was no doorbell and no knocker so I rapped on the red panels with my knuckles. Not too hard, the door might fold.

A big, strong-looking young woman with light-brown hair in a long single braid opened the door. She had on jeans and what looked like a black leotard top. She was obviously braless, and, less noticeably, shoeless.

'Good morning,' I said, 'I'd like to speak with Pam Shepard, please.'

'I'm sorry, there's no Pam Shepard here.'

'Will she be back soon?' I was giving her my most engaging smile. Boyish. Open. Mr Warm.

'I don't know any such person,' she said.

'Do you live here?' I said.

'Yes.'

'Are you Rose Alexander?'

'No.' Once I give them the engaging smile they just slobber all over me.

'Is she in?'

'Who are you?'

'I asked you first,' I said.

Her face closed down and she started to shut the door. I put my hand flat against it and held it open. She shoved harder and I held it open harder. She seemed determined.

'Madam,' I said, 'if you will stop shoving that door at me, I will speak the truth to you. Even though, I do not believe you have spoken the truth to me.'

She paid no attention. She was a big woman and it was getting hard to hold the door open effortlessly.

'I stood outside this house most of yesterday and saw Pam Shepard and another woman come out, go shopping and return with groceries. The phone here is listed to Rose Alexander.' My shoulder was beginning to ache. 'I will talk civilly with Pam Shepard and I won't drag her back to her husband.'

Behind the young woman a voice said, 'What the hell is going on here, Jane?'

Jane made no reply. She kept shoving at the door. The smaller, black-haired woman I'd seen with Pam Shepard yesterday appeared. I said, 'Rose Alexander?' She nodded. 'I need to talk with Pam Shepard,' I said.

'I don't . . .' Rose Alexander started.

'You do too,' I said. 'I'm a detective and I know such things: If you'll get your Amazon to unhand the door we can talk this all out very pleasantly.'

Rose Alexander put her hand on Jane's arm. 'You'd better let him in, Jane,' she said gently. Jane stepped away from the door and glared at me. There were two bright smudges of color on her cheekbones, but no other sign of exertion. I stepped into the hall. My shoulder felt quite numb as I took my hand off the door. I wanted to rub it but was too proud. What price machismo?

'May I see some identification?' Rose Alexander said.

'Certainly.' I took the plastic-coated photostat of my license out of my wallet and showed it to her.

'You're not with the police then?' she said.

'No, I am self-employed,' I said.

'Why do you wish to talk with me?'

'I don't,' I said. 'I wish to talk with Pam Shepard.'

'Why do you wish to talk with her?'

'Her husband hired me to find her.'

'And what were you to do when you did?'

'He didn't say. But he wants her back.'

'And you intend to take her?'

'No, I intend to talk with her. Establish that she's well and under no duress, explain to her how her husband feels and see if she'd like to return.'

'And if she would not like to return?'

'I won't force her.'

Jane said, 'That's for sure,' and glared at me.

55

'Does her husband know she's here?' Rose Alexander asked.

'No.'

'Because you've not told him?'

'That's right.'

'Why?'

'I don't know. I guess I just wanted to see what was happening in the china shop before I brought in the bull.'

'I don't trust you,' Rose Alexander said. 'What do you think, Jane?'

Jane shook her head.

'I'm not here with her husband, am I?'

'But we don't know how close he is,' Rose Alexander said.

'Or who's with him,' Jane said.

'Who's with him?' I was getting confused.

Rose said, 'You wouldn't be the first man to take a woman by force and never doubt your right.'

'Oh,' I said.

'We back down from you now,' Jane said, 'and it will be easier next time. So we'll draw the line here, up front, first time.'

'But if you do,' I said, 'you'll make me use force. Not to take anyone, but to see that she's in fact okay.'

'You saw that yesterday,' Jane said. The color was higher on her cheekbones now, and more intense. 'You told me you saw Pam and Rose go shopping together.'

'I don't think you've got her chained in the attic,' I said. 'But duress includes managing the truth. If she has no

56

chance to hear me and reject me for herself she's not free, she's under a kind of duress.'

'Don't you try to force your way in,' Jane said. 'You'll regret it, I promise you.' She had stepped back away from me and shifted into a martial arts stance, her feet balanced at right angles to each other in a kind of T stance, her open hands held in front of her in another kind of T, the left hand vertical, the right horizontal above it. She looked like she was calling for time out. Her lips were pulled back and her breath made a hissing sound as it squeezed out between her teeth.

'You had lessons?' I asked.

Rose Alexander said, 'Jane is very advanced in karate. Do not treat her lightly. I don't wish to hurt you, but you must leave.' Her black eyes were quite wide and bright as she spoke. Her round pleasant face was flushed. I didn't believe the part about not wishing to hurt me.

'Well, I'm between a rock and a hard place right now. I don't want you to hurt me either, and I don't take Jane lightly. On the other hand the more you don't want me to see Pam Shepard, the more I think I ought to. I could probably go for the cops, but by the time we got back, Pam Shepard would be gone. I guess I'm going to have to insist.'

Jane kicked me in the balls. Groin just doesn't say it. I'd never fought with a woman before and I wasn't ready. It felt like it always does: nausea, weakness, pain and an irresistible compulsion to double over. I did double over. Jane chopped down on the back of my neck. I twisted away and the blow landed on the big trapezius muscles without doing any serious damage. I straightened up. It hurt, but not as much as it was going to if I didn't make a comeback. Jane aimed the heel of her hand at the tip of my nose. I banged her hand aside with my right forearm and hit her as hard a left hook as I've used lately, on the side of her face, near the hinge of her jaw. She went over backward and lay on the floor without motion. I'd never hit a woman before and it scared me a little. Had I hit her too hard? She was a big woman, but I must have outweighed her by forty pounds. Rose Alexander dropped to her knees beside Jane, and having got there didn't know what to do. I got down too, painfully, and felt her pulse. It was nice and strong and her chest heaved and fell steadily. 'She's okay,' I said. 'Probably better than I am.'

At the far end of the hall was a raised panel door that had been painted black. It opened, and Pam Shepard came through it. There were tears running down her face. 'It's me,' she said. 'It's my fault, they were just trying to protect me. If you've hurt her it's my fault.'

Jane opened her eyes and stared up blankly at us. She moved her head. Rose Alexander said, 'Jane?'

I said, 'She's going to be all right, Mrs Shepard. You didn't make her kick me in the groin.'

She too got down on the floor beside Jane. I got out of the way and leaned on the door jamb with my arms folded, trying to get the sick feeling to go away, and trying not to show it. People did not seem to be warming to me down here. I hoped Jane and Eddie never got together.

Jane was on her feet, Pam Shepard holding one arm and Rose Alexander the other. They went down the hall toward the black door. I followed along. Through the door was a big kitchen. A big old curvy-legged gas stove on one wall, a big oilcloth-covered table in the middle of the room, a couch with a brown corduroy spread along another wall. There was a pantry at the right rear and the walls were wainscoted narrow deal boards that reminded me of my grandmother's house. They sat Jane down in a black leather upholstered rocker. Rose went to the pantry and returned with a wet cloth. She washed Jane's face while Pam Shepard squeezed Jane's hand. 'I'm all right,' Jane said and pushed the wet cloth away. 'How the hell did you do that?' she said to me. 'That kick was supposed to finish you right there.'

'I am a professional thug,' I said.

'It shouldn't matter,' she said, frowning in puzzlement. 'A kick in the groin is a kick in the groin.'

'Ever do it for real before?'

'I've put in hours on the mat.'

'No, not instruction. Fighting. For real.'

'No,' she said. 'But I wasn't scared. I did it right.'

'Yeah, you did, but you got the wrong guy. One of the things that a kick in the groin will do is scare the kickee. Aside from the pain and all, it's not something he's used to and he cares about the area and he tends to double over and freeze. But I've been kicked before and I know that it hurts, but it's not fatal. Not even to my sex life. And so I can force myself through the pain.'

59

'But . . .' She shook her head.

'I know,' I said. 'You thought you had a weapon that made you impregnable. That would keep people from shoving you around and the first time you use it you get cold-cocked. It is a ninety-five, I can bench-press three hundred pounds. I used to be a fighter. And I scuffle for a living. The karate will still work for you. But you gotta remember it's not a sport in the street.'

'You think, goddamn you, you think it's because you're a man . . .'

'Nope. It's because a good big person will beat a good small person every time. Most men aren't as good as I am. A lot of them aren't as good as you are.'

They were all looking at me and I felt isolated, unwelcome and uneasy. I wished there were another guy there. I said to Pam Shepard, 'Can we talk?'

Rose Alexander said, 'You don't have to say a word to him, Pam.'

Jane said, 'There's no point in it, Pam. You know how you feel.'

I looked at Pam Shepard. She had sucked in both lips so they were not visible, and her mouth was a thin line. She looked back at me and we held the pose for about thirty seconds.

'Twenty-two years,' I said. 'And you knew him before you got married. More than twenty-two years you've known Harvey Shepard. Doesn't that earn him five minutes of talk. Even if you don't like him? Even simple duration eventually obliges you.'

She nodded her head, to herself, I think, more than to me.

'Tell him about obligation, I've known him since 1950,' she said.

I shrugged. 'He's forking out a hundred dollars a day and expenses to find you.'

'That's his style, the big gesture. "See how much I love you," but is he looking? No, you're looking.'

'Better than no one looking.'

'Is it?' There was color on her cheekbones now. 'Is it really? Why isn't it worse? Why isn't it intrusive? Why isn't it a big pain in the ass? Why don't you all just leave me the goddamned hell alone?'

'I'm guessing,' I said, 'but I think it's because he loves you.'

'Loves me? What the hell has that got to do with anything? He probably does love me. I never doubted that he did. So what. Does that mean I have to love him? His way? By his definition?'

Rose Alexander said, 'It's an argument men have used since the Middle Ages to keep women in subjugation.'

'Was that a master–slave relationship Jane was trying to establish with me?' I said.

'You may joke all you wish,' Rose said, 'but it is perfectly clear that men have used love as a way of obligating women. You even used the term yourself.' Rose was apparently the theoretician of the group.

'Rosie,' I said. 'I am not here to argue sexism with you. It exists and I'm against it. But what we've got here is not a theory, it's a man and a woman who've known each other a long time and conspired to produce children. I want to talk with her about that.'

'You cannot,' Rose said, 'separate the theory from its application. And' – her look was very forceful – 'you cannot get the advantage of me by using the diminutive of my name. I'm quite aware of your tricks.'

'Take a walk with me,' I said to Pam Shepard.

'Don't do it, Pam,' Jane said.

'You'll not take her from this house,' Rose said.

I ignored them and looked at Pam Shepard. 'A walk,' I said, 'down toward the bridge. We can stand and look at the water and talk and then we'll walk back.'

She nodded. 'Yes,' she said, 'I'll walk with you. Maybe you can make him understand.'

9

Protests, excursions and alarums followed Pam Shepard's decision, but in the end it was agreed that we would, in fact, stroll down toward the harbor, and that Jane and Rose would follow along at a discreet distance in case I tried to chloroform her and stuff her in a sack.

As we walked along Front Street the light was strong on her face and I realized she was probably around my age. There were faint lines of adulthood at her eyes and the corners of her mouth. They didn't detract, in fact they added a little, I thought, to her appeal. She didn't look like someone who'd need to pick up overweight shovel operators in bars. Hell, she could have her choice of sophisticated private eyes. I wondered if she'd object to the urine stain on my shoe.

We turned onto the bridge and walked far enough out on it to look at the water. The water made the city look good. Oil slick, cigarette wrappers, dead fish, gelatinous-looking pieces of water-soaked driftwood, an unraveled condom looking like an eel skin against the coffee-colored water. Had it looked like this when Melville shipped out on a whaler 130 years ago? Christ, I hope not.

'What did you say your name was?' Pam Shepard asked.

'Spenser,' I said. We leaned our forearms on the railing and stared out toward the transmitter tower on one of the harbor islands. The wind off the ocean was very pleasant despite the condition of the water.

'What do you want to talk about?' Today she had on a dark-blue polo shirt, white shorts and white Tretorn tennis shoes. Her legs were tan and smooth.

'Mrs Shepard, I've found you and I don't know what to do about it. You are clearly here by choice, and you don't seem to want to go home. I hired onto find you, and if I call your husband and tell him where you are I'll have earned my pay. But then he'll come up here and ask you to come home, and you'll say no, and he'll make a fuss, and Jane will kick him in the vas deferens, and unless that permanently discourages him, and it is discouraging, you'll have to move.'

'So don't tell him.'

'But he's hired me. I owe him something.'

'I can't hire you,' she said. 'I have no money.'

Jane and Rose stood alertly across the roadway on the other side of the bridge and watched my every move. *Semper paratus.*

'I don't want you to hire me. I'm not trying to hold you up. I'm trying to get a sense of what I should do.'

'Isn't that your problem?' Her elbows were resting on the railing and her hands were clasped. The diamond–wedding ring combination on her left hand caught the sun and glinted.

'Yes it is,' I said, 'but I can't solve it until I know who and what I'm dealing with. I have a sense of your husband. I need to get a sense of you.'

'For someone like you, I'd think the *sanctity of marriage* would be all you'd need. A woman who runs out on her family deserves no sympathy. She's lucky her husband will take her back.' I noticed the knuckles of her clasped hands were whitening a little.

'Sanctity of marriage is an abstraction, Mrs Shepard. I don't deal in those. I deal in what it is fashionable to call people. Bodies. Your basic human being. I don't give a goddamn about the sanctity of marriage. But I occasionally worry about whether people are happy.'

'Isn't happiness itself an abstraction?'

'Nope. It's a feeling. Feelings are real. They are hard to talk about so people sometimes pretend they're abstractions, or they pretend that ideas, which are easy to talk about, are more important.'

'Is the quality of men and women an abstraction?'

'I think so.'

She looked at me a little scornfully. 'Yet the failure of that equality makes a great many people unhappy.'

'Yeah. So let's work on the unhappiness. I don't know what in hell quality means. I don't know what it means in the Declaration of Independence. What's making you unhappy with your husband?'

She sighed in a deep breath and heaved it out quickly.

'Oh, God,' she said. 'Where to begin.' She stared at the transmitter tower. I waited. Cars went by behind us.

'He love you?'

She looked at me with more than scorn. I thought for a minute she was going to spit. 'Yes,' she said. 'He loves me. It's as if that were the only basis for a relationship. "I love you. I love you. Do you love me? Love. Love." Shit!'

'It's better than "I hate you. Do you hate me?"' I said.

'Oh, don't be so goddamned superficial,' she said. 'A relationship can't function on one emotion. Love or hate. He's like a . . .' She fumbled for an appropriate comparison. 'He's like when one of the kids eats cotton candy at a carnival on a hot day and it gets all over her and then all over you and you're sticky and sweaty and the day's been a long one, and horrible, and the kids are whiny. If you don't get away by yourself and take a shower you'll just start screaming. You have any children, Mr Spenser?'

'No.'

'Then maybe you don't know. Are you married?'

'No.'

'Then certainly you don't know.'

I was silent.

'Every time I walk by him he wants to hug me. Or he gives me a pat on the ass. Every minute of every day that I am with him I feel the pressure of his love and him wanting a response until I want to kick him.'

'Old Jane would probably help you,' I said.

'She was protecting me,' Pam Shepard said.

'I know,' I said. 'Do you love him?'

'Harvey? Not, probably, by his terms. But in mine. Or at least I did. Until he wore me down. At first it was one of his appeals that he loved me so totally. I liked that. I liked the certainty. But the pressure of that . . .' She shook her head.

I nodded at her encouragingly. Me and Carl Rogers.

'In bed,' she said. 'If I didn't have multiple orgasms I felt I was letting him down.'

'Have many?' I said.

'No.'

'And you're worried about being frigid.'

She nodded.

'I don't know what that means either,' I said.

'It's a term men invented,' she said. 'The sexual model, like everything else, has always been male.'

'Don't start quoting Rose at me,' I said. 'That may or may not be true, but it doesn't do a hell of a lot for our problem at the moment.'

'You have a problem,' Pam Shepard said. 'I do not.'

'Yes you do,' I said. 'I've been talking with Eddie Taylor.'

She looked blank.

'Eddie Taylor,' I said, 'big blond kid, runs a power shovel. Fat around the middle, and a loud mouth.'

She nodded and continued to as I described him, the lines at the corners of her mouth deepening. 'And why is he a problem?'

'He isn't. But unless he made it all up, and he's not bright enough to make it up, you're not as comfortably in charge of your own destiny as you seem to be.'

'I'll bet he couldn't wait to tell you every detail. Probably embellished a great deal.'

'No. As a matter of fact he was quite reluctant. I had to strike him in the solar plexus.'

She made a slight smiling motion with her mouth for a moment. 'I must say you don't talk the way I'd have expected.'

'I read a lot,' I said.

'So what is my problem?'

'I don't read that much,' I said. 'I assume you are insecure about your sexuality and ambivalent about it. But that doesn't mean anything that either one of us can bite into.'

'Well, don't we have all the psychological jargon down pat. If my husband slept around would you assume he was insecure and ambivalent?'

'I might,' I said. 'Especially if he had a paroxysm the morning after and was last seen crying on the bed.'

Her face got a little pink for a moment. 'He was revolting. You've seen him. How I could have, with a pig like that? A drunken, foul, sweaty animal. To let him use me like that.' She shivered. Across the street Jane and Rose stook poised, eyes fixed upon us, ready to spring. I felt like a cobra at a mongoose festival. 'He didn't give a damn about me. Didn't care about how I felt. About what I wanted. About sharing pleasure. He just wanted to rut like a hog and when it was over roll off and go to sleep.'

'He didn't strike me too much as the Continental type,' I said.

'It's not funny.'

'No, it isn't no more than everything else. Laughing is better than crying though. When you can.'

'Well, isn't that just so folksy and down home,' she said. 'What the hell do you know about laughing and crying?'

'I observe it a lot,' I said. 'But what I know isn't an issue. If Eddie Taylor was so revolting, why did you pick him up?'

'Because I goddamned well felt like it. Because I felt like going out and getting laid without complications. Just a simple straightforward screw without a lot of lovey-dovey – did-you-like-that-do-you-love-me crap.'

'You do that much?'

'Yes. When I felt like it, and I've been feeling like it a lot these last few years.'

'You usually enjoy it more than you did with old Eddie?'

'Of course, I – oh hell, I don't know. It's very nice sometimes when it happens, but afterwards I'm still hung up on guilt. I can't get over all those years of nice-girls-don't-do-it, I guess.'

'A guy told me you always went for the big young jocko types. Muscle and youth.'

'You have yourself in mind? You're not all that young.'

'I would love to go to bed with you. You are an excellent-looking person. But I'm still trying to talk about you.'

'I'm sorry,' she said. 'That was flirtatious, and I'm trying to change. Sometimes it's hard after a long time of being something else. Flirtatious was practically the only basis for male–female relationship through much of my life.'

'I know,' I said. 'But what about the guy who says you go for jockos? He right?'

69

She was silent awhile. An old Plymouth convertible went by with the top down and radio up loud. I heard a fragment of Roberta Flack as the sound dopplered past.

'I guess I do. I never really gave it much thought but I guess the kind of guy I seek out is big and young and strong-looking. Maybe I'm hoping for some kind of rejuvenation.'

'And a nice uncomplicated screw.'

'That too.'

'But not with someone who just wants to rut and roll off.'

She frowned. 'Oh, don't split hairs with me. You know what I mean.'

'No,' I said. 'I don't know what you mean. And I don't think you know what you mean. I'm not trying to chop logic with you. I'm trying to find out how your head is. And I think it's a mare's nest.'

'What's a mare's nest?'

'Something confused.'

'Well, I'm not a mare's nest. I know what I want and what I don't want.'

'Yeah? What?'

'What do you mean what?'

'I mean what do you want and what do you not want.'

'I don't want to live the way I have been for twenty years.'

'And what do you want?'

'Something different.'

'Such as?'

'Oh' – tears showed in her eyes – ' I don't know. Goddamn it, leave me alone. How the hell do I know what I want. I want you to leave me the goddamned hell alone.' The tears were on her cheeks now, and her voice had thickened. Across the bridge Rose and Jane were in animated conference. I had the feeling Jane was to be unleashed in a moment. I took out one of my cards and gave it to her.

'Here,' I said. 'If you need me, call me. You got any money?'

She shook her head. I took ten of her husband's ten-dollar bills out of my wallet and gave them to her. The wallet was quite thin without them.

'I won't tell him where you are,' I said, and walked off the bridge and back up the hill toward my car back of the museum.

10

Harvey Shepard had a large purple bruise under his right eye and it seemed to hurt him when he frowned. But he frowned anyway. 'Goddamnit,' he said. 'I laid out five hundred bucks for that information and you sit there and tell me I can't have it. What kind of a goddamned business is that?'

'I'll refund your advance if you want, but I won't tell you where she is. She's well, and voluntarily absent. I think she's confused and unhappy, but she's safe enough.'

'How do I know you've even seen her. How do I know you're not trying to rip me off for five bills and expenses without even looking for her?'

'Because I offered to give it back,' I said.

'Yeah, lots of people offer, but try to get the money.'

'She was wearing a blue polo shirt, white shorts, white Tretorn tennis shoes. Recognize the clothes?'

He shrugged.

'How'd you get the mouse?' I said.

'The what?'

'The bruise on your face. How'd you get it?'

'For crissake, don't change the subject. You owe me

information and I want it. I'll take you right the hell into court if I have to.'

'Hawk lay that on you?'

'Lay what?'

'The mouse. Hawk give it to you?'

'You keep your nose out of my business, Spenser. I hired you to find my wife, and you won't even do that. Never mind about Hawk.'

We were in his office on the second floor overlooking Main Street. He was behind his big Danish modern desk. I was in the white leather director's chair. I got up and walked to the door.

'Come here,' I said. 'I want you to see something in the outer office.'

'What the hell is out there?'

'Just get up and come here, and you'll see.'

He made a snort and got up, slowly and stiffly, and walked like an old man, holding himself very carefully. Keeping his upper body still. When he got to the door, I said, 'Never mind.'

He started to frown, but his eye hurt, so he stopped and swore at me. 'Jesus Christ! What are you trying to do?'

'You been beat up,' I said. He forgot himself for a moment, turned sharply toward me, grunted with pain and put his hand against the wall to keep steady.

'Get out of here,' he said as hard as he could without raising his voice.

'Somebody worked you over. I thought so when I saw

73

the mouse, and I knew so when you tried to walk. You are in money trouble with someone Hawk works for and this is your second notice.'

'You don't know what you're talking about.'

'Yeah, I do. Hawk works that way. Lots of pressure on the body, where it doesn't show. Actually I'm surprised that there's any mark on your face.'

'You're crazy,' Shepard said. 'I fell downstairs yesterday. Tripped on a rug. I don't owe anybody anything. I'm just doing business with Hawk.'

I shook my head. 'Hawk doesn't do business. It bores him. Hawk collects money, and guards bodies, that sort of thing. You're with him one day and the next you can hardly walk. Too big a coincidence. You better tell me.'

Shepard had edged his way back to the desk and gotten seated. His hands shook a little as he folded them in front of him on the desk.

'You're fired,' he said. 'Get out of here. I'm going to sue you for every cent I gave you. You'll be hearing from my lawyer.'

'Don't be a goddamned fool, Shepard. If you don't get out of what you're in, I'll be hearing from your embalmer. You got three kids and no wife. What happens to the kids if you get planted?'

Shepard made a weak attempt at a confident smile. 'Listen, Spenser, I appreciate your concern, but this is a private matter, and it's nothing I can't handle. I'm a businessman, I know how to handle a business deal.' His hands, clasped on the desk in front of him, were rigid, white-

knuckled like his wife's had been on the New Bedford–
Fairhaven bridge. Probably for the same reason. He was
scared to death.

'One last try, Shepard. Are you doing business with King
Powers?'

'I told you, Spenser, it is not your business.' His voice
did a chord change. 'Stop trying to hustle yourself up
some business. You and I are through. I want a check for
five hundred dollars in the mail to me tomorrow or you'll
find yourself in court.' His voice was hitting the upper
registers now. The tin clatter of hysteria.

'You know where to reach me,' I said, and walked out.

Living around Boston for a long time you tend to think
of Cape Cod as the promised land. Sea, sun, sky, health,
ease, boisterous camaraderie, a kind of real-life beer
commercial. Since I'd arrived no one had liked me, and
several people had told me to go away. Two had assaulted
me. You're sure to fall in love with old Cape Cod.

I drove to the end of Sea Street and parked illegally and
walked on the beach. I seemed to be unemployed. There
was no reason I could not pack up and go home. I looked
at my watch. I could call Susan Silverman from the motel
and in two hours we could be having a late lunch and
going to the Museum of Fine Arts to look at the Vermeer
exhibit that had just arrived. Giving Shepard back his
retainer didn't thrill me, maybe Suze would pick up the
lunch tab, but telling Shepard where his wife was didn't
thrill me either.

I liked the idea of seeing Susan. I hadn't seen her in

four days. Lately I had found myself missing her when I didn't see her. It made me nervous.

The beach was crowded and a lot of kids were swimming off a float anchored fifty yards from shore. Down the curve of the beach there was a point and beyond I could see part of the Kennedy compound. I found some open beach and sat down and took off my shirt. A fat woman in a flowered bathing suit eyed the gun clipped to my belt. I took it off and wrapped it in the shirt and used the package for a pillow. The woman got up and folded her beach chair and moved to a different spot. At least people were consistent in their response. I closed my eyes and listened to the sound of the water and the children and occasionally a dog. Down the beach someone's portable radio was playing something about a man who'd been crying for a million years, so many tears. Where have you gone, Cole Porter?

It was a mess, too big a mess. I couldn't walk away from it. How big a mess, I didn't know, but a mess. More mess than even Shepard could handle, I thought.

I got up, clipped the gun back on my hip, stuck the holster in my hip pocket, put on my pale blue madras shirt with the epaulets and let it hang out to cover up the gun. I walked back to my car, got in and drove to my motel. It was nearly noontime.

From my room I called Susan Silverman at home. No answer. I went to the restaurant and had oyster stew and two draft beers, and came back and called again. No answer. I called Deke Slade. He was in.

'Spenser,' I said, 'known in crime-detection circles as Mr Sleuth.'

'Yeah?'

'I have a couple of theories I'd like to share with you on some possible criminal activity in your jurisdiction. Want me to come in?'

'Criminal activity in my jurisdiction? You gotta stop watching those TV crime shows. You sound like Perry Mason.'

'Just because you don't know how to talk right, Slade, is no reason to put me down. You want to hear my theories or not?'

'Come on in,' he said and hung up. He didn't sound excited.

11

'What's Hawk's full name?' Slade said.

'I don't know,' I said. 'Just Hawk.'

'He's gotta have a full name.'

'Yeah, I know, but I don't know what it is. I've known him about twenty years and I've never heard him called anything but Hawk.'

Slade shrugged and wrote Hawk on his pad of yellow, legal-sized lined paper. 'Okay,' he said. 'So you figure that Shepard owes money and isn't paying and the guy he owes it to has sent a bone-breaker down. What's Shepard's story?'

'He has none,' I said. 'He says he's in business with Hawk and it's got nothing to do with me.'

'And you don't believe him.'

'Nope. First place Hawk doesn't do business, with a big B like Shepard means. Hawk's a free spirit.'

'Like you,' Slade said.

I shook my head. 'Nope, not like me. I don't hire out for the things Hawk does.'

'I heard you might,' Slade said.

'From who?'

'Oh, guys I know up in Boston. I made a couple of calls about you.'

'I thought you were too busy keeping a close tail on the litterbugs,' I said.

'I did it on my lunch hour,' Slade said.

'Well, don't believe all you hear,' I said.

Slade almost smiled. 'Not likely,' he said. 'How sure are you he was beat up?'

'Shepard? Certain. I've seen it done before, fact I've had it done before. I know the look and feel of it.'

'Yeah, it does stiffen you up some,' Slade said. 'What's Shepard's story?'

'Says he fell downstairs.'

Slade wrote on his yellow pad again. 'You got thoughts on who hired Hawk?'

'I'm guessing King Powers. Hawk normally gives first refusal to Powers.' Slade wrote some more on his pad. 'Powers is a Shylock,' I said. 'Used to . . .'

'I know Powers,' Slade said.

'Anyway, he's in trouble. Bad, I would guess, and he's too scared to yell for help.'

'Or maybe too crooked.'

I raised both eyebrows at Slade. 'You know something I don't,' I said.

Slade shook his head. 'No, just wondering. Harv has always been very eager to get ahead. Not crooked really, just very ambitious. This leisure community he's building is causing a lot of hassle and it doesn't seem to be going up very fast, and people are beginning to wonder if something's wrong.'

'Is there?'

'Hell,' Slade said, 'I don't know. You ever looked into a land swindle? It takes a hundred CPAs and a hundred lawyers a hundred years just to find out if there's anything to look into.' Slade made a disgusted motion with his mouth. 'You usually can't find out who owns the goddamned property.'

'Shepard doesn't strike me as crooked,' I said.

'Adolf Hitler was fond of dogs,' Slade said. 'Say he's not crooked, say he's just overextended. Could be.'

'Yeah,' I said, 'could be. But what are we going to do about it?'

'How the hell do I know? Am I the whiz-bang from the city? You tell me. We got, to my knowledge, no crime, no victim, no violation of what you big-city types would call the criminal statutes. I'll have the patrol cars swing by his place more often and have everyone keep an eye out for him. I'll see if the AG's office has anything on Shepard's land operation. You got any other thoughts?'

I shook my head.

'You find his wife?' Slade asked.

'Yeah.'

'She coming home?'

'I don't think so.'

'What's he going to do about that?'

'Nothing he can do.'

'He can go get her and drag her ass home.'

'He doesn't know where she is. I wouldn't tell him.'

Slade frowned at me for about thirty seconds. 'You are a pisser,' Slade said. 'I'll give you that.'

'Yeah.'

'Shepard take that okay?'

'No, he fired me. Told me that he was going to sue me.'

'So you're unemployed.'

'I guess so.'

'Just another tourist.'

'Yep.'

Slade did smile this time. A big smile that spread slowly across his face making deep furrows, one on each cheek.

'Goddamn,' he said and shook his head. 'Goddamn.'

I smiled back at him, warmly, got up and left. Back in my car, on the hot seats, with the top down, I thought something I've thought before. I don't know what to do, I thought. I started the car, turned on the radio and sat with the motor idling. I didn't even know where to go. Mrs Shepard sure wasn't happy, and Mr Shepard sure wasn't happy. That didn't make them unusual of course. I wasn't right at the moment all that goddamned happy myself. I supposed I ought to go home. Home's where you can go and they have to take you in. Who said that? I couldn't remember. Cynical bastard though. I put the car in gear and drove slowly down Main Street toward the motel. Course at my home there wasn't any they. There was just me. I'd take me in any time. I stopped for a light. A red-haired girl wearing powder-blue flared denim slacks and a lime-colored halter top strolled by. The slacks were so tight I could see the brief line of her underpants slanting across her buttocks. She looked at the car in a friendly fashion. I could offer her a drink and a swim and dazzle her with my Australian crawl. But she looked like a college kid and she'd probably want me to do some dope and rap about the need for love and a new consciousness. The light turned green and I moved on. A middle-aged grump with nowhere to go. It was a little after one when I pulled into the parking lot at my motel. Time for lunch. With renewed vigor I strode into the lobby, turned left past the desk and headed down the corridor toward my room. A fast wash, and then onto lunch. Who'd have thought but moments ago that I was without purpose. When I opened the door to my room Susan Silverman was lying on the bed reading a book by Erik Erikson and looking like she should.

I said, 'Jesus Christ, I'm glad to see you.'

With her finger in the book to keep her place she turned her head toward me and said, 'Likewise, I'm sure,' and grinned. Often she smiled, but sometimes she didn't smile, she grinned. This was a grin. I never knew for sure, what the difference was but it had something to do with gleeful wickedness. Her smile was beautiful and good, but in her grin there was just a hint of evil. I dove on top of her on the bed, breaking the impact of my weight with my arms, and grabbed her and hugged her.

'Ow,' she said. I eased up a little on the hug, and we kissed each other. When we stopped I said, 'I am not going to ask how you got in here because I know that you can do anything you want to, and getting the management to aid and abet you in a B and E would be child's play for you.'

'Child's play,' she said. 'How has it been with you, blue eyes?'

We lay on our backs on the bed beside each other while I told her. When I finished telling her I suggested an afternoon of sensual delight, starting now. But she suggested that it start after lunch and after a brief scuffle I agreed.

'Suze,' I said in the dining room, starting my first stein of Harp while she sipped a margarita , 'you seemed uncommonly amused by the part where Jane tried to caponize me.'

She laughed. 'I think your hips are beginning to widen out,' she said. 'Are you still shaving?'

'Naw,' I said, 'it did no damage. If it had, all the waitresses here would be wearing black armbands and the flag would fly half-mast at Radcliffe.'

'Well, we'll see, later, when there's nothing better to do.'

'There's never anything better to do,' I said. She yawned elaborately.

The waitress came and took our order. When she'd departed Susan said, 'What are you going to do?'

'Jesus, I don't know.'

'Want me to hang around with you while you do it?'

'Very much,' I said. 'I think I'm in over my head with Pam, Rose and Jane.'

'Good, I brought my suitcase on the chance you might want me to stay.'

'Yeah, and I noted you unpacked it and hung up your clothes. Confidence.'

'Oh, you noticed. I keep forgetting you are a detective.'

'Spenser's the name, clues are my game,' I said. The waitress brought me a half-dozen oysters and Susan six soused shrimp. Susan looked at the oysters.

'Trying to make a comeback?'

'No,' I said, 'planning ahead.'

We ate our seafood.

'What makes you say you're in over your head?' Susan asked.

'I don't feel easy. It's an element I'm not comfortable in. I'm good with my hands, and I'm persevering, but ... Pam Shepard asked me if I had children and I said no. And she said I probably couldn't understand, and she asked if I were married and I said no and she said then for sure I couldn't understand.' I shrugged.

'I've never had children either,' Susan said. 'And marriage wasn't the best thing that ever happened to me. Nor the most permanent. I don't know. There's all the clichés about you don't have to be able to cook a soufflé to know when one's bad. But ... at school, I know, parents come in sometimes for counseling with the kids and they say, but you don't know. You don't have children ... there's probably something to it. Say there is. So what? You've been involved in a lot of things that you haven't experienced firsthand, as I recall. Why is this one different?'

'I don't know that it is,' I said.

'I think it is. I've never heard you talk about things like

84

this before. On a scale of ten you normally test out about fifteen in confidence.'

'Yeah, I think it is too.'

'Of course, as you explain it, the case is no longer your business because the case no longer exists.'

'There's that,' I said.

'Then why worry about it. If it's not your element, anyway, why not settle for that. We'll eat and swim and walk on the beach for a few days and go home.'

The waitress came with steak for each of us, and salad, and rolls and another beer for me. We ate in silence for maybe two minutes.

'I can't think of anything else to do,' I said.

'Try to control your enthusiasm,' Susan said.

'I'm sorry,' I said. 'I didn't mean it that way. It's just bothering me. I've been with two people whose lives are screwed up to hell and I can't seem to get them out of it at all.'

'Of course you can't,' she said. 'You also can't do a great deal about famine, war, pestilence and death.'

'A great backfield,' I said.

'You also can't be everyone's father. It is paternalistic of you to assume that Pam Shepard with the support of several other women cannot work out her own future without you. She may in fact do very well. I have.'

'Me paternalistic? Don't be absurd. Eat your steak and shut up or I'll spank you.'

12

After lunch we took coffee on the terrace by the pool, sitting at a little white table made of curlicued iron shaded by a blue and white umbrella. It was mostly kids in the pool, splashing and yelling while their mothers rubbed oil on their legs. Susan Silverman was sipping coffee from a cup she held with both hands and looking past me. I saw her eyes widen behind her lavender sunglasses and I turned and there was Hawk.

He said, 'Spenser.'

I said, 'Hawk.'

He said, 'Mind if I join you?'

I said, 'Have a seat. Susan, this is Hawk. Hawk, this is Susan Silverman.'

Hawk smiled at her and she said, 'Hello, Hawk.'

Hawk pulled a chair around from the next table, and sat with us. Behind him was a big guy with a sunburned face and an Oriental dragon tattooed on the inside of his left forearm. As Hawk pulled his chair over he nodded at the next table and the tattooed man sat down at it. 'That's Powell,' Hawk said. Powell didn't say anything. He just sat with his arms folded and stared at us.

'Coffee?' I said to Hawk.

He nodded. 'Make it iced coffee though.' I gestured to the waitress, ordered Hawk his iced coffee.

'Hawk,' I said, 'you gotta overcome this impulse toward anonymity you've got. I mean why not start to dress so people will notice you instead of always fading into the background like you do.'

'I'm just a retiring guy, Spenser, just my nature.' He stressed the first syllable in retiring. 'Don't see no reason to be a clotheshorse.' Hawk was wearing white Puma track shoes with a black slash on them. White linen slacks, and a matching white linen vest with no shirt. Powell was more conservatively dressed in a maroon-and-yellow-striped tank top and maroon slacks.

The waitress brought Hawk his iced coffee. 'You and Susan having a vacation down here?'

'Yep.'

'Sure is nice, isn't it? Always like the Cape. Got atmosphere you don't usually find. You know? Hard to define it, but it's kind of leisure spirit. Don't you think, Spenser?'

'I'll tell you if you'll tell me.'

'Susan,' Hawk said, 'this man is a straight-ahead man, you know? Just puts it right out front, hell of a quality, I'd say.'

Susan smiled at him and nodded. He smiled back.

'Come on, Hawk, knock off the Goody Two-Shoes shtick. You want to know what I'm doing with Shepard and I want to know what you're doing with Shepard.'

'Actually, it's a little more than that, babe, or a little

less, whichever way you look at it. It ain't that I so much care what you're doing with Shepard as it is I want you to stop doing it.'

'Ah-ha,' I said. 'A threat. That explains why you brought Eric the Red along. You knew Susan was with me and you didn't want to be outnumbered.'

Powell said from his table, 'What did you call me?'

Hawk smiled. 'Still got that agile mind, Spenser.'

Powell said again, 'What did you call me?'

'It is hard, Powell,' I said to him, 'to look tough when your nose is peeling. Why not try some Sun Ban, excellent, greaseless, filters out the harmful ultraviolet rays.'

Powell stood up. 'Don't smart-mouth me, man. You wising off at me?'

'That a picture of your mom you got tattooed on your left arm?' I said.

He looked down at the dragon tattoo on his forearm for a minute and then back at me. His face got redder and he said, 'You wise bastard. I'm going to straighten you out right now.'

Hawk said, 'Powell, I wouldn't if I was you.'

'I don't have to take a lot of shit from a guy like this,' Powell said.

'Don't swear in front of the lady,' Hawk said. 'You gotta take about whatever he gives you 'cause you can't handle him.'

'He don't look so tough to me,' Powell said. He was standing and people around the pool were beginning to look.

'That's 'cause you are stupid, Powell,' Hawk said. 'He is tough, he may be damn near as tough as me. But you want to try him, go ahead.'

Powell reached down and grabbed me by the shirt front. Susan Silverman inhaled sharply.

Hawk said, 'Don't kill him, Spenser, he runs errands for me.'

Powell yanked me out of the chair. I went with the yank and hit him in the Adam's apple with my forearm. He said something like 'ark' and let go of my shirt front and stepped back. I hit him with two left hooks, the second one with a lot of shoulder turned into it, and Powell fell over backward into the pool. Hawk was grinning as I turned toward him.

'The hayshakers are all the same, aren't they,' he said. 'Just don't seem to know the difference between amateurs and professionals.' He shook his head. 'That's a good lady you got there though.' He nodded at Susan, who was on her feet holding a beer bottle she'd apparently picked up off another table.

Hawk got up and walked to the pool and dragged Powell out of it negligently, with one hand, as if the dead weight of a 200-pound man were no more than a flounder.

The silence around the pool was heavy. The kids were still hanging onto the edge of the pool, staring at us. Hawk said, 'Come on, let's walk out to my car and talk.' He let Powell slump to the ground by the table and strolled back in through the lobby. Susan and I went with him. As we passed the desk we saw the manager come out of his office and hurry toward the terrace.

I said, 'Why don't you go down to the room, Suze? I'll be along in a minute. Hawk just wants me to give him some pointers on poolside fighting.' The tip of her tongue was stuck out through her closed mouth and she was obviously biting on it. 'Don't bite your tongue,' I said. 'Save some for me.' She shook her head.

'I'll stay with you,' she said.

Hawk opened the door on the passenger's side of the Cadillac. 'My pleasure,' he said to Susan. If Hawk and I were going to fight he wouldn't pick a convertible for the place. I got in after Susan. Hawk went around and got in the driver's side. He pushed a button and the roof went up smoothly. He started the engine and turned on the air conditioning. A blue and white Barnstable Township police car pulled into the parking lot and two cops got out and walked into the motel.

Hawk said, 'Let's ride around.' I nodded and he put us in gear and slipped out of the parking lot.

'Where the hell did you get him?' I said to Hawk as we drove.

'Powell? Oh, man, I don't know. He's a local dude. People that hired me told me to work with him.'

'They trying to set up an apprentice program?'

Hawk shrugged. 'Beats me, baby, he got a long way to go though, don't he?'

'It bother you that the cops are going to ask him what he was doing fighting with a tourist, and who the tourist

90

was and who was the black stud in the funny outfit?'

Hawk shook his head. 'He won't say nothing. He dumb, but he ain't that dumb.'

Between us on the front seat Susan Silverman said, 'What are we doing?'

Hawk laughed. 'A fair question, Susan. What in hell are we doing?'

'Let me see if I can guess,' I said. 'I guess that Harv Shepard owes money to a man, probably King Powers, and Hawk has been asked to collect it. Or maybe just oversee the disbursement of funds, whatever, and that things are going the way they should.' I said to Susan, 'Hawk does this stuff, quite well. And then surprise, I appear, and I'm working for Shepard. And Hawk and his employer, probably King Powers, wonder if Harv hired me to counteract Hawk. So Hawk has dropped by to inquire about my relationship with Harv Shepard, and to urge me to sever that relationship.'

The Caddie went almost soundless along the Mid-Cape Highway, down Cape, toward Provincetown. I said, 'How close, Hawk?'

He shrugged. 'I have explained to the people that employ me about how you are. I don't expect to frighten you away, and I don't expect to bribe you, but my employer would like to compensate you for any loss if you were to withdraw from the case.'

'Hawk,' I said. 'All this time I've known you I never could figure out why sometimes you talk like an account exec from Merrill Lynch and sometimes you talk like Br'er Bear.'

'Ah is the product of a ghetto education.' He pronounced both t's in ghetto. 'Sometimes my heritage keep popping up.'

'Lawdy me, yes,' I said. 'What part of the ghetto you living in now?'

Hawk grinned at Susan. 'Beacon Hill,' he said. He U-turned the Caddie over the center strip and headed back up Cape toward Hyannis. 'Anyway, I told the people you weren't gonna do what they wanted, whatever I said, but they give me money to talk to you, so I'm talking. What your interest in Shepard?'

'He hired me to look for his wife.'

'That all?'

'You find her?'

'Yes.'

'Where?'

'I won't say.'

'Don't matter, Shepard'll tell me. If I need to know.'

'No.' I shook my head. 'He doesn't know either.'

'You won't tell him?'

'Nope.'

'Why not, man, That's what you hired on for.'

'She doesn't want to be found.'

Hawk shook his head again. 'You complicate your life, Spenser. You think about things too much.'

'That's one of the things that makes me not you, Hawk.'

'Maybe,' Hawk said, 'and maybe you a lot more like me than you want to say. 'Cept you ain't as good-looking.'

'Yeah, but I dress better.'

Hawk snorted, 'Shit. Excuse me, Susan. Anyway, my problem now is whether I believe you. It sounds right. Sounds just about your speed, Spenser. Course you ain't just fell off the sugar-beet truck going through town, and if you was lying it would sound good. You still work for Shepard?'

'No, he canned me. He says he's going to sue me.'

'Ah wouldn't worry all that much about the suing,' Hawk said. 'Harv's kinda busy.'

'Is it Powers?' I said.

'Maybe it is, maybe it ain't. You gonna stay out of this, Spenser?'

'Maybe I will, maybe I won't.'

Hawk nodded. We drove a way in silence.

'Who's King Powers?' Susan said.

'A thief,' I said. 'Loan-sharking, numbers, prostitution, laundromats, motels, trucking, produce, Boston, Brockton, Fall River, New Bedford.'

Hawk said, 'Not Brockton anymore. Angie Degamo has got Brockton now.'

'Angie chase Powers out?'

'Naw, some kind of business deal. I wasn't in it.'

'Anyway,' I said to Susan, 'Powers is like that.'

'And you work for him?' she said to Hawk.

'Some.'

'Hawk's a freelance,' I said. 'But Powers asks him early when he's got Hawk's kind of work.'

'And what is Hawk's kind of work?' Susan said, still to Hawk.

'He does muscle and gun work.'

'Ah prefer the term soldier of fortune, honey,' Hawk said to me.

'Doesn't it bother you,' Susan said, 'to hurt people for money?'

'No more than it does him.' Hawk nodded to me.

'I don't think he does it for money,' she said.

'That's why ah'm bopping down the Cape in a new Eldorado and he's driving that eight-year-old hog with the gray tape on the upholstery.'

'But . . .' Susan looked for the right words. 'But he does what he must, his aim is to help. Yours is to hurt.'

'Not right,' Hawk said. 'Maybe he aiming to help. But he also like the work. You know? I mean he could be a social worker if he just want to help. I get nothing out of hurting people. Sometimes just happens that way. Just don't be so sure me and old Spenser are so damn different, Susan.'

We pulled back into the parking lot at the motel. The blue and white was gone. I said, 'You people through discussing me yet, I got a couple things to say, but I don't want to interrupt. The subject is so goddamned fascinating.'

Susan just shook her head.

'Okay,' I said. 'This is straight, Hawk. I'm not working for Shepard, or anybody, at the moment. But I can't go home and let you and Powers do what you want. I'm gonna hang around, I think, and see if I can get you off Shepard's back.'

Hawk looked at me without expression. 'That's what I told them,' he said. 'I told them that's what you'd say if I came around and talked. But they paying the money. I'll tell them I was right. I don't think it gonna scare them.'

'I don't suppose it would,' I said.

I opened the door and got out and held it open for Susan. She slid out, and then leaned back in and spoke to Hawk. 'Goodbye,' she said. 'I'm not sure what to say. Glad to have met you wouldn't do, exactly. But' – she shrugged – 'thanks for the ride.'

Hawk smiled at her. 'My pleasure, Susan. Maybe I'll see you again.'

I closed the door and Hawk slid the car out of the parking lot, soundless and smooth, like a shark cruising in still water.

13

Susan said, 'I want a drink.'

We went in and sat on two barstools, at the corner, where the bar turns. Susan ordered a martini and I had a beer. 'Martini?' I said.

She nodded. 'I said I wanted a drink. I meant it.' She drank half the martini in a single pull and put the glass back on the bar.

'How different?' she said, and looked at me.

'You mean me and Hawk?'

'Uh-huh.'

'I don't know. I don't beat people up for money. I don't kill people for money. He does.'

'But sometimes you'll do it for nothing. Like this afternoon.'

'Powell?'

'Powell. You didn't have to fight him. You needled him into it.'

I shrugged.

'Didn't you?' Susan said.

I shrugged again. She belted back the rest of the martini.

'Why?'

I gestured the bartender down. 'Another round,' I said.

We were silent while he put the martini together and drew the beer and placed them before us.

'Got any peanuts?' I said.

He nodded and brought a bowl up from under the bar. The place was almost deserted, a couple having a late lunch across the room, and four guys, who looked like they'd been golfing, drinking mixed drinks at a table behind us. Susan sipped at her second martini.

'How can you drink those things?' I said. 'They taste like a toothache cure.'

'It's how I prove I'm tough,' she said.

'Oh,' I said. I ate some of the peanuts. The voices of the golf foursome were loud. Full of jovial good fellowship like the voice of a game-show host. A little desperate.

'Millions of guys spend their lives that way,' I said. 'Sitting around pretending to be a good fellow with guys they have nothing to say to.'

Susan nodded. 'Not just guys,' she said.

'I always thought women did that better though,' I said.

'Early training,' Susan said, 'at being a phony, so men would like you. You going to answer my question?'

'About why I badgered Powell?'

'Uh-huh.'

'You don't give up easy, do you?'

'Uh-unh.'

'I don't know exactly why I pushed him. He annoyed me sitting there, but it also seemed about the right move to make at the time.'

'To show Hawk you weren't afraid?'

'No, I don't think it impressed Hawk one way or the other. It was a gut reaction. A lot of what I do is a gut reaction. You're a linear thinker, you want to know why and how come and what the source of the problem is and how to work out a solution to it. I assume it comes, in part, with being a guidance type.'

'You're reversing the stereotype, you know,' Susan said.

'What? Women emotional, men rational? Yeah. But that was always horseshit anyway. Mostly, I think it's just the opposite. In my case anyway. I don't think in ABC order. I've gotten to be over forty and done a lot of things, and I've learned to trust my impulses usually. I tend to perceive in images and patterns and – what to call it – whole situations.'

'Gestalt,' Susan said.

'Whatever, so when you say why I feel like the best I can do is describe the situation. If I had a video tape of the situation I would point at it and say, 'See, that's why.'

'Would you have done the same thing if I weren't there?'

'You mean was I showing off?' The bartender came down and looked at our glasses. I nodded and he took them away for refill. 'Maybe.' The bartender brought the drinks back. 'Would you have hit someone with that beer bottle if I needed it?'

'You insufferable egotist,' Susan said. 'Why don't you think I picked the bottle up to defend myself?'

'You got me,' I said. 'I never thought of that. Is that why you picked it up?'

'No,' she said. 'And stop grinning like a goddamned idiot.' She drank some of her third martini. 'Smug bastard,' she said.

'You did it because I'm such terrific tail, didn't you.'

'No,' she said. The force of her face and eyes were on me. 'I did it because I love you.'

The couple across the room got up from the table and headed out. She was Clairol-blond, her hair stiff and brittle; he was wearing white loafers and a matching belt. As they left the dining room their hands brushed and he took hers and held it. I drank the rest of my beer. Susan sipped at her martini. 'Traditionally,' she said, 'the gentleman's response to that remark is, "I love you too."' She wasn't looking at me now. She was studying the olive in the bottom of her martini.

'Suze,' I said. 'Do we have to complicate it?'

'You can't say the traditional thing?'

'It's not saying "I love you," it's what comes after.'

'You mean love and marriage, they go together like a horse and carriage?'

I shrugged. 'I don't suppose they have to. I've seen a lot of marriages without love. I guess it could work the other way.'

Susan said, 'Um-hum' and looked at me steadily again.

'The way we're going now seems nice,' I said.

'No,' she said. 'It is momentary and therefore finally pointless. It has no larger commitment, it involves no risk, and therefore no real relationship.'

'To have a real relationship you gotta suffer?'

'You have to risk it,' she said. 'You have to know that if it gets homely and unpleasant you can't just walk away.'

'And that means marriage? Lots of people walk away from marriage. For crissake, I got a lady client at this moment who has done just that.'

'After what, twenty-two years?' Susan said.

'One point for your side,' I said. 'She didn't run off at the first sprinkle of rain, did she. But does that make the difference? Some JP reading from the Bible?'

'No,' Susan said. 'But the ceremony is the visible symbol of the commitment. We ritualize our deepest meanings usually, and marriage is the way we've ritualized love. Or one of the ways.'

'Are you saying we should get married?'

'At the moment I'm saying I love you and I'm waiting for a response.'

'It's not that simple, Suze.'

'And I believe I've gotten the response.' She got up from the bar and walked out. I finished my beer, left a ten on the bar and walked back to my room. She wasn't there. She also was not on the terrace or in the lobby or in the parking lot. I looked for her small blue Chevy Nova and didn't see it. I went back to the room. Her suitcase was still on the rack, her clothes hanging in the closet. She wouldn't go home without her clothes. Without me maybe, but not without her clothes. I sat down on the bed and looked at the red chair in the corner. The seat was one form of molded plastic, the legs four thin rounds of dark wood with little brass booties on the bottom. Elegant. I was much too damn big and tough to cry. Too old also. It wasn't that goddamned simple.

On the top of the bureau was a card that said, 'Enjoy our health club and sauna.' I got undressed, dug a pair of white shorts and a gray T-shirt out of the bureau, put them on and laced up my white Adidas track shoes with the three black stripes, no socks. Susan always bitched at me about no socks when we played tennis, but I liked the look. Besides, it was a bother putting socks on.

The health club was one level down, plaid-carpeted, several rooms, facilities for steam, sauna, rubdowns, and an exercise room with a Universal Trainer. A wiry middle-aged man in white slacks and a white T-shirt gave me a big smile when I came in.

'Looking for a nice workout, sir?'

'Yeah.'

'Well, we've got the equipment. You familiar with a Universal, sir?'

'Yeah.'

'It is, as you can see, a weightlifting machine that operates on pulleys and runs, thus allowing a full workout without the time-consuming inconvenience of changing plates on a barbell.'

'I know,' I said.

'Let me give you an idea of how ours works. There are eight positions on the central unit here, the bench press, curls, over-the-head press ...'

'I know,' I said.

'The weight numbering on the left is beginning weight,

the markings on the right are overload weights resulting from the diminishment of fulcrum . . .'

I got on the bench, shoved the pin into the slot marked 300, took a big breath and blew the weight up to arm's length and let it back. I did it two more times. The trainer said, 'I guess you've done this before.'

'Yeah,' I said.

He went back toward the trainer's room. 'You want anything, you let me know,' he said.

I moved to the lat machine, did fifteen pull-downs with 150, did fifteen tricep presses with ninety, moved to the curl bar, then to the bench again. I didn't normally lift that heavy on the bench, but I needed to bust a gut or something and 300-pound bench presses were just right for that. I did four sets of everything and the sweat was soaking through my shirt and running down the insides of my arms, so I had to keep wiping my hands to keep a grip on the weight bars. I finished up doing twenty-five dips, and when I stepped away my arms were trembling and my breath was coming in gasps. It was a slow day for the health club. I was the only one in there, and the trainer had come out after a while and watched.

'Hey,' he said, 'you really work out, don't you?'

'Yeah,' I said. There was a heavy bag in one corner of the training room. 'You got gloves for that thing?' I said.

'Got some speed gloves,' the trainer said.

'Gimme,' I said.

He brought them out and I put them on and leaned against the wall, getting my breath under control and waiting for my arms to stop feeling rubbery. It didn't used to take as long. In about five minutes, I was ready for the bag. I stood close to it, maybe six inches away, and punched it in combinations as hard as I could. Two lefts, a right. Left jab, left hook, right cross, left jab, left jab, step-back right uppercut. It's hard to hit a heavy bag with an uppercut. It has no chin. I hit the bag for as long as I could, as hard as I could. Grunting with the effort. Staying up against it and trying to get all the power I could into the six-inch punches. If you've never done it you have no idea how tiring it is to punch something. Every couple of minutes I had to back away and lean on the wall and recover.

The trainer said to me, 'You used to fight?'

'Yeah,' I said.

'You can always tell,' he said. 'Everybody comes in here slaps at the bag, or gives it a punch. They can't resist it. But one guy in a hundred actually hits it and knows what he's doing.'

'Yeah,' I went back to the bag, driving my left fist into it, alternating jabs and hooks, trying to punch through it. The sweat rolled down my face and dripped from my arms and legs. My shirt was soaking and I was beginning to see black spots dancing like visions of sugar plums before my eyes.

'You want some salt?' the trainer said. I shook my head. My gray T-shirt was soaked black with sweat. Sweat ran down my arms and legs. My hair was dripping wet. I stepped back from the bag and leaned on the wall. My breath was heaving in and out and my arms were numb and rubbery. I slid my back down the wall and sat on the floor, knees up, back against the wall, my forearms resting on my knees, my head hanging, and waited while the breath got under control and the spots went away. The speed gloves were slippery with sweat as I peeled them off. I got up and handed them to the trainer.

'Thanks,' I said.

'Sure,' he said. 'When you work out, man, you work out, don't you?'

'Yeah,' I said.

I walked slowly out of the training room and up the stairs. Several people looked at me as I crossed the lobby toward my room. The floor of the lobby was done in rust-colored quarry tile, about 8" × 8". In my room I turned up the air conditioner and took a shower, standing a long time under the hard needle spray. Susan's make-up kit was still on the vanity. I toweled dry, put on a blue and white tank top, white slacks and black loafers. I looked at my gun lying on the bureau. 'Screw it.' I headed clean and tired and unarmed down the corridor, back to the bar, and began to drink bourbon.

14

I woke up at eight fifteen the next morning feeling like a failed suicide. The other bed had not been slept in. At twenty to nine I got out of bed and shuffled to the bathroom, took two aspirin and another shower. At nine fifteen I walked stiffly and slow down to the coffee shop and drank two large orange juices and three cups of black coffee. At ten of ten I walked less stiffly, but still slow, back to my room and called my answering service. In desperate times, habit helps give form to our lives.

Pam Shepard had called and would call again. 'She said it was urgent, Spenser.'

'Thank you, Lillian. When she calls again give her this number.' I hung up and waited. Ten minutes later the phone rang.

'Spenser,' I said.

'I need help,' she said. 'I've got to talk with you.'

'Talk,' I said.

'I don't want to talk on the phone, I need to see you, and be with you when I talk. I'm scared. I don't know who else to call.'

'Okay, I'll come up to your place.'

'No, we're not there anymore. Do you know where Plimoth Plantation is?'

'Yes.'

'I'll meet you there. Walk down the main street of the village. I'll see you.'

'Okay, I'll leave now. See you there about noon?'

'Yes. I mustn't be found. Don't let anyone know you're going to see me. Don't let anyone follow you.'

'You want to give me a hint of what your problem is?'

'No,' she said. 'Just meet me where we said.'

'I'll be there.'

We hung up. It was ten thirty. Shouldn't take more than half an hour to drive to Plymouth. Susan's clothes were still in the closet. She'd come back for them, and the make-up kit. She must have been incensed beyond reason to have left that. She'd probably checked into another motel. Maybe even another room in this one. I could wait an hour. Maybe she'd come back for her clothes. I got a piece of stationery and an envelope from the drawer of the desk, wrote a note, sealed it in the envelope and wrote Susan's name on the outside. I got Susan's cosmetic case from the bathroom and put it on the desk. I propped the note against it, and sat down in a chair near the bath-room door.

At eleven-thirteen someone knocked softly on my door. I got up and stepped into the bathroom, out of sight, behind the open bathroom door. Another knock. A wait. And then a key in the lock. Through the crack of the hinge end of the bathroom door I could see the motel room door open. Susan came in. Must have gotten the key at the desk. Probably said she'd lost hers. She walked out of sight toward the desk top where the note was. I heard her tear open the envelope. The note said. 'Lurking in the bathroom is a horse's ass. It requires the kiss of a beautiful woman to turn him into a handsome prince again.' I stepped out from behind the door, into the room. Susan put the note down, turned and saw me. With no change of expression she walked over and gave me a small kiss on the mouth. Then she stepped back and studied me closely. She shook her head. 'Didn't work,' she said. 'You're still a horse's ass.'

'It was the low-voltage kiss,' I said. 'Transforming a horse's ass into a handsome prince is a high-intensity task.'

'I'll try once more,' she said. And put both arms around me and kissed me hard on the mouth. The kiss held, and developed into much more and relaxed in postclimactic languor without a sound. Without even breaking the kiss. At close range I could see Susan's eyes still closed.

I took my mouth from hers and said, 'You wanta go to Plimoth Plantation?'

Susan opened her eyes and looked at me. 'Anywhere at all,' she said. 'You are still a horse's ass, but you are my horse's ass.'

I said, 'I love you.'

She closed her eyes again and pushed her face against the hollow of my neck and shoulder for a moment. Then she pulled her head back and opened her eyes and nodded her head. 'Okay, prince,' she said. 'Let's get to Plimoth.'

Our clothes were in a scattered tangle on the floor and by the time we sorted them out and got them back on it was noon. 'We are late,' I said.

'I hurried as fast as I could,' Susan said. She was putting on her lipstick in the mirror, bending way over the dresser to do it.

'We were fast,' I said. 'A half-hour from horse's ass to handsome prince. I think that fulfills the legal definition of a quickie.'

'You're the one in a hurry to go see Plimoth Plantation. Given the choice between sensual delight and historical restoration, I'd have predicted a different decision on your part.'

'I've got to see someone there, and it may help if you're with me. Perhaps later we can reconsider the choice.'

'I'm ready,' she said. And we went out of the room to my car. On the drive up Route 3 to Plymouth I told Susan what little I knew about why we were going.

Susan said, 'Won't she panic or something if I show up with you? She did say something about alone.'

'We won't go in together,' I said. 'When I find her, I'll explain who you are and introduce you. You been to the Plantation before?'

She nodded. 'Well, then, you can just walk down the central street a bit ahead of me and hang around till I holler.'

'Always the woman's lot,' she said.

I grunted. A sign on my left said Plimoth Plantation Road and I turned in. The road wound up through a meadow toward a stand of pines. Behind the pines was a parking lot and at one edge of the parking lot was a ticket booth. I parked and Susan got out and walked ahead, bought a ticket and went through the entrance. When she was out of sight I got out and did the same thing. Beyond the ticket booth was a rustic building containing a gift shop, lunch room and information service. I went on past it and headed down the soft path between the high pines toward the Plantation itself. A few years back I had been reading Samuel Eliot Morison's big book of American history, and got hooked and drove around the East going to Colonial restorations. Williamsburg is the most dazzling, and Sturbridge is grand, but Plimoth Plantation is always a small pleasure.

I rounded the curve by the administration building and saw the blockhouse of dark wood and the stockade around the little town and beyond it the sea. The area was entirely surrounded by woods and if you were careful you could see no sign of the twentieth century. If you weren't careful and looked too closely you could see Bert's Restaurant and somebody else's motel down along the shore. But for a moment I could go back, as I could every time I came, to the small cluster of zealous Christians in the wilderness of seventeenth century America, and experience a sense of the desolation they must have felt, minute and remote and resolute in the vast woods.

I saw Susan on top of the blockhouse, looking out at the village, her arms folded on the parapet, and I came back to business and walked up the hill, past the blockhouse and into the Plantation. There was one street, narrow and rutted, leading downhill toward the ocean. Thatched houses along each side, behind the herb gardens, some livestock and a number of people dressed in Colonial costume. Lots of children, lots of Kodak Instamatics. I walked down the hill, slowly, letting Pam Shepard have ample time to spot me and see that I wasn't followed. I went the whole length of the street and started back up. As I passed Myles Standish's house, Pam came out of the door wearing huge sunglasses and fell into step beside me.

'You're alone.'

'No, I have a friend with me. A woman.' It seemed important to say it was a woman.

'Why,' she said. Her eyes were wide and dark.

'You are in trouble, and maybe she could help. She's an A-1 woman. And I had the impression you weren't into men much lately.'

'Can I trust her?'

'Yes.'

'Can I trust you?'

'Yes.'

'I suppose you wouldn't say so if I couldn't anyway, would you?' She was wearing a faded denim pants and jacket combo over a funky-looking multicolored T-shirt. She was exactly as immaculate and neat and fresh-from-the-shower-and-make-up-table as she had been the last time I saw her.

'No, I wouldn't. Come on, I'll introduce you to my friend,

then we can go someplace and sit down and maybe have a drink or a snack or both and talk about whatever you'd like to talk about.'

She looked all around her as if she might dart back into one of the thatched houses and hide in the loft. Then she took a deep breath and said, 'Okay, but I mustn't be seen.'

'Seen by who?'

'By anyone, by anyone who would recognize me.'

'Okay, we'll get Susan and we'll go someplace obscure.' I walked back up the street toward the gate to the block-house, Pam Shepard close by me as if trying to stay in my shadow. Near the top of the hill Susan Silverman met us. I nodded at her and she smiled.

'Pam Shepard,' I said. 'Susan Silverman.' Susan put out her hand and smiled.

Pam Shepard said, 'Hello.'

I said, 'Come on, we'll head back to the car.'

In the car Pam Shepard talked with Susan. 'Are you a detective too, Susan?'

'No, I'm a guidance counselor at Smithfield High School,' Susan said.

'Oh, really? That must be very interesting.'

'Yes,' Susan said, 'it is. It's tiresome, sometimes, like most things, but I love it.'

'I never worked,' Pam said. 'I always just stayed home with the kids.'

'But that must be interesting too,' Susan said. 'And tiresome. I never had much chance to do that.'

'You're not married?'

'Not now, I was divorced quite some time ago.'

'Children?'

Susan shook her head, I pulled into the parking lot at Bert's. 'You know anybody in this town?' I said to Pam.

'No.'

'Okay, then this place ought to be fairly safe. It doesn't look like a spot people would drive up from the Cape to go to.'

Bert's was a two-storey building done in weathered shingles fronting on the ocean. Inside, the dining room was bright, pleasant, informal and not very full. We sat by the window and looked at the waves come in and go out. The waitress came. Susan didn't want a drink. Pam Shepard had a stinger on the rocks. I ordered a draft beer. The waitress said they had none. 'I've learned,' I said, 'to live with disappointment.' The waitress said she could bring me a bottle of Heineken. I said it would do. The menu leaned heavily toward fried seafood. Not my favorite, but the worst meal I ever had was wonderful. At least they didn't feature things like the John Alden Burger or Pilgrim Soup.

The waitress brought the drinks and took our food order. I drank some of my Heineken. 'Okay, Mrs Shepard,' I said, 'what's up?'

She looked around. There was no one near us. She drank some of her stinger. 'I . . . I'm involved in a murder.'

I nodded. Susan sat quietly with her hands folded in front of her on the table.

'We ... there was ...' She took another gulp of the stinger. 'We robbed a bank in New Bedford, and the bank guard, an old man with a red face, he ... Jane shot him and he's dead.'

The tide was apparently ebbing. The mark was traced close to the restaurant by an uneven line of seaweed and driftwood and occasional scraps of rubbish. Much cleaner than New Bedford harbor. I wondered what flotsam was. I'd have to look that up sometime when I got home. And jetsam.

'What bank?' I said.

'Bristol Security,' she said. 'On Kempton Street.'

'Were you identified?'

'I don't know. I was wearing these sunglasses.'

'Okay, that's a start. Take them off.'

'But ...'

'Take them off, they're no longer a disguise, they are an identification.' She reached up quickly and took them off and put them in her purse.

'Not in your purse, give them to me.' She did, and I slipped them in Susan Silverman's purse. 'We'll ditch them on the way out,' I said.

'I never thought,' she said.

'No, probably you don't have all that much experience at robbery and murder. You'll get better as you go along.'

Susan said, 'Spenser.'

I said, 'Yeah, I know. I'm sorry.'

'I didn't know,' Pam Shepard said. 'I didn't know Jane would really shoot. I just went along. It seemed ... it seemed I ought to – they'd stood by me and all.'

Susan was nodding. 'And you felt you had to stand by them. Anyone would.'

The waitress brought the food: crab salad for Susan, lobster stew for Pam, fisherman's plate for me. I ordered another beer.

'What was the purpose of the robbery?' Susan said.

'We needed money for guns.'

'Jesus Christ!' I said.

'Rose and Jane are organizing ... I shouldn't tell you this ...'

'Babe,' I said, 'you better goddamned well tell me everything you can think of. If you want me to get your ass out of this.'

Susan frowned at me.

'Don't be mad at me,' Pam Shepard said.

'Bullshit,' I said. 'You want me to bring you flowers for being a goddamn thief and a murderer? Sweets for the sweet, my love. Hope the old guy didn't have an old wife who can't get along without him. Once you all get guns you can liberate her too.'

Susan said, 'Spenser,' quite sharply. 'She feels bad enough.'

'No she doesn't,' I said. 'She doesn't feel anywhere near bad enough. Neither do you. You're so goddamned empathetic you've jumped into her frame. "And you felt you had to stand by them. Anyone would." Balls. Anyone wouldn't. You wouldn't.'

I snarled at Pam Shepard. 'How about it. You thought

you were going to a dance recital when you went into that bank with guns to steal the money? You thought you were Faye Dunaway, la de da, we'll take the money and run and the theme music will come up and the banjos will play and all the shots will miss?' I bit a fried shrimp in half. Not bad. Tears were rolling down Pam Shepard's face. Susan looked very grim. But she was silent.

'All right? Okay. We start there. You committed a vicious and mindless goddamned crime and I'm going to try and get you out of the consequences. But let's not clutter up the surface with a lot of horseshit about who stood by who and how you shouldn't tell secrets, and oh-of-course-anyone-would-have.'

Susan said, between her teeth, 'Spenser.'

I drank some beer and ate a scallop. 'Now start at the beginning and tell me everything that happened.'

Pam Shepard said, 'You will help me?'

'Yes.'

She dried her eyes with her napkin. Snuffled a little. Susan gave her a Kleenex and she blew her nose. Delicately. My fisherman's platter had fried haddock in it. I pushed it aside, over behind the French fries, and ate a fried clam.

'Rose and Jane are organizing a women's movement. They feel we must overcome our own passivity and arouse our sisters to do the same. I think they want to model it on the Black Panthers, and to do that we need guns. Rose says we won't have to use them. But to have them will make a great psychological difference. It will increase the level of militancy and it will represent power, even, Jane says, a threat to phallic power.'

'Phallic power?'

She nodded.

I said, 'Go ahead.'

'So they talked about it, and some other women came over and we had a meeting, and decided that we either had to steal the guns or the money to buy them. Jane had a gun, but that was all. Rose said it was easier to steal money than guns, and Jane said that it would be easy as pie to steal from a bank because banks always instruct their employees to cooperate with robbers anyway. What do they care, they are insured. And banks are where the money is. So that's where we should go.'

I didn't say anything. Susan ate some crab salad. Pam Shepard seemed to have no interest in her lobster stew. Looked good too.

'So Rose and Jane said they would do the actual work,' she said. 'And I – I don't know exactly why – I said I'd go with them. And Jane said that was terrific of me and proved that I was really into the women's movement. And Rose said a bank was the ideal symbol of masculine-capitalist oppression. And one of the other women, I don't know her name, she was a black woman, Cape Verdean I think, said that capitalism was itself masculine, and racist as well, so that the bank was a really perfect place to strike. And I said I wanted to go.'

'Like an initiation,' I said.

Susan nodded. Pam Shepard looked puzzled and shrugged.

'Maybe, I don't know. Anyway we went and Jane and Rose and I all wore sunglasses and big hats. And Jane had the gun.'

'Jane has all the fun,' I said. Susan glared at me. Pam Shepard didn't seem to notice.

'Anyway, we went in and Rose and Jane went to the counter and I stayed by the door as a . . . a lookout . . . and Rose gave the girl, woman, behind the counter a note and Jane showed her the gun. And the woman did what it said. She took all her money from the cash drawer and put it in a bag that Rose gave her and we started to leave when that foolish old man tried to stop us. Why did he do that? What possessed him to take that chance?'

'Maybe he thought that was his job.'

She shook her head. 'Foolish old man. What is an old man like that working as a bank guard for anyway?'

'Probably a retired cop. Stood at an intersection for forty years and directed traffic and then retired and couldn't live on the pension. So he's got a gun and he hires out at the bank.'

'But why try to stop us, an old man like that? I mean he saw Jane had a gun. It wasn't his money.'

'Maybe he thought he ought to. Maybe he figured that if he were taking the money to guard the bank when the robbers didn't come, he ought to guard it when they did. Sort of a question of honor, maybe.'

She shook her head. 'Nonsense, that's the machismo convention. It gets people killed and for what? Life isn't a John Wayne movie.'

'Yeah, maybe. But machismo didn't kill that old guy. Jane killed him.'

'But she had to. She's fighting for a cause. For freedom. Not only for women but for men as well, freedom from all the old imperatives, freedom from the burden of machismo for you as well as for us.'

'Right on,' I said. 'Off the bank guard.'

Susan said, 'What happened after Jane shot the guard?'

'We ran,' Pam said. 'Another woman, Grace something, I never knew her last name, was waiting for us in her Volkswagen station wagon, and we got in and drove back to the house.'

'The one on Centre Street?' I asked.

She nodded. 'And we decided there that we better split up. That we couldn't stay there because maybe they could identify us from the cameras. There were two in the bank that Rose spotted. I didn't know where to go so I went to the bus station in New Bedford and took the first bus going out, which was coming to Plymouth. The only time I'd ever been to Plymouth was when we took the kids to Plimoth Plantation when they were smaller. So I got off the bus and walked here. And then I didn't know what to do, so I sat in the snack bar at the reception center for a while and I counted what money I had, most of the hundred dollars you gave me, and I saw your card in my wallet and called you.' She paused and stared out the window. 'I almost called my husband. But that would have just been running home with my tail between my legs. And I started to call you and hung up a couple of times.

I . . . Did I have to have a man to get me out of trouble? But then I had nowhere else to go and nothing else to try so I called.' She kept looking out the window. The butter in her lobster stew was starting to form a skin as the stew cooled. 'And after I called you I walked up and down the main street of the village and in and out of the houses and thought, here I am, forty-three years old and in the worst trouble of my life and I've got no one to call but a guy I've met once in my life, that I don't even know, no one else at all.' She was crying now and her voice shook as she talked. She turned her head away farther toward the window to hide it. The tide had gone out some more since I'd last looked and the dark water rounded rocks beyond the beach and made a kind of cobbled pattern with the sea breaking and foaming over them. It had gotten quite dark now, though it was early afternoon, and spits of rain splattered on the window. 'And you think I'm a goddamned fool,' she said. She had her hand on her mouth and it muffled her speech. 'And I am.'

Susan put her hand on Pam Shepard's shoulder. 'I think I know how you feel,' Susan said. 'But it's the kind of thing he can do and others can't. You did what you felt you had to do, and you need help now, and you have the right person to help you. You did the right thing to call him. He can fix this. He doesn't think you are a fool. He's grouchy about other things, about me, and about himself, a lot of things and he leaned on you too hard. But he can help you with this. He can fix it.'

'Can he make that old man alive again?'

'We don't work that way,' I said. 'We don't look around and see where we were. And we don't look down the road and see what's coming. We don't have anything to do but deal with what we know. We look at the facts and we don't speculate. We just keep looking right at this and we don't say what if, or I wish or if only. We just take it as it comes. First you need someplace to stay besides Plimoth Plantation. I'm not using my apartment because I'm down here working on things. So you can stay there. Come on, we'll go there now.' I gestured for the check. 'Suze,' I said, 'you and Pam go get in my car, I'll pay up here.'

Pam Shepard said, 'I have money.'

I shook my head as the waitress came. Susan and Pam got up and went out. I paid the check, left a tip neither too big nor too small – I didn't want her to remember us – and went to the car after them.

15

It's forty-five minutes from Plymouth to Boston and the traffic was light in midafternoon. We were on Marlborough Street in front of my apartment at three fifteen. On the ride up Pam Shepard had given me nothing else I could use. She didn't know where Rose and Jane were. She didn't know how to find them. She didn't know who had the money, she assumed Rose. They had agreed, if they got separated, to put an ad in the New Bedford *Standard Times* personals column. She didn't know where Rose and Jane had expected to get the guns. She didn't know if they had any gun permit or FID card.

'Can't you just go someplace and buy them?' she said.

'Not in this state,' I said.

She didn't know what kind of guns they had planned to buy. She didn't really know that guns came in various kinds. She didn't know anyone's name in the group except Rose and Jane and Grace, and the only last name she knew was Alexander.

'It's a case I can really sink my teeth into,' I said. 'Lot of hard facts, lot of data. You're sure I've got your name right?'

She nodded.

'What's the wording for your ad,' I said.

'If we get separated? We just say, 'Sisters, call me at' – then we give a phone number and sign our first name.'

'And you run it in the *Standard Times*?'

'Yes, in the personal column.'

We got out of the car and Pam said, 'Oh, what a pretty location. There's the Common right down there.'

'Actually the Public Garden. The Common's on the other side of Charles Street,' I said. We went up to my apartment, second floor front. I opened the door.

Pam Shepard said, 'Oh, very nice. Why it's as neat as a pin. I always pictured bachelor apartments with socks thrown around and whiskey bottles on the floor and wastebaskets spilling onto the floor.'

'I have a cleaning person, comes in once a week.'

'Very nice. Who did the woodcarvings?'

'I have a woodcarver come in once a week.'

Susan said, 'Don't listen to him. He does them.'

'Isn't that interesting, and look at all the books. Have you read all these books?'

'Most of them, my lips get awful tired though. The kitchen is in here. There should be a fair supply of food laid in.'

'And booze,' Susan said.

'That too,' I said. 'In case the food runs out you can starve to death happy.'

I opened the refrigerator and took out a bottle of Amstel. 'Want a drink?' Both Susan and Pam said no. I opened the beer and drank some from the bottle.

'There's some bread and cheese and eggs in the refrigerator. There's quite a bit of meat in the freezer. It's labeled. And Syrian bread. There's coffee in the cupboard here.' I opened the cupboard door. 'Peanut butter, rice, canned tomatoes, flour, so forth. We can get you some vegetables and stuff later. You can make a list of what else you need.'

I showed her the bathroom and the bedroom. 'The sheets are clean.' I said. 'The person changes them each week, and she was here yesterday. You will need clothes and things.' She nodded. 'Why don't you make a list of food and clothes and toiletries and whatever that you need and Suze and I will go out and get them for you.' I gave her a pad and pencil. She sat at the kitchen counter to write. While she did I talked at her. 'When we leave,' I said, 'stay in here. Don't answer the door. I've got a key and Suze has a key and no one else has. So you won't have to open the door for us and no one else has reason to come here. Don't go out.'

'What are you going to do?' she asked.

'I don't know,' I said. 'I'll have to think about it.'

'I think maybe I'll have that drink you offered,' she said.

'Okay, what would you like?'

'Scotch and water?'

'Sure.'

I made her the drink, lots of ice, lots of Scotch, a dash of water. She sipped it while she finished her list.

When she gave it to me she also offered me her money. 'No,' I said. 'You may need it. I'll keep track of all this

123

and when it's over I'll give you a bill.'

She nodded. 'If you want more Scotch,' I said, 'you know where it is.'

Susan and I went out to shop. At the Prudential Center on Boylston Street we split up. I went into the Star Market for food and she went up to the shopping mall for clothes and toiletries. I was quicker with the food than she was with her part, and I had to hang around for a while on the plaza by the funny statue of Atlas or Prometheus or whoever he was supposed to be. Across the way a movie house was running an action-packed double feature: *The Devil in Miss Jones* and *Deep Throat*. They don't make them like they used to. Whatever happened to Ken Maynard and his great horse, Tarzan? I looked some more at the statue. It looked like someone had done a takeoff on Michelangelo, and been taken seriously. Did Ken Maynard really have a great horse named Tarzan? If Ken were still working, his great horse would probably be named Bruce and be a leather freak. A young woman went by wearing a white T-shirt and no bra. On the T-shirt was stenciled TONY'S PX, GREAT FALLS, MONTANA. I was watching her walk away when Susan arrived with several ornate shopping bags.

'That a suspect?' Susan said.

'Remember I'm a licensed law officer. I was checking whether those cut-off jeans were of legal length.'

'Were they?'

'I don't think so.' I picked up groceries and one of Susan's shopping bags and we headed for the car. When we got home Pam Shepard was sitting by the front window looking out at Marlborough Street. She hadn't so far as I could see done anything else except perhaps freshen her drink. It was five o'clock and Susan agreed to join Pam for a drink while I made supper. I pounded some lamb steaks I'd bought for lamb cutlets. Dipped them in flour, then egg, then bread crumbs. When they were what Julia Child calls nicely coated I put them aside and peeled four potatoes. I cut them into little egg-shaped oblongs, which took a while, and started them cooking in a little oil, rolling them around to get them brown all over. I also started the cutlets in another pan. When the potatoes were evenly browned I covered them, turned down the heat and left them to cook through. When the cutlets had browned, I poured off the fat, added some Chablis and some fresh mint, covered them and let them cook. Susan came out into the kitchen once to make two new drinks. I made a Greek salad with feta cheese and ripe olives and Susan set the table while I took the lamb cutlets out of the pan and cooked down the wine. I shut off the heat, put in a lump of unsalted butter, swirled it through the wine essence and poured it over the cutlets. With the meal we had warm Syrian bread and most of a half gallon of California Burgundy. Pam Shepard told me it was excellent and what a good cook I was.

'I never liked it all that much,' Pam said. 'When I was a kid my mother never wanted me in the kitchen. She said I'd be messy. So when I got married I couldn't cook anything.'

Susan said, 'I couldn't cook, really, when I got married either.'

'Harv taught me,' Pam said. 'I think he kind of liked to cook, but . . .' She shrugged. 'That was the wife's job. So I did it. Funny how you cut yourself off from things you like because of . . . of nothing. Just convention, other people's assumptions about what you ought to be and do.'

'Yet often they are our own assumptions, aren't they,' Susan said. 'I mean where do we get our assumptions about how things are or ought to be? How much is there really a discrete identifiable self trying to get out?' I drank some Burgundy.

'I'm not sure I follow,' Pam said.

'It's the old controversy,' Susan said. 'Nature-nurture. Are you what you are because of genetics or because of environment? Do men make history or does history make men?'

Pam Shepard smiled briefly. 'Oh yes, nature–nurture, *Child Growth and Development*, ed. 103. I don't know, but I know I got shoved into a corner I didn't want to be in.' She drank some of her wine, and held her glass toward the bottle. Not fully liberated. Fully liberated you pour the wine yourself. Or maybe the half-gallon bottle was too heavy. I filled her glass. She looked at the wine a minute. 'So did Harvey,' she said.

'Get shoved in a corner?' Susan said.

'Money?' Susan asked.

'No, not really. Not money exactly. It was more being important, being a man that mattered, being a man that knew the score, knew what was happening. A mover and shaker. I don't think he cared all that much about the money, except it proved that he was on top. Does that make sense?' She looked at me.

'Yeah, like making the football team,' I said. 'I understand that.'

'You ought to,' Susan said.

Pam Shepard said, 'Are you like that?'

I shrugged. Susan said, 'Yes, he's like that. In a specialized way.'

Pam Shepard said, 'I would have thought he wasn't but I don't know him very well.'

Susan smiled. 'Well, he isn't exactly, but he is if that makes any sense.'

I said, 'What the hell am I, a pot roast, I sit here and you discuss me?'

Susan said, 'I think you described yourself quite well this morning.'

'Before or after you smothered me with passionate kisses?'

'Long before,' she said.

'Oh,' I said.

Pam Shepard said, 'Well, why aren't you in the race? Why aren't you grunting and sweating to make the team, be a star, whatever the hell it is that Harvey and his friends are trying to do?'

'It's not easy to say. It's an embarrassing question because it requires me to start talking about integrity and self-respect and stuff you recently lumped under John

Wayne movies. Like honor. I try to be honorable. I know that's embarrassing to hear. It's embarrassing to say. But I believe most of the nonsense that Thoreau was preaching. And I have spent a long time working on getting myself to where I could do it. Where I could live life largely on my own terms.'

'Thoreau?' Pam Shepard said. 'You really did read all those books, didn't you?'

'And yet,' Susan said, 'you constantly get yourself involved in other lives and in other people's troubles. This is not Walden Pond you've withdrawn to.'

I shrugged again. It was hard to say it all. 'Everybody's got to do something,' I said.

'But isn't what you do dangerous?' Pam Shepard said.

'Yeah, sometimes.'

'He likes that part,' Susan said. 'He's very into tough. He won't admit it, maybe not even to himself, but half of what he's doing all the time is testing himself against other men. Proving how good he is. It's competition, like football.'

'Is that so?' Pam Shepard said to me.

'Maybe. It goes with the job.'

'It's a job that lets me choose,' I said.

'And yet it cuts you off from a lot of things,' Susan said. 'You've cut yourself off from family, from home, from marriage.'

'I don't know,' I said. 'Maybe.'

'More than maybe,' Susan said. 'It's autonomy. You are the most autonomous person I've ever seen and you don't let anything into that. Sometimes I think the muscle you've built is like a shield, like armor, and you keep yourself private and alone inside there. The integrity complete, unviolated, impervious, safe even from love.'

'We've gone some distance away from Harv Shepard, Suze,' I said. I felt as if I'd been breathing shallow for a long time and needed a deep inhale.

'Not as far as it looks,' Susan said. 'One reason you're not into the corner that Pam's husband is in is because he took the chance. He married. He had kids. He took the risk of love and relationship and the risk of compromise that goes with it.'

'But I don't think Harvey was working for us, Susan,' Pam Shepard said.

'It's probably not that easy,' I said. 'It's probably not something you can cut up like that. Working for us, working for him.'

'Well,' Pam Shepard said. 'There's certainly a difference.'

'Sometimes I think there's never a difference and things never divide into column A and column B,' I said. 'Perhaps he had to be a certain kind of man for you, because he felt that was what you deserved. Perhaps to him it meant manhood, and perhaps he wanted to be a man for you.'

Pam said, 'Machismo again.'

'Yeah, but machismo isn't another word for rape and murder. Machismo is really about honorable behavior.'

'Then why does it lead so often to violence?'

'I don't know that it does, but if it does it might be because that's one of the places that you can be honorable.'

'That's nonsense,' Pam Shepard said.

'You can't be honorable when it's easy,' I said. 'Only when it's hard.'

'When the going gets tough, the tough get going?' The scorn in Pam Shepard's voice had more body than the wine. 'You sound like Nixon.'

I did my David Frye impression. 'I am not a crook,' I said and looked shifty.

'Oh, hell, I don't know,' she said. 'I don't even know what we're talking about anymore. I just know it hasn't worked. None of it, not Harv, not the kids, not me, not the house and the business and the club and growing older, nothing.'

'Yeah,' I said, 'but we're working on it, my love.' She nodded her head and began to cry.

16

I couldn't think of much to do about Pam Shepard crying so I cleared the table and hoped that Susan would come up with something. She didn't. And when we left, Pam Shepard was still snuffling and teary. It was nearly eleven and we were overfed and sleepy. Susan invited me up to Smithfield to spend the night and I accepted, quite graciously, I thought, considering the aggravation she'd been giving me.

'You haven't been slipping off to encounter groups under an assumed name, have you?' I said.

She shook her head. 'I don't quite know why I'm so bitchy lately,' she said.

'It's not bitchy, exactly. It's pushy. I feel from you a kind of steady pressure. An obligation to explain myself.'

'And you don't like a pushy broad, right?'

'Don't start up again, and don't be so goddamned sensitive. You know I don't mean the cliché. If you think I worry about role reversal and who keeps in whose place, you've spent a lot of time paying no attention to me.'

'True,' she said. 'I'm getting a little hyped about the whole subject.'

'What whole subject? That's one of my problems. I think I know the rules of the game all right, but I don't know what the game is.'

'Man–woman relationships, I guess.'

'All of them or me and you.'

'Both.'

'Terrific, Suze, now we've got it narrowed down.'

'Don't make fun. I think being middle-aged and female and single one must think about feminism, if you wish, women's rights and women vis-à-vis men. And of course that includes you and me. We care about each other, we see each other, we go on, but it doesn't develop. It seems directionless.'

'You mean marriage?'

'I don't know. I don't think I mean just that. My God, am I still that conventional? I just know there's a feeling of incompleteness in us. Or, I suppose I can only speak for me, in me, and in the way I perceive our relationship.'

'It ain't just wham-bam-thank-you-ma'am.'

'No, I know that. That's not a relationship. I know I'm more than good tail. I know I matter to you. But . . .'

I paid my fifteen cents on the Mystic River Bridge and headed down its north slope, past the construction barricades that I think were installed when the bridge was built.

'I don't know what's wrong with me,' she said.

'Maybe it's wrong with me,' I said.

There weren't many cars on the Northeast Expressway at this time of night. There was a light fog and the headlights made a scalloped apron of light in front of us as we drove.

'Maybe,' she said. Far right across the salt marshes the lights of the G.E. River Works gleamed. Commerce never rests.

'Explaining myself is not one of the things I do really well, like drinking beer, or taking a nap. Explaining myself is clumsy stuff. You really ought to watch what I do, and, pretty much, I think, you'll know what I am. Actually I always thought you knew what I am.'

'I think I do. Much of it is very good, a lot of it is the best I've ever seen.'

'Ah-ha,' I said.

'I don't mean that,' Susan said. The mercury arc lights at the newly renovated Saugus Circle made the wispy fog bluish and the Blue Star Bar look stark and unreal across Route 1.

'I know pretty well what you are,' she said. 'It's what we are that is bothersome. What the hell are we, Spenser?'

I swung off Route 1 at the Walnut Street exit and headed in toward Smithfield. 'We're together,' I said. 'Why have we got to catalogue. Are we a couple? A pair? I don't know. You pick one.'

'Are we lovers?'

On the right Hawkes Pond gleamed through a very thin fringe of trees. It was a long narrow pond and across it the land rose up in a wooded hill crowned with power lines. In the moonlight, with a wispy fog, it looked pretty good.

'Yeah,' I said. 'Yeah. We're lovers.'

'For how long?' Susan said.

'For as long as we live,' I said. 'Or until you can't bear me anymore. Whichever comes first.'

We were in Smithfield now, past the country club on the left, past the low reedy meadow that was a bird sanctuary, and the place where they used to have a cider mill, to Summer Street, almost to Smithfield Center. Almost to Susan's house.

'For as long as we live will come first,' Susan said.

I drove past Smithfield Center with its old meeting house on the triangular common. A banner stretched across the street announced some kind of barbecue, I couldn't catch what in the dark. I put my hand and Susan took and we held hands to her house.

Everything was wet and glistening in the dark, picking up glints from the streetlights. It wasn't quite raining, but the fog was very damp and the dew was falling. Susan's house was a small cape, weathered shingles, flagstone walk, lots of shrubs. The front door was a Colonial red with small bull's-eye glass windows in the top. Susan unlocked it and went in. I followed her and shut the door. In the dark silent living room, I put my hands on Susan's shoulders and turned her slowly toward me, and put my arms around her. She put her face against my chest and we stood that way, wordless and still for a long time.

'For as long as we live,' I said.

'Maybe longer,' Susan said. There was an old steeple clock with brass works on the mantel in the living room, and while I couldn't see in the dark, I could hear it ticking loudly as we stood there pressed against each other. I thought about how nice Susan smelled, and about how strong her body felt, and about how difficult it is to say what you feel. And I said, 'Come on, honey, let's go to bed.' She didn't move, just pressed harder against me and I reached down with my left hand and scooped up her legs and carried her to the bedroom. I'd been there before and had no trouble in the dark.

17

In the morning, still damp from the shower, we headed back for the Cape, stopped on the way for steak and eggs in a diner and got to the hotel room I still owned about noon. The fog had lifted and the sun was as clean and bright as we were, though less splendidly dressed. In my mailbox was a note to call Harv Shepard.

I called him from my room while Susan changed into her bathing suit.

'Spenser,' I said, 'what do you want?'

'You gotta help me.'

'That's what I was telling you just a little while back,' I said.

'I gotta see you, it's, it's outta control. I can't handle it. I need help. That, that goddamned nigger shoved one of my kids. I need help.'

'Okay,' I said. 'I'll come over.'

'No,' he said. 'I don't want you here. I'll come there. You in the hotel?'

'Yep.' I gave him my room number. 'I'll wait for you.'

Susan was wiggling her way into a one-piece bathing suit.

'Anything?' she said.

136

'Yeah, Shepard's coming apart. I guess Hawk made a move at one of the kids and Shepard's in a panic. He's coming over.'

'Hawk scares me,' Susan said. She slipped her arms through the shoulder straps.

'He scares me too, my love.'

'He's . . .' She shrugged. 'Don't go against him.'

'Better me than Shepard,' I said.

'Why better you than Shepard?'

'Because I got a chance and Shepard has none.'

'Why not the police?'

'We'll have to ask Shepard that. Police are okay by me. I got no special interest in playing Russian roulette with Hawk. Shepard called him a nigger.'

Susan shrugged. 'What's that got to do?'

'I don't know,' I said. 'But I wish he hadn't done that. It's insulting.'

'My God, Spenser. Hawk has threatened this man's life, beaten him up, abused his children, and you're worried about a racial slur?'

'Hawk's kind of different,' I said.

She shook her head. 'So the hell are you,' she said. 'I'm off to the pool to work on my tan. When you get through you can join me there. Unless you decide to elope with Hawk.'

'Miscegenation,' I said. 'Frightful.'

She left. About two minutes later Shepard arrived. He was moving better now. Some of the stiffness had gone from his walk, but confidence had not replaced it. He had on a western-cut, black-checked leisure suit and a white shirt with black stitching, the collar out over the lapels of the suit. There was a high shine on his black-tassled loafers and his face was gray with fear.

'You got a drink here,' he said.

'No, but I'll get one. What do you like?'

'Bourbon.'

I called room service and ordered bourbon and ice. Shepard walked across the room and stared out the window at the golf course. He sat down in the armchair by the window and got right up again. 'Spenser,' he said. 'I'm scared shit.'

'I don't blame you,' I said.

'I never thought ... I always thought I could handle business, you know? I mean I'm a businessman and a businessman is supposed to be able to handle business. I'm supposed to know how to put a deal together and how to make it work. I'm supposed to be able to manage people. But this. I'm no goddamned candy-ass. I been around and all, but these people ...'

'I know about these people.'

'I mean that goddamned nigger ...'

'His name's Hawk,' I said. 'Call him Hawk.'

'What are you, the NAACP?'

'Call him Hawk.'

'Yeah, okay, Hawk. My youngest came in the room while they were talking to me and Hawk grabbed him by the shirt and put him out the door. Right in front of me. The black bastard.'

'Who are they?'

'They?'

'You said your kid came in while they were talking to you.'

'Oh, yeah,' Shepard walked back to the window and looked out again. 'Hawk and a guy named Powers. White guy. I guess Hawk works for him.'

'Yeah, I know Powers.'

The room service waiter came with the booze on a tray. I signed the check and tipped him a buck. Shepard rummaged in his pocket. 'Hey, let me get that,' he said.

'I'll put it on your bill,' I said. 'What did Powers want? No, better, I'll tell you what he wanted. You owe him money and you can't pay him and he's going to let you off the hook a little if you let him into your business a lot.'

'Yeah.' Shepard poured a big shot over ice from the bottle of bourbon and slurped at it. 'How the hell did you know?'

'Like I said, I know Powers. It's also not a very new idea. Powers and a lot of guys like him have done it before. A guy like you mismanages the money, or sees a chance for a big break or overextends himself at the wrong time and can't get financing. Powers comes along, gives you the break, charges an exorbitant weekly interest. You can't pay, he sends Hawk around to convince you it's serious. You still can't pay, so Powers comes around and says you can give me part of the business or you can cha-cha once more with Hawk. You're lucky, you got me to run to. Most guys got no one but the cops.'

139

'I didn't mismanage the money.'

'Yeah, course not. Why not go to the cops?'

'No cops,' Shepard said. He drank some more bourbon.

'Why not?'

'They'll start wanting to know why I needed money from Powers.'

'And you were cutting a few corners?'

'Goddamnit, I had to. Everybody cuts a few corners.'

'Tell me about the ones you cut.'

'Why? What do you need to know that for?'

'I won't know till you tell me.'

Shepard drank some more bourbon. 'I was in a box. I had to do something.' The drape on the right side of the window hung crookedly. Shepard straightened it. I waited. 'I was in business with an outfit called Estate Management Corporation. They go around to different vacation-type areas and develop leisure homes in conjunction with a local guy. Around here I was the local guy. What we did was set up a separate company with me as president. I did the developing, dealt with the town-planning board, building inspector, that stuff, and supervised the actual construction. They provided architects, planners and financing and the sales force. It's a little more complicated than that, but you get the idea. My company was a wholly owned subsidiary of Estate Management. You follow that okay?'

'Yeah. I got that. I'm not a shrewd-o-business tycoon like you, but if you talk slowly and I can watch your lips move, I can keep up, I think. What was the name of your company?'

'We called the development Promised Land. And the company was Promised Land, Inc.'

'Promised Land.' I whistled. 'Cu-ute,' I said. 'Were you aiming at an exclusive Jewish clientele?'

'Huh? Jewish? Why Jewish? Anybody was welcome. I mean we wouldn't be thrilled if the Shvartzes moved in maybe, but we didn't care about religion.'

I wished I hadn't said it. 'Okay,' I said. 'So you're president of Promised Land, Inc., a wholly owned subsidiary of Estate Management, Inc. Then what?'

'Estate Management went under.'

'Bankrupt?'

'Yeah.' Shepard emptied his bourbon and I poured some more in the glass. I offered ice and he shook his head. 'The way it worked was the Estate Management people would see the land, really high-powered stuff, contact people, closers, free trips to Florida, the whole bag. The buyer would put a deposit on the land and would also sign a contract for the kind of house he wanted. We had about six models to choose from. He'd put a deposit on the house as well, and that deposit would go into an escrow account.'

'What happened to the land deposit?'

'Went to Estate Management.'

'Okay, and who controlled the house escrow?'

Shepard said, 'Me.'

'And when Estate Management pulled out, and you were stuck with a lot of money invested and no backing, you dipped into the escrow.'

'Yeah, I used it all. I had to. When Estate Management folded, the town held up on the building permits. All there was was the building sites staked off. We hadn't brought the utilities in yet. You know, water, sewage, that kind of thing.'

I nodded.

'Well, the town said, nobody gets a permit to build anything until the utilities are in. They really screwed me. I mean, I guess they had to. Things smelled awful funny when Estate went bankrupt. A lot of money disappeared, all those land deposits, and a lot of people started wondering about what happened. It smelled awful bad. But I was humped. I had all my capital tied up in the goddamned land and the only way I was going to get it back was to build the houses and sell them. But I couldn't do that because I couldn't get a permit until I put in the utilities. And I couldn't put in the utilities because I didn't have any money. And nobody wanted to finance the thing. Banks only want to give you money when you can prove you don't need it, you know that. And they really didn't want to have anything to do with Promised Land, because by now the story was all around financial circles and the IRS and the SEC and the Mass attorney general's office and the FCC and a bunch of other people were starting to investigate Estate Management, and a group of people who'd bought land were suing Estate Management. So I scooped the escrow money. I was stuck. It was that or close up shop and start looking for work without enough money to have my résumé typed. I'm forty-five years old.'

'Yeah, I know. Let me guess the next thing that happened. The group that was suing Estate Management also decided to get its house deposit back.'

Shepard nodded.

'And of course, since you'd used it to start bringing in utilities, you couldn't give it back.'

He kept nodding as I talked.

'So you found Powers someplace and he lent you the dough. What was the interest rate? Three percent a week?'

'Three and a half.'

'And, of course, payment on the principal.'

Shepard nodded some more.

'And you couldn't make it.'

Nod.

'And Hawk beat you up.'

'Yeah. Actually he didn't do it himself. He had two guys do it, and he, like, supervised.'

'Hawk's moving up. Executive level. He was always a comer.'

'He said he just does the killing now; the sweaty work he delegates.'

'And so here we are.'

'Yeah,' Shepard said. He leaned his head against the window. 'The thing is, Powers' money bailed me out. I was coming back. The only money I owe is Powers and I can't pay. It's like – I'm so close and the only way to win is to lose.'

18

Shepard looked at me expectantly when he was through telling me his sins.

'What do you want,' I said, 'absolution? Say two Our Fathers and three Hail Marys and make a good act of contrition? Confession may be good for the soul but it's not going to help your body any if we can't figure a way out.'

'What could I do,' he said. 'I was in a corner, I had to crib on the escrow money. Estate Management got off with four or five million bucks. Was I supposed to watch it all go down the pipe? Everything I've been working for? Everything I am?'

'Someday we can talk about just what the hell you were working for, and maybe even what you are. Not now. How hot is Powers breathing on your neck?'

'We've got a meeting set up for tomorrow.'

'Where?'

'At Hawk's room in the Holiday Inn.'

'Okay, I'll go with you.'

'What are you going to do?'

'I don't know. I've got to think. But it's better than going alone, isn't it.'

Shepard's breath came out in a rush. 'Oh, hell, yes,' he said, and finished the bourbon.

'Maybe we can talk them into an extension,' I said. 'The more time I got, the more chance to work out something.'

'But what can we do?'

'I don't know. What Powers is doing, remember, is illegal. If we get really stuck we can blow the whistle and you can be state's evidence against Powers and get out of it with a tongue-lashing.'

'But I'm ruined.'

'Depends how you define ruined,' I said. 'Being King Powers' partner, rich or poor, would be awful close to ruination. Being dead also.'

'No,' he said. 'I can't go to the cops.'

'Not yet you can't. Maybe later you'll have to.'

'How would I get Pam back? Broke, no business, my name in the papers for being a goddamned crook? You think she'd come back and live with me in a four-room cottage while I collected welfare?'

'I don't know. She doesn't seem to be coming back to you while, as far as she knows, you're up on top.'

'You don't know her. She's always watching. Who's got how much, whose house is better or worse than ours, whose lawn is greener or browner. You don't know her.'

'She's another problem,' I said. 'We'll work on her too, but we can't get into marriage encounter until this problem is solved.'

'Yeah, but just remember, what I told you is absolutely

confidential. I can't risk everything. There's got to be another way.'

'Harv,' I said. 'You're acting like you got lots of options. You don't. You don't. You reduced your options when you dipped into the escrow, and you goddamned near eliminated them when you took some of Powers' money. We're talking about people who might shoot you. Remember that.'

Shepard nodded. 'There's got to be a way.'

'Yeah, there probably is. Let me think about it. What time's the meeting tomorrow?'

'One o'clock.'

'I'll pick you up at your house about twelve forty-five. Go home, stay there. If I need you I want to be able to reach you.'

'What are you going to do?'

'I'm going to think.'

Shepard left. Half sloshed and a little relieved. Talking about a problem sometimes gives you the illusion you've done something about it. At least he wasn't trying to handle it alone. Nice clientele I had. The cops wanted Pam and the crooks wanted Harv.

I went out to the pool. Susan was sitting in a chaise in her red-flowered one-piece suit reading *The Children of the Dream*, by Bruno Bettelheim. She had on big, gold-rimmed sunglasses and a large white straw hat with a red band that matched the bathing suit. I stopped before she saw me and looked at her. Jesus Christ, I thought. How could anyone have ever divorced her? Maybe she'd divorced him.

We'd never really talked much about it. But even so, where was he? If she'd divorced me, I'd have followed her around for the rest of our lives. I walked over, put my arms on either side of her and did a push-up on the chaise. Lowering myself until our noses touched.

'If you and I were married, and you divorced me, I would follow you around the rest of my life,' I said.

'No you wouldn't,' she said. 'You'd be too proud.'

'I would assault anyone you dated.'

'That I believe. But you're not married to me and get off of me, you goof. You're just showing off.'

I did five or six push-ups over her on the chaise.

'Why do you say that?' I said.

She poked me with her index finger in the solar plexus. 'Off,' she said.

I did one more push-up. 'You know what this makes me think of?'

'Of course I know what it makes you think of. Now get the hell off me, you're bending my book.'

I snapped off one more push-up and bounced off the chaise the way a gymnast dismounts the parallel bars. Straightening to attention as my feet hit.

'Once you put adolescence behind you,' Susan said, 'you'll be quite an attractive guy, a bit physical but ... attractive. What did Shepard want?'

'Help,' I said. 'He's into a loan shark as we assumed, and the loan shark wants his business.' I got a folding chair from across the pool and brought it back and sat beside Susan and told her about Shepard and his problem.

'That means you are going to have to deal with Hawk,' Susan said.

'Maybe,' I said.

She clamped her mouth in a thin line and took a deep breath through her nose. 'What are you going to do?'

'I don't know. I thought I'd go down and sit in the bar and think. Want to come?'

She shook her head. 'No, I'll stay here and read and maybe swim in a while. When you think of something, let me know. We can have lunch or something to celebrate.'

I leaned over and kissed her on the shoulder, and went to the bar. There were people having lunch, but not many drinking. I sat at the far end of the bar, ordered a Harp on draft and started in on the peanuts in the dark wooden bowl in front of me.

I had two problems. I had to take King Powers off of Shepard's back and I had to get Pam Shepard off the hook for armed robbery and murder. Saps. I was disgusted with both of them. It's an occupational hazard, I thought. Everyone gets contemptuous after a while of his clients. Teachers get scornful of students, doctors of patients, bartenders of drinkers, salesmen of buyers, clerks of customers. But, Jesus, they were saps. The Promised Land. Holy Christ! I had another beer. The peanut bowl was empty. I rattled it on the bar until the bartender came down and refilled it. Scornfully, I thought. Guns, I thought. Get guns and disarm phallic power. Where the hell were they going to get guns? They could look in the Yellow

Pages under gunrunner. I could put them in touch with somebody like King Powers. Then when he sold them the guns they could shoot him and that would solve Shepard's problem ... or I could frame Powers. No, frame wasn't right. Entrapment. That's the word. I could entrap Powers. Not for sharking: that would get Shepard in the soup too. But for illegal gun sales. Done right it would get him off Shepard's back for quite a long time. It would also get Rose and Jane out of Pam Shepard's life. But why wouldn't they take Pam with them? Because I could deal with the local DA: Powers and two radical feminists on a fresh roll, if he kept the Shepards out of it. I liked it. It needed a little more shape and substance. But I liked it. It could work. My only other idea was appealing to Powers' better instincts. That didn't hold much promise. Entrapment was better. I was going to flimflam the old King. A little Scott Joplin music in the background, maybe. I had another beer and ate more peanuts and thought some more.

Susan came in from the pool with a thigh-length white lace thing over her bathing suit, and slid onto the barstool next to me.

'Cogito ergo sum,' I said.

'Oh absolutely,' she said. 'You've always been sicklied over with the pale cast of thought.'

'Wait'll you hear,' I said.

19

After lunch I called the New Bedford *Standard Times* and inserted an ad in the personals column of the classified section: 'Sisters, call me at 555–1434. Pam.'

Then I called 555–1434. Pam Shepard answered the first ring.

'Listen,' I said. And read her the ad. 'I just put that in the New Bedford *Standard Times*. When the sisters call you arrange for us to meet. You, me, them.'

'Oh, they won't like that. They won't trust you.'

'You'll have to get them to do it anyway. Talk to them of obligation and sororal affiliation. Tell them I've got a gun dealer who wants to talk. How you get us together is up to you, but do it.'

'Why is it so important?'

'To save your hide and Harv's and make the world safe for democracy. Just do it. It's too complicated to explain. You getting stir-crazy there?'

'No, it's not too bad. I've seen a lot of daytime tele-vision.'

'Don't watch too much, it'll rot your teeth.'

'Spenser?'

'Yeah.'

'What's wrong with Harvey? What did you mean about saving Harvey's hide?'

'Nothing you need worry about now. I'm just concerned with his value system.'

'He's all right?'

'Sure.'

'And the kids?'

'Of course. They miss you, Harv, too, but they're fine otherwise.' Ah, Spenser, you glib devil you. How the hell did I know how they were? I'd seen one of them my first day on the case.

'Funny,' she said. 'I don't know if I miss them or not, sometimes I think I do, but sometimes I just think I ought to and am feeling guilty because I don't. It's hard to get in touch with your feelings sometimes.'

'Yeah, it is. Anything you need right now before I hang?'

'No, no thanks, I'm okay.'

'Good. Suze or I will be in touch.'

I hung up.

Susan in faded jeans and a dark-blue blouse was heading down Cape to look at antiques. 'And I may pick up some young stud still in college and fulfill my wildest fantasies,' she said.

I said, 'Grrrrrr.'

'Women my age are at the peak of their erotic power,' she said. 'Men your age are in steep decline.'

'I'm young at heart,' I said. Susan was out the door. She stuck her head back in. 'I wasn't talking about heart,' she said. And went. I looked at my watch. It was one fifteen. I went in the bathroom, splashed some water on my face, toweled dry and headed for New Bedford.

At five after two I was illegally parked outside the New Bedford police station on Spring Street. It was three stories, brick, with A dormers on the roof and a kind of cream yellow trim. Flanking the entrance, just like in the Bowery Boys movies, were white globes on black iron columns. On the globes it said NEW BEDFORD POLICE in black letters. A couple of tan police cruisers with blue shields on the door were parked out front. One of them was occupied, and I noticed that the New Bedford cops wore white hats. I wondered if the crooks wore black ones.

At the desk I asked a woman cop who was handling the Bristol Security robbery. She had light hair and blue eye-shadow and shiny lipstick, and she looked at me hard for about ten seconds.

'Who wants to know?' she said.

Not sex nor age nor national origin makes any difference. Cops are cops.

'My name's Spenser,' I said. 'I'm a private license from Boston and I have some information that's going to get someone promoted to sergeant.'

'I'll bet you do,' she said. 'Why don't you lay a little on me and see if I'm impressed.'

'You on the case?'

'I'm on the desk, but impress me anyway.'

I shook my head. 'Detectives,' I said. 'I only deal with detectives.'

'Everybody only deals with detectives. Every day I sit here with my butt getting wider, and every day guys like you come in and want to talk with a detective.' She picked up the phone on the desk, dialed a four-digit number and said into the mouthpiece, 'Sylvia there? Margaret on the desk. Yeah. Well, tell him there's a guy down here says he's got information on Bristol Security. Okay.' She hung up. 'Guy in charge is a detective named Jackie Sylvia. Sit over there, he'll be down in a minute.'

It was more like five before he showed up. A squat bald man with dark skin. He was as dapper as a guy can be who stands five six and weighs two hundred. Pink-flowered shirt, a beige leisure suit, coppery-brown patent leather loafers with a couple of bright gold links on the tops. It was hard to tell how old he was. His round face was without lines, but the close-cropped hair that remained below his glistening bald spot was mostly gray. He walked over to me with a light step, and I suspected he might not be as fat as he looked.

'My name's Sylvia,' he said. 'You looking for me?'

'I am if you're running the Bristol Security investigation.'

'Yeah.'

'Can we go someplace and talk?'

Sylvia nodded toward the stairs past the desk and I followed him to the second floor. We went through a door marked ROBBERY and into a room that overlooked Second Street. There were six desks butted together in groups of two, each with a push-button phone and a light maple swivel chair. In the far corner an office had been partitioned off. On the door was a sign that read SGT CRUZ. At one of the desks a skinny cop with scraggly blond hair sat with his feet up talking on the phone. He was wearing a black T-shirt, and on his right forearm he had a tattoo of a thunderbird and the words FIGHTING 45TH. A cigarette burned on the edge of the desk, a long ash forming. Sylvia grabbed a straight chair from beside one of the other desks and dragged it over beside his. 'Sit,' he said. I sat and he slid into his swivel chair and tilted it back, his small feet resting on the base of the chair. He wasn't wearing socks. A big floor fan in the far corner moved hot air back and forth across the desk tops as it scanned the room.

On Sylvia's desk was a paper coffee cup, empty, and part of a peanut-butter sandwich on white bread. 'Okay,' Sylvia said. 'Shoot.'

'You know who King Powers is?' I said.

'Yeah.'

'I can give you the people who did the Bristol Security and I can give you Powers, but there's got to be a trade.'

'Powers don't do banks.'

'I know. I can give him to you for something else, and I can give you the bank people and I can tie them together, but I gotta have something back from you.'

'What do you want?'

'I want two people who are in this, left out of this.'

'One of them you?'

'No, I don't do banks either.'

'Let me see something that tells me what you do do.'

I showed him my license. He looked at it, handed it back. 'Boston, huh. You know a guy named Abel Markum up there, works out of Robbery?'

'Nope.'

'Who do you know?'

'I know a homicide lieutenant named Quirk. A dick named Frank Belson. Guy in Robbery named Herschel Patton. And I have a friend that's a school-crossing guard in Billerica named . . .'

Sylvia cut me off. 'Okay, okay, I done business with Patton.' He took some grape-flavored sugarless bubble gum from his shirt pocket and put two pieces in his mouth. He didn't offer any to me. 'You know, if you're in possession of evidence of the commission of a felony that you have no legal right to withhold that evidence.'

'Can I have a piece of bubble gum?'

Sylvia reached into his pocket, took out the pack and tossed it on the desk in front of me. There were three pieces left. I took one.

'Take at least two,' Sylvia said. 'You can't work up a bubble with one. Stuff's lousy.'

I took another piece, peeled off the paper and chewed it. Sylvia was right. It was lousy.

'Remember when Double Bubble used to put out the nice lump of pink bubble gum and it was all you needed to get a good bubble?'

'Times change,' Sylvia said. 'Withholding information of a felony is illegal.'

I blew a small purple bubble. 'Yeah, I know. You want to talk about trade?'

'How about we slap you in a cell for a while as an accessory to a felony?'

I worked on the bubble gum. It wasn't elastic enough. I could only produce a small bubble, maybe as big as a ping-pong ball, before it broke with a sharp little snap.

'How about while you're in the cell we interrogate you a while. We got some guys down here can interrogate the shit out of a person. You know?'

'This stuff sticks to your teeth,' I said.

'Not if you don't have any,' Sylvia said.

'Why the hell would someone make gum that sticks to your teeth?' I said. 'Christ, you can't trust anyone.'

'You don't like it, spit it out. I don't make you chew it.'

'It's better than nothing,' I said.

'You gonna talk to me about the Bristol Security job?'

'I'm gonna talk to you about a trade.'

'Goddamnit, Spenser, you can't come waltzing in here and tell me what kind of deal you'll make with me. I don't know what kind of crap you get away with up in Boston, but down here I tell you what kind of deal there is.'

'Very good,' I said. 'One look at my license and you remembered my name. I didn't even see your lips move when you looked at it either.'

'Don't smart-ass with me, Johnny, or you'll be looking very close at the floor. Understand what I'm saying to you?'

'Aw come on, Sylvia, stop terrifying me. When I get panicky I tend to violence and there's only two of you in the room.' The scraggly-haired cop with the tattoo had hung up the phone and drifted over to listen.

'Want me to open the window, Jackie,' he said. 'Then if he gets mean we can scream for help?'

'Or jump,' Sylvia said. 'It's two floors but it would be better than trying to deal with an animal like this.'

I said, 'You guys want to talk trade yet, or are you working up a nightclub act?'

'How do I know you can deliver?' Sylvia said.

'If I don't what have you lost? You're no worse off than you are now.'

'No entrapment,' scraggly hair said. 'At least nothing that looks like entrapment in court. We been burned on that a couple of times.'

'No sweat,' I said.

'How bad are the people you want left out?'

'They are no harm to anybody but themselves,' I said. 'They ran after the wrong promise and got into things they couldn't control.'

'The bank guard that got killed,' Sylvia said, 'I knew him. Used to be in the department here, you know.'

'I know,' I said. 'My people didn't want it to happen.'

'Homicide during the commission of a felony is murder one.'

'I know that too,' I said. 'And I know that these people are a good swap for what I can give you. Somebody's got to go down for the bank guard.'

Sylvia interrupted. 'Fitzgerald, his name was. Everybody called him Fitzy.'

'Like I say, somebody has to go down for that. And somebody will. I just want to save a couple of goddamned fools.'

Scraggly hair looked at Sylvia. 'So far we got zip on the thing, Jackie. Air.'

'You got a plan?' Sylvia said.

I nodded.

'There's no guarantee. Whatever you got, I'm going to have to check you out first.'

'I know that.'

'Okay, tell me.'

'I thought you'd never ask,' I said.

20

Scraggly hair's name turned out to be McDermott. He and Jackie Sylvia listened without comment while I laid it out and when I was through Sylvia said, 'Okay, we'll think about it. Where can I reach you?'

'Dunfey's in Hyannis. Or my service if I'm not there. I check with the service every day.' I gave him the number.

'We'll get back to you.'

On the drive back to Hyannis the grape bubble gum got harder and harder to chew. I gave up in Wareham and spat it out the window in front of the hospital. The muscles at my jaw hinges were sore, and I felt slightly nauseous. When I pulled into the parking lot at Dunfey's it was suppertime and the nausea had given way to hunger.

Susan was back from her antiquing foray and had a Tiffany-style glass lampshade for which she'd paid $125. We went down to the dining room, had two vodka gimlets each, parslied rack of lamb and blackberry cheesecake. After dinner we had some cassis and then went down to the ballroom and danced all the slow numbers until midnight. We brought a bottle of champagne back to the room and drank it and went to bed and didn't sleep until nearly three.

It was ten forty when I woke up. Susan was still asleep, her back to me, the covers up tight around her neck. I picked up the phone and ordered breakfast, softly. 'Don't knock,' I said. 'Just leave it outside the door. My friend is still asleep.'

I showered and shaved and with a towel around my waist opened the door and brought in the cart. I drank coffee and ate from a basket of assorted muffins while I dressed. Susan woke up as I was slipping my gun into the hip holster. I clipped the holster onto my belt. She lay on her back with her hands behind her head and watched me. I slipped on my summer blazer with the brass buttons and adjusted my shirt collar so it rolled out nicely over the lapels. Seductive.

'You going to see Hawk and whatsisname?' Susan said.

'Powers,' I said. 'Yeah. Me and Harv Shepard.'

She continued to look at me.

'Want some coffee?' I said.

She shook her head. 'Not yet.'

I ate a corn muffin.

'Are you scared? Susan asked.

'I don't know. I don't think much about it. I don't see anything very scary happening today.'

'Do you like it?'

'Yeah. I wouldn't do it if I didn't like it.'

'I mean this particularly. I know you like the work. But do you like this? You are going to frame a very dangerous man. That should scare you, or excite you or something.'

'I'm not going to frame him. I'm going to entrap him, in fact.'

'You know what I mean. If it doesn't work right he'll kill you.'

'No, he'll have it done.'

'Don't do that. Don't pick up the less important part of what I'm saying. You know what I'm after. What kind of man does the kinds of things you do? What kind of man gets up in the morning and showers and shaves and checks the cartridges in his gun?'

'Couldn't we talk over the transports of delight in which we soared last evening?'

'Do you laugh at everything?'

'No, but we're spending too much time on this kind of talk. The kind of man I am is not a suitable topic, you know. It's not what one talks about.'

'Why?'

'Because it's not.'

'The code? A man doesn't succumb to self-analysis? It's weak? It's womanish?'

'It's pointless. What I am is what I do. Finding the right words for it is no improvement. It isn't important whether I'm scared or excited. It's important whether or not I do it. It doesn't matter to Shepard why. It matters to Shepard if.'

'You're wrong. It matters more than that. It matters why.'

'Maybe it matters mostly how.'

'My, aren't we epigrammatic. Spencer Tracy and Katharine Hepburn. Repartee.'

'He spells his name differently,' I said.

Susan turned over on her side, her back to me, and was quiet. I had some more coffee. The murmurous rush of the air conditioner seemed quite loud. I'd asked for the New Bedford *Standard Times* with breakfast, and in the quiet, I picked it up and turned to the classified section. My ad was there under personals. 'Sisters, call me at 555–1434, Pam.' I looked at the sports page and finished my coffee. It was ten after twelve. I folded the paper and put it on the room-service cart.

'Gotta go, Suze,' I said.

She nodded without turning over.

I got up, put on my sunglasses and opened the door. 'Spenser,' she said, 'I don't want us to be mad at each other.'

'Me neither,' I said. I still had hold of the doorknob.

'Come back when you can,' she said. 'I miss you when you're gone.'

'Me too,' I said. I left the door open and went back and kissed her on the cheekbone, up near the temple. She rolled over on her back and looked up at me. Her eyes were wet. 'Bye-bye,' I said.

'Bye-bye.'

I went out and closed the door and headed for Harv Shepard's place with my stomach feeling odd.

I don't know if I was scared or not, but Shepard was so scared his face didn't fit. The skin was stretched much too tight over the bones and he swallowed a lot, and loudly, as we drove out Main Street to the Holiday Inn.

'You don't need to know what I'm up to,' I said. 'I think

162

you'll do better if you don't. Just take it that I've got something working that might get you out of this.'

'Why can't you tell me?'

'Because it requires some deception and I don't think you're up to it.'

'You're probably right,' he said.

Hawk had a room on the second floor, overlooking the pool. He answered the door when we knocked, and Shepard and I went in. There was assorted booze on the bureau to the right, and a thin guy with horn-rimmed glasses reading the *Wall Street Journal* on one of the beds. King Powers was sitting at a round table with an open ledger in front of him, his hands folded on the edge of the table. Stagey bastard.

'What is that you have with you?' Powers said in a flat Rudy Vallée voice.

'We're friends,' I said. 'We go everywhere together.'

Powers was a tall, soft-looking man with pale skin and reddish hair trimmed long like a Dutch boy, and augmented with fuzzy mutton-chop sideburns. His wardrobe looked like Robert Hall Mod. Maroon-checked doubleknit leisure suit, white belt, white shoes, white silk shirt with the collar out over the lapels. A turquoise arrowhead was fastened around his neck on a leather thong and stuck straight out, like a gesture of derision.

'I didn't tell you to bring no friends,' Powers said to Shepard.

'You'll be glad he did,' I said. 'I got a package for you that will put a lot of change in your purse.'

'I don't use no goddamned purse,' Powers said.

'Oh,' I said. 'I'm sorry. I thought that was your mistress on the bed.'

Behind me Hawk murmured. 'Hot damn' to himself. The guy on the bed looked up from his *Wall Street Journal* and frowned.

Powers said, 'Hawk, get him the fuck out of here.'

Hawk said. 'This is Spenser. I told you about him. He likes to kid around but he don't mean harm. Leastwise he don't always mean harm.'

'Hawk, you hear me. I told you move him out.'

'He talking money, King. Maybe you should listen.'

'You working for me, Hawk? You do what you're told.'

'Naw, I only do what I want. I never do what I'm told. Same with old Spenser here. You yell your ass off at him, if you want, but he ain't going to do a goddamned thing he don't want to do. You and Macey listen to him. He talking about money, he probably ain't bullshitting. You don't like what you hear, then I'll move him out.'

'Aw right, aw right. Let's hear it, for crissake. Spit it out.' Powers' pale face was a little red and he was looking at me hard. Macey, on the bed, had sat up, and put his feet on the floor. He still held the *Journal* in his left hand, his forefinger keeping the place.

'Okay, King. First. Harv can't pay up, at this time.'

'Then his ass is grass and I'm a fucking lawnmower,' Powers said.

'Trendy,' I said.

'Huh?'

'Trendy as a bastard, that slick maroon and white combo. And to top it off you talk so good. You're just an altogether with-it guy.'

'You keep fucking around with me, Spenser, and you're going to wish you never did.'

'Whyn't you get to the part about the bread, Spenser?' Hawk said. 'In the purse. Whyn't you talk on that?'

'I got a buyer with about a hundred thousand dollars who is looking for some guns. I will trade you the buyer for Shepard.'

'What makes you think I can get guns?'

'King, for a hundred thousand skins you could get a dancing aardvark.' He smiled. His lips were puffy and when he smiled the inside of his upper lip turned out. And his gums showed above his top teeth.

'Yeah, maybe I could,' he said. 'But Shepard's into me for a lot of fucking dough.' He ran his eyes down the ledger page in front of him. 'Thirty big ones. I took a lot of risk with that dough, just on a handshake, you know? It ain't easy to trade that off.'

'Okay,' I said. 'See you, we'll take it elsewhere,' I said. 'Come on, Harv.'

Powers said, 'You're choice, but your pal better have the payment on him now, or we're going to be awful mad.'

'The payment's in the offer. You turned it down, you got no bitch.' I turned to go. Hawk was between us and the door. His hands resting delicately on his hips.

'Hawk,' Powers said. 'Shepard don't leave.'

'Hundred thousand's a lotta vegetable matter, King,' Hawk said.

'Hawk's right, Mr Powers.' Macey on the bed had dropped his *Journal* and brought out a neat-looking little .25 automatic with a pearl handle and nickel plating. Probably matched his cufflinks.

'What's in it for you, Spencer?' Powers said.

'Thirty percent,' I said. 'You can use it to pay off Shepard's loan.'

Powers was quiet. We all were. It was like a stop frame in instant replay.

Hawk at ease in front of the door. Shepard with his skin squeezing tight on his body, Macey with his cute gun. Powers sitting at the table, thinking.

The window was behind him and the light coming in framed him like a back-lit photograph. The little tendrils of fuzz in the double-knit were silhouetted and clear along his coat sleeves and the tops of the shoulders. The mutton-chop sideburns where the whiskers individuated at the outer edge were more gold than copper against the light.

'Who's your customer?' King said. Hawk whistled shave-and-a-haircut-two-bits between his teeth. Softly.

'If I told you that I probably wouldn't be needed as go-between, would I?'

Powers turned his lip up again and giggled. Then he turned to the thin guy. 'Macey,' he said, 'I got some golf to play. Set this thing up.' He looked at me. 'This better be straight,' he said. 'If it ain't you are going to be pushing up your fucking daisies. You unnerstand? Fucking daisies

166

you'll be pushing up.' He got up and walked past me toward the door.

'Daisies,' I said.

He went out. Macey put the .25 away and said, 'Okay, let's get to work.'

I said, 'Is he going to play golf in his Anderson-Little cutaway?'

'He's going to change in the clubhouse,' Macey said. 'Haven't you ever played golf?'

'Naw, we were into aggravated assault when I was a kid.'

Macey smiled once, on and off like a blinking light. Hawk went and lay down on the bed and closed his eyes. Shepard went stiffly to the bureau where the booze was and made a big drink. Macey sat down at the round table and I joined him. 'Okay,' he said, 'give me the deal.'

21

There wasn't all that much to set up with Macey yet. I told him I'd have to get in touch with the other principals first and get back to him, but that the 100 grand was firm and he should start getting in touch with his sources.

'The guns would be top dollar,' Macey said. 'There's the risk factor, and the added problem of market impact. Large quantity like this causes ripples, as you must know.'

'I know. And I know you can manage it. That's why I came to you.'

Macey said, 'Um-hum' and took a business card from the breast pocket of his seersucker suit. 'Call me,' he said, 'when you've talked to the other party.'

I took the card and put it in my wallet. 'We're in business then,' I said.

'Certainly,' Macey said. 'Assuming the deal is as you represent it.'

'Yeah, that too,' I said. 'That means if we're in business that you folks will lay off old Harv here. Right?'

'Of course,' Macey said. 'You heard Mr Powers. We borrow and lend, we're not animals. There's no problem there.'

'Maybe not,' I said. 'But I want a little more reassurance. Hawk?'

Hawk was motionless on the bed, his hands folded over his solar plexus, his eyes closed. Without opening his eyes he said, 'Shepard'll be okay.'

I nodded. 'Okay,' I said. 'Let's go, Harv.'

Shepard put down what was left of his drink, and went out of the room without even looking around. I followed him. Nobody said goodbye.

When we got in my car and started out of the parking lot, Shepard said, 'How do we know they'll keep their word?'

'About staying off your back?' I said.

Shepard nodded.

'Hawk said so,' I said.

'Hawk? The nigger? He's the one beat me up last time.'

'He keeps his word,' I said. 'And I told you before, call him Hawk. I'm not going to tell you again.'

'Yeah, sure, sorry, I forgot. But, Jesus, trusting him. I mean the guy Macey seems reasonable, like a guy you can do business with. But Hawk—'

'You don't know anything,' I said. 'Macey would take out your eyeballs for a dollar. You think he's a guy you can deal with 'cause he talks like he went to the Wharton School. Maybe he did, but he's got no more honor than a toad. He'll do anything. Hawk won't. There's things Hawk won't do.'

'Like what?'

'He won't say *yes* and do *no*.'

169

'Well, I guess you know your business. Where the hell are you getting the money?'

'That's not your problem,' I said. We pulled up in front of Shepard's house. He'd banged back two big drinks while I was talking with Macey and his mouth was a little slow.

'Thanks, Spenser,' he said. 'Just for going, let alone for making that gun deal. I was scared shit.'

'You should have been,' I said. We shook hands, Shepard got out and went in the house. I cruised back to the motel. Susan wasn't around and her car wasn't in the lot. I called Pam Shepard from my hotel room.

'You hear from the girls?' I said.

'From Rose, yes. They'll meet us. I know you're being funny, but please don't call them girls.'

'Where?'

'Where will they meet us?'

'Yeah.'

'In Milton. There's an observatory on top of the Great Blue Hill. Do you know where that is?'

'Yeah.'

'They'll meet us in the observatory. This afternoon at five.'

I looked at my watch: 1:25. There was time. 'Okay,' I said. 'I'll come pick you up and we'll go. I'll leave now, should be there around three. Start looking out the window then. I'll park on the street and when you see me, come on down.'

'What are we going to do?'

'I'll talk with you about it while we drive to Milton.'

'All right.'

'You bored?'

'Oh God, I'm going crazy.'

'Not too much longer,' I said.

'I hope not.'

We hung up. I went back to my car and set out for Boston again. If I made the trip many more times I'd be able to sleep on the way. I pulled up in front of my apartment at ten after three. In about forty seconds Pam Shepard came out the front door and got in the car. And we were off again for the Blue Hills.

The top was down and Pam Shepard leaned her head back against the seat and took a big inhale. 'Good God, it's good to get out of there,' she said.

'That's my home you're speaking of,' I said. 'I was kind of wishing I could get in there.'

'I didn't mean it's not nice, and it's not even so much that it's been that long, it's just that, when you know you can't go out, it's almost like claustrophobia.'

Her clean brown hair was pulled back, still in the French twist she'd worn since I met her, and the wind didn't bother it much. I went out along Park Drive and the Jamaicaway and the Arborway south on Route 28. Just across the Neponset River, Route 138 branched off from Route 28 and we went with it, taking our time. We pulled into the Blue Hills Reservation and parked near the Trailside Museum at four o'clock.

'We're awfully early,' Pam Shepard said.

Plan ahead,' I said. 'I want to be here waiting. I don't

want them to get nervous waiting for us and leave.'

'I don't mind,' she said. 'What are we going to do?'

'We'll walk up to the observatory on the top. And when they come, I'll tell them I have a seller for them.'

'A seller?'

'A gun broker. I've got a guy who'll sell them all the guns they can afford.'

'But why? Why would you do that?'

'Isn't that why you stole the money?'

'Yes, but you don't approve of us, do you? You don't want to arm us certainly.'

'That doesn't matter. I'm working on a very fancy move, and I don't want you trying to pretend you don't know. So I won't tell you. Then you won't have to pretend. You just assume I'm in your corner, and you vouch for me every time the question comes up.'

'I've done that already. On the phone when they called. They don't trust you and they don't like you.'

'Hard to imagine, isn't it,' I said.

She smiled, and closed her eyes and shook her head slightly.

'Come on,' I said, 'let's get out and walk.'

The blue hills are actually spruce green and they form the center of a large reservation of woods and ponds in an upper-middle-class suburb that abuts Boston. The biggest of the blue hills supports on its flank a nature museum, and on its crest a fieldstone observatory from which one gets a fine view of Boston's skyline, and an excellent wind for kite-flying on the downside pitch of the hill below the building. It's a hike of maybe fifteen minutes to the top, through woods and over small gullies, and there are usually Cub Scout packs and Audubon members clambering among the slate-colored outcroppings. I offered Pam Shepard a hand over one of the gullies and she declined. I didn't offer on the next one. I'm a quick study.

The observatory at the top had two sets of stairs and two balconies, and kids were running up and down the stairs and shouting at each other from the balconies. Several kites danced above us, one of them shaped like a large bat. 'That's auspicious,' I said to Pam, and nodded at the bat.

She smiled. 'They have all sorts of fancy ones like that now,' she said. 'The kids went through the kite stage. Harvey and I could never get them to fly ... Or us either, now that I think of it.'

'It can be done,' I said. 'I've seen it done.'

She shrugged and smiled again and shook her head. We stood on the upper balcony of the observatory and looked at the Boston skyline to the north. 'What is it,' Pam Shepard said, 'about a cluster of skyscrapers in the distance that makes you feel ... What? ... Romantic? Melancholy? Excited? Excited probably.'

'Promise,' I said.

'Of what?'

'Of everything,' I said. 'From a distance they promise everything, whatever you're after. They look clean and permanent against the sky like that. Up close you notice dog litter around the foundations.'

'Are you saying it's not real? The look of the skyscrapers from a distance?'

'No. It's real enough, I think. But so is the dog litter and if you spend all your time looking at the spires you're going to step in it.'

'Into each life some shit must fall?'

'Ah,' I said, 'you put it so much more gracefully than I.'

She laughed.

Below us to the left Jane emerged from behind some trees where the trail opened out into a small meadow below the observatory. She looked around carefully and then looked up at us on the balcony. Pam Shepard waved. I smiled inoffensively. Jane turned her head and said something and Rose emerged from the trees and stood beside her. Pam waved again and Rose waved back. My smile became even more inoffensive. And earnest. I fairly vibrated with earnestness. This was going to be the tough part. Guys like Powers you can get with money, or the hope of it. Or fear, if you're in a position to scare them. But people like Rose, they were hard. Zealots were always hard. Zeal distorts them. Makes the normal impulses convolute. Makes people fearless and greedless and loveless and finally monstrous. I was against zeal. But being against it didn't make it go away. I had to persuade these two zealots to go along with the plan or the plan washed away and maybe so did the Shepards.

They trudged up the hill to the observatory warily, alert for an ambush among the kite-flying kids and the Cub

Scouts looking at lichen growth on the north side of rocks. They disappeared below us as they went into the stairwell and then appeared coming up the stairs behind us. As Rose reached the top of the stairs Pam Shepard went to her and embraced her. Rose patted her back as they hugged. With one arm still around Rose, Pam took Jane's hand and squeezed it.

'It's good to see you both,' she said.

Rose said, 'Are you all right?'

Jane said, 'Have you got a place to stay?'

'Yes, yes, I'm all right, I'm fine. I've been using his apartment.'

'With him?' Rose looked suddenly menopausal.

'No,' I said. The way I used to say it to my mother. 'No, I've been down the Cape, working on a case. Besides I have a girlfriend, ah woman, ah, I have a person, I . . . I'm with Susan Silverman.'

Rose said to Pam Shepard, 'That's good of him.'

Jane said to Rose and Pam Shepard, 'I still don't trust him.'

'You can,' Pam said. 'You really can. I trust him. He's a good man.'

I smiled harder. Ingratiation. Jane eyes me for vulnerable points.

Rose said, 'Well, whether or not we can trust him, we can talk some business with him at least. I'll reserve my opinion of his trustworthiness. What is his offer exactly?' And, while she hadn't yet addressed me directly, she looked at me. Once they did that I always had them. I think it was the puckish charm. 'Well?' she said. Yeah, it was the puckish charm.

'I can get you all the guns you need, one hundred thousand dollars' worth. And bullets. No questions asked.'

'Why?'

'I get a broker's fee.'

Rose nodded. Jane said, 'Perhaps that's why we can trust him.'

Rose said, 'I suppose we give you the money and then you have the guns delivered? Something like that perhaps? And when we get tired of waiting for delivery and call you up you seem to have moved?'

Pam Shepard said, 'No. Rose, believe me, you can trust him. He's not dishonest.'

'Pam, almost everyone is dishonest. He's as dishonest as anyone else. I don't want to do business with him.'

'That's dumb,' I said. 'It's the kind of dumb that smart people get because they think they're smart.'

'What the hell does that mean?' Jane said.

'It means that if everyone's dishonest you aren't going to do better elsewhere. And the devil you know is better than the devil you don't know. I got one character witness. Where you going to find a gun dealer that has that many?'

Rose said, 'We are not fools. You assume women can't manage this sort of thing? That gunrunning is a masculine profession?'

'I don't assume anything. What I know is that amateurs can't handle this sort of thing. You will get ripped off if you're lucky and ripped off and busted if you're not.' Ah,

Spenser, master of the revolutionary argot. Word maven of the counterculture.

'And why should we believe you won't rip us off?' Jane said.

'You got my word, and the assurance of one of your own people. Have I lied to you yet? Have I turned Pam in to her husband, or the fuzz? You held up a bank and killed an old man. He used to be a cop and the New Bedford cops are not going to forget that. They are going to be looking for you until Harvard wins the Rose Bowl. You are fugitives from justice as the saying goes. And you are in no position to be advertising for a gun dealer. If the word gets out that a group of women are looking to make a gun buy, who do you think the first dealer will be? The easy one, the one that shows up one day and says he's got what you want?'

'So far,' Rose said, 'it seems to be you.'

'Yeah, and you know who I am. The next one will be somebody undercover. An FBI informant, a special services cop, an agent from the Treasury Department, maybe a woman, a nice black woman with all the proper hatreds who wants to help a sister. And you show up with the cash and she shows up with thirteen cops and the paddy wagon.'

'He's right, you know,' Pam Shepard said. 'He knows about this kind of thing, and we don't. Who would get us guns that we could trust better?'

'Perhaps,' Rose said, 'we can merely sit on the money for a while.'

I shook my head. 'No, you can't. Then you're just a felon, a robber and murderer. Now you're a revolutionary who killed because she had to. If you don't do what you set out to do then you have no justification for murdering that old man and the guilt will get you.'

'I killed the guard,' Jane said. 'Rose didn't. He tried to stop us and I shot him.' She seemed proud.

'Same, same,' I said. 'She's an accessory and as responsible as you are. Doesn't matter who squeezed off the round.'

'We can do without the amateur psychoanalyzing, Spenser,' Rose said. 'How do we prevent you from taking our money and running?'

'I'll just be the broker. You and the gun dealer meet face to face. You see the guns, he sees the money.'

'And if they're defective?'

'Examine them before you buy.'

They were silent.

'If you're not familiar with the particular type of weapon, I'll examine it too. Have you thought of what kinds of guns you want?'

'Any kind,' Jane said. 'Just so they fire.'

'No, Jane. Let's be honest. We don't know much about guns. You know that anyway. We want guns appropriate for guerrilla fighting. Including handguns that we can conceal easily, and, I should think, some kind of machine guns.'

'You mean hand-held automatic weapons; you don't mean something you'd mount on a tripod.'

'That's right. Whatever the proper terminology. Does that seem sensible to you?'

'Yeah. Let me check with my dealer. Any other preferences?'

'Just so they shoot,' Jane said.

'Are we in business?' I said.

'Let us talk a bit, Mr Spenser,' Rose said. And the three women walked to the other end of the balcony and huddled.

On the walls of the observatory, mostly in spray paint, were graffiti. Mostly names, but also a pitch for gay liberation, a suggestion that blacks be bused to Africa and some remarks about the sister of somebody named Mangan. The conference broke up and Rose came back and said, 'All right, we're agreed. When can you get the guns?'

'I'll have to be in touch with you,' I said. 'Couple days, probably.'

'We're not giving you an address or phone number.'

'No need to.' I gave her my card. 'You have my number. I'll leave a message with my answering service. Call every day at noon and check in. Collect is okay.'

'We'll pay our way, Mr Spenser.'

'Of course you will, I was just being pleasant.'

'Perhaps you shouldn't bother, Mr Spenser. It seems very hard for you.'

22

Rose and Jane left as furtively as they'd come. They were hooked. I might pull it off. Jane hadn't even kicked me.

'It's going to work,' I said to Pam Shepard.

'Are they going to get hurt?'

'That's my worry, not yours.'

'But I'm like the Judas goat if they are. They are trusting you because of me.'

We were driving back into Boston passing the outbound commuting traffic. 'Somebody has to go down,' I said, 'for the bank guard. It isn't going to be you and that's all you have to concentrate on.'

'Dammit, Spenser, am I selling them out?'

'Yes,' I said.

'You son of a bitch.'

'If you kick me in the groin while I'm driving a traffic accident might ensue.'

'I won't do it. I'll warn them now. As soon as I get home.'

'First, you don't know how to reach them except through an ad in the paper, which you can't do right now. Second, if you warn them you will screw yourself and your husband, whose troubles are as serious as yours and whose salvation is tied to selling out Rose and Jane.'

'What's wrong? What's the matter with Harvey? Are the kids okay?'

'Everyone's okay at the moment. But Harv's in hock to a loan shark. I didn't want to tell you all this but you can't trust me if I lie to you. You kept asking.'

'You have no right to manipulate me. Not even for my own good. You have not got that right maybe especially for my own good.'

'I know. That's why I'm telling you. You're better off not knowing, but you have the right to know and I don't have the right to decide for you.'

'So what in hell is going on?'

I told her. By the time I got through we were heading down Boylston Street through Copley Square with the sun reflecting off the empty John Hancock Building and the fountain sparkling in the plaza. I left out only the part about Hawk shoving one of the kids. Paternalism is hard to shake.

'Good Jesus,' she said. 'What the hell have we become?'

'You've become endangered species among other things. The only way out for you is to do what I say. That includes throwing Rose and Jane off the back of the sleigh.'

'I can't . . . double-cross them. I know that sounds melo-dramatic but I don't know how else to put it.'

'It's better than saying you can't betray them. But however you put it, you're wrong. You've gotten yourself into a place where all the choices are lousy. But they seem clear. You've got kids that need a mother, you've got a husband that needs a wife. You've got a life and it needs you to live it. You're a handsome intelligent broad in the middle of something that could still be a good life.' I turned left at Bonwit's onto Berkeley Street. 'Somebody has got to go inside for that old cop. And I won't be crying if it's Rose and Jane. They snuffed him like a candle when he got in their way. And if we can hook King Powers on the same line, I say we've done good.'

I turned right onto Marlborough Street and pulled into the curb by the hydrant in front of my apartment. We went up in silence. And we were silent when we got inside. The silence got awkward inside because it was pregnant with self-awareness. We were awkwardly aware that we were alone together in my apartment and that awareness hung between us as if Kate Millett had never been born. 'I'll make us some supper,' I said. 'Want a drink first?' My voice was a little husky but I didn't want to clear my throat. That would have been embarrassing, like an old Leon Errol movie.

'Are you having one?' she said.

'I'm having a beer.' My voice had gone from husky to hoarse. I coughed to conceal the fact that I was clearing it.

'I'll have one too,' she said.

I got two cans of Utica Club cream ale out of the refrigerator.

'Glass?' I said.

'No, can's fine,' she said.

'Ever try this?' I said. 'Really very good. Since they stopped importing Amstel, I've been experimenting around.'

'It's very nice,' she said.

'Want spaghetti?'

'Sure, that would be fine.'

I took a container of sauce from the freezer and ran it under hot water and popped the crimson block of frozen sauce out into a saucepan. I put the gas on very low under the pan, covered it and drank some Utica Club cream ale.

'When I was a kid, I remember being out in western Mass some and they used to advertise Utica Club with a little character made out of the U and the C. I think he was called Ukie.' I coughed again, and finished the beer. Pam Shepard was leaning her backside on one of the two counter stools in my kitchen, her legs straight out in front of her and slightly apart so that the light summer print dress she wore pulled tight over the tops of her thighs. I wondered if tumescent could be a noun. I am a tumescent? Sounded good. She sipped a little of the beer from the can.

'Like it?' I said.

She nodded.

'And the plan? How about that.'

She shook her head.

'All right, you don't like it. But will you go along? Don't waste yourself. Go along. I can get you out of this mess. Let me.'

'Yes,' she said. 'I'm not pleased with myself, but I'll go

183

along. For Harvey and for the children and for myself. Probably mostly for myself . . .'

Ah-ha, the old puckish charm. I must use this power only for good.

I said, 'Whew!' and popped the top off another can of Utica Club. I put the water on for the spaghetti and started to tear lettuce for the salad.

'Want another beer?' I said. I put the lettuce in some ice water to crisp.

'Not yet,' she said. She sat still and sipped on the beer and watched me. I glanced at her occasionally and smiled and tried not to look too long at her thighs.

'I can't figure you out,' she said. I sliced a red onion paper-thin with a wide-bladed butcher knife.

'You mean how someone with my looks and talent ended up in this kind of business?'

'I was thinking more about all the conflicts in your character. You reek of machismo, and yet you are a very caring person. You have all these muscles and yet you read all those books. You're sarcastic and a wise guy and you make fun of everything; and yet you were really afraid I'd say no a little while ago and two people you don't even like all that well would get into trouble. And now here you are cooking me my supper and you're obviously nervous at being alone with me in your apartment.'

'Obviously?'

'Obviously.'

'And you?'

'I too. But I'm just somebody's middle-class housewife.

I would have assumed that you were used to such things. Surely I can't be the first woman you've made supper for?'

'I cook for Suze a lot,' I said. I cut some native tomatoes into wedges. And started on a green pepper.

'And for no one else?'

'Lately, just for Suze.'

'So what's different about me? Why is there this sense of strain?'

'I'm not sure. It has to do with you being desirable and me being randy. I know that much. But it also has to do with a sense that we should leave it at that.'

'Why?' She had put the beer can down and her arms were folded under her breasts.

'I'm trying to get you and Harv back together and making a move at you doesn't seem the best way to get that done. And, I don't think Suze would like it all that much either.'

'Why would she have to know?'

'Because if I didn't tell her then there would be things I kept from her. She couldn't trust me.'

'But she wouldn't know she couldn't trust you.'

'Yeah, but she couldn't.'

'That's crazy.'

'No. See the fact would be that she couldn't trust me. That I am not trustworthy. The fact that she didn't know it would be simply another deception.'

'So you confess every indiscretion?'

'Every one she has a right to know about.'

'Have there been many?'

'Some.'

'And Susan objects?'

'No. Not generally. But she doesn't know them. And she knows you. I think this would hurt her. Especially now. We're at some kind of juncture. I'm not quite sure what, but I think this would be wrong. Damnit.'

'She is, I think, a very lucky woman.'

'Would you be willing to swear to that? Just recently she called me a horse's ass.'

'That's possible,' Pam Shepard said.

I sliced up three small pickling cucumbers, skin and all, and added them to my salad. I took the lettuce out of the water and patted it with a towel and then wrapped it and put it in the refrigerator. I checked my sauce, it was nearly melted. I added some seedless green grapes to the salad bowl. 'The thing is, all that explanation didn't do much for the randiness. I don't think it's fatal, but you can't say I'm resting comfortably.'

Pam Shepard laughed. 'That's good to know. In fact, I thought about us going to bed together and the thought was pleasant. You look like you'd hurt and somehow I know you wouldn't.'

'Tough but oh so gentle,' I said.

'But it isn't going to happen, and it's probably just as well. I don't usually feel so good about myself after I've made it with someone but Harvey.' She laughed again, but this time harshly. 'Come to think about it, I didn't feel all that good the last few times I made it with Harvey.'

'Was that recently?'

She looked away from me. 'Two years ago.'

'That embarrass you?'

She looked back. 'Yes,' she said. 'Very much. Don't you think it should?'

'Yeah, maybe. On the other hand you're not a sex vendomatic. He drops in two quarters and you come across. I guess you didn't want to sleep with him.'

'I couldn't stand it.'

'And you both figured you were frigid. So you hustled out evenings to prove you weren't.'

'I guess so. Not very pretty, is it?'

'Nope. Unhappiness never is. How about Harv, what was he doing to dissipate tension?'

'Dissipate tension? My God, I don't think I've ever heard anyone talk the way you do. I don't know what he was doing. Masturbation perhaps. I don't think he was with other women.'

'Why not?'

'Loyalty, masochism, maybe love, who knows?'

'Maybe a way to grind the guilt in deeper too.'

'Maybe, maybe all that.'

'It's almost always all that. It seems the longer I'm in business, the more it's always everything working at the same time.' I took two cans of Utica Club from the refrigerator and popped the tops and handed one to her.

'The thing is,' she said, 'I never found out.'

'If you were frigid?'

'Yes. I'd get drunk and I'd thrash around and bite and moan and do anything anyone wanted done, but part of it all was faking and the next day I was always disgusted. I think one reason I wanted to ball you was so I could ask you afterwards if you thought I was frigid.' Her voice had a harsh sound to it, and when she said 'ball you' it sounded wrong in her mouth. I knew the harsh sound. Disgust, I'd heard it before.

'For one thing, you're asking the wrong question. Frigid isn't a very useful word. You pointed that out to me a while ago. It doesn't have a meaning. It simply means you don't want to do something that someone else wants you to do. If you don't enjoy screwing old Harv then why not say that? Why generalize? Say, I don't enjoy screwing Harvey, or, even better, I didn't enjoy it last evening. Why turn it into an immutable law?'

'It's not that simple.'

'Sometimes I wonder. Sometimes I think everything is that simple. But you're probably right. Sex is as natural as breathing except it takes a partner and what one can do with ease, two mangle.'

'Does Susan . . . ? I'm sorry, I have no right to ask that.'

'Does Susan like to have sexual intercourse? Sometimes she does and sometimes she doesn't. Occasionally, just occasionally now, that's true of me. The occasions are more frequent than they were when I was nineteen.'

She smiled.

I took the lettuce out of the refrigerator, unwrapped it and tossed it in the bowl with the rest of the vegetables. My sauce was starting to bubble gently and I took enough spaghetti for two and tossed it into my boiling pot. 'Plenty of water,' I said, 'makes it less sticky, and it comes right back to a boil so it starts cooking right away. See that. I am a spaghetti superstar.'

'Why do you want Harvey and me back together? I'm not sure that's your business. Or is it just American and apple pie? Marriages are made in heaven, they should never break up.'

'I just don't think you've given it a real shot.'

'A real shot? Twenty-two years? That's not a real shot?'

'That's a long shot, but not a real one. You've been trying to be what you aren't until you can't swallow it anymore, and now you think you're frigid. He's been panting after greatness all his life and he can't catch it because he thinks it's success.'

'If I'm not what I've been trying to be, what am I?'

'I don't know. Maybe you could find out if you no longer decided that what you ought to be was what your husband expected you to be.'

'I'm not sure I know what you're talking about.'

'You too, huh? Well, look, if he's disappointed in you it doesn't mean you're wrong. It could mean he's wrong.'

She shook her head. 'Of course, I mean that's no news flash. That's every woman's problem. I know that.'

'Don't generalize on me. I don't know if it's every woman's problem, or if it's only a woman's problem. What I do know is that it might be one of your problems. If so, it can be solved. It's one thing to know something. It's another to feel it, to act as if it were so, in short, to believe it.'

'And how does one learn to believe something?'

'One talks for a while with a good psychotherapist.'

'Oh God, a shrink?'

'There's good ones and bad ones. Like private eyes. I can put you in touch with some good ones.'

'Former clients?'

'No, Suze knows a lot about that stuff. She's a guidance person and takes it seriously.'

'Is that the answer, a damned shrink? Everything that happens some psychiatrist is in on it. Every time some kid gets an F the shrink's got to have his two cents' worth.'

'You ever try it?'

'No.'

'Harv?'

'No. He wanted me to, see if they could find out why I was frigid. But he didn't want to go too. Said there was nothing wrong with him. Didn't want some goddamned headshrinker prying around in his business trying to convince him he was sick.'

'Doesn't have to be a psychiatrist, you know. Could be a good social worker. You ought to talk with Suze about it. But Harv's got the wrong language again, just like frigid. Doesn't help to talk about "wrong" with a big W. You got a problem. They can help. Sometimes.'

'What about all these people they commit to asylums for no reason and how in murder cases they can't agree on anything? One side gets a shrink to say he's crazy and the other side gets one to say he's sane.'

'Okay, psychiatry boasts as many turkeys as any other

business, maybe more. But the kinds of things you're talking about aren't relevant. Those things come from asking psychiatrists to do what they aren't equipped to do. Good ones know that, I think. Good ones know that what they can do is help people work out problems. I don't think they are very good at curing schizophrenia or deciding whether someone is legally sane. That's bullshit. But they might be quite useful in helping you get over defining yourself in your husband's terms, or helping your husband get over defining himself in Cotton Mather's terms.'

'Cotton Mather?'

'Yeah, you know, the old Puritan ethic.'

'Oh, that Cotton Mather. You do read the books, don't you?'

'I got a lotta time,' I said. The timer buzzed and I twirled out a strand of spaghetti and tried it. 'Al dente,' I said. 'His brother Sam used to play for the Red Sox.' The spaghetti was done. I turned it into a colander, emptied the pan, shook the colander to drain the spaghetti, turned it back into the pan, added a little butter and some Parmesan cheese and tossed it.

'You made that up.'

'What?'

'About Al Dente's brother.'

'Nope, truth. Sam Dente used to play with the Sox about thirty years ago. Infielder. Left-handed batter.' The spaghetti sauce was bubbling. I poured it into a big gravy boat and put two big heaps of spaghetti on two plates. I poured the salad dressing over the salad, tossed it and set everything on the kitchen counter. 'Silverware in the drawer there,' I said. I got some Gallo Burgundy in a half-gallon bottle and two wine glasses out of the cupboard.

We sat at the counter and ate and drank. 'Did you make the spaghetti sauce?' she said.

'Yeah. A secret recipe I got off the back of the tomato paste can.'

'And the salad dressing? Is there honey in it?'

'Yep. Got that from my mother.'

She shook her head. 'Fighter, lover, gourmet cook? Amazing.'

'Nope. I'll take the fighter, lover, but the gourmet cook is a sexist remark.'

'Why?'

'If you'd cooked this no one would say you were a gourmet cook. It's because I'm a man. A man who cooks and is interested in it is called a gourmet. A woman is called a housewife. Now eat the goddamned spaghetti,' I said. She did. Me too.

23

I slept on the couch. A triumph once more of virtue over tumescence. I was up and showered and away before Pam Shepard woke up. At 10 a.m. I was having coffee with King Powers' man Macey in the Holiday Inn in Hyannis.

'Care for some fruit?' Macey said.

'No thanks. The coffee will do. When can you deliver the guns?'

'Tomorrow maybe, day after for sure.'

'What you got?'

'M2 carbines, in perfect condition, one hundred rounds apiece.'

'How many?'

'Four hundred and fifty.'

'Jesus Christ, that's more than two bills apiece.'

Macey shrugged. 'Ammo's included, don't forget.'

'Christ, you can pick 'em up in the gun shop for less than half that.'

'Four hundred and fifty of them? M2s?'

'There's that,' I said. 'But a hundred grand for four hundred and fifty pieces. I don't think my people will like that.'

'You came to us, Spence. You asked us. Remember?'

I loved being called Spence. 'And remember there's thirty thousand out for your share.'

'Which you're keeping.'

'Hey, Spence, it's owed us. We wouldn't be long in business if we didn't demand financial responsibility from our clients. We didn't go to Harvey either. He came to us. Just like you. You don't like the deal, you're free to make another one someplace else. Just see to it that Harvey comes up with the thirty thousand dollars he owes us. Which, incidentally, will increase as of Monday.'

'Oh yeah, you private-service firms seem to work on an escalated interest scale, don't you.'

Macey smiled and shrugged and spread his hands. 'What can I tell you, Spence? We have our methods and we attract clients. We must be doing something right.' He folded his arms. 'You want the guns or don't you?'

'Yes.'

'Good, then we have a deal. When do you wish to take delivery? I can guarantee day after tomorrow.' He checked his calendar watch. 'The twenty-seventh. Sooner is iffy.'

'The twenty-seventh is fine.'

'And where do you wish to take delivery?'

'Doesn't matter. You got a spot?'

'Yes. Do you know the market terminal in Chelsea?'

'Yeah.'

'There, day after tomorrow at 6 a.m. There are a lot of trucks loading and unloading at that time. No one will pay us any mind. Your principals have a truck?'

'Yeah.'

'Okay. We've got a deal. You going to be there with your people?'

'Yeah.'

'I won't be. But you should have ready for the man in charge one hundred thousand dollars in cash. Go to the restaurant there in the market center. You know where it is?' I nodded. 'Have a cup of coffee or whatever. You'll be contacted.'

'No good,' I said.

'Why not?'

'King's got to deliver them himself.'

'Why?'

'My people want to do business with the principals. They don't like working through me. They might want to do more business and they want to deal direct.'

'Perhaps I can go.'

'No. It's gotta be King. They want to be sure they don't get burned. They figure doing business with the boss is like earnest money. If he does it himself they figure it'll go right, there won't be anything sour, like selling us ten crates of lead pipe. Or shooting us and taking the money and going away. They figure King wouldn't want to be involved in that kind of goings-on himself. Too much risk. So, King delivers personally or it's no deal.'

'Mr Powers doesn't like being told what to do,' Macey said.

'Me neither, but we been reasonable, and you're getting your price. He can bend on this one.'

'I can assure you there will be no contrivances or double-dealing on this. This is an on-the-table, straightahead business deal.'

'That's good to know, Macey. And I believe you 'cause I'm here looking into your sincere brown eyes, but my clients, they're not here. They don't know how sincere you are and they don't trust you. Even after I mentioned how you been to college and everything.'

'How about we just cancel the whole thing and foreclose on Harvey.'

'We go to the cops.'

'And Harvey explains why he needed all that money we advanced him?'

'Better than explaining to you people why he can't pay.'

'That would be a bad mistake.'

'Yeah, maybe, but it would be a bad one for you too. Even if you wasted Harvey you'd have the fuzzy-wuzzies following you around and you'd have me mad at you and trying to get you busted, and for what? All because King was too lazy to get up one morning for a six o'clock appointment?'

Macey looked at me for maybe thirty seconds.

'You don't want to maneuver me and Harv into a place where we got no options. You don't want to make the law look more attractive than you guys. You don't want to arrange something where Harv's got nothing to lose by talking to the DA. My people are adamant on this. They are interested in doing business with the man. And you ain't him. King is the man.'

Macey said, 'I'll check with him. I'm not authorized to commit him to something like this.'

'You're not authorized to zip your fly without asking King. We both know that, preppy. Call him.' Macey looked at me another thirty seconds. Then he got up and went into the next room.

He was gone maybe fifteen minutes. I drank my coffee and admired my Adidas Varsities, in rust-colored suede. Excellent for tennis, jogging and avoiding injury through flight. I poured another cup of coffee from the room-service thermos pitcher. It was not hot. I left the cup on the table and went to the window and looked down at the pool. It was as blue as heaven and full of people, largely young ones, splashing and swimming and diving. A lot of flesh was darkening on beach chairs around the pool and some of it was pleasant to see. I should probably call Susan. I hadn't been back last night. Maybe she'd be worried. I should have called her last night. Hard to keep everything in my head sometimes. Pam Shepard and Harvey and Rose and Jane and King Powers and Hawk, and the New Bedford cops and getting it to work. And the tumescence. There was that to deal with too. A girl with long straight blond hair appeared from under one of the sun umbrellas wearing a bikini so brief as to seem pointless. I was looking at her closely when Macey came back into the room.

'King okayed it.'

'Say, isn't that good,' I said. 'Not only is he a King but he's a Prince. Right, Macey?'

'He wasn't easy to persuade, Spence. You've got me to thank for this deal. He was going to have you blown away when I first told him what you wanted.'

'And you saved me. Macey, you've put it all together today, kid.'

'You laugh, but I'm telling you it was a near thing. This better go smooth or King'll do it. Take my word. He'll do it, Spence.'

'Macey,' I said. 'If you call me Spence again I'll break your glasses.'

24

It was eleven twenty when I got back to my motel. There was a note on the bureau. 'I'm walking on the beach,' it said. 'Be back around lunchtime. Maybe I didn't come home all night either.' I looked at my watch: 11:22. I called my service and left word for Rose to call me at the motel. At five past twelve she did.

'You know where the New England Produce Center is in Chelsea?' I said.

'No.'

'I'm going to tell you, so get a pencil and write it down.'

'I have one.'

I told her. 'When you get there,' I said, 'go to the restaurant and sit at the counter and have a cup of coffee. I'll be there by quarter of six.'

'I want Pamela to be there as well.'

'Why?'

'I'll trust you more if she's there.'

'That's sort of like using a sister,' I said.

'We use what we must. The cause requires it.'

'Always does,' I said.

'She'll be there?'

'I'll bring her with me.'

'We will be there, with our part of the bargain.'

'You'll need a truck.'

'How large?'

'Not large, an Econoline van, something like that.'

'We'll rent one. Will you help us load?'

'Yes.'

'Very well. See you there.' She hung up.

I wrote a note to Susan, told her I'd be back to take her to dinner, put twenty-seven X's at the bottom and replaced the one she'd written me. Then I called New Bedford. Jackie Sylvia said he and McDermott would meet me at the Bristol County Court House on County Street. They were there when I arrived, leaning on each side of a white pillar out front.

'Come on,' Sylvia said when I got out of the car. 'We got to talk with Linhares.'

We went into the red-brick courthouse, past the clerk's office, up some stairs and into an office that said ANTON LINHARES, ASST. DIST. ATT., on the door. Linhares stood, came around the desk and shook hands with me when we went in. He was medium-size and trim with a neat Afro haircut, a dark three-piece suit and a white shirt with a black and red regimental stripe tie. His shoes looked like Gucci and his suit looked like Pierre Cardin and he looked like a future DA. His handshake was firm and he smelled of aftershave lotion. Canoe I bet.

'Sit down, Spenser, good to see you. Jackie and Rich have me wired in on the case. I don't see any problem. When's it going down?'

'Day after tomorrow,' I said, 'at six in the morning, at the market terminal in Chelsea.'

'That Suffolk or Middlesex County?'

'Suffolk,' I said.

'You sure?'

'I used to work for the Suffolk County DA. Everett's Middlesex, Chelsea's Suffolk.'

'Okay. I'm going to need some cooperation from Suffolk.' He looked at his wristwatch. It was big and had a luminous green face and you pressed a button to get the time displayed in digits. 'That's no sweat,' he said. 'I'll get Jim Clancy on the horn up there. He'll go along.'

He leaned back in his swivel chair, cocked one foot up on a slightly open drawer and looked at me. 'What's the setup?' he said. I told him.

'So we set up around there ahead of time,' Sylvia said, 'and when they are in the middle of the transaction . . .' He raised an open hand and clamped it shut.

Linhares nodded. 'Right. We've got them no matter what part of the swap they're in. One of them will have stolen money and the others will have stolen guns. I want to be there. I want part of this one.'

McDermott said. 'We thought you might, Anton.'

Linhares smiled without irritation. 'I didn't take this job to stay in it all my life.'

Sylvia said, 'Yeah, but let's make sure this doesn't get leaked to the press before it happens.'

Linhares grinned again. 'Gentlemen,' he said. He shook his head in friendly despair. 'Gentlemen. How unkind.'

'Sylvia's right,' I said. 'These are very careful people. King Powers by habit. Rose and Jane by temperament. They'll be very skittish.'

'Fair enough,' Linhares said. 'Now what about your people? How you want to handle that?'

'I want them not to exist,' I said. 'They can be referred to as two anonymous undercover operatives whose identity must be protected. Me too. If my name gets into this it may drag theirs in with it. They're both clients.'

Linhares said, 'I'll need the names. Not to prosecute but to bury. If they get scooped up in the net I've got to know who to let go.'

I told him. 'They're related?' he said.

'Yeah, husband and wife.'

'And you put this thing together for them?'

'Yeah.'

'How'd Suffolk ever let you get away?'

'Hard to figure,' I said.

'Okay.' Linhares looked at his watch again. He liked pushing the button. 'Jackie, you and Rich get up there tomorrow with Spenser here and set this thing up. I'll call Jimmy Clancy and have him waiting for you.'

'We gotta check with the squad,' McDermott said.

'I'll take care of that,' Linhares said. 'I'll call Sergeant Cruz and have you assigned to me for a couple of days. Manny and I are buddies. He'll go along. You get hold of Bobby Santos, he'll go up with you tomorrow so he can brief me for the bust.' He reached over and punched an intercom on his phone and said into it, 'Peggy, get me

Jimmy Clancy up in the Suffolk DA's office.' With one hand over the mouthpiece he said to me, 'Good seeing you, Spenser. Nice job on this one.' And to Sylvia and McDermott, 'You, too, guys, nice job all around.'

He took his hand away and said into the phone, 'Jimmy, Anton Linhares. I got a live one for you, kid.' We got up and went out.

'Who's this Santos?' I said to Jackie Sylvia.

'State dick, works out of this office. He's okay. Wants to be public safety commissioner, but what the hell, nothing wrong with ambition. Right Rich?'

'I don't know,' McDermott said. 'I never had any. You want to ride up with us tomorrow, Spenser, or you want to meet us there?'

'I'll meet you there,' I said. 'In Clancy's office. About ten.'

'Catch you then,' Sylvia said. We reached my car. There was a parking ticket under the windshield wiper. I took it out and slipped it into the breast pocket of Sylvia's maroon blazer. 'Show me the kind of clout you got around here,' I said. 'Fix that.' I got in the car. As I pulled away Sylvia took the ticket out of his pocket and tore it in two. As I pulled around the corner on County Street he was giving half to McDermott.

I was into the maze again and on my first pass at the Fairhaven Bridge I ended up going out Acushnet Street parallel to the river. There was a parking lot by the unemployment office and I pulled in to turn around. There was a long line at the unemployment office and a man with a pushcart and a striped umbrella was selling hot dogs, soft drinks, popcorn and peanuts. Festive.

I made the bridge on my second try, and headed back down the Cape. The sun was at my back now and ahead was maybe a swim, some tennis and supper. I hoped Susan hadn't eaten. It was five twenty when I got back to the motel. I spotted Susan's Nova in the lot. When I unlocked the door to the room she was there. Sitting in front of the mirror with a piece of Kleenex in her hand, her hair up in big rollers, a lot of cream on her face, wearing a flowered robe and unlaced sneakers.

'Arrrgh,' I said.

'You weren't supposed to be back yet,' she said, wiping at some of the cream with her Kleenex.

'Never mind that shit, lady,' I said. 'What have you done with Susan Silverman?'

'It's time you knew, sweetie: this is the real me.'

'Heavens,' I said.

'Does this mean it's over?'

'No, but tell me the fake you will reappear in a while.'

'Twenty minutes,' she said, 'I've made us reservations at the Coonamessett Inn for seven.'

'How about a swim first and then some tennis, or vice versa?'

'No. I just washed my hair. I don't want to get it wet and sweaty. Or vice versa. Why don't you swim while I conceal the real me. Then we can have a drink and a leisurely drive to the inn and you can explain yourself and where the hell you've been and what you've been doing and with or to whom, and that sort of thing.'

I swam for a half-hour. The pool was only about fifty feet long so I did a lot of turns, but it was a nice little workout and I went back to the room with the blood moving in my veins. Susan didn't do anything to slow it down. The hair was unrolled and the robe and cream had disappeared. And she was wearing a pale sleeveless dress the color of an eggshell, and jade earrings. She was putting her lipstick on when I came in, leaning close to the mirror to make sure it was right.

I took a shower and shaved and brushed my teeth with a fluoride toothpaste that tasted like Christmas candy. I put on my dark-blue summer suit with brass buttons on the coat and vest, a pale-blue oxford button-down shirt and a white tie with blue and gold stripes. Dark socks, black tassel loafers. I checked myself in the mirror. Clear-eyed, and splendid. I clipped my gun on under my coat. I really ought to get a dress gun sometime. A pearl handle perhaps, in a patent leather holster.

'Stay close to me,' I said to Susan on the way out to the car. 'The Hyannis Women's Club may try to kidnap me and treat me as a sex object.'

Susan put her arm through mine. 'Death before dishonor,' she said.

In the car Susan put a kerchief over her hair and I drove slowly with the top down to the inn. We had a margarita in the bar and a table by the window where you could look out on the lake.

We had a second margarita while we looked at the menu. 'No beer?' Susan asked.

'Didn't seem to go with the mood or the occasion,' I said. 'I'll have some with dinner.'

I ordered raw oysters and lobster thermidor. Susan chose oysters and baked stuffed lobster.

'It's all falling into place, Suze,' I said. 'I think I can do it.'

'I hope so,' she said. 'Have you seen Pam Shepard?'

'Last night.'

'Oh?'

'Yeah, I slept in my apartment last night.'

'Oh? How is she?'

'Oh, nowhere near as good as you,' I said.

'I don't mean that. I mean how is her state of mind?'

'Okay, I think you should talk with her. She's screwed up pretty good, and I think she needs some kind of therapy.'

'Why? You made a pass at her and she turned you down?'

'Just talk with her. I figure you can direct her someplace good. She and her husband can't agree on what she ought to be and she feels a lot of guilt about that.'

Susan nodded. 'Of course I'll talk with her. When?'

'After this is over, day after tomorrow it should be.'

'I'll be glad to.'

'I didn't make a pass at her.'

'I didn't ask,' Susan said.

'It was a funny scene though. I mean we talked about it a lot. She's not a fool, but she's misled, maybe unadult, it's hard to put my finger on it. She believes some very destructive things. What's that Frost line, "He will not go behind his father's saying"?'

'"Mending Wall,"' Susan said.

'Yeah, she's like that, like she never went beyond her mother's sayings, or her father's, and when they didn't work she still didn't go beyond them. She just found someone with a new set of sayings, and never went beyond them.'

'Rose and Jane?' Susan said.

'You have a fine memory,' I said. 'It helps make up for your real appearance.'

'There's a lot of women like that. I see a lot of them at school, and a lot of them at school parties. Wives of teachers and principals. I see a lot of them coming in with their daughters and I see a lot of daughters that will grow into that kind of woman.'

'Frost was writing about a guy,' I said.

'Yes, I know. I see.' The waitress brought our oysters. 'It's not just women, is it.'

'No, ma'am. Old Harv is just as bad, just as far into the sayings of his father and just as blind to what's beyond them as Pam is.'

'Doesn't he need therapy too?'

The oysters were outstanding. Very fresh, very young. 'Yeah, I imagine. But I think she might be brighter, and have more guts. I don't think he's got the guts for therapy. Maybe not the brains either. But I've only seen him under stress. Maybe he's better than he looks,' I said. 'He loves her. Loves the crap out of her.'

'Maybe that's just another saying of his father's that he can't go behind.'

'Maybe everything's a saying. Maybe there isn't anything but sayings. You have to believe in something. Loving the crap out of someone isn't the worst one.'

'Ah, you sweet talker you,' Susan said. 'How elegantly you put it. Do you love the crap out of anyone?'

'You got it, sweetheart,' I said.

'Is that your Bogart impression again?'

'Yeah, I work on it in the car mirror driving back and forth between here and Boston and New Bedford.'

The oysters departed and the lobster came. While we worked on it I told Susan everything we had set up for next day. Few people can match Susan Silverman for lobster eating. She leaves no claw uncracked, no crevice unpried. And all the while she doesn't get any on her and she doesn't look savage.

I tend to hurt myself when I attack a baked stuffed lobster. So I normally get thermidor, or salad, or stew or whatever they offered that had been shelled for me.

When I got through talking Susan said, 'It's hard to keep it all in your head, isn't it. So many things depend on so many other things. So much is unresolved and will remain so unless everything goes in sequence.'

'Yeah, it's nervous-making.'

'You don't seem nervous.'

'It's what I do,' I said. 'I'm good at it. It'll probably work.'

'And if it doesn't?'

'Then it's a mess and I'll have to think of something else. But I've done what I can. I try not to worry about things I can't control.'

'And you assume if it breaks you can fix it, don't you?'

'I guess so. Something like that. I've always been able to do most of what I needed to do.'

We each had a very good wild blueberry tart for dessert and retired to the bar for Irish coffee. On the ride back to the motel, Susan put her head back against the seat without the kerchief and let her hair blow about.

'Want to go look at the ocean,' I said. 'Yes,' she said.

I drove down Sea Street to the beach and parked in the lot. It was late and there was no one there. Susan left her shoes in the car and we walked along the sand in the bright darkness with the ocean rolling in gently to our left. I took her hand and we walked in silence. Off somewhere to the right, inland, someone was playing an old Tommy Dorsey album and a vocal group was singing 'Once in a while.' The sound in the late stillness drifted out across the water. Quaint and sort of old-fashioned now, and familiar.

'Want to swim?' I said.

We dropped our clothes in a heap on the beach and went into the ebony water and swam beside each other parallel to the shore perhaps a quarter of a mile. Susan was a strong swimmer and I didn't have to slow down for her. I dropped back slightly so I could watch the white movement of her arms and shoulders as they sliced almost soundlessly through the water. We could still hear the stereo. A boy singer was doing 'East of the Sun and West of the Moon' with a male vocal group for backing. Ahead of me Susan stopped and stood breast-deep in the water. I stopped beside her and put my arms around her slick body. She was breathing deeply, though not badly out of breath, and I could feel her heart beating strongly against my chest. She kissed me and the salt taste of ocean mixed with the sweet taste of her lipstick. She pulled her head back and looked up at me with her hair plastered tight against her scalp. And the beads of sea water glistening on her face. Her teeth seemed very shiny to me, up close like that when she smiled.

'In the water?' she said.

'Never tried it in the water,' I said. My voice was hoarse again.

'I'll drown,' she said and turned and dove toward the shore. I plunged after her and caught her at the tidal margin and we lay in the wet sand and made love while Frank Sinatra and the Pied Pipers sang 'There Are Such Things' and the waves washed about our legs. By the time we had finished the late-night listener had put on an Artie Shaw album and we were listening to 'Dancing in the Dark.' We were motionless for a bit, letting the waves flow over us. The tide seemed to be coming in. A wave larger than the ones before it broke over us, and for a moment we were underwater. We came up, both of us blowing water from our mouths, and looked at each other and began to laugh. 'Deborah Kerr,' I said.

'Burt Lancaster,' she said.

'From here to eternity,' I said.

'That far, at least,' she said. And we snuggled in the wet sand with the sea breaking over us until our teeth began to chatter.

25

We got dressed and went back to the motel and took a long hot shower together and ordered a bottle of Burgundy from room service and got into bed and sipped the wine and watched the late movie, *Fort Apache*, one of my favorites, and fell asleep.

In the morning we had breakfast in the room and when I left for Boston about eight thirty, Susan was still in bed, drinking a cup of coffee and watching the *Today* program.

The Suffolk County Court House in Pemberton Square is a very large gray building that's hard to see because it's halfway up the east flank of Beacon Hill and the new Government Center buildings shield it from what I still call Bowdoin Square and Scollay Square. I parked down in Bowdoin Square in front of the Saltonstall State Office Building and walked up the hill to the courthouse.

Jim Clancy had an Errol Flynn mustache, and it looked funny because his face was round and shiny and his light hair had receded hastily from his forehead. Sylvia and McDermott were there already, along with a guy who looked like Ricardo Montalban and one who looked like a Fed. McDermott introduced me. Ricardo turned out in fact to be Bobby Santos who might someday be public safety commissioner. The Fed turned out to be a man named Klaus from Treasury.

'We'll meet some people from Chelsea over there,' McDermott said. 'We've already filled Bobby in, and we're about to brief these gentlemen.'

McDermott was wearing a green T-shirt today, with a pocket over the left breast, and gray corduroy pants, and sandals. His gun was stuck in his belt under the T-shirt, just above his belt buckle, and bulged like a prosthetic device. Klaus, in a Palm Beach suit, white broadcloth shirt and polka-dot bow tie, looked at him like a virus. He spoke to Sylvia.

'What's Spenser's role in this?'

Sylvia said, 'Why not ask him?'

'I'm asking you,' Klaus said.

Sylvia looked at McDermott and raised his eyebrows. McDermott said, 'Good heavens.'

'Did I ever explain to you,' Sylvia said to McDermott, 'why faggots wear bow ties?'

I said to Klaus, 'I'm the guy set it up. I'm the one knows the people and I'm the one that supervises the swap. I'm what you might call your key man.'

Clancy said, 'Go ahead, McDermott. Lay it out for us, we want to get the arrangements set.'

McDermott lit a miserable-looking cigarette from the pack he kept in the pocket of his T-shirt.

'Well,' he said, 'me and Jackie was sitting around the squad room one day, thinking about crime and stuff, it was kind of a slow day, and here comes this key man here.'

Klaus said, 'For crissake, get on with it.'

Santos said, 'Rich.'

McDermott said, 'Yeah, yeah, okay, Bobby. I just don't want to go too fast for the G-man.'

'Say it all, Rich,' Santos said.

He did. The plan called for two vans, produce trucks, with Sylvia, McDermott, Santos, Linhares, Klaus and several Chelsea cops and two Staties from Clancy's staff to arrive in the area about five thirty, park at a couple of unloading docks, one on one side and one on the other side of the restaurant, and await developments. When the time was right I'd signal by putting both hands in my hip pockets, and 'Like locusts,' McDermott said, 'me and Jackie and J. Edgar over here will be on 'em.'

Clancy opened a manila folder on his desk and handed around 8 × 10 glossy mugshots of King Powers. 'That's Powers,' Clancy said. 'We have him on file.'

'The two women,' I said, 'I'll have to describe.' And I did. Klaus took notes, Sylvia cleaned his fingers with the small blade of a pocketknife. The others just sat and looked at me. When I got through, Klaus said, 'Good descriptions, Spenser.'

McDermott and Sylvia looked at each other. Tomorrow it would be good if they were in one truck and Klaus was in another.

Clancy said, 'Okay, any questions?'

Santos said, 'Warrants?'

Clancy said, 'That's in the works; we'll have them ready for tomorrow.'

Santos said, 'How about entrapment?'

'What entrapment?' Sylvia said. 'We got a tip from an informant that an illegal gun sale was going down, we staked it out and we were lucky.'

Clancy nodded. 'It should be clean: all we're arranging is the stakeout. We had nothing to do with Spenser double-crossing them.'

'One of my people's going to be there: Pam Shepard. You'll probably have to pick her up. If you do, keep her separate from the others and give her to me as soon as the others are taken away.'

'Who in hell are you talking to, Spenser?' Klaus said. 'You sound like you're in charge of the operation.'

McDermott said, 'Operation, Jackie. That's what we're in, an operation.'

Clancy said, 'We agreed, Clyde. We trade the broad and her husband for Powers and the libbers.'

'Clyde?' Sylvia said to McDermott.

'Clyde Klaus?' McDermott's face was beautiful with pleasure.

Klaus's face flushed slightly.

'Clyde Klaus.' McDermott and Sylvia spoke in unison, their voices breaking on the very edge of a giggle.

Santos said, 'You two clowns wanna knock off the horse-shit. We got serious work to do here. Cruz got you detached to me on this thing, you know. You listen to what I tell you.'

Sylvia and McDermott forced their faces into solemnity behind which the giggles still smirked.

'Anything else?' Clancy said. He turned his head in a half circle, covering all of us, one at a time. 'Okay, let's go look at the site.'

'I'll skip that one,' I said. 'I'll take a look at it later. But if any of the bad persons got it under what Klaus would call surveillance I don't want to be spotted with a group of strange, fuzzy-looking men.'

'And if they see you looking it over on your own,' Santos said, 'they'll assume you're just careful. Like they are. Yeah. Good idea.'

'You know the place?' Clancy said.

'Yeah.'

'Okay, the Chelsea people are going to be under command of a lieutenant named Kaplan if you want to check on something over there.'

I nodded. 'Thanks, Clancy. Nice to have met you gentlemen. See you tomorrow.' I went out of Clancy's office. With the door ajar I reached back in with my right hand, gave it the thumbs-up gesture and said, 'Good hunting, Clyde,' and left. Behind me I could hear Sylvia and McDermott giggling again, now openly. Klaus said, 'Listen,' as I closed the door.

Outside I bought two hot dogs and a bottle of cream soda from a street vendor and ate sitting by the fountain in City Hall Plaza. A lot of women employed in the Government Center buildings were lunching also on the plaza and I ranked them in the order of general desirability.

I was down to sixteenth when my lunch was finished and I had to go to work. I'd have ranked the top twenty-five in that time normally, but there was a three-way tie for seventh and I lost a great deal of time trying to resolve it.

Chelsea is a shabby town, beloved by its residents, across the Mystic River from Boston. There was a scatter of junk dealers, rag merchants and wholesale tire outlets, a large weedy open area where a huge fire had swallowed half the city, leaving what must be the world's largest vacant lot. On the northwest edge of the city where it abuts Everett is the New England Produce Center, one of two big market terminals on the fringes of Boston that funnel most of the food into the city. It was an ungainly place, next door to the Everett oil farm, but it sports a restaurant housed in an old railroad car. I pulled my car in by the restaurant and went in. It bothered me a little, as I sat at the counter and looked out at it, that my car seemed to integrate so aptly with the surroundings.

I had a piece of custard pie and a cup of black coffee and looked things over. It was a largely idle gesture. There was no way I could know where the swap would take place. There wasn't a hell of a lot for me to gain by surveying the scene. I had to depend on the buttons to show up, like they would when I put my hands in my hip pockets.

The restaurant wasn't very busy, more empty than full, and I glanced around to see if anyone was casing me. Or looked suspicious. No one was polishing a machine gun, no one was picking his teeth with a switchblade, no one was paying me any attention at all. I was used to it. I sometimes went days when people paid no attention to me at all. The bottom crust on my custard pie was soggy. I paid the bill and left.

I drove back into Boston through Everett and Charlestown. The elevated had been dismantled in Charlestown and City Square looked strangely naked and vulnerable without it. Like someone without his accustomed eyeglasses. They could have left it up and hung plants from it.

For reasons that have never been clear to me the midday traffic in Boston is as bad as the commuter traffic, and it took me nearly thirty-five minutes to get to my apartment. Pam Shepard let me in looking neat but stir-crazy.

'I was just having a cup of soup,' she said. 'Want some?'

'I ate lunch,' I said, 'but I'll sit with you and have a cup of coffee while you eat. We're going to have to spend another night together.'

'And?'

'And then I think we'll have it whipped. Then I think you can go home.'

We sat at my counter and she had her tomato soup and I had a cup of instant coffee.

'Home,' she said. 'My God, that seems so far away.'

'Homesick?'

'Oh, yes, very much. But . . . I don't know. I don't know about going home. I mean, what has changed since I left?'

'I don't know. I guess you'll have to go home and find out. Maybe nothing has changed. But tomorrow Rose and

Jane are going to be in the jug and you can't sleep here forever. My restraint is not limitless.'

She smiled. 'It's kind of you to say so.'

'After tomorrow we can talk about it. I won't kick you out.'

'What happens tomorrow?'

'We do it,' I said. 'We go over to the Chelsea Market about six in the morning and we set up the gun sale and when it is what you might call consummated, the cops come with the net and you and Harv get another crack at it.'

'Why do I have to go? I don't mean I won't, or shouldn't, but what good will I do?'

'You're kind of a hostage . . . Rose figures if you're implicated too, I won't double-cross them. She doesn't trust me, but she knows I'm looking out for you.'

'You mean if she gets arrested, I'll get arrested too?'

'That seems her theory. I told her that didn't seem sisterly. She said something about the cause.'

'Jesus Christ, maybe you are the only person I can depend on.'

I shrugged.

26

It was raining like hell and still dark when I woke up with a crick in my neck on the sofa in my living room. I shut off the alarm and dragged myself out of bed. It was quarter of five. I took a shower, and got dressed before I banged on my bedroom door, at five o'clock.

Pam Shepard said, 'I'm awake.'

She came out of the bedroom wearing my bathrobe and looking her age and went into the bathroom. I checked my gun. I stood in my front window and looked down at Marlborough Street and at the rain circles forming in the wet street. I thought about making coffee and decided we wouldn't have time and we could get some in the railroad car. I got out my red warm-up jacket that said LOWELL CHIEFS on it and put it on. I tried getting the gun off my hip while wearing it, and I left it unbuttoned, it wasn't bad. At five twenty Pam Shepard came out of the bathroom with her hair combed and her make-up on and my robe still folded around her, and went back into my bedroom and shut the door. I took my car keys out of my hip pocket and put them in my coat pocket. I went to the window and looked at the rain some more. It always excited me when it rained. The wet streets seemed more promising than the dry ones, and the city was quieter. At five thirty Pam Shepard came out of my bedroom wearing yellow slacks and a chocolate-colored blouse with long lapels. She put on a powder-blue slicker and a widebrimmed rain hat that matched and said, 'I'm ready.'

'The wardrobe for every occasion,' I said. 'I have the feeling you had Susan buy you a safari hat just in case you had to shoot tiger while you stayed here.'

She smiled but there wasn't much oomph in it. She was scared.

'This is going to be a milk run,' I said. 'There will be more cops than fruit flies there. And me, I will be right with you.'

We went down the front stairs and got in my car and it started and we were off.

'I know,' she said. 'I know it'll be all right. There's just been so much, and now this. Police and gangsters and it's early in the morning and raining and so much depends on this.'

'You and me babe,' I said, 'we'll be fine.' I patted her leg. It was a gesture my father used to make. It combined, when he did it, affection and reassurance. It didn't seem to do a hell of a lot for Pam Shepard. At twelve minutes of six in the morning we pulled into the restaurant parking lot. It was daylight now, but a gray and dismal daylight, cold as hell, for summer, and the warm yellow of the lighted windows in the railroad car looked good. There were a lot of trucks and cars parked. The terminal does its work very early. I assumed that two of the trucks contained our side but there was no telling which ones.

Inside we sat in a booth and ordered two coffees and two English muffins. Pam didn't eat hers. At about two minutes past six King Powers came in wearing a trench coat and a plaid golf cap. Macey was with him in a London Fog, and outside in the entryway I could see Hawk in what looked like a white leather cape with a hood.

'Good morning, Kingo-babe,' I said. 'Care for a cup of java? English muffin? I think my date's not going to eat hers.'

Powers sat down and looked at Pam Shepard. 'This the buyer?' he said.

'One of them. The ones with the bread haven't shown up yet.'

'They fucking better show up,' King said. Macey sat in the booth beside Powers.

'That's a most fetching hat, King,' I said. 'I remember my Aunt Bertha used to wear one very much like it on rainy days. Said you get your head wet you got the miseries.'

Powers paid no attention to me. 'I say fucking six o'clock I mean fucking six o'clock. I don't mean five after. You know what I'm saying?'

Rose and Jane came into the restaurant.

'Speak of coincidence, King,' I said. 'There they are.'

I gestured toward Rose and Jane and pointed outside. They turned and left. 'Let us join them,' I said, 'outside where fewer people will stand around and listen to us.'

Powers got up, Macey went right after him and Pam and I followed along. As we went out the door I looked closely at Hawk. It was a white leather cape. With a hood. Hawk said, 'Pow'ful nice mawning, ain't it, boss.'

I said, 'Mind if I rub your head for luck?'

I could see Hawk's shoulders moving with silent laughter. He drifted along behind me. In the parking lot I said, 'King, Macey, Hawk, Rose, Jane, Pam. There now, we're all introduced, let us get it done.'

Powers said, 'You got the money?'

Jane showed him a shopping bag she was carrying under her black rubber raincoat.

'Macey, take it to the truck and count it.'

Rose said, 'How do we know he won't run off with it?'

Powers said, 'Jesus Christ, sister, what's wrong with you?'

Rose said, 'We want to see the guns.'

'They're in the back of the truck,' Macey said. 'We'll get in and you can look at the guns while I count the money. That way we don't waste time and we both are assured.'

Powers said, 'Good. You do that. I'm getting out of the fucking rain. Hawk, you and Macey help them load the pieces when Macey's satisfied.'

Powers got up in the cab of a yellow Ryder Rental Truck and closed the door. Rose and Jane and Macey went to the back of the truck. Macey opened the door and the three of them climbed in. Hawk and I and Pam Shepard stood in the rain. In about one minute Rose leaned out of the back of the truck.

'Spenser,' she said, 'would you check this equipment for us?'

I said to Pam, 'You stand right there. I'll be right back.'

Hawk was motionless beside her, leaning against the front fender of the truck. I went around back and climbed in. The guns were there. Still in the original cases. M2 carbines. I checked two or three. 'Yeah,' I said, 'they're good. You can waste platoons of old men now.'

Rose ignored me. 'All right, Jane bring the truck over here. Spenser, you said you'd help us load the truck.'

'Yes, ma'am,' I said. 'Me and Hawk.'

Macey took the shopping bag that said FILENE'S on it, jumped down and went around to where Powers sat in the cab. He handed the money in to Powers and came back to the tailgate. 'What do you think, Spenser. This okay to make the swap.'

We were to the side of and nearly behind the restaurant. 'Sure,' I said. 'This looks fine. Nobody around. Nobody pays any attention anyway. They load and unload all day around here.'

Macey nodded. Jane backed in a blue Ford Econoline van, parked it tail to tail with Powers' truck, got out and opened the back doors. I went back to the front of the truck where Pam and Hawk were standing. 'Hawk,' I said softly, 'the cops are coming. This is a setup.' Macey and Rose and Jane were conspiring to move one case of guns from the truck to the van. 'Hawk,' Macey yelled, 'you and Spenser want to give us a hand.' Hawk walked silently around the front of the truck behind the restaurant and disappeared. I put my hands in my hip pockets. 'Stay right beside me,' I said to Pam Shepard.

From a truck that said ROLLIE'S PRODUCE Sylvia and

McDermott and two state cops emerged with shotguns.

Jane screamed, 'Rose,' and dropped her end of the crate. She fumbled in the pocket of her raincoat and came out with a gun. Sylvia chopped it out of her hand with the barrel of the shotgun and she doubled over, clutching her arm against her. Rose said, 'Jane,' and put her arms around her. Macey dodged around the end of the van and ran into the muzzle of Bobby Santos' service revolver, which Santos pressed firmly into Macey's neck. King Powers never moved. Klaus and three Chelsea cops came around the other side of the truck and opened the door. One of the Chelsea cops, a fat guy with a boozer's nose, reached in and yanked him out by the coat front. Powers said nothing and did nothing except look at me.

I said to King. 'Peekaboo, I see you,' nodded at Jackie Sylvia, took Pam Shepard's hand and walked away. At seven we were in a deli on Tremont Street eating hash and eggs and toasted bagels and cream cheese and looking at the rain on the Common across the street.

'Why did you warn that black man?' Pam Shepard said, putting cream cheese on her bagel. She had skipped the hash and eggs, which showed you what she knew about breakfasts. The waitress came and poured more coffee in both our cups.

'I don't know. I've known him a long time. He was a fighter when I was. We used to train together sometimes.'

'But isn't he one of them? I mean isn't he the, what, the muscle man, the enforcer, for those people?'

'Yeah.'

'Doesn't that make a difference? I mean you just let him go.'

'I've known him a long time,' I said.

27

It was still raining when we drove back to my apartment to get Pam's things, and it was still raining when we set out at about eight thirty for Hyannis. There's an FM station in Boston that plays jazz from six in the morning until eleven. I turned it on. Carmen McRae was singing 'Skyliner.' The rain had settled in and came steadily against the windshield as if it planned to stay awhile. My roof leaked in one corner and dripped on the back seat.

Pam Shepard sat quietly and looked out the side window of the car. The Carmen McRae record was replaced by an album of Lee Wiley singing with Bobby Hackett's cornet and Joe Bushkin's piano. Sweet Bird of Youth. There wasn't much traffic on Route 3. Nobody much went to the Cape on a rainy midweek morning.

'When I was a little kid,' I said, 'I used to love to ride in the rain, in a car. It always seemed so self-contained, so private.' There we were in the warm car with the music playing, and the rest of the world was out in the rain getting wet and shivering. 'Still like it, in fact.'

Pam Shepard kept looking out the side window. 'Is it over, do you think?' she said.

'What?'

'Everything. The bank robbery, the trouble Harvey is in, the hiding out and being scared? The feeling so awful?'

'I think so,' I said.

'What is going to happen to Harvey and me?'

'Depends, I guess. I think you and he can make it work better than it has worked.'

'Why?'

'Love. There's love in the relationship.'

'Shit,' she said.

'Not shit,' I said. 'Love doesn't solve everything and it isn't the only thing that's important, but it has a big head start on everything else. If there's love, then there's a place to begin.'

'That's romantic goo,' Pam Shepard said. 'Believe me. Harvey's preached the gospel of love at me for nearly twenty years. It's crap. Believe me, I know.'

'No, you don't know. You've had a bad experience, so you think it's the only experience. You're just as wrong as Harvey. It didn't work, doesn't mean it won't work. You're intelligent, and you've got guts. You can do therapy. Maybe you can get Harv to do it. Maybe when you've gotten through talking about yourself with someone intelligent you'll decide to roll Harv anyway. But it'll be for the right reasons, not because you think you're frigid, or he thinks you're frigid. And if you decide to roll Harv you'll have some alternatives beside screwing sweaty drunks in one-night cheap hotels, or living in a feminist commune with two cuckoos.'

'Is it that ugly?' she said.

'Of course it's that ugly. You don't screw people to prove things. You screw people because you like the screwing or the people or both. Preferably the last. Some people even refer to it as making love.'

'I know,' she said, 'I know.'

'And the two dimwits you took up with. They're theoreticians. They have nothing much to do with life. They have little connection with phallic power and patterns of dominance and blowing away old men in the service of things like that.'

She stopped looking out the window and looked at me. 'Why so angry?' she said.

'I don't know exactly. Thoreau said something once about judging the cost of things in terms of how much life he had to expend to get it. You and Harv aren't getting your money's-worth. Thrift, I guess. It violates my sense of thrift.'

She laughed a little bit and shook her head. 'My God, I like you,' she said. 'I like you very much.'

'It was only a matter of time,' I said.

She looked back out the window and we were quiet most of the rest of the drive down. I hadn't said it right. Maybe Suze could. Maybe nobody could. Maybe saying didn't have much effect anyway.

We got to the motel a little after ten and found Susan in the coffee shop drinking coffee and reading the *New York Times*.

'Was it okay?' Susan said.

'Yeah, just the way it should have been.'

'He warned one of them,' Pam Shepard said. 'And he got away.'

Susan raised her eyebrows at me.

'Hawk,' I said.

'Do you understand that?' Pam Shepard said.

'Maybe,' Susan said.

'I don't.'

'And I'll bet he didn't give you a suitable explanation, did he?' Susan said.

'Hardly,' Pam said.

'Everything else was good though?' Susan said.

I nodded.

'Are you going home, Pam?'

'I guess I am. I haven't really faced that, even driving down. But here I am, half a mile from my house. I guess I am going home.'

'Good.'

'I'm going to call Harv,' I said. 'How about I ask him to join us and we can talk about everything and maybe Suze can talk a little?'

'Yes,' she said. 'I'm scared to see him again. I'd like to see him with you here and without the children.'

I went back to the room and called Shepard and told him what had happened. It took him ten minutes to arrive. I met him in the lobby.

'Is Powers in jail?' he said.

I looked at my watch. 'No, probably not. They've booked him by now, and his lawyer is there arranging bail and

King's sitting around in the anteroom waiting to go home.'

'Jesus Christ!' Shepard said. 'You mean he's going to be out loose knowing we set him up?'

'Life's hard sometimes,' I said.

'But, for crissake, won't he come looking for us? You didn't tell me they'd let him out on bail. He'll be after us. He'll know we double-crossed him. He'll be coming.'

'If I'd told you, you wouldn't have done it. He won't come after you.'

'What the hell is wrong with them, letting him out on bail? You got no right to screw around with my life like that.'

'He won't come after you, Shepard. Your wife's waiting for you in the coffee shop.'

'Jesus, how is she?'

'She's fine.'

'No, I mean, like what's her frame of mind? I mean, what's she been saying about me? Did she say she's going to come back?'

'She's in the coffee shop with my friend Susan Silverman. She wants to see you and she wants us to be there and what she's going to do is something you and she will decide. She's planning, right now, I think, to stay. Don't screw it up.'

Shepard took a big inhale and let it out through his nose. We went into the coffee shop. Susan and Pam Shepard were sitting opposite each other in a booth. I slid in beside Susan. Shepard stood and looked down at Pam Shepard. She looked up at him and said, 'Hello, Harv.'

'Hello, Pam.'

'Sit down, Harv,' she said. He sat, beside her. 'How have you been?' she said.

He nodded his head. He was looking at his hands, close together on the table before him.

'Kids okay?'

He nodded again. He put his right hand out and rested it on her back between the shoulder blades, the fingers spread. His eyes were watery and when he spoke his voice was very thick. 'You coming back?'

She nodded. 'For now,' she said and there was strain now in her voice too.

'Forever?' he said.

'For now, anyway,' she said.

His hand was moving in a slow circle between her shoulder blades. His face was wet now. 'Whatever you want,' he said in his squeezed voice. 'Whatever you want. I'll get you anything you want, we can start over and I'll be back up on top for you in a year. Anything. Anything you want.'

'It's not up on top I want, Harvey.' I felt like a voyeur. 'It's, it's different. They think we need psychiatric help.' She nodded toward me and Suze.

'What do they know about it or us, or anything?'

'I won't stay if we don't get help, Harvey. We're not just unhappy. We're sick. We need to be cured.'

'Who do we go to? I don't even know any shrinks.'

'Susan will tell us,' Pam said. 'She knows about these things.'

'If that's what will bring you back, that's what I'll do.'
His voice was easing a little, but the tears were still running
down his face. He kept rubbing her back in the little
circles. 'Whatever you want.'

I stood up. 'You folks are going to make it. And while
you are, I'm going to make a call.'

They paid me very little heed and I left feeling about
as useful as a faucet on a clock. Back in the room I called
Clancy in the Suffolk County DA's office.

'Spenser,' I said when he came on. 'Powers out of the
calaboose yet?'

'Lemme check.'

I listened to the vague sounds that a telephone makes
on hold for maybe three minutes. Then Clancy came back
on. 'Yep.'

'Dandy,' I said.

'You knew he would be,' Clancy said. 'You know the
score.'

'Yeah, thanks.' I hung up.

Back in the coffee shop Pam was saying, 'It's too heavy.
It's too heavy to carry the weight of being the center of
everybody's life.'

The waitress brought me another cup of coffee.

'Well, what are we supposed to do?' Harv said. 'Not love
you? I tell the kids, knock it off on the love, it's too much
for your mother? Is that what we do?'

Pam Shepard shook her head. 'It's just . . . no of course,
I want to be loved, but it's being the *only* thing you love,
and the kids, being so central, feeling all that . . . I don't

know . . . responsibility, maybe. I want to scream and run.'

'Boy' – Harv shook his head – 'I wish I had that problem, having somebody love me too much. I'd trade you in a goddamned second.'

'No you wouldn't.'

'Yeah, well, I wouldn't be taking off on you either. I don't even know where you been. You know where I been.'

'And what you've been doing,' she said. 'You goddamned fool.'

Harv looked at me. 'You bastard, Spenser, you told her.'

'I had to,' I said.

'Well, I was doing it for you and the kids. I mean, what kind of man would I be if I let it all go down the freaking tube and you and the kids had shit? What kind of a man is that?'

'See,' Pam said. 'See, it's always me, always my responsibility. Everything you do is for me.'

'Bullshit. I do what a man's supposed to do. There's nothing peculiar about a man looking out for the family. Dedicating his life to his family. That's not peculiar. That's right.'

'Submerging your own ego that extent is unusual,' Susan said.

'Meaning what?'

Shepard's voice had lost its strangled quality and had gotten tinny. He spoke too loudly for the room.

'Don't yell at Suze, Harv,' I said.

'I'm not yelling, but I mean, Christ, Spenser, she's telling me that dedication and self-sacrifice is a sign of being sick.'

'No she's not, Harv. She's asking you to think why you can't do anything in your own interest. Why you have to perceive it in terms of self-sacrifice.'

'I, I don't perceive . . . I mean I can do things I want to . . . for myself.'

'Like what?' I said.

'Well, shit, I . . . Well, I want money too, and good things for the family . . . and . . . aw, bullshit. Whose side are you on in this?'

Pam Shepard put her face in her hands. 'Oh God,' she said. 'Oh God, Jesus goddamned Christ,' she said.

28

The Shepards went home after a while, uneasy, uncertain, but in the same car with the promise that Susan and I would join them for dinner that night. The rain stopped and the sun came out. Susan and I went down to Sea Street beach and swam and lay on the beach. I listened to the Sox play the Indians on a little red Panasonic portable that Susan had given me for my birthday. Susan read Erikson and the wind blew very gently off Nantucket Sound. I wondered when Powers would show up. Nothing much to do about that. When he showed he'd show. There was no way to prepare for it.

The Sox lost to Cleveland and a disc jockey came on and started to play 'Fly Robin Fly.'

I shut off the radio.

'You think they'll make it?' I said.

Susan shrugged. 'He's not encouraging, is he?'

'No, but he loves her.'

'I know.' She paused. 'Think we'll make it?'

'Yeah. We already have.'

'Have we?'

'Yeah.'

'That means that the status remains quo?'

'Nope.'

'What does it mean?'

'Means I'm going to propose marriage.'

Susan closed her book. She looked at me without saying anything. And she smiled. 'Are you really?' she said.

'Yeah.'

'Was that it?'

'I guess it was, would you care to marry me?'

She was quiet. The water on the sound was quiet. Easy swells looking green and deep rolled in quietly toward us and broke gently onto the beach.

Susan said, 'I don't know.'

'I was under a different impression,' I said.

'So was I.'

'I was under the impression that you wanted to marry me and were angry that I had not yet asked.'

'That was the impression I was under too,' Susan said. 'Songs unheard are sweeter far,' I said.

'No, it's not that, availability makes you no less lovable. It's ... I don't know. Isn't that amazing. I think I wanted the assurance of your asking more than I wanted the consummated fact.'

'Consummation would hardly be a new treat for us,' I said.

'You know what I mean,' she said.

'Yeah, I do. How are you going to go about deciding whether you want to marry me or not?'

'I don't know. One way would be to have you threaten to leave. I wouldn't want to lose you.'

'You won't lose me,' I said.

'No, I don't think I will. That's one of the lovely qualities about you. I have the freedom, in a way, to vacillate. It's safe to be hesitant, if you understand that.'

I nodded. 'You also won't shake me,' I said.

'I don't want to.'

'And this isn't free-to-be-you-and-me stuff. This is free to be us, no sharesies. No dibs, like we used to say in the schoolyard.'

'How dreadfully conventional of you.' Susan smiled at me. 'But I don't want to shake you and take up with another man. And I'm not hesitating because I want to experiment around. I've done that. I know what I need to know about that. Both of us do. I'm aware you might be difficult about sharing me with guys at the singles bar.'

'I'll say.'

'There are things we have to think about though.'

'Like what?'

'Where would we live?'

I was still lying flat and she was half sitting, propped up on her left elbow, her dark hair falling a little forward. Her interior energy almost tangible. 'Ah-ha,' I said.

She leaned over and kissed me on the mouth. 'That's one of your great charms, you understand so quickly.'

'You don't want to leave your house, your work.'

'Or a town I've lived in nearly twenty years where I

have friends, and patterns of life I care about.'

'I don't belong out there, Suze,' I said.

'Of course you don't. Look at you. You are the ultimate man, the ultimate adult in some ways, the great powerful protecting father. And yet you are the biggest goddamned kid I ever saw. You would have no business in the suburbs, in a Cape Cod house, cutting the lawn, having a swim at the club. I mean you once strangled a man to death, did not you?'

'Yeah, name was Phil. Never knew his other name, just Phil. I didn't like it.'

'No, but you like the kind of work where that kind of thing comes up.'

'I'm not sure that's childish.'

'In the best sense it is. There's an element of play in it for you, a concern for means more than ends. It comes very close to worrying about honor.'

'It often has to do with life and death, sweetie.'

'Of course it does, but that only makes it a more significant game. My neighbors in Smithfield are more serious. They are dealing with success or failure. For most of them it's no fun.'

'You've thought about me some,' I said.

'You bet your ass I have. You're not going to give up your work, I'm not going to stop mine. I'm not going to move to Boston. You're not going to live in Smithfield.'

'I might,' I said. 'We could work something out there, I think. No one's asking you to give up your work, or me to give up mine.'

'No, I guess not. But it's the kind of thing we need to think on.'

'So a firm I-don't-know is your final position on this?'

'I think so.'

I put my hands up and pulled her down on top of me. 'You impetuous bitch,' I said. Her faced pressed against my chest. It made her speech muffled.

'On the other hand,' she mumbled, 'I ain't never going to leave you.'

'That's for sure,' I said. 'Let's go have dinner and consummate our friendship.'

'Maybe,' Susan said as we drove back to the motel, 'we should consummate it before dinner.'

'Better still,' I said, 'how about before and after dinner?'

'You're as young as you feel, lovey,' Susan said.

29

We rang the bell at the Shepards' house at seven-thirty, me with a bottle of Hungarian red wine in a brown paper bag, and Hawk opened the door and pointed a Colt .357 Magnum at me.

'Do come in,' he said.

We did. In the living room were King Powers and Powell, the stiff I had knocked in the pool, and Macey and the Shepards. The Shepards were sitting on the couch together with Powell standing by with his gun out, looking at them, hard as nails. Macey stood by the mantel with his slim-line briefcase and Powers was in a wing chair by the fireplace. Shepard's face was damp and he looked sick. Getting beaten up tends to take a lot of starch out of a person and Shepard looked like he was having trouble holding it together. His wife had no expression at all. It was as if she'd gone inside somewhere and was holding there, waiting.

'Where's the kids?' I said.

Hawk smiled. 'They not here. Harv and the Mrs, I guess, thought they'd have a quiet time together, 'fore you come, so they shipped 'em off to neighbors for the night. That do make it cozier, I say.'

Powers said, 'Shut up, Hawk. You'd fuck around at your own funeral.'

Hawk winked at me. 'Mr Powers a very grumpy man and I do believe I know who he grumpy at, babe.'

'I figured I'd be seeing you, King,' I said.

'You figured fucking right, too, smart guy. I got something for you, you son of a bitch. You think you can drop me into the bag like that and walk away, you don't know nothing about King Powers.'

Macey said, 'King, this is just more trouble. We don't need this. Why don't we just get going.'

'Nope, first I burn this son of a bitch.' Powers stood up. He was a paunchy man who looked like he'd once been thin, and his feet pointed out to the side like a duck's. 'Hawk, take his gun away.'

'On the wall, kid, you know the scene.'

I turned and leaned against the wall and let him take the gun off my hip. He didn't have to search around. He knew right where it was. Probably smelled it. I stepped away from the wall. 'How come you walk like a duck, King?' I said. Powers' red face deepened a bit. He stepped close to me and hit me in the face with his closed fist. I rocked back from the waist and didn't fall.

'Quack,' I said. Powers hit me again, and cut my lip. It would be very fat in an hour. If I was around in an hour.

Susan said, 'Hawk.'

He shook his head at her. 'Sit on the couch,' he said.

Shepard said, 'You gonna shoot us?' There wasn't much vitality in his voice.

'I'm fucking-A-well going to shoot this smart scumbag,' Powers said. 'Then maybe I'll like it so much I'll shoot the whole fucking bag of you. How's that sound to you, you fucking welcher?'

'She's not in it,' Shepard said, moving his head toward his wife. 'Let her go. We got three kids. They never done anything to you.'

Powers laughed with the inside of his upper lip showing. 'But you did. You screwed me out of a lot of money, you gonna have to make that good to me.'

'I'll make it good, with interest. Let her go.'

'We'll talk about it, welcher. But I want to finish with this smart bastard first.' He turned back to me and started to hit me again. I stepped inside and hit him hard in the side over the kidneys. His body was soft. He grunted with pain and buckled to his knees.

Macey brought out his little automatic and Powell turned his gun from the Shepards toward me.

Hawk said, 'Hold it.' There was no Amos and Andy mockery in it now.

Powers sat on the floor, his body twisted sideways, trying to ease the pain. His face red and the freckles looking pale against it.

'Kill him,' he said. 'Kill the fucker. Kill him, Hawk.'

Susan said, 'Hawk.'

I kept my eyes on Hawk. Macey wouldn't have the stomach for it. He'd do it to save his ass, if he couldn't run. But not just standing there; that took something Macey didn't get in business school. Powell would do what he was told, but so far no one had told him. Hawk was the one. He stood as motionless as a tree. From the corner of my eye, I could see Shepard's hand go out and rest in the middle of his wife's back, between the shoulder blades.

Susan said again, 'Hawk.'

Powers, still sitting on the floor with his knees up and his white socks showing above his brown loafers, said, 'Hawk, you bastard, do what you're told. Burn him. Blow him away. Right now. Kill him.'

Hawk shook his head. 'Naw.'

Powers was on his knees now, struggling to his feet. He was so out of shape that just getting off the floor was hard for him. 'No? Who the fuck you saying no to, nigger? Who pays your fucking ass? You do what you're told . . .'

Hawk's face widened into a bright smile. 'Naw, I don't guess I am going to do what I'm told. I think I'm going to leave that up to you, boss.'

Powell said, 'I'll do it, Mr Powers.'

Hawk shook his head. 'No, not you, Powell. You put the piece down and take a walk. You too, Macey. This gonna be King and Spenser here, one on one.'

'Hawk, you gotta be out of your mind,' Macey said.

'Hawk, what the fuck are you doing?' Powers said.

'Move it out, Macey,' Hawk said. 'You and Powell lay the piece down on the coffee table and walk on away.'

Powell said, 'Hawk, for crissake . . .'

Hawk said. 'Do it. Or you know I'll kill you.'

Macey and Powell put the guns on the coffee table and walked toward the front door.

'What the fuck is happening here?' Powers said. The color was down in his face now, and his voice was up an octave. 'You don't take orders from this fucking coon, you take them from me.'

'Racial invective,' Hawk said to me.

'It's ugly,' I said. 'Ugly talk.'

Powers said, 'Macey. Call the cops when you get out, Macey. You hear me, you call the cops. They're going to kill me. This crazy nigger is trying to kill me.'

Macey and Powell went out and closed the door. Powers' voice was high now. 'Macey, goddamnit. Macey.'

Hawk said, 'They gone, King. Time for you to finish Spenser off, like you started to.'

'I don't have a gun. You know that, Hawk. I never carry a piece. Lemme have Macey's.'

'No guns, King. Just slap him around like you was doing before.' Hawk put his .357 under his coat and leaned against the door with his arms folded and his glistening ebony face without expression. Powers, on his feet now, backed away two steps.

'Hey, wait up, now, hey, Hawk, you know I can't go on Spenser just me and him. I don't even know if you could. I mean that ain't fair, you know. I mean that ain't the way I work.'

Hawk's face was blank. Harvey Shepard got off the couch and took a looping amateurish roundhouse righthand haymaker at Powers. It connected up high on the side of Powers' head near his right ear and staggered him. It also probably broke a knuckle in Shepard's hand. It's a dumb way to hit someone, but Harv didn't seem to mind. He plowed on toward Powers, catching him with a left hand on the face and knocking him down. Powers scrambled for the two guns on the coffee table as Shepard tried to kick him. I stepped between him and the guns and he lunged at my leg and bit me in the right calf.

I said, 'Jesus Christ,' and reached down and jerked him to his feet. He clawed at my face with both hands and I twisted him away from me and slammed him hard against the wall. He stayed that way for a moment, face against the wall, then turned slowly away from the wall, rolling on his left shoulder so that when he got through turning, his back was against the wall. Shepard started toward him again and I put my hand out. 'Enough,' I said. Shepard kept coming and I had to take his shoulder and push him back. He strained against me.

From the couch Pam Shepard said, 'Don't, Harvey.' Shepard stopped straining and turned toward her. 'Jesus!' he said and went and sat on the couch beside her and put his arms awkwardly around her and she leaned against him, a little stiffly but without resistance.

Susan got up and walked over and put her hands on Hawk's shoulders and, standing on her toes to reach, kissed him on the mouth.

'Why not, Hawk? I knew you wouldn't, but I don't know why.'

Hawk shrugged. 'Me and your old man there are a lot alike. I told you that already. There ain't all that many of us left, guys like old Spenser and me. He was gone there'd be one less. I'd have missed him. And I owed him one from this morning.'

'You wouldn't have done it anyway,' Susan said. 'Even if he hadn't warned you about the police.'

'Don't be too sure, honey. I done it lots of times before.'

'Anyway, babe,' Hawk said to me, 'we even. Besides' – Hawk looked back at Susan and grinned – 'Powers a foul-mouthed bastard, never did like a guy swore in front of ladies that way.' He stepped across, dropped my gun on the table, picked up those belonging to Macey and Powell and walked out. 'See y'all again,' he said. And then he was gone.

I looked at Powers. 'I think we got you on assault with intent to murder, King. It ain't gonna help iron out the trouble you're already in in Boston, is it?'

'Fuck you,' Powers said, and let his legs go limp and slid onto the floor and sat still.

'Hawk was right, King,' I said. 'Nobody likes a garbage mouth.'

LOOKING FOR RACHEL WALLACE

1

Locke-Ober's Restaurant is on Winter Place, which is an alley off Winter Street just down from the Common. It is Old Boston the way the Custom House tower is Old Boston. The decor is plain. The waiters wear tuxedos. There are private dining rooms. Downstairs is a room which used to be the Men's Bar until it was liberated one lunchtime by a group of humorless women who got into a shouting match with a priest. Now anybody can go in there and do what they want. They take Master Charge.

I didn't need Master Charge. I wasn't paying, John Ticknor was paying. And he didn't need Master Charge because he was paying with the company's money. I ordered lobster Savannah. The company was Hamilton Black Publishing, and they had ten million dollars. Ticknor ordered scrod.

'And two more drinks, please.'

'Very good.' The waiter took our menus and hurried off. He had a hearing aid in each ear.

Ticknor finished his Negroni. 'You drink only beer, Mr Spenser?'

The waiter returned with a draft Heineken for me and another Negroni for Ticknor.

'No. I'll drink wine sometimes.'

'But no hard liquor?'

'Not often. I don't like it. I like beer.'

'And you always do what you like.'

'Almost always. Sometimes I can't.'

He sipped some more Negroni. Sipping didn't look easy for him.

'What might prevent you?' he said.

'I might have to do something I don't like in order to get to do something I like a lot.'

Ticknor smiled a little. 'Metaphysical,' he said.

I waited. I knew he was trying to size me up. That was okay, I was used to that. People didn't know anything about hiring someone like me, and they almost always vamped around for a while.

'I like milk, too,' I said. 'Sometimes I drink that.'

Ticknor nodded. 'Do you carry a gun?' he said.

'Yes.'

The waiter brought our salad.

'How tall are you?'

'Six one and something.'

'How much do you weigh?'

'Two-oh-one and a half, this morning, after running.'

'How far do you run?'

The salad was made with Boston lettuce and was quite fresh.

'I do about five miles a day,' I said. 'Every once in a while I'll do ten to sort of stretch out.'

'How did your nose get broken?'

'I fought Joe Walcott once when he was past his prime.'

'And he broke your nose?'

'If he'd been in his prime, he'd have killed me,' I said.

'You were a fighter then?'

I nodded. Ticknor was washing down a bite of salad with the rest of his Negroni.

'And you've been on the police?'

I nodded.

'And you were dismissed?'

'Yeah.'

'Why?'

'They said I was intractable.'

'Were they right?'

'Yeah.'

The waiter brought our entrée.

'I am told that you are quite tough.'

'You betcha,' I said. 'I was debating here today whether to have lobster Savannah or just eat one of the chairs.'

Ticknor smiled again, but not like he wanted me to marry his sister.

'I was also told that you were – I believe the phrase was, and I'm quoting – 'a smart-mouthed bastard' – though it was not said without affection.'

I said, 'Whew.'

Ticknor ate a couple of green peas from the side dish. He was maybe fifty and athletic-looking. Squash probably or tennis. Maybe he rode. He wore rimless glasses, which you don't see all that often anymore, and had a square-jawed Harvardy face, and an unkempt gray crew cut like

Archibald Cox. Not a patsy even with the Bryn Mawr accent. Not soft.

'Were you thinking of commissioning a biography of me, or do you want to hire me to break someone's arm?'

'I know some book reviewers,' he said, 'but . . . no, neither of those.' He ate five more peas. 'Do you know very much about Rachel Wallace?'

'*Sisterhood*,' I said.

'Really?'

'Yeah. I have an intellectual friend. Sometimes she reads to me.'

'What did you think of it?'

'I thought Simone de Beauvoir already said most of it.'

'Have you read *The Second Sex*?'

'Don't tell the guys down the gym,' I said. 'They'll think I'm a fairy.'

'We published *Sisterhood*.'

'Oh, yeah?'

'Nobody ever notices the publisher. But yes, we did. And we're publishing her new book.'

'What is that called?'

'*Tyranny*.'

'Catchy title.'

'It is an unusual book,' Ticknor said. 'The tyrants are people in high places who discriminate against gay women.'

'Catchy idea,' I said.

Ticknor frowned for a moment. 'The people in high places are named. Ms Wallace has already had threats against her if the book is published.'

'Ah-hah,' I said.

'I beg your pardon?'

'My role in this is beginning to take on definition.'

'Oh, yes, the threats. Well, yes. That's it essentially. We want you to protect her.'

'Two hundred dollars a day,' I said. 'And expenses.'

'Expenses?'

'Yeah, you know. Sometimes I run out of ammunition and have to buy more. Expenses.'

'There are people I can get for half that.'

'Yeah.'

The waiter cleared the lunch dishes and poured coffee.

'I'm not authorized to go that high.'

I sipped my coffee.

'I can offer one hundred thirty-five dollars a day.'

I shook my head.

Ticknor laughed. 'Have you ever been a literary agent?' he said.

'I told you, I don't do things I don't like to do if I can avoid it.'

'And you don't like to work for a hundred and thirty-five a day.'

I nodded.

'Can you protect her?'

'Sure. But you know as well as I do that it depends on what I protect her from. I can't prevent a psychopath from sacrificing himself to kill her. I can't prevent a horde of hate-crazed sexists from descending on her. I can make her harder to hurt, I can up the cost to the hurter. But if she wishes to live anything like a normal life, I can't make her completely safe.'

'I understand that,' Ticknor said. He didn't look happy about it, though.

'What about the cops?' I said.

'Ms Wallace doesn't trust them. She sees them as, quote, "agents of repression."'

'Oh.'

'She has also said she refuses to have, and once again I quote, "a rabble of armed thugs following me about day and night." She has agreed to a single bodyguard. At first she insisted on a woman.'

'But?'

'But if there were to be but one, we felt a man might be better. I mean if you had to wrestle with an assassin, or whatever. A man would be stronger, we felt.'

'And she agreed?'

'Without enthusiasm.'

'She gay?' I said.

'Yes,' Ticknor said.

'And out of the closet?'

'Aggressively out of the closet,' Ticknor said. 'Does that bother you?'

'Gay, no. Aggressive, yes. We're going to spend a lot of time together. I don't want to fight with her all day.'

'I can't say it will be pleasant, Spenser. She's not an easy person. She has a splendid mind, and she has forced the world to listen to her. It has been difficult. She's tough and cynical and sensitive to every slight.'

'Well, I'll soften her up,' I said. 'I'll bring some candy and flowers, sweet-talk her a little ...'

Ticknor looked like he'd swallowed a bottle cap.

'My God, man, don't joke with her. She'll simply explode.'

Ticknor poured some more coffee for me and for himself from the small silver pot. There was only one other table occupied now. It made no difference to our waiter. He sprang forward when Ticknor put the coffeepot down, took it away, and returned almost at once with a fresh pot.

'The only reservation I have,' Ticknor said when the waiter had retreated, 'is the potential for a personality clash.'

I leaned back in my chair and folded my arms.

'You look good in most ways,' Ticknor said. 'You've got the build for it. People who should know say you are as tough as you look. And they say you're honest. But you work awfully hard sometimes at being a wise guy. And you look like everything Rachel hates.'

'It's not hard work,' I said.

'What isn't?'

'Being a wise guy. It's a gift.'

'Perhaps,' Ticknor said. 'But it is not a gift that will endear you to Rachel Wallace. Neither will the muscles and the machismo.'

'I know a guy would lend me a lavender suit,' I said.

'Don't you want this work?' Ticknor said.

I shook my head. 'What you want, Mr Ticknor, is

someone feisty enough to get in the line of someone else's fire, and tough enough to get away with it. And you want him to look like Winnie-the-Pooh and act like Rebecca of Sunnybrook Farm. I'm not sure Rebecca's even got a gun permit.'

He was silent for a moment. The other table cleared, and now we were alone in the upstairs dining room, except for several waiters and the maître d'.

'God damn it,' Ticknor said. 'You are right. If you'll take the job, it's yours. Two hundred dollars a day and expenses. And God help me, I hope I'm right.'

'Okay,' I said. 'When do I meet Ms Wallace?'

2

I met Rachel Wallace on a bright October day when Ticknor and I walked down from his office across the Common and the Public Garden through the early turn-of-fall foliage and visited her in her room at the Ritz.

She didn't look like Carry Nation. She looked like a pleasant woman about my age with a Diane von Furstenberg dress on and some lipstick, and her hair long and black and clean.

Ticknor introduced us. She shook hands firmly and looked at me carefully. If I'd had tires, she'd have kicked them. 'Well, you're better than I expected,' she said.

'What did you expect?' I said.

'A wide-assed ex-policeman with bad breath wearing an Anderson Little suit.'

'Everybody makes mistakes,' I said.

'Let's have as few as possible between us,' she said. 'To insure that, I think we need to talk. But not here. I hate hotel rooms. We'll go down to the bar.'

I said okay. Ticknor nodded. And the three of us went down to the bar. The Ritz is all a bar should be – dark and quiet and leathery, with a huge window that looks out onto Arlington Street and across it to the Public Garden. The window is tinted so that the bar remains dim. I always like to drink in the Ritz Bar. Ticknor and Rachel Wallace had martinis on the rocks. I had beer.

'That figures,' Rachel Wallace said, when I ordered the beer.

'Everybody laughs at me when I order a Pink Lady,' I said.

'John has warned me that you are a jokester. Well, I am not. If we are to have any kind of successful association, you'd best understand right now that I do not enjoy humor. Whether or not successful.'

'Okay if now and then I enjoy a wry, inward smile if struck by one of life's vagaries?'

She turned to Ticknor, and said, 'John, he won't do. Get rid of him.'

Ticknor took a big drink of his martini. 'Rachel, damn it. He's the best around at what we need. You did needle him about the beer. Be reasonable, Rachel.'

I sipped some beer. There were peanuts in a small bowl in the center of the table. I ate some.

'He's read your book,' Ticknor said. 'He'd read it even before I approached him.'

She took the olive on a toothpick out of her drink and bit half of it off and held the other half against her bottom lip and looked at me. 'What did you think of *Sisterhood*?'

'I think you are rehashing Simone de Beauvoir.'

Her skin was quite pale and the lipstick mouth was very bright against it. It made her smile more noticeable.

'Maybe you'll do,' she said. 'I prefer to think that I'm re-applying Simone de Beauvoir to contemporary issues. But I'll accept "rehashing." It's direct. You speak your mind.'

I ate some more peanuts.

'Why did you read Simone de Beauvoir?'

'My friend gave it to me for my birthday. She recommended it.'

'What did you feel was her most persuasive insight?'

'Her suggestion that women occupied the position of *other*. Are we having a quiz later?'

'I wish to get some insight into your attitude toward women and women's issues.'

'That's dumb,' I said. 'You ought to be getting insight into how well I can shoot and how hard I can hit and how quick I can dodge. That's what somebody is giving me two hundred a day for. My attitude toward women is irrelevant. So are my insights into *The Second Sex*.'

She looked at me some more. She leaned back against the black leather cushions of the corner banquette where we sat. She rubbed her hands very softly together.

'All right,' she said. 'We shall try. But there are ground rules. You are a big attractive man. You have probably been successful in your dealings with some women. I am not like those women. I am a lesbian. I have no sexual interest in you or any other man. Therefore there is no need for flirtatious behavior. And no need to take it personally. Does the idea of a gay woman offend you or titillate you?'

'Neither of the above,' I said. 'Is there a third choice?'

'I hope so,' she said. She motioned to the waiter and ordered another round. 'I have work to do,' she went on.

'I have books to write and publicize. I have speeches to give and causes to promote and a life to live. I will not stay in some safe house and hide while my life goes by. I will not change what I am, whatever the bigots say and do. If you want to do this, you'll have to understand that.'

'I understand that,' I said.

'I also have an active sex life. Not only active but often diverse. You'll have to be prepared for that, and you'll have to conceal whatever hostility you may feel toward me or the women I sleep with.'

'Do I get fired if I blush?'

'I told you before, I have no sense of humor. Do you agree or disagree?'

'Agree.'

'Finally, except when you feel my life is in danger, I want you to stay out of my way. I realize you will have to be around and watchful. I don't know how serious the threats are, but you have to assume they are serious. I understand that. But short of a mortal situation I do not want to hear from you. I want a shadow.'

I said, 'Agree,' and drank the rest of my beer. The waiter came by and removed the empty peanut bowl and replaced it. Rachel Wallace noticed my beer was gone and gestured that the waiter should bring another. Ticknor looked at his glass and at Rachel Wallace's. His was empty, hers wasn't. He didn't order.

'Your appearance is good,' she said. 'That's a nice suit, and it's well tailored. Are you dressed up for the occasion or do you always look good?'

'I'm dressed up for the occasion. Normally I wear a light-blue body stocking with a big red S on the front.' It was dim in the bar, but her lipstick was bright, and I thought for a moment she smiled, or nearly smiled, or one corner of her mouth itched.

'I want you presentable,' she said.

'I'll be presentable, but if you want me appropriate, you'll have to let me know your plans ahead of time.'

She said, 'Certainly.'

I said thank you. I tried to think of things other than the peanuts. One bowl was enough.

'I've had my say, now it is your turn. You must have some rules or questions, or whatever. Speak your mind.'

I drank beer. 'As I said to Mr Ticknor when he and I first talked, I cannot guarantee your safety. What I can do is increase the odds against an assassin. But someone dedicated or crazy can get you.'

'I understand that,' she said.

'I don't care about your sex life. I don't care if you elope with Anita Bryant. But I do need to be around when it happens. If you make it with strangers, you might be inviting your murderer to bed.'

'Are you suggesting I'm promiscuous?'

'You suggested it a little while ago. If you're not, it's not a problem. I don't assume your friends will kill you.'

'I think we'll not discuss my sex life further. John, for

God's sake order another drink. You look so uncomfortable, I'm afraid you'll discorporate.'

He smiled and signaled the waiter.

'Do you have any other statements to make?' she said to me.

'Maybe one more,' I said. 'I hired onto guard your body, that's what I'll do. I will work at it. Part of working at it will include telling you things you can do and things you can't do. I know my way around this kind of work a lot better than you do. Keep that in mind before you tell me to stick it. I'll stay out of your way when I can, but I can't always.'

She put her hand out across the table, and I took it. 'We'll try it, Spenser,' she said. 'Maybe it won't work, but it could. We'll try.'

3

'Okay,' I said, 'tell me about the death threats.'

'I've always gotten hate mail. But recently I have gotten some phone calls.'

'How recently?'

'As soon as the bound galleys went out.'

'What are bound galleys? And who do they go out to?'

Ticknor spoke. 'Once a manuscript is set in type, a few copies are run off to be proofread by both author and copy editor. These are called galley proofs.'

'I know that part,' I said. 'What about the bound ones going out?'

'Galleys normally come in long sheets, three pages or so to the sheet. For reviewers and people from whom we might wish to get a favorable quote for promotional purposes, we cut the galleys and bind them in cheap card-board covers and send them out.' Ticknor seemed more at ease now, with the third martini half inside him. I was still fighting off the peanuts.

'You have a list of people to whom you send these?'

Ticknor nodded. 'I can get it to you tomorrow.'

'Okay. Now, after the galleys went out, came the phone calls. Tell me about them.'

She was eating her martini olive. Her teeth were small and even and looked well cared for. 'A man's voice,' she said. 'He called me a dyke, "a fucking dyke," as I recall. And told me if that book was published, I'd be dead the day it hit the streets.'

'Books don't hit the streets,' I said. 'Newspapers do. The idiot can't get his clichés straight.'

'There has been a call like that every day for the last week.'

'Always say the same thing?'

'Not word for word, but approximately. The substance is always that I'll die if the book is published.'

'Same voice all the time?'

'No.'

'That's too bad.'

Ticknor said, 'Why?'

'Makes it seem less like a single cuckoo getting his rocks off on the phone,' I said. 'I assume you've rejected the idea of withdrawing the book.'

Rachel Wallace said, 'Absolutely.'

Ticknor said, 'We suggested that. We said we'd not hold her to the contract.'

'You also mentioned returning the advance,' Rachel Wallace said.

'We run a business, Rachel.'

'So do I,' she said. 'My business is with women's rights and with gay liberation and with writing.' She looked at

264

me. 'I cannot let them frighten me. I cannot let them stifle me. Do you understand that?'

I said yes.

'That's your job,' she said. 'To see that I'm allowed to speak.'

'What is there in the new book,' I said, 'that would cause people to kill you?'

'It began as a book about sexual prejudice. Discrimination in the job market against women, gay people, and specifically gay women. But it has expanded. Sexual prejudice goes hand in hand with other forms of corruption. Violation of the equal employment laws is often accompanied by violation of other laws. Bribery, kickbacks, racket tie-ins. I have named names as I found them. A lot of people will be hurt by my book. All of them deserve it.'

'Corporations,' Ticknor said, 'local government agencies, politicians, city hall, the Roman Catholic Church. She has taken on a lot of the local power structure.'

'Is it all Greater Boston?'

'Yes,' she said. 'I use it as a microcosm. Rather than trying to generalize about the nation, I study one large city very closely. Synecdoche, the rhetoricians would call it.'

'Yeah,' I said, 'I bet they would.'

'So,' Ticknor said, 'you see there are plenty of potential villains.'

'May I have a copy of the book to read?'

'I brought one along,' Ticknor said. He took his briefcase off the floor, opened it, and took out a book with a green dust jacket. The title, in salmon letters, took up most of the front. Rachel Wallace's picture took up most of the back. 'Just out,' Ticknor said.

'I'll read it tonight,' I said. 'When do I report for work?'

'Right now,' Rachel Wallace said. 'You are here. You are armed. And quite frankly I have been frightened. I won't be deflected. But I am frightened.'

'What are your plans for today?' I said.

'We shall have perhaps three more drinks here, then you and I shall go to dinner. After dinner I shall go to my room and work until midnight. At midnight I shall go to bed. Once I am in my room with the door locked, I should think you could leave. The security here is quite good, I'm sure. At the slightest rustle outside my door I will call the hotel security number without a qualm.'

'And tomorrow?'

'Tomorrow you should meet me at my room at eight o'clock. I have a speech in the morning and an autographing in the afternoon.'

'I have a date for dinner tonight,' I said. 'May I ask her to join us?'

'You're not married,' she said.

'That's true,' I said.

'Is this a casual date or is this your person?'

'It's my person,' I said.

Ticknor said, 'We can't cover her expenses, you know.'

'Oh, damn,' I said.

'Yes, of course, bring her along. I hope that you don't plan to cart her everywhere, however. Business and pleasure, you know.'

'She isn't someone you cart,' I said. 'If she joins us, it will be your good fortune.'

'I don't care for your tone, buster,' Rachel Wallace said. 'I have a perfectly legitimate concern that you will not be distracted by your lady friend from doing what we pay you to do. If there's danger, would you look after her first or me?'

'Her,' I said.

'Then certainly I can suggest that she not always be with us.'

'She won't be,' I said. 'I doubt that she could stand it.'

'Perhaps I shall change my mind about this evening,' Rachel Wallace said.

'Perhaps I shall change mine, too,' I said.

Ticknor said, 'Wait. Now just wait. I'm sure Rachel meant no harm. Her point is valid. Surely, Spenser, you understand that.'

I didn't say anything.

'Dinner this evening, of course, is perfectly understandable,' Ticknor said. 'You had a date. You had no way to know that Rachel would require you today. I'm sure Rachel will be happy to have dinner with you both.'

Rachel Wallace didn't say anything.

'Perhaps you could call the lady and ask her to meet you.'

Rachel Wallace didn't like Ticknor saying 'lady,' but she held back and settled for giving him a disgusted look. Which he missed, or ignored – I couldn't tell which.

'Where are we eating?' I said to Rachel.

'I'd like the best restaurant in town,' she said. 'Do you have a suggestion?'

'The best restaurant in town is not *in* town. It's in Marblehead, place called Rosalie's.'

'What's the cuisine?'

'Northern Italian Eclectic. A lot of it is just Rosalie's.'

'No meatball subs? No pizza?'

'No.'

'Do you know this restaurant, John?'

'I've not been out there. I've heard that it is excellent.'

'Very well, we'll go. Tell your friend that we shall meet her there at seven. I'll call for reservations.'

'My friend is named Susan. Susan Silverman.'

'Fine,' Rachel Wallace said.

4

Rosalie's is in a renovated commercial building in one of the worst sections of Marblehead. But the worst section of Marblehead is upper-middle-class. The commercial building had probably once manufactured money clips.

The restaurant is up a flight and inside the door is a small stand-up bar. Susan was at the bar drinking a glass of Chablis and talking to a young man in a corduroy jacket and a plaid shirt. He had a guardsman's mustache twirled upward at the ends. I thought about strangling him with it.

We paused inside the door for a moment. Susan didn't see us, and Wallace was looking for the maître d'. Susan had on a double-breasted camel's-hair jacket and matching skirt. Under the jacket was a forest-green shirt open at the throat. She had on high boots that disappeared under the skirt. I always had the sense that when I came upon her suddenly in a slightly unusual setting, a pride of trumpets ought to play alarms and flourishes. I stepped up to the bar next to her and said, 'I beg your pardon, but the very sight of you makes my heart sing like an April day on the wings of spring.'

She turned toward me and smiled and said, 'Everyone tells me that.'

She gestured toward the young man with the guardsman's mustache. 'This is Tom,' she said. And then with the laughing touch of evil in her eyes she said, 'Tom was nice enough to buy me a glass of Chablis.'

I said to Tom, 'That's *one*.'

He said, 'Excuse me?'

I said, 'It's the tag line to an old joke. Nice to meet you.'

'Yeah,' Tom said, 'same here.'

The maître d', in a dark velvet three-piece suit, was standing with Rachel Wallace. I said, 'Bring your wine and come along.'

She smiled at Tom and we stepped over to Wallace. 'Rachel Wallace,' I said, 'Susan Silverman.'

Susan put out her hand. 'Hi, Rachel,' she said. 'I think your books are wonderful.'

Wallace smiled, took her hand, and said, 'Thank you. Nice to meet you.'

The maître d' led us to our table, put the menus in front of us, and said, 'I'll have someone right over to take your cocktail order.'

I sat across from Susan, with Rachel Wallace on my left. She was a pleasant-looking woman, but next to Susan she looked as if she'd been washed in too much bleach. She was a tough, intelligent national figure, but next to Susan I felt sorry for her. On the other hand I felt sorry for all women next to Susan.

Rachel said, 'Tell me about Spenser. Have you known him long?'

'I met him in 1973,' Susan said, 'but I've known him forever.'

'It only seems like forever,' I said, 'when I'm talking.'

Rachel ignored me. 'And what is he like?'

'He's like he seems,' Susan said. The waitress came and took our cocktail order.

'No, I mean in detail, what is he like? I am perhaps dependent on him to protect my life. I need to know about him.'

'I don't like to say this in front of him, but for that you could have no one better.'

'Or as good,' I said.

'You've got to overcome this compulsion to understate your virtues,' Susan said. 'You're too self-effacing.'

'Can he suspend his distaste for radical feminism enough to protect me properly?'

Susan looked at me and widened her eyes. 'Hadn't you better answer that, snookie?' she said.

'You're begging the question, I think. We haven't established my distaste for radical feminism. We haven't even in fact established that you are a radical feminist.'

'I have learned,' Rachel Wallace said, 'to assume a distaste for radical feminism. I rarely err in that.'

'Probably right,' I said.

'He's quite a pain in the ass, sometimes,' Susan said. 'He knows you want him to reassure you and he won't.

271

But I will. He doesn't much care about radical feminism one way or the other. But if he says he'll protect you, he will.'

'I'm not being a pain in the ass,' I said. 'Saying I have no distaste for her won't reassure her. Or it shouldn't There's no way to prove anything to her until something happens. Words don't do it.'

'Words can,' Susan said. 'And tone of voice. You're just so goddamned autonomous that you won't explain yourself to anybody.'

The waitress came back with wine for Susan and Beck's beer for me, and another martini for Rachel Wallace. The five she'd had this afternoon seemed to have had no effect on her.

'Maybe I shouldn't cart her around everyplace,' I said to Rachel.

'Machismo,' Rachel said. 'The machismo code. He's locked into it, and he can't explain himself, or apologize, or cry probably, or show emotion.'

'I throw up good, though. And I will in a minute.'

Wallace's head snapped around at me. Her face was harsh and tight. Susan patted her arm. 'Give him time,' she said. 'He grows on you. He's hard to classify. But he'll look out for you. And he'll care what happens to you. And he'll keep you out of harm's way.' Susan sipped her wine. 'He really will,' she said to Rachel Wallace.

'And you,' Rachel said, 'does he look out for you?'

'We look out for each other,' Susan said. 'I'm doing it now.'

Rachel Wallace smiled, her face loosened. 'Yes,' she said. 'You are, aren't you?'

The waitress came again, and we ordered dinner.

I was having a nice time eating Rosalie's cream of carrot soup when Rachel Wallace said, 'John tells me you used to be a prizefighter.'

I nodded. I had a sense where the discussion would lead.

'And you were in combat in Korea?'

I nodded again.

'And you were a policeman?' Another nod.

'And now you do this.'

It was a statement. No nod required.

'Why did you stop fighting?'

'I had plateaued,' I said.

'Were you not a good fighter?'

'I was good. I was not great. Being a good fighter is no life. Only great ones lead a life worth too much. It's not that clean a business, either.'

'Did you tire of the violence?'

'Not in the ring,' I said.

'You didn't mind beating someone bloody.'

'He volunteered. The gloves are padded. It's not pacifism, but if it's violence, it is controlled and regulated and patterned. I never hurt anyone badly. I never got badly hurt.'

'Your nose has obviously been broken.'

'Many times,' I said. 'But that's sort of minor. It hurts, but it's not serious.'

'And you've killed people?'

'Yes.'

'Not just in the army?'

'No.'

'What kind of a person does that?' she said.

Susan was looking very closely at some of the decor in Rosalie's. 'That is a magnificent old icechest,' she said. 'Look at the brass hinges.'

'Don't change the subject for him,' Rachel Wallace said. 'Let him answer.'

She spoke a little sharply for my taste. But if there was anything sure on this earth, it was that Susan could take care of herself. She was hard to overpower.

'Actually,' she said, 'I was changing the subject for me. You'd be surprised at how many times I've heard this conversation.'

'You mean we are boring you?'

Susan smiled at her. 'A tweak,' she said.

'I bore a lot of people,' Rachel said. 'I don't mind. I'm willing to be boring to find out what I wish to know.'

The waitress brought me veal Giorgio. I ate a bite.

'What is it you want to know?'

'Why you engage in things that are violent and dangerous.'

I sipped half a glass of beer. I took another bite of veal. 'Well,' I said, 'the violence is a kind of side-effect, I think. I have always wanted to live life on my own terms. And I have always tried to do what I can do. I am good at certain kinds of things; I have tried to go in that direction.'

'The answer doesn't satisfy me,' Rachel said.

'It doesn't have to. It satisfies me.'

'What he won't say,' Susan said, 'and what he may not even admit to himself is that he'd like to be Sir Gawain. He was born five hundred years too late. If you understand that, you understand most of what you are asking.'

'Six hundred years,' I said.

5

We got through the rest of dinner. Susan asked Rachel about her books and her work, and that got her off me and onto something she liked much better. Susan is good at that. After dinner I had to drive Rachel back to the Ritz. I said goodbye to Susan in the bank parking lot behind Rosalie's where we'd parked.

'Don't be mean to her,' Susan said softly. 'She's scared to death, and she's badly ill at ease with you and with her fear.'

'I don't blame her for being scared,' I said. 'But it's not my fault.'

From the front seat of my car Rachel said, 'Spenser, I have work to do.'

'Jesus Christ,' I said to Susan.

'She's scared,' Susan said. 'It makes her bitchy. Think how you'd feel if she were your only protection.'

I gave Susan a pat on the fanny, decided a kiss would be hokey, and opened the door for her before she climbed into her MG. I was delighted. She'd gotten rid of the Nova. She was not Chevy. She was sports car.

Through the open window Susan said, 'You held the door just to spite her.'

'Yeah, baby, but I'm going home with her.'

Susan slid into gear and wheeled the sports car out of the lot. I got in beside Rachel and started up my car.

'For heaven's sake, what year is this car?' Rachel said.

'1968,' I said. 'I'd buy a new one, but they don't make convertibles anymore.' Maybe I should get a sports car. Was I old Chevy?

'Susan is a very attractive person,' Rachel said.

'That's true,' I said.

'It makes me think better of you that she likes you.'

'That gets me by in a lot of places,' I said.

'Your affection for each other shows.'

I nodded.

'It is not my kind of love, but I can respond to it in others. You are lucky to have a relationship as vital as that.'

'That's true, too,' I said.

'You don't like me.'

I shrugged.

'You don't,' she said.

'It's irrelevant,' I said.

'You don't like me, and you don't like what I stand for.'

'What is it you stand for?' I said.

'The right of every woman to be what she will be. To shape her life in conformity to her own impulse, not to bend her will to the whims of men.'

I said, 'Wow.'

'Do you realize I bear my father's name?'

'I didn't know that,' I said.

'I had no choice,' she said. 'It was assigned me.'

'That's true of me, too,' I said.

She looked at me.

'It was assigned me. Spenser. I had no choice. I couldn't say I'd rather be named Spade. Samuel Spade. That would have been a terrific name, but no. I had to get a name like an English poet. You know what Spenser wrote?'

'*The Faerie Queen.*'

'Yeah. So what are you bitching about?'

We were out of Marblehead now and driving on Route 1A through Swampscott.

'It's not the same,' she said.

'Why isn't it?'

'Because I'm a woman and was given a man's name.'

'Whatever name would have been without your consent. Your mother's, your father's, and if you'd taken your mother's name, wouldn't that merely have been your grandfather's?'

There was a blue Buick Electra in front of me. It began to slow down as we passed the drive-in theater on the Lynnway. Behind me a Dodge swung out into the left lane and pulled up beside me.

'Get on the floor,' I said.

She said, 'What—' and I put my right hand behind her neck and pushed her down toward the floor. With my left hand I yanked the steering wheel hard over and went inside the Buick. My right wheels went up on the curb. The Buick pulled right to crowd me, and I floored the Chevy and dragged my bumper along his entire righthand side and spun off the curb in front of him with a strong smell of skun rubber behind me. I went up over the General Edwards Bridge with the accelerator to the floor and my elbow on the horn, and with the Buick and the Dodge behind me. I had my elbow on the horn because I had my gun in my hand.

The Lynnway was too bright and too busy, and it was too early in the evening. The Buick swung off into Point of Pines, and the Dodge went with it. I swerved into the passing lane to avoid a car and swerved back to the right to avoid another and began to slow down.

Rachel Wallace crouched, half fetal, toward the floor on the passenger's side. I put the gun down on the seat beside me. 'One of the advantages of driving a 1968 Chevy,' I said, 'is you don't care all that much about an occasional dent.'

'May I sit up?' she said. Her voice was strong.

'Yeah.'

She squirmed back up onto the seat.

'Was that necessary?'

'Yeah.'

'Was there someone really chasing us?'

'Yeah.'

'If there was, you handled it well. My reactions would not have been as quick.'

I said, 'Thank you.'

'I'm not complimenting you. I'm merely observing a fact. Did you get their license numbers?'

'Yes, 469AAG, and D60240, both Mass. But it won't do us any good unless they are bad amateurs, and the way they boxed me in on the road before I noticed, they aren't amateurs.'

'You think you should have noticed them sooner?'

'Yeah. I was too busy arguing patristic nomenclature with you. I should never have had to hit the curb like that.'

'Then partly it is my fault for distracting you.'

'It's not your line of work. It is mine. You don't know better. I do.'

'Well,' she said, 'no harm done. We got away.'

'If the guy in front of us in the Buick was just a mohair better, we wouldn't have.'

'He would have cut you off?'

I nodded. 'And the Dodge would have blasted us.'

'Actually would he not have blasted you? I was on the floor, and you were much closer anyway.'

I shrugged. 'It wouldn't have mattered. If you survived the crash they'd have waited and blasted you.'

'You seem, so, so at ease with all of this.'

'I'm not. It scares me.'

'Perhaps. It scares me, too. But you seem to expect it. There's no moral outrage. You're not appalled. Or offended. Or . . . aghast. I don't know. You make this seem so commonplace.'

'*Aghast* is irrelevant, too. It's useless. Or expressing it is useless. On the other hand I'm not one of the guys in the other car.'

We went past the dog track and around Bell Circle. There was no one noticeable in the rearview mirror.

'Then you do what you do in part from moral outrage.'

I looked at her and shook my head. 'I do what I do because I'm comfortable doing it.'

'My God,' she said, 'you're a stubborn man.'

'Some consider it a virtue in my work,' I said.

She looked at the gun lying on the seat.

'Oughtn't you to put that away?'

'I think I'll leave it there till we get to the Ritz.'

'I've never touched a gun in my life.'

'They're a well-made apparatus,' I said. 'If they're good. Very precise.'

'Is this good?'

'Yes. It's a very nice gun.'

'No gun is nice,' she said.

'If those gentlemen from the Lynnway return,' I said, 'you may come to like it better.'

She shook her head. 'It's come to that. Sometimes I feel sick thinking about it.'

'What?'

'In this country – the land of the free and all that shit – I need a man with a gun to protect me simply because I am what I am.'

'That's fairly sickening,' I said.

6

I picked Rachel Wallace up at her door at eight thirty the next morning, and we went down to breakfast in the Ritz Café. I was wearing my bodyguard outfit – jeans, T-shirt, corduroy Levi jacket, and a daring new pair of Pumas: royal-blue suede with a bold gold stripe. Smith and Wesson .38 Police Special in a shoulder holster.

Rachel Wallace said, 'Well, we are somewhat less formal this morning, aren't we? If you're dressed that way tonight, they won't let you in the dining room.'

'Work clothes,' I said. 'I can move well in them.'

She nodded and ate an egg. She wore a quiet gray dress with a paisley scarf at her throat. 'You expect to have to move?'

'Probably not,' I said. 'But like they say at the Pentagon, you have to plan for the enemy's capacity, not his intentions.'

She signed the check. 'Come along,' she said. She picked up her briefcase from under the table, and we walked out through the lobby. She got her coat from the check room, a pale-tan trenchcoat. It had cost money. I made no effort to hold it for her. She ignored me while she put it on. I looked at the lobby. There were people, but they looked like they belonged there. No one had a Gatling gun. At least no one had one visible. In fact I'd have been the only one I would have been suspicious of if I hadn't known me so well, and so fondly.

A young woman in a green tweed suit and a brown beret came toward us from the Arlington Street entrance.

'Ms Wallace. Hi. I've got a car waiting.'

'Do you know her?' I said.

'Yes,' Rachel said. 'Linda Smith.'

'I mean by sight,' I said. 'Not just by hearing of her or getting mail from her.'

'Yes, we've met several times before.'

'Okay.'

We went out onto Arlington Street. I went first. The street was normal 9 a.m. busy. There was a tan Volvo sedan parked at the yellow curb with the motor running and the doorman standing with his hand on the passenger door. When he saw Linda Smith, he opened the passenger door. I looked inside the car and then stepped aside. Rachel Wallace got in; the doorman closed the door. I got in the back, and Linda Smith got in the driver's seat.

As we pulled into traffic Rachel said, 'Have you met Mr Spenser, Linda?'

'No, I haven't. Nice to meet you, Mr Spenser.'

'Nice to meet you, Ms Smith,' I said. Rachel would like the *Ms*.

'Spenser is looking after me on the tour,' Rachel said.

'Yes, I know. John told me.' She glanced at me in the

rearview mirror. 'I don't think I've ever met a bodyguard before.'

'We're just regular folks,' I said. 'If you cut us, do we not bleed?'

'Literary, too,' Linda Smith said.

'When are we supposed to be in Belmont?'

'Ten o'clock,' Linda said. 'Belmont Public Library.'

'What for?' I said.

'Ms Wallace is speaking there. They have a Friends of the Library series.'

'Nice liberal town you picked.'

'Never mind, Spenser,' Rachel Wallace said. Her voice was brusque. 'I told them I'd speak wherever I could and to whom I could. I have a message to deliver, and I'm not interested in persuading those who already agree with me.'

I nodded.

'If there's trouble, all right. That's what you're being paid for.'

I nodded.

We got to the Belmont Library at a quarter to ten. There were ten men and women walking up and down in front of the library with placards on poles made of strapping.

A Belmont Police cruiser was parked across the street, two cops sitting in it quietly.

'Park behind the cops,' I said.

Linda swung in behind the cruiser, and I got out. 'Stay in the car a second,' I said.

'I will not cower in here in front of a few pickets.'

'Then look menacing while you sit there. This is what I'm paid for. I just want to talk to the cops.'

I walked over to the cruiser. The cop at the wheel had a young wise-guy face. He looked like he'd tell you to stick it, at the first chance he got. And laugh. He was chewing a toothpick, the kind they put through a club sandwich. It still had the little cellophane frill on the end he wasn't chewing.

I bent down and said through the open window, 'I'm escorting this morning's library speaker. Am I likely to have any trouble from the pickets?'

He looked at me for ten or twelve seconds, worrying the toothpick with his tongue.

'You do, and we'll take care of it,' he said. 'You think we're down here waiting to pick up a copy of *Gone with the Wind*?'

'I figured you more for picture books,' I said.

He laughed. 'How about that, Benny?' he said to his partner. 'A hot shit. Haven't had one today.' His partner was slouched in the seat with his hat tipped over his eyes. He didn't say anything or move. 'Who's the speaker you're escorting?'

'Rachel Wallace,' I said.

'Never heard of her.'

'I'll try to keep that from her,' I said. 'I'm going to take her in now.'

'Good show,' he said. 'Shouldn't be any trouble for a hot shit like you.'

I went back to the car and opened the door for Rachel Wallace.

'What did you do?' she said as she got out.

'Annoyed another cop,' I said. 'That's 361 this year, and October's not over yet.'

'Did they say who the pickets were?'

I shook my head. We started across the street, Linda Smith on one side of Rachel and me on the other. Linda Smith's face looked tight and colorless; Rachel's was expressionless.

Someone among the pickets said, 'There she is.' They all turned and closed together more tightly as we walked toward them. Linda looked at me, then back at the cops. We kept walking.

'We don't want you here!' a woman shouted at us.

Someone else yelled, 'Dyke!'

I said, 'Is he talking to me?'

Rachel Wallace said, 'No.'

A heavy-featured woman with shoulder-length gray hair was carrying a placard that said, A Gay America is a Communist Goal. A stylish woman in a tailored suit carried a sign that read, Gay's Can't Reproduce. They Have to Convert.

I said, 'I bet she wanted to say proselytize; but no one knew how to spell it.'

No one laughed; I was getting used to that. As we approached the group they joined arms in front of us, blocking the entrance. In the center of the line was a large man with a square jaw and thick brown hair. Looked like he'd been a tight end perhaps, at Harvard. He wore a dark suit and a pale-gray silk tie. His cheeks were rosy, and his eye was clear. Probably still active in his alumni association. A splendid figure of a man, the rock upon which the picket line was anchored. Surely a foe of atheism, Communism, and faggotry. Almost certainly a perfect asshole.

Rachel Wallace walked directly up to him and said, 'Excuse me, please.'

There was no shouting now. It was quiet. Square Jaw shook his head, slowly, dramatically.

Rachel said, 'You are interfering with my right of free speech and free assembly, a right granted me by the Constitution.'

Nobody budged. I looked back at the cops. The wise-guy kid was out of the squad car now, leaning against the door on the passenger side, his arms crossed, his black leather belt sagging with ammunition, Mace, handcuffs, nightstick, gun, come-along, and a collection of keys on a ring. He probably wanted to walk over and let us through, but his gunbelt was too heavy.

I said to Rachel, 'Would you like me to create an egress for you?'

'How do you propose to do it?' she said.

'I thought I would knock this matinee idol on his kiester, and we could walk in over him.'

'It might be a mistake to try, fellow,' he said. His voice was full of money, like Daisy Buchanan.

'No,' I said. 'It would not be a mistake.'

Rachel said, 'Spenser.' Her voice was sharp. 'I don't stand for that,' she said. 'I won't resort to it.'

I shrugged and looked over at the young cop. His partner appeared not to have moved. He was still sitting in the squad car with his hat over his eyes. Maybe it was an economy move; maybe the partner was really an inflatable dummy. The young cop grinned at me.

'Our civil rights are in the process of violation over here!' I yelled at him. 'You have any plans for dealing with that?'

He pushed himself away from the car and swaggered over. His half-chewed toothpick bobbed in his mouth as he worked it back and forth with his tongue. The handle of his service revolver thumped against his leg. On his uniform blouse were several military service ribbons. Vietnam, I figured. There was a Purple Heart ribbon and a service ribbon with battle stars and another ribbon that might have been the Silver Star.

'You could look at it that way,' he said when he reached us. 'Or you could look at it that you people are causing a disturbance.'

'Will you escort us inside, officer?' Rachel Wallace said. 'I would say that is your duty, and I think you ought to do it.'

'We are here to prevent the spreading of an immoral and pernicious doctrine, officer,' Square Jaw said. 'That is *our* duty. I do not think you should *aid* people who wish to destroy the American family.'

The cop looked at Rachel.

'I will not be caught up in false issues,' Rachel said. 'We have a perfect right to go into that library and speak. I have been invited, and I will speak. There is no question of right here. I have a right and they are trying to violate it. Do your job.'

Other people were gathering, passing cars slowed down and began to back up traffic while the drivers tried to see what was happening. On the fringes of the crowd post-high-school kids gathered and smirked.

Square Jaw said, 'It might help you to keep in mind, officer, that I am a close personal friend of Chief Garner, and I'm sure he'll want to hear from me exactly what has happened and how his men have behaved.'

The young cop looked at me. 'A friend of the chief,' he said.

'That's frightening,' I said. 'You better walk softly around him.'

The young cop grinned at me broadly. 'Yeah,' he said. He turned back to Square Jaw. 'Move it, Jack,' he said. The smile was gone.

Square Jaw rocked back a little as if someone had jabbed at him.

'I beg your pardon?' he said.

'I said, move your ass. This broad may be a creep, but she didn't try to scare me. I don't like people to try and scare me. These people are going in – you can tell the chief that when you see him. You can tell him they went in past you or over you. You decide which you'll tell him.'

The young cop's face was half an inch away from Square

Jaw's, and since he was three inches shorter, it was tilted up. The partner had appeared from the car. He was older and heavier, with a pot belly and large hands with big knuckles. He had his night stick in his right hand, and he slapped it gently against his thigh.

The people on either side of Square Jaw unlinked their arms and moved away. Square Jaw looked at Rachel, and when he spoke he almost hissed. 'You foul, contemptible woman,' he said. 'You bulldyke. We'll never let you win. You queer . . .'

I pointed down the street to the left and said to the two cops, 'There's trouble.'

They both turned to look, and when they did I gave Square Jaw a six-inch jab in the solar plexus with my right fist. He gasped and doubled up. The cops spun back and looked at him and then at me. I was staring down the street where I'd pointed. 'Guess I was mistaken,' I said.

Square Jaw was bent over, his arms wrapped across his midsection, rocking back and forth. A good shot in the solar plexus will half-paralyze you for a minute or two.

The young cop looked at me without expression. 'Yeah, I guess you were,' he said, 'Well, let's get to the library.'

As we walked past Square Jaw the older cop said to him, 'It's a violation of health ordinances, Jack, to puke in the street.'

7

Inside the library, and downstairs in the small lecture room, there was no evidence that a disturbance had ever happened. The collection of elderly people, mostly women, all gray-haired, mostly overweight, was sitting placidly on folding chairs, staring patiently at the small platform and the empty lectern.

The two cops left us at the door. 'We'll sit around outside,' the young one said, 'until you're through.' Rachel Wallace was being introduced to the Friends of the Library president, who would introduce her to the audience. The young cop looked at her. 'What did you say her name was?'

'Rachel Wallace,' I said.

'She some kind of queer or something?'

'She's a writer,' I said. 'She's a feminist. She's gay. She's not easy to scare.'

The cop shook his head, 'A goddamned lezzy,' he said to his partner. 'We'll be outside,' he said to me. They started up the stairs. Three steps up the young cop stopped and turned back to me. 'You got a good punch,' he said. 'You don't see a lot of guys can hit that hard on a short jab.' Then he turned and went on up after his partner. Inside the room Rachel Wallace was sitting on a folding chair beside the lectern, her hands folded in her lap, her ankles crossed. The president was introducing her. On a table to the right of the lectern were maybe two dozen of Rachel Wallace's books. I leaned against the wall to the right of the door in the back and looked at the audience. No one looked furtive. Not all of them looked awake. Linda Smith was standing next to me.

'Nice booking,' I said to her.

She shrugged. 'It all helps,' she said. 'Did you hit that man outside?'

'Just once,' I said.

'I wonder what she'll say about that,' Linda Smith said.

I shrugged.

The president finished introducing Rachel and she stepped to the lectern. The audience clapped politely.

'I am here,' Rachel said, 'for the same reason I write. Because I have a truth to tell, and I will tell it.'

I whispered to Linda Smith, 'You think many of these people have read her books?'

Linda shook her head. 'Most of them just like to come out and look at a real live author.'

'The word *woman* is derived from the Old English *wifman* meaning "wife-person." The very noun by which our language designates us does so only in terms of men.'

The audience looked on loyally and strained to understand. Looking at them, you'd have to guess that the majority of them couldn't find any area where they could agree with her. At least a plurality probably couldn't find an area where they understood what she was talking about. They were library friends, people who had liked to read all their lives, and liked it in the library and had a lot of free time on their hands. Under other circumstances they would have shot a lesbian on sight.

'I am not here,' Rachel Wallace was saying, 'to change your sexual preference. I am here only to say that sexual preference is not a legitimate basis for discriminatory practices, for maltreatment in the marketplace. I am here to say that a woman can be fulfilled without a husband and children, that a woman is not a breeding machine, that she need not be a slave to her family, a whore for her husband.'

An elderly man in a gray sharkskin suit leaned over to his wife and whispered something. Her shoulders shook with silent laughter. A boy about four years old got up from his seat beside his grandmother and walked down the center aisle to sit on the floor in front and stare up at Rachel. In the very last row a fat woman in a purple dress read a copy of *Mademoiselle*.

'How many books does this sell?' I whispered to Linda Smith.

She shrugged. 'There's no way to know, really,' she whispered. 'The theory is that exposure helps. The more the better. Big scenes like the *Today Show*, small ones like this. You try to blanket a given area.'

'Are there any questions?' Rachel said. The audience stared at her. A man wearing white socks and bedroom slippers was asleep in the front row, right corner. In the silence the pages turning in *Mademoiselle* were loud. The woman didn't seem to notice.

'If not, then thank you very much.'

Rachel stepped off the low platform past the small boy and walked down the center aisle toward Linda and me. Outside the hall there were multicolored small cookies on a table and a large coffee maker with a thumbprint near the spigot. Linda said to Rachel, 'That was wonderful.'

Rachel said, 'Thank you.'

The president of the Friends said, 'Would you like some coffee and refreshments?'

Rachel said, 'No, thank you.' She jerked her head at me, and the three of us headed for the door.

'You sure you don't want any refreshment?' I said, as we went out the side door of the library.

'I want two maybe three martinis and lunch,' Rachel said. 'What have I this afternoon, Linda?'

'An autographing in Cambridge.'

Rachel shivered. 'God,' she said.

There was no one outside now except the two cops in the squad car. The pickets were gone, and the lawn was empty and innocent in front of the library. I shot at the young cop with my forefinger and thumb as we got into Linda Smith's car. He nodded. We drove away.

'You and the young officer seem to have developed some sort of relationship. Have you met him before?'

'Not him specifically, but we know some of the same things. When I was his age, I was sort of like him.'

'No doubt,' she said, without any visible pleasure. 'What

sort of things do you both know? And how do you know you know them?'

I shrugged. 'You wouldn't get it, I don't think. I don't even know how we know, but we do.'

'Try,' Rachel said. 'I am not a dullard. Try to explain.'

'We know what hurts,' I said, 'and what doesn't. We know about being scared and being brave. We know applied theory.'

'You can tell that, just by looking?'

'Well, partly. He had some combat decorations on his blouse.'

'Military medals?'

'Yeah, cops sometimes wear them. He does. He's proud of them.'

'And that's the basis of your judgment?'

'No, not just that. It's the way he walks. How his mouth looks, the way he holds his head. The way he reacted to the protest leader.'

'I thought him a parody of machismo.'

'No, not a parody,' I said. 'The real thing.'

'The real thing is a parody,' she said.

'I didn't think you'd get it,' I said.

'Don't you patronize me,' she said. 'Don't use that oh-women-don't-understand tone with me.'

'I said you didn't understand. I didn't say other women don't. I didn't say it was because you're a woman.'

'And,' she snapped, 'I assume you think you were some kind of Sir Galahad protecting my good name when you punched that poor sexist fool at the library. Well, you were not. You were a stupid thug. I will not have you acting on my behalf in a manner I deplore. If you strike another person except to save my life, I will fire you at that moment.'

'How about if I stick my tongue out at them and go *bleaaah*?'

'I'm serious,' she said.

'I'll say.'

We were perfectly quiet then. Linda Smith drove back through Watertown toward Cambridge.

'I really thought the talk went very well, Rachel,' she said. 'That was a tough audience, and I thought you really got to them.'

Rachel Wallace didn't answer.

'I thought we could go into Cambridge and have lunch at the Harvest,' Linda said. 'Then we could stroll up to the bookstore.'

'Good,' Rachel said. 'I'm hungry, and I need a drink.'

8

In my mouth there was still the faint taste of batter-fried shrimp with mustard fruits as I hung around the front door of the Crimson Book Store on Mass. Ave. and watched Rachel Wallace sign books. Across the street Harvard Yard glistened in the fall rain that had started while we were eating lunch.

Rachel was at a card table near the check-out counter in the front of the store. On the card table were about twenty copies of her new book and three blue felt-tipped pens. In the front window a large sign announced that she'd be there from one until three that day. It was now two ten, and they had sold three books. Another half dozen people had come in and looked at her and gone out.

Linda Smith hung around the table and drank coffee and steered an occasional customer over. I looked at everyone who came in and learned nothing at all. At two fifteen a teenage girl came in wearing Levi jeans and a purple warm-up jacket that said Brass Kaydettes on it.

'You really an author?' she said to Rachel.

Rachel said, 'Yes, I am.'

'You write this book?'

'Yes.'

Linda Smith said, 'Would you like to buy one? Ms Wallace will autograph a copy.'

The girl ignored her. 'This book any good?' she said.

Rachel Wallace smiled. 'I think so,' she said.

'What's it about?'

'It's about being a woman and about the way people discriminate against women, and about the way that corruption leads to other corruption.'

'Oh, yeah? Is it exciting?'

'Well, I wouldn't, ah, I wouldn't say it was exciting, exactly. It is maybe better described as powerful.'

'I was thinking of being a writer,' the kid said.

Rachel's smile was quite thin. 'Oh, really?'

'Where do you get your ideas?'

'I think them up,' Rachel said. The smile was so thin it was hard to see.

'Oh, yeah?' The girl picked up a copy of Rachel's book and looked at it, and turned it over and looked at the back. She read the jacket flap for a minute, then put the book down.

'This a novel?' the girl said.

'No,' Rachel said.

'It's long as a novel.'

'Yes,' Rachel said.

'So why ain't it a novel?'

'It's nonfiction.'

'Oh.'

The girl's hair was leaf-brown and tied in two pigtails

that lapped over her ears. She had braces on her teeth. She picked the book up again and flipped idly through the pages. There was silence.

Rachel Wallace said, 'Are you thinking of buying a copy?'

The girl shook her head, 'Naw,' she said, 'I got no money anyway.'

'Then put the book down and go somewhere else,' Rachel said.

'Hey, I ain't doing any harm,' the girl said. Rachel looked at her.

'Oh, I'm through anyway,' the girl said and left the store.

'You got some smooth way with the reading public,' I said.

'Little twerp,' Rachel said. 'Where do I get my ideas? Jesus Christ, where does she think I get them? Everyone asks me that. The question is inane.'

'She probably doesn't know any better,' I said.

Rachel Wallace looked at me and said nothing. I didn't have a sense that she thought me insightful.

Two young men came in. One was small and thin with a crew cut and gold-rimmed glasses. He had on a short yellow slicker with a hood up and blue serge pants with cuffs that stopped perhaps two inches above the tops of his wing-tipped cordovan shoes. He had rubbers on over the shoes. The other one was much bigger. He had the look of a fat weightlifter. He couldn't have been more than twenty-five, but he was starting to get bald. He wore a red-and-black plaid flannel shirt, a black down vest, and chino pants rolled up over laced work boots. The sleeves of his shirt were turned up.

The small one carried a white cardboard pastry box. I edged a little closer to Rachel when they came in. They didn't look bookstorish. As they stopped in front of Rachel's table I put my hand inside my jacket on the butt of my gun. As the small one opened the pastry box I moved. He came out with a chocolate cream pie and had it halfway into throwing position when I hit him with my shoulder. He got it off, side-armed and weakly, and it hit Rachel in the chest. I had the gun out now, and when the fat one grabbed at me I hit him on the wrist with the barrel. The small one bowled over backwards and fell on the floor.

I said, 'Everybody freeze,' and pointed my gun at them. Always a snappy line.

The fat one was clutching his wrist against his stomach. 'It was only a freaking pie, man,' he said.

The small one had scrunched up against the wall by the door. The wind was knocked out of him, and he was working on getting it back. I looked at Rachel. The pie had hit her on the left breast and slid down her dress to her lap, leaving a wide trail of chocolate and whipped cream.

I said to the men, 'Roll over on the floor, face down. Clasp your hands back of your head.'

The little one did what I said. His breath was back. The fat one said, 'Hey, man, I think you broke my freaking wrist.'

'On the floor,' I said.

He went down. I knelt behind them and searched them quickly with my left hand, keeping the gun clear in my right. They had no weapons.

The bookstore manager and Linda Smith were busy with paper towels trying to wipe the chocolate cream off Rachel; customers gathered in a kind of hushed circle – not frightened, embarrassed rather. I stood up.

Rachel's face was flushed, and her eyes were bright. 'Sweets for the sweet, my dear,' I said.

'Call the police,' she said.

'You want to prefer charges?' I said.

'Absolutely,' she said. 'I want these two boars charged with assault.'

From the floor the fat one said, 'Aw, lady, it was only a freaking pie.'

'Shut up,' she said. 'Shut your foul, stupid mouth now. You grunting ass. I will do everything I can to put you in jail for this.'

I said, 'Linda, could you call the buttons for us?'

She nodded and went over to the telephone behind the counter.

Rachel turned and looked at the five customers and two clerks in a small semicircle looking uncomfortable.

'What are you people looking at?' she said. 'Go about your business. Go on. Move.'

They began to drift away. All five customers went out. The two clerks went back to arranging books on a display table downstairs.

'I think this autographing is over,' Rachel said.

'Yeah,' I said, 'but the cops are coming. You gotta wait for them. They get grouchy as hell when you call them and screw.'

Linda Smith hung up the phone. 'They'll be right along,' she said.

And they were – a prowl car with two cops in uniform. They wanted to see my license and my gun permit, and they shook down both the assault suspects routinely and thoroughly. I didn't bother to tell them I'd already done it; they'd have done it again anyway.

'You want to prefer assault charges against these two, lady?' one of the prowlies said.

'My name is Rachel Wallace. And I certainly do.'

'Okay, Rachel,' the cop said. There was a fine network of red veins in each cheek. 'We'll take them in. Sergeant's gonna like this one, Jerry. Assault with a pie.'

They herded the two young men toward the door. The fat one said, 'Geez, lady, it was just a freaking pie.'

Rachel leaned toward him a little and said to him very carefully, 'Eat a shit sandwich.'

9

We drove back to the Ritz in silence. The traffic wasn't heavy yet, and Linda Smith didn't have to concentrate on driving as much as she did. As we went over the Mass. Ave. Bridge I looked at the way the rain dimpled the surface of the river. The sweep of the Charles from the bridge down toward the basin was very fine from the Mass. Ave. Bridge – much better when you walked across it, but okay from a car. The red-brick city on Beacon Hill, the original one, was prominent from here, capped by the gold dome of the Bulfinch State House. The high-rises of the modern city were all around it, but from here they didn't dominate. It was like looking back through the rain to the way it was, and maybe should have been.

Linda Smith turned off Mass. Ave. and onto Commonwealth. 'You don't think I should have preferred charges,' Rachel said to me.

'Not my business to think about that,' I said.

'But you disapprove.'

I shrugged. 'Tends to clog up the court system.'

'Was I to let them walk away after insulting and degrading me?'

'I could have kicked each one in the fanny,' I said.

'That's your solution to everything,' she said, and looked out the window.

'No, but it's a solution to some things. You want them punished. What do you think will happen to them? A night in jail and a fifty-dollar fine, maybe. To get that done will involve two prowl-car cops, a desk sergeant, a judge, a prosecutor, a public defender, and probably more. It will cost the state about two thousand dollars, and you'll probably have to spend the morning in court and so will the two arresting officers. I could have made them sorry a lot sooner for free.'

She continued to stare out the window.

'And,' I said, 'it was only a freaking pie, lady.'

She looked at me and almost smiled. 'You were very quick,' she said.

'I didn't know it was going to be a pie.'

'Would you have shot him?' she said. She wasn't looking out the window now; she stared straight at me.

'If I had to. I almost did before I saw it was a pie.'

'What kind of a man would do that?'

'Throw a pie at someone?'

'No,' she said. 'Shoot someone.'

'You asked me that before,' I said. 'I don't have a better answer this time except to say, isn't it good you've got one? At the rate we're going, you'll be attacked by a horde of chauvinist cameldrivers before the week is out.'

'You sound as if it were my fault. It is not. I do not cause trouble – I am beset by it because of my views.'

Linda Smith pulled the car onto Arlington Street and

into the open space in front of the Ritz. I said, 'Stay in the car till I tell you.'

I got out and looked both ways and into the lobby. The doorman hustled forward to open the door for Rachel. She looked at me. I nodded. She stepped out of the car and walked into the hotel.

'We'll have a drink in the bar,' she said.

I nodded and followed her in. There were a couple of business types having Scotch on the rocks at a table by the window, and a college-age boy and girl sitting at another table, very dressed up and a little ill at ease. He had beer. She had a champagne cocktail. Or at least it looked like a champagne cocktail. I hoped it was.

Rachel slid onto a bar stool, and I sat next to her and turned my back to the bar and surveyed the room. No one but us and the business types and the college kids. Rachel's coat had a hood. She slid the hood off but kept the coat on to cover up the pie smear down the front of her dress.

'Beer, Spenser?'

'Yes, please.'

She ordered. Beer for me and a martini for her. For the Ritz Bar I was spectacularly underdressed. I thought the bartender paled a little when I came in, but he said nothing and tended the bar just as if I were not offensive to his sight.

A young woman came into the bar alone. She had on a long cream-colored wool skirt and heavy black boots, the kind that seem to have extra leather. Her blouse was white. There was a black silk scarf at her neck, and she carried a gray leather coat over her arm. Very stylish. The skirt fitted well, I noticed, especially around the hips. She looked around the room and spotted us at the bar and came directly to us. The kid can still attract them, I thought. Still got the old whammo.

The young woman reached us and said, 'Rachel,' and put her hand out.

Rachel Wallace turned and looked at her and then smiled. She took the outstretched hand in both of hers. 'Julie,' she said. 'Julie Wells.' She leaned forward and Julie Wells put her face down and Rachel kissed her. 'How lovely to see you,' she said. 'Sit down.'

Julie slid onto the bar stool on the other side of Rachel.

'I heard you were in town again,' she said, 'and I knew you'd be staying here, so I got through work early and came over. I called your room, and when there was no answer, I thought, well, knowing Rachel, chances are she's in the bar.'

'Well, you do know me,' Rachel said. 'Can you stay? Can you have dinner with me?'

'Sure,' Julie said, 'I was hoping you'd ask.'

The bartender came over and looked questioningly at Julie. 'I'll have a Scotch sour on the rocks,' she said.

Rachel said, 'I'll have another martini. Spenser, another beer?'

I nodded. The bartender moved away. Julie looked at me. I smiled at her. 'We're on tour,' I said. 'Rachel plays the hand organ, and I go around with a little cup and collect money.'

Julie said, 'Oh, really,' and looked at Rachel.

'His name is Spenser,' Rachel said. 'There have been

some threats about my new book. The publisher thought I should have a bodyguard. He thinks he's funny.'

'Nice to meet you,' Julie said.

'Nice to meet you, too,' I said. 'Are you an old friend of Rachel's?'

She and Rachel smiled at each other. 'Sort of, I guess,' Julie said. 'Would you say so, Rachel?'

'Yes,' Rachel said, 'I would say that. I met Julie when I was up here doing the research for *Tyranny*, last year.'

'You a writer, Julie?'

She smiled at me, very warm. *Zing* went the strings of my heart. 'No,' she said, 'I wish I were. I'm a model.'

'What agency?'

'Carol Cobb. Do you know the modeling business?'

'No, I'm just a curious person.'

Rachel shook her head. 'No, he's not,' she said. 'He's screening you. And I don't like it.' She looked at me. 'I appreciate that you have to do your job, and that today may have made you unduly suspicious. But Julie Wells is a close personal friend of mine. We have nothing to fear from her. I'll appreciate it if in the future you trust my judgment.'

'Your judgment's not as good as mine,' I said. 'I have no involvement. How close a personal friend can someone be that you met only last year?'

'Spenser, that's enough,' Rachel said. There was force in her voice and her face.

Julie said, 'Rachel, I don't mind. Of course he has to be careful. I pray that he is. What are these threats? How serious are they?'

Rachel turned toward her. I sipped a little beer. 'I've had phone calls threatening me if *Tyranny* is published.'

'But if you're on the promotion tour, it means it's been published already.'

'In fact, yes, though technically publication date isn't until October 15th. The book is already in a lot of bookstores.'

'Has anything happened?'

'There was an incident last night, and there have been protests. But I don't think they're related.'

'The incident last night was the real goods,' I said. 'The other stuff was probably what it seemed.'

'What happened last night?' Julie said.

'Spenser contends that someone tried to run us off the road last night in Lynn.'

'Contends?' Julie said.

'Well, I was on the floor, and he swerved around a lot and then the car behind us was gone. I can't speak for sure myself. And if I were convinced no one was after me, Spenser would be out of work.'

'Aw, you'd want me around anyway. All you chicks like a guy to look after you.'

She threw her drink at me. She threw like a girl; most of it landed on my shirt front.

'Now we're both messy,' I said. 'A his-and-hers outfit.'

The bartender slid down toward us. Julie put her hand on Rachel's arm. The bartender said, 'Is there something wrong, ma'am?'

Rachel was silent. Her breath blew in and out through her nose.

I said to the bartender, 'No, it's fine. She was kidding with me, and the drink slipped.'

The bartender looked at me as if I were serious, smiled as if he believed me, and moved off down the bar. In maybe thirty seconds he was back with a new martini for Rachel. 'This is on the house, ma'am,' he said.

Julie said to me, 'Why do you feel last night was serious?'

'It was professional,' I said. 'They knew what they were doing. We were lucky to get out of it.'

'Rachel is hard sometimes,' Julie said. She was patting the back of Rachel's left hand. 'She doesn't mean everything she says and does always. Sometimes she regrets them, even.'

'Me, too,' I said. I wondered if I should pat the other hand. My T-shirt was wet against my chest, but I didn't touch it. It's like getting hit with a pitch. You're not supposed to rub.

Rachel said, 'Julie and I will dine in our room tonight. I won't need you until tomorrow at eight.'

'I better wait until Julie leaves,' I said.

They both looked at me. Then Rachel said, 'That's when she is going to leave.'

I said, 'Oh.' Always the smooth comeback, even when I've been dumb. Of course they were very good friends.

'I'll walk up with you and hang around in the hall till the waiter has come and gone.'

'That won't be necessary,' Rachel said. She wouldn't look at me.

'Yeah, it will,' I said. 'I work at what I do, Rachel. I'm not going to let someone buzz you in the lobby just because you're mad at me.'

She looked up at me. 'I'm not mad at you,' she said. 'I'm ashamed of the way I behaved a moment ago.'

Behind her Julie beamed at me. *See?* her smile said, *See? She's really very nice.*

'Either way,' I said. 'I'll stick around and wait till you've locked up for the night. I won't bother you – I'll lurk in the hall.'

She nodded. 'Perhaps that would be best,' she said.

We finished our drinks, Rachel signed the bar tab, and we headed for the elevators. I went first; they followed. When we got in the elevator, Julie and Rachel were holding hands. The skirt still fitted Julie's hips wonderfully. Was I a sexist? Was it ugly to think, *what a waste*? On Rachel's floor I got out first. The corridor was empty. At her room I took the key from Rachel and opened the door. The room was dark and silent. I went in and turned on the lights. There was no one there and no one in the bathroom. Rachel and Julie came in.

I said, 'Okay, I'll say goodnight. I'll be in the hall. When room service comes, open the door on the chain first, and don't let him in unless I'm there, too. I'll come in with him.'

Rachel nodded. Julie said, 'Nice to have met you, Spenser.'

I smiled at her and closed the door.

10

The corridor was silent and Ritzy, with gold-patterned wallpaper. I wondered if they'd make love before they ordered dinner. I would. I hoped they wouldn't. It had been a while since lunch and would be a long wait for dinner if it worked out wrong.

I leaned against the wall opposite their door. If they were making love, I didn't want to hear. The concept of love between two women didn't have much effect on me in the abstract. But if I imagined them at it, and speculated on exactly how they went about it, it seemed sort of too bad, demeaning. Actually maybe Susan and I weren't all that slick in the actual doing ourselves. When you thought about it, maybe none of us were doing *Swan Lake*. 'What's right is what feels good afterwards,' I said out loud in the empty corridor. Hemingway said that. Smart man, Hemingway. Spent very little time hanging around hotel corridors with no supper.

Down the corridor to my left a tall thin man with a black mustache and a double-breasted gray pinstripe suit came out of his room and past me, heading for the elevator. There was a silver pin in his collar under the modest knot of his tie. His black shoes glistened with polish. Class. Even more class than a wet Adidas T-shirt. The hell with him. He probably did not have a Smith and Wesson .38 caliber revolver with a four-inch barrel. And I did. *How's that for class?* I mumbled at his back as he went into the elevator.

About fifteen minutes later a housekeeper went bustling past me down the corridor and knocked on a door. No one answered, and the housekeeper let herself in with a key on a long chain. She was in for maybe a minute and came back past me and into the service elevator. She probably didn't have a .38 either.

I amused myself by trying to see how many lyrics I could sing to songs written by Johnny Mercer. I was halfway through 'Memphis in June' when a pleasant-looking gray-haired man with a large red nose got out of the elevator and walked down the corridor toward me. He had on gray slacks and a blue blazer. On the blazer pocket was a small name plate that said Asst. Mgr.

His blazer also hung funny over his right hip, the way it does when you are carrying a gun in a hip holster. He smiled as he approached me. I noticed that the blazer was unbuttoned and his left hand was in a half fist. He sort of tapped it against his thigh, knuckles toward me.

'Are you locked out of your room, sir?' he said with a big smile. He was a big guy and had a big stomach, but he didn't look slow and he didn't look soft. His teeth had been capped.

I said, 'House man, right?'

'Callahan,' he said. 'I'm the assistant night manager.'

'Spenser,' I said. 'I'm going to take out my wallet and show you some ID.'

'You're not registered here, Mr Spenser.'

'No, I'm working. I'm looking out for Rachel Wallace, who is registered here.'

I handed him my license. He looked at it and looked at me. 'Nice picture,' he said.

'Well, that's my bad side,' I said.

'It's full face,' he said.

'Yeah,' I said.

'Do I detect a weapon of some sort under your left arm, Mr Spenser?'

'Yes. It makes us even – you got one on your right hip.'

He smiled again. His half-clenched left fist tapped against his thigh.

'I'm in kind of a puzzle, Mr Spenser. If you really are guarding Miss Wallace, I can't very well ask you to leave. On the other hand you could be lying. I guess we better ask her.'

'Not right now,' I said. 'I think she's busy.'

''Fraid we'll have to anyway.'

'How do I know you're really the house dick?'

'Assistant manager,' he said. 'Says so right on my coat.'

'Anyone can get a coat. How do I know this isn't a ploy to get her to open the door?'

He rolled his lower lip out. 'Got a point there,' he said. 'What we do is go down the end of the hall by the elevators and call on the house phone. You can see the whole corridor and I can see you that way.'

I nodded. We walked down to the phone side by side, watching each other and being careful. I was paying most attention to the half-closed fist. For a man his size it was a small fist. At the phones he tucked the phone between his cheek and shoulder and dialed with his right hand. He knew the number without looking. She took a long while to answer.

'Sorry to bother you, Miss Wallace ... Ms Wallace ... Yeah ... Well, this is Callahan, the assistant manager. Do you have a man named Spenser providing personal security for you? ... Unh-huh ... Describe him to me, if you would ... No, we just spotted him outside your room and thought we'd better check ... Yes, ma'am. Yes, that'll be fine. Thank you.' He hung up.

'Okay,' he said with a big friendly smile. 'She validated you.' He put his left hand into the side pocket of his blazer and took it out.

'What did you have in your hand?' I said. 'Roll of quarters?'

'Dimes,' he said. 'Got a small hand.'

'Who whistled on me – the housekeeper?'

He nodded.

I said, 'Are you looking out for Ms Wallace special?'

'We're a little special on her,' he said. 'Got a call from a homicide dick said there'd been threats on her life.'

'Who called you – Quirk?'

'Yeah, know him?'

I nodded.

'Friend of his?'

'I wouldn't go that far,' I said.

We walked back down the corridor toward Rachel's room. 'Good cop,' Callahan said.

I nodded. 'Very tough,' I said.

'So I hear. I hear he's as tough as there is in this town.'

'Top three,' I said.

'Who else?'

'Guy named Hawk,' I said. 'He ever shows up in your hotel, don't try to take him with a roll of dimes.'

'Who's the third?'

I smiled at him and ducked my head. 'Aw, hell,' I said.

He did his big friendly smile again. 'Well, good we don't have to find that out,' he said. His voice was steady. He seemed able to repress his terror. 'Not tonight anyway.' He nodded at me. 'Have a good day,' he said, and moved off placidly down the corridor. I must have frightened him to death.

I went back to my Johnny Mercer lyrics. I was on the third verse of 'Midnight Sun' when a room-service waiter came off the elevator pushing a table. He stopped at Rachel's door and knocked. He smiled at me as he waited. The door opened on the chain and a small vertical plane of Rachel Wallace's face appeared.

I said, 'It's okay, Rachel. I'm here.' The waiter smiled at me again, as if I'd said something clever. The door closed and in a moment reopened. The waiter went in, and I came in behind him. Rachel was in a dark-brown full-length robe with white piping. She wore no makeup. Julie Wells wasn't in the room. The bathroom door was closed, and I could hear the shower going. Both beds were a little rumpled but still made.

The waiter opened up the table and began to lay out the supper. I leaned against the wall by the window and watched him. When he was through, Rachel Wallace signed the bill, added in a tip, and gave it back to him. He smiled – smiled at me – and went out.

Rachel looked at the table. There were flowers in the center.

'You can go for tonight, Spenser,' she said. 'We'll eat and go to bed. Be here at eight tomorrow.'

'Yes, ma'am,' I said. 'Where we going first?'

'We're going out to Channel Four and do a talk show.'

Julie Wells came out of the bathroom. She had a small towel wrapped around her head and a large one wrapped around her body. It covered her but not by much. She said, 'Hi, Spenser,' and smiled at me. Everyone smiled at me. Lovable. A real pussycat.

'Hello.' I didn't belong there. There was something powerfully non-male in the room, and I felt its pressure. 'Okay, Rachel. I'll say goodnight. Don't open the door. Don't even open it to push that cart into the hall. I'll be here at eight.'

They both smiled. Neither of them said anything. I went to the door at a normal pace. I did not run. 'Don't forget the chain,' I said. 'And the deadbolt from inside.'

They both smiled at me and nodded. Julie Wells's towel seemed to be shrinking. My mouth felt a little dry. 'I'll stay outside until I hear the bolt turn.'

Smile. Nod.

'Goodnight,' I said, and went out and closed the door. I heard the bolt slide and the chain go in. I went down in the elevator and out onto Arlington Street with my mouth still dry, feeling a bit unlovely.

11

I leaned against the cinder-block wall of studio two at Channel Four and watched Rachel Wallace prepare to promote her book and her cause. Off camera a half-dozen technician types in jeans and beards and sneakers hustled about doing technical things.

Rachel sat in a director's chair at a low table. The interviewer was on the other side, and on the table between them was a copy of *Tyranny*, standing upright and visible on a small display stand. Rachel sat calmly looking at the camera. The interviewer, a Styrofoam blonde with huge false eyelashes, was smoking a kingsized filter-tipped mentholated Salem cigarette as if they were about to tie her to a post and put on the blindfold. A technician pinned a small microphone to the lapel of Rachel's gray flannel jacket and stepped out of the way. Another technician with a clipboard crouched beneath one of the cameras a foot and a half from the interviewer. He wore earphones.

'Ten seconds, Shirley,' he said. The interviewer nodded and snuffed her cigarette out in an ashtray on the floor behind her chair. A man next to me shifted in his folding chair and said, 'Jesus Christ, I'm nervous.' He was scheduled to talk about raising quail after Rachel had finished. The technician squatting under the front camera pointed at the interviewer.

She smiled. 'Hi,' she said to the camera. 'I'm Shirley. And this is *Contact*. We have with us today feminist and lesbian activist Rachel Wallace. Rachel has written a new book, *Tyranny*, which takes the lid off of some of the ways government and business exploit women and especially gay women. We'll be back to talk with Rachel about her book and these issues after this word.' A commercial for hair coloring came on the monitor overhead.

The guy with the earphones crouching beneath the camera said, 'Good, Shirl.' Shirl took another cigarette from a box on the table behind Rachel's book and lit up. She was able to suck in almost half of it before the guy under the camera said, 'Ten seconds.' She snuffed this one out, leaned forward slightly, and when the picture came on the monitor, it caught her profile looking seriously at Rachel.

'Rachel,' she said, 'do you think lesbians ought to be allowed to teach at a girls' school?'

'Quite the largest percentage,' Rachel said, 'of child molestations are committed by heterosexual men. As I pointed out in my book, the incidence of child molestation by lesbians is so small as to be statistically meaningless.'

'But what kind of role model would a lesbian provide?'

'Whatever kind she was. We don't ask other teachers about their sexual habits. We don't prevent so-called frigid women from teaching children, or impotent men. Children do not, it seems to me, have much chance in public school to emulate the sexual habits of their teachers. And if the teacher's sexual preference is so persuasive to his or her students, why aren't gays made straight by exposure to heterosexual teachers?'

'But might not the gay teacher subtly persuade his or her students toward a homosexual preference?'

Rachel said, 'I just answered that, Shirley.'

Shirley smiled brilliantly. 'In your book you allege frequent violations of civil rights in employment both by the government and the private sector. Many of the offenders are here in Massachusetts. Would you care to name some of them?'

Rachel was beginning to look annoyed. 'I named all of them in my book,' she said.

'But,' Shirley said, 'not all of our viewers have read it.'

'Have you?' Rachel said.

'I haven't finished it yet,' Shirley said. 'I'm sorry to say.' The guy crouching below the camera lens made a gesture with his hand, and Shirley said, 'We'll be right back with more interesting revelations from Rachel Wallace after this message.'

I whispered to Linda Smith, who stood in neat tweeds beside me, 'Shirley doesn't listen to the answers.'

'A lot of them don't,' Linda said. 'They're busy looking ahead to the next question.'

'And she hasn't read the book.'

Linda smiled and shook her head. 'Almost none of them ever do. You can't blame them. Sometimes you get several authors a week plus all the other stuff.'

'The pressure must be fearful,' I said. 'To spend your working life never knowing what you're talking about.'

'Lots of people do that,' Linda said. 'I only hope Rachel doesn't let her annoyance show. She's a good interview, but she gets mad too easy.'

'That's because if *she* had been doing the interview, she'd have read the book first.'

'Maybe,' Linda said, 'but Shirley North has a lot of fans in the metropolitan area, and she can sell us some books. The bridge club types love her.'

A commercial for pantyhose concluded with a model holding out the crotch to show the ventilated panel, then Shirley came back on.

'In your book, Rachel, you characterize lesbianism as an alternative way of loving. Should everyone try it?'

'Everyone should do what she wants to do,' Rachel said. 'Obviously people to whom the idea is not attractive should stay straight. My argument is, and has been, that those who do find that alternative desirable should not be victimized for that preference. It does no one any harm at all.'

'Is it against God's law?'

'It would be arrogant of me to tell you God's law. I'll leave that to the people who think they have God's ear. All I can say is that I've had no sign that He disapproves.'

'How about the argument that it is unnatural?'

'Same answer. That really implies a law of nature that exists immutably. I'm not in a position to know about that. Sartre said that perhaps existence precedes essence, and maybe we are in the process of making the laws of nature as we live.'

'Yes, certainly. Do you advocate lesbian marriage?'

'Shirley,' Rachel said. 'I have documented corruption on several levels of local and state government, in several of the major corporations in the country, and you've asked me only about titillating things. In essence you've asked only about sex. That seems unbalanced to me.'

Shirley's smile glowed. Her splendiferous eyelashes fluttered. 'Isn't that an interesting thought, Rachel? I wish we could spend more time, but I know you have to rush.' She picked up *Tyranny*. 'Get Rachel's book, *Tyranny*, published by Hamilton Black. You'll love it, as I did. Thanks a million, Rachel. Come back again.'

Rachel muttered, 'Thank you.'

Shirley said, 'Now this message.'

The guy squatting under the camera stood up and said, 'Okay, next segment. Thanks a lot Mrs Wallace. Shirley, you're on the den set.' A technician took off Rachel's lapel mike, and she got up and walked away. Shirley didn't say goodbye. She was getting as much mentholated smoke into her as she could before the deodorant commercial ended.

Linda Smith said, 'Oh, Rachel, you were dynamite.'

Rachel looked at me. I shrugged. Rachel said, 'What's that mean?'

I said, 'It means you did your best in a difficult situation. You can't look good being interviewed by Shirley North.'

Rachel nodded. Linda said, 'Oh, no, I thought you were super.'

Rachel said nothing as we walked out of the studio and down the long corridor past the news set, empty now and shabby, then along the corridor where people sat in small offices and typed, and out into the lobby and reception area. On the big monitor opposite the reception desk Shirley was leaning toward the man who raised quail.

I frowned the way Shirley did and said in a high voice, 'Tell me, do quails like to do it with anything but other quails?'

Rachel gave a snort. Linda smiled. Outside we parted – Rachel and I in my car, Linda in hers.

We wheeled along Soldiers' Field Road with the Charles, quite small and winding this far up, on our left. I looked at Rachel. She was crying. Tears ran in silence down her cheeks. Her hands were folded in her lap. Her shoulders were a little hunched, and her body shook slightly. I looked back at the road. I couldn't think of anything to say. She didn't cry any harder and she didn't stop. The only sound was the unsteady inhaling and exhaling as she cried. We went past Harvard Stadium.

I said, 'Feel like a freak?'

She nodded.

'Don't let them do that to you,' I said.

'A freak,' she said. Her voice was a little thick and a little unsteady, but if you didn't see the tears, you wouldn't be sure she was crying. 'Or a monster. That's how everyone seems to see us. Do you seduce little girls? Do you carry them off for strange lesbian rites? Do you use a dildo? God. God damn. Bastards.' Her shoulders began to shake harder.

I put my right hand out toward her with the palm up. We passed the business school that way – me with my hand out, her with her body shaking. Then she put her left hand in my right. I held it hard.

'Don't let them do that to you,' I said.

She squeezed back at me and we drove the rest of the way along the Charles like that – our hands quite rigidly clamped together, her body slowly quieting down. When I got to the Arlington Street exit, she let go of my hand and opened her purse. By the time we stopped in front of the Ritz, she had her face dry and a little makeup on and herself back in place.

The doorman looked like I'd made a mess on his foot when I got out and nodded toward the Chevy. But he took it from me and said nothing. A job is a job. We went up in the elevator and walked to her room without saying a word. She opened the door. I stepped in first; she followed.

'We have to go to First Mutual Insurance Company at one. I'm addressing a women's group there. Could you pick me up about twelve thirty?' Her voice was quite calm now.

'Sure,' I said.

'I'd like to rest for a while,' she said, 'so please excuse me.'

'Sure,' I said. 'I'll be here at quarter to one.'

'Yes,' she said. 'Thank you.'

'Lock the door behind me,' I said.

She nodded. I went out and waited until I heard the bolt click behind me. Then I went to the elevator and down.

12

'I'm meeting with a caucus of women employees at First Mutual Insurance,' Rachel said. 'This is their lunch hour and they've asked me to eat with them. I know you have to be close by, but I would like it if you didn't actually join us.' We were walking along Boylston Street.

'Okay,' I said. 'As I recall from your book, First Mutual is one of the baddies.'

'I wouldn't put it that way, but yes. They are discriminatory in their hiring and wage practices. There are almost no women in management. They have systematically refused to employ gay people and have fired any that they discovered in their employ.'

'Didn't you turn up discriminatory practices in their sales policy?'

'Yes. They discourage sales to blacks.'

'What's the company slogan?'

Rachel smiled. 'We're in the people business.'

We went into the lobby of First Mutual and took an elevator to the twentieth floor. The cafeteria was at one end of the corridor. A young woman in camel's-hair slacks and vest topped with a dark-brown blazer was waiting outside. When she saw Rachel she came forward and said, 'Rachel Wallace?' She wore small gold-rimmed glasses and no makeup. Her hair was brown and sensible.

Rachel put out her hand. 'Yes,' she said. 'Are you Dorothy Collela?'

'Yes, come on in. We're all at a table in the corner.' She looked at me uncertainly.

'My name is Spenser,' I said. 'I just hang around Ms Wallace. Don't think about me for a moment.'

'Will you be joining us?' Dorothy said.

Rachel said, 'No. Mr Spenser is just going to stay by if I need anything.'

Dorothy smiled a little blankly and led Rachel to a long table at one end of the cafeteria. There were eight other women gathered there. I leaned against the wall maybe twenty feet away where I could see Rachel and not hear them and not be in the flow of diners.

There was a good deal of chair-scraping and jostling at the table when Rachel sat down. There were introductions and people standing and sitting, and then all but two of the women got up and went to the food line to get lunch. The luncheon special was Scrambled Hamburg Oriental, and I decided to pass on lunch.

The cafeteria had a low ceiling with a lot of fluorescent panels in it. The walls were painted a brilliant yellow on three sides with a bank of windows looking out over Back Bay on the fourth side. The bright yellow paint was almost painful. Music filtered through the cafeteria noise. It sounded like Mantovani, but it always does.

Working with a writer, you get into the glamour scene. After we left here, we'd probably go down to Filene's basement and autograph corsets. Maybe Norman would be there, and Truman and Gore. Rachel took her tray and sat down. She had eschewed the Oriental hamburg. On her tray was a sandwich and a cup of tea.

A girl not long out of the high-school corridors came past me wearing very expensive clothes, very snugly. She had on blue harlequin glasses with small jewels on them, and she smelled like a French sunset.

She smiled at me and said, 'Well, foxy, what are you looking at?'

'A size-nine body in a size-seven dress,' I said.

'You should see it without the dress,' she said.

'I certainly should,' I said.

She smiled and joined two other kids her age at a table. They whispered together and looked at me and laughed. The best-dressed people in the world are the single kids that just started working.

Two men in business suits and one uniformed guard came into the cafeteria and walked over to Rachel's table. I slid along behind and listened in. It looked like my business. It was.

'We invited her here,' Dorothy was saying.

One of the business suits said, 'You're not authorized to do that.' He looked like Clark Kent. Three-piece suit with a small gray herringbone in it. Glasses, square face.

His hair was short, his face was clean-shaved. His shoes were shined. His tie was knotted small but asserted by a simple pin. He was on the way up.

'Who are you?' Rachel said.

'Timmons,' he said. 'Director of employee relations.' He spoke very fast. 'This is Mr Boucher, our security co-ordinator.' Nobody introduced the uniformed guard; he wasn't on the way up. Boucher was sort of plumpish and had a thick mustache. The guard didn't have a gun, but the loop of a leather strap stuck out of his right hip pocket.

'And why are you asking me to leave?' Rachel was saying.

'Because you are in violation of company policy.'

'How so?'

'No soliciting is allowed on the premises,' Timmons said. I wondered if he was nervous or if he always spoke that fast. I drifted around behind Rachel's chair and folded my arms and looked at Timmons.

'And what exactly am I supposed to be soliciting?' Rachel said.

Timmons didn't like me standing there, and he didn't quite know what to do about it. He looked at me and looked away quickly and then he looked at Boucher and back at me and then at Rachel. He started to speak to Rachel and stopped and looked at me again.

'Who are you?' he said.

'I'm the Tooth Fairy,' I said.

'The what?'

'The Tooth Fairy,' I said. 'I loosen teeth.'

Timmons's mouth opened and shut. Boucher said, 'We don't need any smart answers, mister.'

I said, 'You wouldn't understand any.'

Rachel said, 'Mr Spenser is with me.'

'Well,' Boucher said, 'you'll both have to leave or we'll have you removed.'

'How many security people you got?' I said to Boucher.

'That's no concern of yours,' Boucher said. Very tough.

'Yeah, but it could be a concern of yours. It will take an awful lot of people like you to remove us.'

The uniformed guard looked uncomfortable. He probably knew his limitations, or maybe he just didn't like the company he was keeping.

'Spenser,' Rachel said, 'I don't want any of that. We will resist, but we will resist passively.'

The dining room was very quiet except for the yellow walls. Timmons spoke again – probably encouraged by the mention of passive resistance.

'Will you leave quietly?' he said.

'No,' Rachel said, 'I will not.'

'Then you leave us no choice,' Boucher said. He turned to the uniformed guard. 'Spag,' he said, 'take her out.'

'You can't do that,' Dorothy said.

'You should wait and discuss this with your supervisor,' Timmons said, 'because I certainly will.'

Spag stepped forward and said softly, 'Come on, miss.'

Rachel didn't move.

Boucher said, 'Take her, Spag.'

Spag took her arm, gently. 'Come on, miss, you gotta

go,' he said. He kept a check on me with frequent side-shifting glances. He was probably fifty and no more than 170 pounds, some of it waistline. He had receding brown hair and tattoos on both forearms. He pulled lightly at Rachel's arm. She went limp.

Boucher said, 'God damn it, Spag, yank her out of that chair. She's trespassing. You have the right.'

Spag let go of Rachel's arm and straightened up. 'No,' he said. 'I guess not.'

Timmons said, 'Jesus Christ.'

Boucher said to him, 'All right, we'll do it. Brett, you take one arm.' He stepped forward and took Rachel under the left arm. Timmons took her right arm, and they dragged her out of the chair. She went limp on them, and they weren't ready for it. They couldn't hold her dead weight, and she slipped to the floor, her legs spread, her skirt hitched halfway up her thighs. She pulled it down.

I said to Spag, 'I am going to make a move here. Are you in or out?'

Spag looked at Rachel on the floor and at Timmons and Boucher. 'Out,' he said. 'I used to do honest work.'

Boucher was behind Rachel now and had both his arms under hers. I said to him, 'Let her go.'

Rachel said, 'Spenser, I told you we were going to be passive.'

Boucher said, 'You stay out of this, or you'll be in serious trouble.'

I said, 'Let go of her, or I'll hit you while you're bent over.'

Timmons said, 'Hey,' but it wasn't loud.

Boucher let Rachel go and stood up. Everyone in the dining room was standing and watching. There was a lot on the line for Boucher. I felt sorry for him. Most of the onlookers were young women. I reached my hand down to Rachel. She took it and got up.

'God damn you,' she said. I turned toward her and Boucher took a jump at me. He wasn't big, but he was slow. I dropped my shoulder and caught him in the chest. He grunted. I straightened up, and he staggered backwards and bumped into Timmons.

I said, 'If you annoy me, I will knock you right over that serving counter.' I pointed my finger at him.

Rachel said, 'You stupid bastard,' and slapped me across the face. Boucher made another jump. I hit him a stiff jab in the nose and then crossed with my right, and he went back into the serving line and knocked down maybe fifty plates off the counter and slid down to the floor. 'Into is almost as good as over,' I said. Timmons was stuck. He had to do something. He took a swing at me; I pulled my head back, slapped his arm on past me with my right hand. It half turned him. I got his collar in my left hand and the seat of his pants in my right and ran him three steps over to the serving counter, braced my feet, arched my back a little, and heaved him up and over it. One of his arms went in the gravy. Mashed potatoes smeared his chest, and he went over the counter rolling and landed on his side on the floor behind it.

The young girl with the tight clothes said, 'All *right*, foxy,' and started to clap. Most of the women in the cafeteria joined in. I went back to Rachel. 'Come on,' I said. 'Someone must have called the cops. We'd best walk out with dignity. Don't slap me again till we're outside.'

13

'You dumb son of a bitch,' Rachel said. We were walking along Boylston Street back to the Ritz. 'Don't you realize that it would have been infinitely more productive to allow them to drag me out in full view of all those women?'

'Productive of what?'

'Of an elevated consciousness on the part of all those women who were standing there watching the management of that company dramatize its sexism.'

'What kind of a bodyguard stands around and lets two B-school twerps like those drag out the body he's supposed to be guarding?'

'An intelligent one. One who understands his job. You're employed to keep me alive, not to exercise your Arthurian fantasies.' We turned left on Arlington. Across the street a short gray-haired man wearing two topcoats vomited on the base of the statue of William Ellery Channing.

'Back there you embodied everything I hate,' Rachel said. 'Everything I have tried to prevent. Everything I have denounced – machismo, violence, that preening male arrogance that compels a man to defend any woman he's with, regardless of her wishes and regardless of her need.'

'Don't beat around the bush,' I said. 'Come right out and say you disapprove of my conduct.'

'It demeaned me. It assumed I was helpless and dependent, and needed a big strong man to look out for me. It reiterated that image to all those young women who broke into mindless applause when it was over.'

We were in front of the Ritz. The doorman smiled at us – probably pleased that I didn't have my car.

'Maybe that's so,' I said. 'Or maybe that's a lot of theory which has little to do with practice. I don't care very much about theory or the long-range consequences to the class struggle, or whatever. I can't deal with that. I work close up. Right then I couldn't let them drag you out while I stood around.'

'Of course from your viewpoint you'd be dishonored. I'm just the occasion for your behavior, not the reason. The reason is pride – you didn't do that for me, and don't try to kid yourself.'

The doorman's smile was getting a little forced.

'I'd do it again,' I said.

'I'm sure you would,' Rachel said, 'but you'll have to do it with someone else. You and I are terminated. I don't want you around me. Whatever your motives, they are not mine, and I'll not violate my life's convictions just to keep your pride intact.'

She turned and walked into the Ritz. I looked at the doorman. He was looking at the Public Garden. 'The hell of it is,' I said to him, 'I think she was probably right.'

'That makes it much worse,' he said.

I walked back along Arlington and back up Boylston for a block to Berkeley Street. I had several choices. I could go down to the Dockside Saloon and drink all their beer, or I could drive up to Smithfield and wait till Susan came home from school and tell her I flunked Women's Lib. Or I could do something useful. I opted for useful and turned up Berkeley.

Boston Police Headquarters was a block and a half up Berkeley Street on the right, nestled in the shadows of big insurance companies – probably made the cops feel safe. Martin Quirk's office at the end of the Homicide squadroom was just as it always was. The room was neat and spare. The only thing on the desk was a phone and a plastic cube with pictures of his family in it.

Quirk was on the phone when I appeared in his doorway. He was tilted back in his chair, his feet on the desk, the phone hunched against his ear with his shoulder. He pointed at the straight chair beside his desk, and I sat down.

'Physical evidence,' Quirk said into the phone. 'What have you got for physical evidence?' He listened. His tweed jacket hung on the back of his chair. His white shirt was crisp and starchy. The cuffs were turned under once over his thick wrists. He was wearing over the ankle cordovan shoes with brass buckles. The shoes shined with fresh polish. The gray slacks were sharply creased. The black knit tie was knotted and in place. His thick black hair was cut short with no sign of gray.

'Yeah, I know,' he said into the phone. 'But we got no

choice. Get it.' He hung up and looked at me. 'Don't you ever wear a tie?' he said.

'Just the other day,' I said. 'Dinner at the Ritz.'

'Well, you ought to do it more often. You look like a goddamned overage hippie.'

'You're jealous of my youthful image,' I said. 'Just because you're a bureaucrat and have to dress up like Calvin Coolidge doesn't mean I have to. It's the difference between you and me.'

'There's other differences,' Quirk said. 'What do you want?'

'I want to know what you know about threats on the life of Rachel Wallace.'

'Why?'

'Until about a half hour ago I was her bodyguard.'

'And?'

'And she fired me for being too masculine.'

'Better than the other way around, I guess,' Quirk said.

'But I figured since I'd been hired by the day I might as well use the rest of it to see what I could find out from you.'

'There isn't much to tell. She reported the threats. We looked into it. Nothing much surfaced. I had Belson ask around on the street. Nobody knew anything.'

'You have any opinion on how serious the threats are?'

Quirk shrugged. 'If I had to guess, I'd guess they could be. Belson couldn't find any professional involvement. She names a lot of names and makes a lot of embarrassing charges about local businesses and government figures, but that's all they are – embarrassing. Nobody's going to go to jail or end his career, or whatever.'

'Which means,' I said, 'if the threats are real, they are probably from some coconut, or group of coconuts, that are anti-feminist or anti-gay, or both.'

'That would be my guess,' Quirk said. 'The busing issue in this town has solidified and organized all the redneck crazies. So any radical issue comes along, there's half a dozen little fringe outfits available to oppose it. A lot of them don't have anything to do now that busing is getting to be routine. For crissake, they took the state cops out of South Boston High this year.'

'Educational reform,' I said. 'One comes to expect such innovation in the Athens of America.'

Quirk grunted and locked his hands behind his head as he leaned back further in his chair. The muscles in his upper arm swelled against the shirt sleeve.

'So who's looking after her now?' he said.

'Nobody that I know of. That's why I'm interested in the reality of the threats.'

'You know how it is,' Quirk said. 'We got no facts. How can we? Anonymous phone calls don't lead anywhere. If I had to guess, I guess there might be some real danger.'

'Yeah, me too,' I said. 'What bothers you?'

'Well, the threat to harm her if the book wasn't suppressed. I mean, there were already copies of the damned thing around in galleys or whatever they are. The damage had been done.'

'Why doesn't that make you feel easier?' I said. 'Why

isn't it just a crank call, or a series of crank calls?'

'How would a crank caller even know about the book? Or her? I'm not saying it's sure. I mean it could be some numb-nuts in the publishing company, or at the printer, or anywhere that they might see the book. But it feels worse than that. It has a nice, steady hostile feel of organized opposition.'

'Balls,' I said.

'You don't agree,' Quirk said.

'No. I do. That's what bothers me. It feels real to me, too. Like people who want that book suppressed not because it tells secrets, but because it argues something they don't want to hear.'

Quirk nodded. 'Right. It's not a matter of keeping a secret. If we're right, and we're both guessing, it's opposition to her opinion and her expression of it. But we are both guessing.'

'Yeah, but we're good guessers,' I said. 'We have some experience in the field.'

Quirk shrugged. 'We'll see,' he said.

'Also, somebody made what looked like a professional try at her a couple of nights ago.'

'Good how promptly you reported it to the authorities,' Quirk said.

'I'm doing that now,' I said. 'Listen.'

He listened.

I told him about the two-car incident on the Lynnway. I told him about the pickets in Belmont and the pie-throwers in Cambridge. I told him about the recent unpleasantness in the First Mutual cafeteria.

'Don't you freelance types have an exciting time of it?' Quirk said.

'It makes the time pass,' I said.

'The business on the Lynnway is the only thing that sounds serious,' Quirk said. 'Gimme the license numbers.'

I did.

'Course they could be merely harassing you like the others.'

'They seemed to know their way around.'

'Shit, everybody knows his way around. They watch *Baretta* and *Kojak*. They know all about that stuff.'

'Yeah,' I said. 'Could be. Could even be a pattern.'

'Conspiracy?' Quirk raised both eyebrows.

'Possible.'

'But likely?'

I shrugged. 'There are stranger things in this world than in all your philosophies, Horatio.'

'The only other guy I ever met as intellectual as you,' Quirk said, 'was a child molester we put away in the late summer of 1967.'

'Smart doesn't mean good,' I said.

'I've noted that,' Quirk said. 'Anyway, I'm not ready to buy a conspiracy without more.'

'Me neither,' I said. 'Can you do anything about keeping an eye on her?'

'I'll call Callahan over at the Ritz again. Tell him you're off the thing, and he should be a little carefuller.'

'That's it?'

339

'Yeah,' Quirk said, 'that's it. I need more people than I've got now. I can't put a guard on her. If she makes a public appearance somewhere, maybe I can arrange to beef up her security a little. But we both know the score – I can't protect her and neither can you, unless she wants us to. And even then' – he shrugged – 'depends on how bad somebody wants her.'

'But after someone does her in, you'll swing into action. Then you'll be able to spare a dozen men.'

'Take a walk,' Quirk said. The lines from his nose to the corners of his mouth were deep. 'I don't need to get lectured about police work. I'm still here – I didn't quit.'

I stood up. 'I apologize,' I said. 'I feel very sour about things now. I'm blaming you.'

Quirk nodded. 'I get anything on those numbers, you want to know?'

'Yeah.'

'Okay.'

I left.

14

Susan and I were at the raw bar in the middle of Quincy Market eating oysters and drinking beer, and arguing. Sort of.

'So why didn't you keep out of it?' Susan said. 'Rachel had asked you to.'

'And stand there and let them drag her out?'

'Yes.' Susan slurped an oyster off the shell. They don't offer forks at the raw bar. They just serve oysters or clams or shrimp, with beer in paper cups. There are bowls of oyster crackers and squeeze bottles of cocktail sauce. They named the place the Walrus and the Carpenter, but I like it anyway.

'I couldn't do that,' I said. Under the vaulted ceiling of the market, people swirled up and down the main aisle. A bearded man wearing a ski cap and a green turtleneck sweater eyed Susan and whispered something to the man with him. The man with him looked at Susan and nodded. They both smiled, and then they both caught me looking at them and looked away and moved on. I ordered another beer. Susan sipped a little of hers.

'Why couldn't you do that?' Susan said.

'It violates something.'

'What?'

I shrugged. 'My pride?'

Susan nodded. 'Now we're getting somewhere. And while we're at it, if somebody wants to admire my figure, why not let them? I am pleased. Would it be better if they didn't?'

'You mean those two clowns a minute ago?'

'Yes. And a man who admires my ass isn't necessarily a clown.'

'I didn't do anything,' I said.

'You glared at them.'

'Well, they scare easy.'

'Would you have liked it better if they'd told me to start wearing a girdle?'

I said, 'Grrrrr.'

'Exactly. So what are you glaring at them for?'

'My pride?'

'Now we're getting somewhere.'

'Didn't we just have this conversation?'

She smiled and gestured at the bartender for another beer. 'Yes, but we haven't finished it.'

'So what should I have done when those two upwardly mobile assholes took hold of her?'

'Stood by, made sure they didn't hurt her. Been available if she called for help. Held the door as they went out.'

'Jesus Christ,' I said.

'Or you could have locked arms with her and gone limp

342

when they touched you and made it that much harder.'

'No,' I said. 'I couldn't do that. Maybe I could have stood by, or maybe if there were a next time I could. But I couldn't lie down and let them drag me out.'

'No. You couldn't. But you didn't have to deprive Rachel of a chance for a triumph.'

'I didn't think of it in just that way.'

'Of course you didn't – just as you don't perceive it that way when we're at a party and someone makes a pass at me and you're at his shoulder with the look.'

'Depriving you of the chance to deal with it success-fully yourself.'

'Of course,' she said. There was a small streak of cock-tail sauce at one corner of her mouth. I reached over and wiped it away with my thumb. 'I don't normally need you to protect me. I got along quite well without you for quite some years. I fended off the people I wanted to fend off, all by myself.'

'And if they don't fend?'

'I call you. You're not far. I've not seen you ten feet from me at a party since we met.'

I finished my beer. 'Let's walk up toward the Faneuil Hall end,' I said. It was nearly four thirty and the crowds were thin, for the market. 'Maybe I'll buy you a croissant.'

'I'm not bitching about me,' she said. She put her arm through mine. Her head came a little above my shoulder. Her hair had a faint flowery smell. 'I understand you, and I kind of like your proprietary impulses. Also I love you, and it changes one's perspective sometimes.'

'We could slip into that stairwell and make out,' I said.

'Later. You promised a lot of walking and eating and drinking and looking at people.'

'And after that?'

'Who knows?' Susan said. 'Maybe ecstasy.'

'Let's walk faster then.'

Quincy Market is old and lovingly restored. It is vast and made of granite blocks. Along each side of the long center aisle there were stalls selling yogurt with fruit topping, kielbasy on a roll with sauerkraut, lobster rolls, submarine sandwiches, French bread, country pâté, Greek salad, sweet and sour chicken, baklava, cookies, bagels, oysters, cheese, fresh fruit on a stick, ice cream, cheese-cake, barbecued chicken, pizza, doughnuts, galantine of duck, roast-beef sandwiches with chutney on fresh-baked bread, beansprouts, dried peaches, jumbo cashews and other nuts. There are also butchers' shops, cheese stores, a place that sells custom-ground coffee, fruit stands, and a place that sells Korean ginseng root. Outside on either side are arcades with more stalls and terrace cafés, and in restored brick buildings parallel were clothing stores and specialty shops and restaurants. It claims to be the number-one tourist attraction in Boston, and it should be. If you were with a girl in the market area, it would be hard not to hold hands with her. Jugglers and strolling musicians moved around the area. The market is never empty, and in prime time it is nearly unmanageable. We stopped and bought two skewers of fresh fruit and melon, and ate them as we walked.

'What you say makes sense, babe,' I said, 'but it doesn't feel right.'

'I know,' she said. 'It probably never will for you. You were brought up with a fierce sense of family. But you haven't got a family, and so you transfer that great sea of protective impulse to clients, and me.'

'Maybe not you, but usually clients need protection.'

'Yes. That's probably why you're in business. You need people who need protection. Otherwise what would you do with the impulse?'

I threw my empty skewer in a trash barrel. 'Concentrate it all on you, chickie,' I said.

Susan said, 'Oh, God.'

'I don't think I'm going to change,' I said.

'Oh, I hope you don't. I love you. And I understand you, and you should stay as sweet as you are. But you can see why Rachel Wallace might have reservations about you.'

'Yeah, except I'm so goddamned cute,' I said.

'You certainly are that,' Susan said. 'Want to split a yogurt?'

15

It was three weeks before Christmas, and it was snowing big sporadic flakes outside my office window when I found out that they'd taken Rachel Wallace.

I was sitting with my feet up, drinking black coffee and eating a doughnut and waiting for a guy named Anthony Gonsalves to call me from Fall River when the phone rang. It wasn't Gonsalves.

A voice said, 'Spenser? John Ticknor from Hamilton Black. Could you get over here right now? It appears Rachel Wallace has been kidnaped.'

'Did you call the cops?' I said.

'Yes.'

'Okay, I'm on my way.'

I hung up, put my fleece-lined jacket on over my black turtleneck and shoulder holster, and went. My office that year was on the corner of Mass. Ave. and Boylston Street, on the second floor, in a small three-sided turret over a smokeshop. My car was parked by a sign that said NO PARKING BUS STOP. I got in and drove straight down Boylston. The snow was melting as it hit the street but collecting on the margins of the road and on the sidewalks and building ledges.

The Christmas tree in the Prudential Center was lit already although it was only three forty-five. I turned left at Charles and right onto Beacon and parked at the top of the hill in front of the State House in a space that said Reserved for Members of the General Court. They meant the legislature, but Massachusetts calls it the Great and General Court for the same reason they call themselves a Commonwealth. It has something to do I think with not voting for Nixon. To my right the Common sloped down to Tremont Street, its trees strung with Christmas lights, a very big Nativity scene stretching out near the Park Street end. The snow was holding on the grass part of the Common and melting on the walkways. Down near the information booth they had some reindeer in pens, and a guy with a sandwich board was standing by the pens handing leaflets to people who were trying to feed popcorn to the deer.

Ticknor's office was on the top floor looking out over the Common. It was high-ceilinged and big-windowed and cluttered with books and manuscripts. Across from the desk was a low couch, and in front of the couch was a coffee table covered with manila folders. Ticknor was sitting on the couch with his feet on the coffee table looking out at the guy on the Common who was handing out leaflets by the reindeer pens. Frank Belson, who was a detective-sergeant, sat on the couch beside him and sipped some coffee. A young guy with a face from County Mayo and a three-piece suit from Louis was standing behind Ticknor's desk talking on the phone.

Belson nodded at me as I came in. I looked at the kid with the County Mayo face and said, 'DA's office?'

Belson nodded. 'Cronin,' he said. 'Assistant prosecutor.'

Ticknor said, 'Spenser, I'm glad you could come. You know Sergeant Belson, I gather.'

I nodded.

Ticknor said, 'This is Roger Forbes, our attorney.'

I shook hands with a tall gray-haired man with high cheekbones and sunken cheeks who stood – a little uncomfortably, I thought – in the corner between the couch and a book shelf.

Cronin said into the phone, 'We haven't said anything to the media yet.'

I said to Belson, 'What have you got?'

He handed me a typewritten sheet of paper. It was neatly typed, double-spaced. No strikeovers, no x-ed out portions. Margins were good. Paragraphs were indented five spaces. It was on a plain sheet of Eaton's Corrasable Bond. It read:

Whereas Rachel Wallace has written several books offensive to God and country; whereas she has advocated lesbian love in direct contradiction of the Bible and common decency; whereas she has corrupted and continues to corrupt our nation and our children through the public media, which mindlessly exploits her for greed; and whereas our public officials, content to be the dupes of any radical conspiracy, have taken no action, therefore we have been forced to move.

We have taken her and are holding her. She has not been harmed, and unless you fail to follow our instructions, she will not be. We want no money. We have taken action in the face of a moral imperative higher than any written law, and we shall follow that imperative though it lead to the grave.

Remain alert for further communication. We will submit our demands to you for communication to the appropriate figures. Our demands are not negotiable. If they are not met, the world will be better for the death of Rachel Wallace.

R(estore) A(merican) M(orality)

RAM

I read it twice. It said the same thing both times. 'Some prose style,' I said to Ticknor.

'If you'd been able to get along with her,' Ticknor said, 'perhaps the note would never have been written.' His face was a little flushed.

I said to Belson, 'And you've checked it out?'

'Sure,' Belson said. 'She's nowhere. Her hotel room is empty. Suitcases are still there, stuff still in drawers. She was supposed to be on a radio talk show this afternoon and never showed. Last time anyone saw her was last night around nine o'clock, when the room-service waiter brought up some sandwiches and a bottle of gin and one of vermouth and two glasses. He says there was someone taking a shower, but he doesn't know who. The bathroom door was closed, and he heard the water running.'

'And you got nothing for a lead?'

'Not a thing,' Belson said. He was lean and thin-faced with a beard so heavy that the lower half of his face had a blue cast to it, even though he shaved at least twice a day. He smoked five-cent cigars down to the point where the live end burned his lip, and he had one going now that was only halfway there but already chewed and battered-looking.

'Quirk coming in on this?' I said.

'Yeah, he'll be along in a while. He had to be in court this afternoon, and he sent me down to get started. But now that you showed up, he probably won't need to.'

Cronin hung up the phone and looked at me. 'Who are you?'

Ticknor said, 'Mr Spenser was hired to protect her. We thought he might be able to shed some light on the situation.'

'Sure did a hell of a job protecting,' Cronin said. 'You know anything?'

'Not much,' I said.

'Didn't figure you would. They want you around, okay by me, but don't get in the way. You annoy me, and I'll roast your ass.'

I looked at Belson. He grinned. 'They're turning them out tougher and tougher up the heights,' Belson said.

'This must be their supreme achievement,' I said. 'They'll never get one tougher than this.'

'Knock off the shit,' Cronin said. 'Sergeant, you know this guy?'

'Oh, yes, sir, Mr Cronin. I know him. You want me to shoot him?'

'What the hell is wrong with you, Belson? I asked you a simple question.'

'He's all right,' Belson said. 'He'll be a help.'

'He better be,' Cronin said. 'Spenser, I want you to give Sergeant Belson a rundown on anything you know about this case. Belson, if there's anything worth it, get a formal statement.'

'Yeah, sure,' Belson said. 'Get right on it.' He winked at me.

Cronin turned to Ticknor. 'You're in the word business. You recognize anything from the way it's written, the prose style?'

'If it were a manuscript, we'd reject it,' Ticknor said. 'Other than that I haven't anything to say about it. I can't possibly guess who wrote it.'

Cronin wasn't really listening. He turned toward Forbes, the lawyer. 'Is there a room around here where we can meet with the media people, Counselor?' He addressed Forbes almost like an equal; law-school training probably gave him an edge.

'Certainly,' Forbes said. 'We've a nice conference room on the second floor that will do, I think.' He spoke to Ticknor. 'I'll take him to the Hamilton Room, John.'

'Good idea,' Ticknor said. Forbes led the way out. Cronin stopped at the door. 'I want everything this guy knows, Sergeant. I want him empty when he leaves.'

I said to Belson, 'I don't want my face marked up.'

'Who could tell?' he said.

Cronin went out after Forbes.

I sat on the edge of Ticknor's desk. 'I hope he doesn't go armed,' I said.

'Cronin?' Belson laughed. 'He got out of law school in 1973, the year I first took the lieutenant's exam. He thinks if he's rough and tough, people won't notice that he doesn't know shit and just wants to get elected to public office.'

'He figures wrong,' Ticknor said. Belson raised his eyebrows approvingly. Ticknor was behind him and didn't see.

I said to Ticknor, 'How'd you get the letter?'

'Someone delivered it to the guard at the desk downstairs,' Ticknor said. He handed me the envelope. It was blank except for Ticknor's name typed on the front.

'Description?'

Belson answered. 'They get a hundred things a day delivered down there. Guard paid no attention. Can't remember for sure even whether it was a man or a woman.'

'It's not his fault,' Ticknor said. 'We get all sorts of deliveries from the printers – galleys, pages, blues – as well as manuscripts from agents, authors, and readers, artwork, and half a dozen other kinds of material at the desk every day. Walt isn't expected to pay attention to who brings it.'

I nodded. 'Doesn't matter. Probably someone hired a cabby to bring it in anyway, and descriptions don't help much, even if they're good ones.'

Belson nodded. 'I already got somebody checking the

cab companies for people who had things delivered here. But they could just as easy have delivered it themselves.'

'Should the press be in on this?' Ticknor said.

'I don't think it does much harm,' I said. 'And I don't think you could keep them out of here if Cronin has any say. This sounds like an organization that wants publicity. They said nothing about keeping it from the press, just as they said nothing about keeping the police out.'

'I agree,' Belson said. 'Most kidnapings have something about "don't go to the police," but these political or social or whatever-the-hell-they-are kidnapings usually are after publicity. And anyway Cronin has already told the press so the question is – what? What word am I after?'

Ticknor said, 'Academic. Hypothetical. Aimless. Too late. Merely conjectural.'

'Okay, any of those,' Belson said.

'So what do we do?' Ticknor said.

'Nothing much,' Belson said. 'We sit. We wait. Some of us ask around on the street. We check with the FBI to see if they have anything on RAM. We have the paper analyzed and the ink, and learn nothing from either. In a while somebody will get in touch and tell us what they want.'

'That's all?' Ticknor was offended. He looked at me.

'I don't like it either,' I said. 'But that's about all. Mostly we have to wait for contact. The more contact the better. The more in touch they are, the more we have to work on, the better chance we have to find them. And her.'

'But how can we be sure they'll make contact?'

Belson answered. 'You can't. But you figure they will.

353

They said they would. They did this for a reason. They want something. One of the things you can count on is that everybody wants something.' The cigar had burned down far enough now so that Belson had to tilt his head slightly to keep the smoke from getting in his eyes.

'But in the meantime – what about Rachel? My God, think how she must feel. Suppose they abuse her? We can't just sit here and wait.'

Belson looked at me. I said, 'We haven't got anything else to do. There's no profit in thinking about alternatives when you don't have any. She's a tough woman. She'll do as well as anyone.'

'But alone,' Ticknor said, 'with these maniacs . . .'

'Think about something else,' Belson said. 'Have you any idea who this group might be?'

Ticknor shook his head briskly, as if he had a fly in his ear. 'No,' he said. 'No. No idea at all. What do they call themselves? RAM?'

Belson nodded. 'Anyone in the publishing community that you know of that has any hostility toward Ms Wallace?'

'No, well, I mean, not like this. Rachel is abrasive and difficult, and she advocates things not everyone likes, but nothing that would cause a kidnaping.'

'Let us decide that. You just give me a list of everybody you can think of that didn't like her, that argued with her, that disagreed with her.'

'My God, man, that would include half the reviewers in the country.'

'Take your time,' Belson said. He had a notebook out and leaned back in his chair.

'But, my God, Sergeant, I can't just start listing names indiscriminately. I mean, I'll be involving these people in the investigation of a capital crime.'

'Aren't you the one who was worried about how poor Rachel must be feeling?' Belson said.

I knew the conversation. I'd heard variations on it too many times. I said, 'I'm going to go out and look for Rachel. Let me know when you hear from them.'

'I'm not authorized to employ you on this, Spenser,' Ticknor said.

Belson said, 'Me neither.' His thin face had the look of internal laughter.

'All part of the service,' I said.

I went out of Ticknor's office, past two detectives questioning a secretary, into the elevator down to the street, and out to start looking.

16

The *Boston Globe* is in a building on Morrissey Boulevard which looks like the offspring of a warehouse and a suburban junior high school. It used to be on Washington Street in the middle of the city and looked like a newspaper building should. But that was back when the *Post* was still with us, and the *Daily Record*. Only yesterday. When the world was young.

It was the day after they took Rachel, and snowing again. I was talking to Wayne Cosgrove in the city room about right-wing politics, on which he'd done a series three years earlier.

'I never heard of RAM,' he said. Cosgrove was thirty-five, with a blond beard. He had on wide-wale corduroy pants and a gray woolen shirt and a brown tweed jacket. His feet were up on the desk. On them he wore leather boots with rubber bottoms and yellow laces. A blue down parka with a hood hung on the back of his chair.

'God you look slick, Wayne,' I said. 'You must have been a Nieman Fellow some time.'

'A year at Harvard,' he said, 'picks up your taste like a bastard.' He'd grown up in Newport News, Virginia, and still had the sound of it when he talked.

'I can see that,' I said. 'Why don't you look in your files and see if you have anything on RAM?'

'Files,' Cosgrove said. 'I don't need to show no stinking files, gringo.' He told me once that he'd seen *The Treasure of the Sierra Madre* four times at a revival house in Cambridge.

'You don't have any files?'

He shrugged. 'Some, but the good stuff is up here, in the old coconut. And there ain't nothing on RAM. Doesn't matter. Groups start up and fold all the time, like sub sandwich shops. Or they change the name, or a group splinters off from another one. If I had done that series day before yesterday, I might not have heard of RAM, and they might be this week's biggie. When I did the series, most of the dippos were focused on busing. All the mackerel-snappers were afraid of the niggers fucking their daughters, and the only thing they could think of to prevent that was to keep the niggers away from their daughters. Don't seem to speak too highly of their daughters' self-control, but anyway if you wanted to get a group started, then you went over to Southie and yelled *nigger nigger*.'

He pronounced it *niggah*.

'Isn't that a technique that was developed regionally?'

'Ahhh, yes,' Cosgrove said. 'Folks down home used to campaign for office on that issue, whilst you folks up north was just a tsk-tsking at us and sending in the feds. Fearful racism there was, in the South, in those days.'

'Didn't I hear you were involved in freedom riding, voter registration, and Communist subversion in Mississippi some years back?'

'I had a northern granddaddy,' Cosgrove said. 'Musta come through on a gene.'

'So where are all the people in this town who used to stand around chanting *never* and throwing rocks at children?'

Cosgrove said, 'Most of them are saying, "Well, hardly ever." But I know what you're after. Yeah, I'd say some of them, having found out that a lot of the niggers don't want to fuck their daughters, are now sweating that the faggots will bugger their sons and are getting up a group to throw rocks at fairies.'

'Any special candidates?'

Cosgrove shrugged. 'Aw, shit, I don't know, buddy. You know as well as I do that the hub of any ultra-right-wing piece of business in this metropolitan area is Fix Farrell. For Christ's sake, he's probably anti-Eskimo.'

'Yeah, I know about Farrell, but I figure a guy like him wouldn't involve himself in a thing like this.'

''Cause he's on the city council?' Cosgrove said. 'How the hell old are you?'

'I don't argue he's honest, I just argue he doesn't need this kind of action. I figure a guy like him benefits from people like Rachel Wallace. Gives him someone to be against. Farrell wouldn't want her kidnaped and her book suppressed. He'd want her around selling it at the top of her lungs so he could denounce her and promulgate plans to thwart her.'

Cosgrove tapped his teeth with the eraser end of a yellow pencil. 'Not bad,' he said. 'You probably got a pretty good picture of Fix at that.'

'You think he might have any thoughts on who I should look into?'

Cosgrove shook his head very quickly. 'No soap. Farrell's never going to rat on a possible vote – and anybody opposed to a gay feminist activist can't be all bad in Fix's book.'

'You think the RAM people would trust him?' I said.

'How the fuck would I know?' Cosgrove said. 'Jesus, Spenser, you are a plugger, I'll say that for you.'

'Hell of a bodyguard, too,' I said.

Cosgrove shrugged. 'I'll ask around; I'll talk it up in the city room. I hear anything, I'll give you a buzz.'

'Thank you,' I said, and left.

17

I knew a guy who was in the Ku Klux Klan. His name was Manfred Roy, and I had helped bust him once, when I was on the cops, for possession of pornographic materials. It was a while ago, when possession of pornographic materials was more serious business than it is now. And Manfred had weaseled on the guy he bought it from and the friends who were with him when he bought it, and we dropped the charges against him and his name never got in the papers. He lived with his mother, and she would have been disappointed in him if she had known. After I left the cops, I kept track of Manfred. How many people do you know that actually belong to the Ku Klux Klan? You find one, you don't lose him.

Manfred was working that year cutting hair in a barbershop on the ground floor of the Park Square Building. He was a small guy, with white-blond hair in a crew cut. Under his barber coat he had on a plaid flannel shirt and chino pants and brown penny-loafers with a high shine. It wasn't a trendy shop. The only razor cut you got was if somebody nicked you while they were shaving your neck.

I sat in the waiting chair and read the *Globe*. There was an article on the city council debate over a bond issue. I read the first paragraph because Wayne Cosgrove had a byline, but even loyalty flagged by paragraph two.

There were four barbers working. One of them, a fat guy with an Elvis Presley pompadour sprayed into rigid stillness, said, 'Next?'

I said, 'No thanks. I'll wait for him,' and pointed at Manfred.

He was cutting the hair of a white-haired man. He glanced toward me and then back at the man and then realized who I was and peeked at me in the mirror. I winked at him, and he jerked his eyes back down at the white hair in front of him.

In five minutes he finished up with Whitey and it was my turn. I stepped to the chair. Manfred said, 'I'm sorry, sir, it's my lunch hour, perhaps another barber . . . ?'

I gave him a big smile and put my arm around him. 'That's even better, Manfred. Actually I just wanted to have a good rap with you anyway. I'll buy you lunch.'

'Well, actually, I was meeting somebody.'

'Swell, I'll rap with them, too. Come on, Manfred. Long time no see.'

The barber with the pompadour was looking at us. Manfred slipped off his white barber coat, and we went together out the door of the shop. I took my coat from the rack as I went by.

In the corridor outside Manfred said, 'God damn you, Spenser, you want to get me fired?'

'Manfred,' I said, 'Manfred. How unkind. Un-Christian even. I came by to see you and buy you lunch.'

'Why don't you just leave me alone?' he said.

'You still got any of those inflatable rubber nude girls you used to be dealing?'

We were walking along the arcade in the Park Square Building. The place had once been stylish and then gotten very unstylish and was now in renaissance. Manfred was looking at his feet as we walked.

'I was different then,' Manfred said. 'I had not found Christ yet.'

'You, too?' I said.

'I wouldn't expect you to understand.'

Near the St James Avenue exit was a small stand that sold sandwiches. I stopped. 'How about a sandwich and a cup of coffee, Manfred? On me, any kind. Yogurt too, and an apple if you'd like. My treat.'

'I'm not hungry,' he said.

'Okay by me,' I said. 'Hope you don't mind if I dine.'

'Why don't you just go dine and stop bothering me?'

'I'll just grab a sandwich here and we'll stroll along, maybe cross the street to the bus terminal, see if any miscegenation is going on or anything.'

I bought a tuna on whole wheat, a Winesap apple, and a paper cup of black coffee. I put the apple in my pocket and ate the sandwich as we walked along. At the far end of the arcade, where the Park Square Cinema used to be, we stopped. I had finished my sandwich and was sipping my coffee.

'You still with the Klan, Manfred?'

'Certainly.'

'I heard you were regional manager or Grand High Imperial Alligator or whatever for Massachusetts.'

He nodded.

'Dynamite,' I said, 'next step up is playing intermission piano at a child-abuse convention.'

'You're a fool, like all the other liberals. Your race will be mongrelized; a culture that took ten thousand years and produced the greatest civilization in history will be lost. Drowned in a sea of half-breeds and savages. Only the Communists will gain.'

'Any culture that produced a creep like you, Manfred,' I said, 'is due for improvement.'

'Dupe,' he said.

'But I didn't come here to argue ethnic purity with you.'

'You'd lose,' he said.

'Probably,' I said. 'You're a professional bigot. You spend your life arguing it. You are an expert. It's your profession. And it ain't mine. I don't spend two hours a month debating racial purity. But even if I lose the argument, I'll win the fight afterwards.'

'And you people are always accusing us of violence,' Manfred said. He was standing very straight with his back against the wall near the barren area where the advertisements for the Cinema used to be. There was some color on his cheeks.

'*You people*?' I said. '*Us*? I'm talking about me and you.

I'm not talking about *us* and about *you people*.'

'You don't understand politics,' Manfred said. 'You can't change society talking about *you* and *me*.'

'Manfred, I would like to know something about a group of people as silly as you are. Calls itself RAM, which stands for Restore American Morality.'

'Why ask me?'

'Because you are the kind of small dogturd who hangs around groups like this one and talks about restoring morality. It probably helps you to feel like less of a dogturd.'

'I don't know anything about RAM.'

'It is opposed to feminism and gay activism – probably in favor of God and racial purity. You must've heard about them?'

Manfred shook his head. He was looking at his feet again. I put my fist under his chin and raised it until he was looking at me. 'I want to know about this group, Manfred,' I said.

'I promise you, I don't know nothing about them,' Manfred said.

'Then you should be sure to find out about them, Manfred.'

He tried to twist his chin off my fist, but I increased the upward pressure a little and held him still.

'I don't do your dirty work.'

'You do. You do anyone's. You're a piece of shit, and you do what you're told. Just a matter of pressure,' I said.

His eyes shifted away from me. Several people coming

out of the bank to my right paused and looked at us, and then moved hurriedly along.

'There are several kinds of pressure, Manfred. I can come into work every day and harass you until they fire you. I can go wherever you go and tell them about how we busted you for possession of an inflatable lover, and how you sang like the Mormon Tabernacle Choir to get off.' There was more color in his cheeks now. 'Or,' I said, 'I could punch your face into scrapple once a day until you had my information.'

With his teeth clenched from the pressure of my fist, Manfred said, 'You miserable prick.' His whole face was red now. I increased the pressure and brought him up on his toes.

'Vilification,' I said. 'You people are always vilifying us.' I let him go and stepped away from him. 'I'll be around tomorrow to see what you can tell me,' I said.

'Maybe I won't be here,' he said.

'I know where you live, Manfred. I'll find you.'

He was still standing very straight and stiff against the wall. His breath was hissing between his teeth. His eyes looked bright to me, feverish.

'Tomorrow, Manfred. I'll be by tomorrow.'

18

I went out to Arlington Street and turned left and walked down to Boylston eating my Winesap apple. On Boylston Street there were lots of Christmas decorations and pictures of Santa Claus and a light, pleasant snow falling. I wondered if Rachel Wallace could see the snow from where she was. 'Tis the season to be jolly. If I had stayed with her ... I shook my head. Hard. No point to that. It probably wasn't much more unpleasant to be kidnaped in the Christmas season than any other time. I hadn't stayed with her. And thinking I should have wouldn't help find her. Got to concentrate on the priority items, babe. Got to think about finding her. Automatically, as I went by Brentano's, I stopped and looked in the window at the books. I didn't have much hope for Manfred – he was mean and bigoted and stupid. Cosgrove was none of those things, but he was a working reporter on a liberal newspaper. Anything he found out, he'd have to stumble over. No one was going to tell him.

I finished my apple and dropped the core in a trash basket attached to a lamp post. I looked automatically in Malben's window at the fancy food. Then I could cross and see what new Japanese food was being done at Hai Hai, then back this side and stare at the clothes in Louis, perhaps stop off at the Institute of Contemporary Art. Then I could go home and take a nap. Shit. I walked back to my office and got my car and drove to Belmont.

The snow wasn't sticking as I went along Storrow Drive, and it was early afternoon with no traffic. On my right the Charles was very black and cold-looking. Along the river people jogged in their winter running clothes. A very popular model was longjohns under shorts, with a hooded sweatshirt and blue New Balance shoes with white trim. I preferred a cut-off sweat shirt over black turtleneck sweater, with blue warm-up pants to match the New Balance 320's. Diversity. It made America great.

I crossed the Charles to the Cambridge side near Mt Auburn Hospital and drove through a slice of Cambridge through Watertown, out Belmont Street to Belmont. The snow was beginning to collect as I pulled into a Mobil station on Trapelo Road and got directions to the Belmont Police Station on Concord Avenue.

I explained to the desk sergeant who I was, and he got so excited at one point that he glanced up at me for a moment before he went back to writing in a spiral notebook.

'I'm looking for one of your patrol-car people. Young guy, twenty-five, twenty-six. Five ten, hundred eighty pounds, very cocky, wears military decorations on his uniform blouse. Probably eats raw wolverine for breakfast.'

Without looking up the desk sergeant said, 'That'd be Foley. Wise mouth.'

'Man's gotta make his mark somehow,' I said. 'Where do I find him?'

The sergeant looked at something official under the counter. 'He's cruising up near the reservoir,' he said. 'I'll have the dispatcher call him. You know the Friendly's up on Trapelo?'

'Yeah, I passed it coming in,' I said.

'I'll have him meet you in the parking lot there.'

I thanked him and went out and drove up to Friendly's ice-cream parlor. Five minutes after I got there, a Belmont cruiser pulled in and parked. I got out of my car in the steady snowfall and walked over to the cruiser and got in the back seat. Foley was driving. His partner was the same older cop with the pot belly, still slouched in the passenger seat with his hat over his eyes.

Foley shifted sideways and grinned at me over the seat. 'So someone snatched your lez, huh?'

'How gracefully you put it,' I said.

'And you got no idea who, and you come out grabbing straws. You want me to ID the cluck you hit in the gut, don't you?'

I said to the older cop, 'How long you figure before he's chief?'

The older cop ignored me.

'Am I right or wrong?'

'Right,' I said, 'you know who he is?'

'Yeah, after we was all waltzing together over by the

library that day, I took down his license number when he drove off, and I checked into him when I had time. Name's English – Lawrence Turnbull English, Junior. Occupation, financial consultant. Means he don't do nothing. Family's got twelve, fifteen million bucks. He consults with their trust officer on how to spend it. That's as much as he works. Spends a lot of time taking the steam, playing racquetball, and protecting democracy from the coons and the queers and the commies and the lower classes, and the libbers and like that.'

The old cop shifted a little in the front seat and said, 'He's got an IQ around eight, maybe ten.'

'Benny's right,' Foley said. 'He snatched that broad, he'd forget where he hid her.'

'Where's he live?' I said.

Foley took a notebook out of his shirt pocket, ripped out a page, and handed it to me. 'Watch your ass with him though. Remember, he's a friend of the chief's,' Foley said.

'Yeah,' I said. 'Thanks.'

A plow rumbled by on Trapelo Road as I got out of the cruiser and went back to my car. The windows were opaque with snow, and I had to scrape them clean before I could drive. I went into the same Mobil station and got my tank filled and asked for directions to English's house.

It was in a fancy part of Belmont. A rambling, gabled house that looked like one of those old nineteenth-century resort hotels. Probably had a hunting preserve in the snow behind it. The plow had tossed up a small drift in front of the driveway, and I had to shove my car through it. The driveway was clear and circled up behind the house to a wide apron in front of a garage with four doors. To the right of the garage there was a back door. I disdained it. I went back around to the front door. A blow for the classless society. A young woman in a maid suit answered the bell. Black dress, little white apron, little hat – just like in the movies.

I said, 'Is the master at home?'

She said, 'Excuse me?'

I said, 'Mr English? Is he at home?'

'Who shall I say is calling, please?'

'Spenser,' I said, 'representing Rachel Wallace. We met once, tell him, at the Belmont Library.'

The maid said, 'Wait here, please,' and went off down the hall. She came back in about ninety seconds and said, 'This way, please.'

We went down the hall and into a small pine-paneled room with a fire on the hearth and a lot of books on built-in shelves on either side of the fireplace. English was sitting in a red-and-gold wing chair near the fire, wearing an honest-to-God smoking jacket with black velvet lapels and smoking a meerschaum pipe. He had on black-rimmed glasses and a book by Harold Robbins was closed in his right hand, the forefinger keeping the place.

He stood up as I came in but did not put out his hand – probably didn't want to lose his place. He said, 'What do you want, Mr Spenser?'

'As you may know, Rachel Wallace was kidnaped yesterday.'

'I heard that on the news,' he said. We still stood.

'I'm looking for her.'

'Yes?'

'Can you help?'

'How on earth could I help?' English said. 'What have I to do with her?'

'You picketed her speech at the library. You called her a bulldyke. As I recall, you said you'd "never let her win" or something quite close to that.'

'I deny saying any such thing,' English said. 'I exercised my Constitutional right of free speech by picketing. I made no threats whatsoever. You assaulted me.'

So he hadn't forgotten.

'We don't have to be mad at each other, Mr English. We can do this easy.'

'I wish to do nothing with you. It is preposterous that you'd think I knew anything about a crime.'

'On the other hand,' I said, 'we can do it the other way. We can talk this all over with the Boston cops. There's a sergeant named Belson there who'll be able to choke back the terror he feels when you mention your friend, the chief. He'd feel duty bound to drag your tail over to Berkeley Street and ask you about the reports that you'd threatened Rachel Wallace before witnesses. If you annoyed him, he might even feel it necessary to hold you overnight in the tank with the winos and fags and riffraff.'

'My attorney—' English said.

'Oh, yeah,' I said, 'Belson just panics when an attorney shows up. Sometimes he gets so nervous, he forgets where he put the client. And the attorney has to chase all over the metropolitan area with his writ, looking into assorted pens and tanks and getting puke on his Chesterfield over-coat to see if he can find his client.'

English opened his mouth and closed it and didn't say anything.

I went and sat in his red-and-gold wing chair. 'How'd you know Rachel Wallace was going to be at the library?' I said.

'It was advertised in the local paper,' he said.

'Who organized the protest?'

'Well, the committee had a meeting.'

'What committee?'

'The vigilance committee.'

'I bet I know your motto,' I said.

'Eternal vigilance—' he said.

'I know,' I said. 'I know. Who is the head of the committee?'

'I am chairman.'

'Gee, and still so humble,' I said.

'Spenser, I do not find you funny,' he said.

'Puts you in excellent company,' I said. 'Could you account for your movements since Monday night at nine o'clock if someone asked you?'

'Of course I could. I resent being asked.'

'Go ahead,' I said.

'Go ahead what?'

'Go ahead and account for your movements since nine o'clock Monday night.'

'I certainly will not. I have no obligation to tell you anything.'

'We already did this once, Lawrence. Tell me, tell Belson – I don't care.'

'I have absolutely nothing to hide.'

'Funny how I knew you'd say that. Too bad to waste it on me though. It'll dazzle the cops.'

'Well, I don't,' he said. 'I don't have anything to hide. I was at a committee meeting from seven thirty Monday night until eleven fifteen. Then I came straight home to bed.'

'Anybody see you come home?'

'My mother, several of the servants.'

'And the next day?'

'I was at Old Colony Trust at nine fifteen, I left there at eleven, played racquetball at the club, then lunched at the club. I returned home after lunch, arrived here at three fifteen. I read until dinner. After dinner—'

'Okay, enough. I'll check on all of this, of course. Who'd you play racquetball with?'

'I simply will not involve my friends in this. I will not have you badgering and insulting them.'

I let that go. He'd fight that one. He didn't want his friends at the club to know he was being investigated, and a guy like English will dig in to protect his reputation. Besides I could check it easily. The club and the committee, too.

'Badger?' I said. 'Insult? Lawrence, how unkind. I am clearly not of your social class, but I am not without grace.'

'Are you through?'

'I am for now,' I said. 'I will authenticate your – if you'll pardon the expression – alibi, and I may look further into your affairs. If the alibi checks, I'll still keep you in mind, however. You didn't have to do it, to have it done, or to know who did it.'

'I shall sue you if you continue to bother me,' English said.

'And if you are involved in any way in anything that happened to Rachel Wallace,' I said, 'I will come back and put you in the hospital.'

English narrowed his eyes a little. 'Are you threatening me?' he said.

'That's exactly it, Lawrence,' I said. 'That is exactly what I am doing. I am threatening you.'

English looked at me with his eyes narrowed for a minute, and then he said, 'You'd better leave.'

'Okay by me,' I said, 'but remember what I told you. If you are holding out on me, I'll find out, and I'll come back. If you know something and don't tell me, I will find out, and I will hurt you.'

He stood and opened the study door.

'A man in my position has resources, Spenser.' He was still squinting at me. I realized that was his tough look.

'Not enough,' I said, and walked off down the hall and out the front door. The snow had stopped. Around back, a Plymouth sedan was parked next to my car. When I walked over to it, the window rolled down and Belson looked out at me.

'Thought this was your heap,' he said. 'Learn anything?'

I laughed. 'I just got through threatening English with

you,' I said, 'so he'd talk to me. Now here you are, and he could just as well not have talked to me.'

'Get in,' Belson said. 'We'll compare notes.'

I got in the backseat. Belson was in the passenger seat. A cop I didn't know sat behind the wheel. Belson didn't introduce us.

'How'd you get here?' I said.

'You told Quirk about the library scene,' Belson said, 'and we questioned Linda Smith along with everybody else and she mentioned it to me. I had it on my list when Quirk mentioned it to me. So we called the Belmont Police and found ourselves about an hour behind you. What you get?'

'Not much,' I said. 'If it checks out, he's got an alibi for all the time that he needs.'

'Run it past us,' Belson said. 'We won't mention you, and we'll see if the story stays the same.'

I told Belson what English had told me. The cop I didn't know was writing a few things in a notebook. When I was through, I got out of the Plymouth and into my own car. Through the open window I said to Belson, 'Anything surfaces, I'd appreciate hearing.'

'Likewise,' Belson said.

I rolled up the window and backed out and turned down the drive. As I pulled onto the street I saw Belson and the other cop get out and start toward the front door. The small drift of snow that had blocked the driveway when I'd arrived was gone. A man in English's position was not without resources.

19

The main entrance to the Boston Public Library used to face Copley Square across Dartmouth Street. There was a broad exterior stairway and inside there was a beautiful marble staircase leading up to the main reading room with carved lions and high-domed ceilings. It was always a pleasure to go there. It felt like a library and looked like a library, and even when I was going in there to look up Duke Snider's lifetime batting average, I used to feel like a scholar.

Then they grafted an addition on and shifted the main entrance to Boylston Street. *Faithful to the spirit*, the architect had probably said. *But making a contemporary statement*, I bet he said. The addition went with the original like Tab goes with pheasant. Now, even if I went into study the literary influence of Eleanor of Aquitaine, I felt like I'd come out with a pound of hamburger and a loaf of Wonder bread.

By the big glass doors a young woman in Levi's jeans and a rabbit fur coat told me she was trying to raise money to get a bus back to Springfield. She had one tooth missing and a bruise on her right cheekbone. I didn't give her anything.

I went through the new part to the old and walked around a bit and enjoyed it, and then I went to the periodical section and started looking at the *Globe* on microfilm to see what I could find out about the Belmont Vigilance Committee. I was there all day. Next to me a fragrant old geezer in a long overcoat slept with his head resting on the microfilm viewer in front of him. The overcoat was buttoned up to his neck even though the room was hot. No one bothered him.

At noon I went out and went across the street to a Chinese restaurant and ate some Peking ravioli and some mushu pork for lunch. When I went back for the afternoon session the old man was gone, but the broad with the missing tooth was still working the entrance. At five o'clock I had seven pages of notes, and my eyes were starting to cross. If I weren't so tough, I would have thought about reading glasses. I wonder how Bogie would have looked with specs. Here's looking at you, four-eyes. I shut off the viewer, returned the last microfilm cassette, put on my coat, and went out to a package store, where I bought two bottles of Asti Spumante.

I was driving up to Smithfield to have dinner with Susan, and the traffic northbound was stationary a long way back onto Storrow Drive. I deked and dived up over the Hill and down across Cambridge Street past the Holiday Inn, behind Mass. General and got to the traffic light at Leverett Circle almost as quick as the people who just sat in line on Storrow. The radio traffic-reporter told me from his helicopter that there was a 'fender-bender' on the bridge, so I turned off onto 93 and went north that way. A magician with the language – *fender-bender*, wow! It was six when I turned off of Route 128 at the Main Street–Smithfield exit. Out in the subs most of the snow was still white. There were candles in all the windows and wreaths on all the doors, and some people had Santas on their rooftops, and some people had colored lights on their shrubbery. One house had a drunken Santa clutching a bottle of Michelob under the disapproving stare of a red-nosed reindeer. Doubtless the antichrist lurks in the subs as well.

Susan's house had a spotlight on the front and a sprig of white pine hanging on the brass doorknocker. I parked in her driveway and walked to her front door, and she opened it before I got there.

'Fa-la-la-la-la,' I said.

She leaned against the doorjamb and put one hand on her hip.

'Hey, Saint Nick,' she said, 'you in town long?'

'Trouble with you Jews,' I said, 'is that you mock our Christian festivals.'

She gave me a kiss and took the wine, and I followed her in. There was a fire in her small living room and on the coffee table some caponata and triangles of Syrian bread. There was a good cooking smell mixed with the wood-smoke. I sniffed. 'Onions,' I said, 'and peppers.'

'Yes,' she said, 'and mushrooms. And rice pilaf. And when the fire burns down and the coals are right, you can grill two steaks, and we'll eat.'

'And then?' I said.

'Then maybe some Wayne King albums on the stereo and waltz till dawn.'

'Can we dip?'

'Certainly, but you have to wait for the music. No dipping before it starts. Want a beer?'

'I know where,' I said.

'I'll say.'

'White wine and soda for you?'

She nodded. I got a bottle of Beck's out of her poppy-red refrigerator and poured white wine from a big green jug into a tall glass. I put in ice, soda, and a twist of lime, and gave it to her. We went back into the living room and sat on her couch, and I put my arm around her shoulder and laid my head back against the couch and closed my eyes.

'You look like the dragon won today,' she said.

'No, didn't even see one. I spent the day in the BPL looking at microfilm.'

She sipped her wine and soda. 'You freebooters do have an adventurous life, don't you?' With her left hand she reached up and touched my left hand as it rested on her shoulder.

'Well, some people find the search for truth exciting.'

'Did you find some?' she said.

'Some,' I said. Susan drew a series of small circles on the back of my hand with her forefinger. 'Or at least some facts. Truth is a little harder, maybe.'

I took a small triangle of Syrian bread and picked up

some caponata with it and ate it and drank some beer.

'It's hard to hug and eat simultaneously,' I said.

'For you that may be the definition of a dilemma,' she said.

She sipped at her wine. I finished my beer. A log on the fire settled. I heaved myself off the couch and went to the kitchen for more beer. When I came back, I stood in the archway between the living room and dining room and looked at her.

She had on a white mannish-looking shirt of oxford cloth with a button-down collar, and an expensive brown skirt and brown leather boots, the kind that wrinkle at the ankles. Her feet were up on the coffee table. Around her neck two thin gold chains showed where the shirt was open. She wore them almost all the time. She had on big gold earrings; her face was thoroughly made up. There were fine lines around her eyes, and her black hair shone. She watched me looking at her. There stirred behind her face a sense of life and purpose and mirth and caring that made her seem to be in motion even as she was still. There was a kind of rhythm to her, even in motionless repose. I said, 'Energy contained by grace, maybe.'

She said, 'I beg your pardon?'

I said, 'I was just trying to find a phrase to describe the quality you have of festive tranquility.'

'That's an oxymoron,' she said.

'Well, it's not my fault,' I said.

'You know damn well what an oxymoron is,' she said. 'I just wanted you to know that I know.'

'You know everything you need to,' I said.

'Sit down,' she said, 'and tell me what you found out in the library.'

I sat beside her, put my feet up beside hers and my arm back around her shoulder, leaned my head back on the couch, closed my eyes, and said, 'I found out that the Belmont Vigilance Committee is a somewhat larger operation that I would have thought. It was founded during the Korean war by English's father to combat the clear menace of Communist subversion in this country. Old man English managed to stave off the commies until his death in 1965, at which time the family business, which as far as I can tell is anti-Communism, passed into the hands of his only son, Lawrence Turnbull English, Junior. There was a daughter, Geraldine Julia English, but she went off to Goucher College and then got married and dropped out of things. Probably got radicalized in college, mixing with all those com-symp professors. Anyway there's Lawrence Junior, Harvard '61, and his momma, who looks like Victor McLaglen, living in the old homestead, with fifteen million or so to keep them from the cold, running the committee and spreading the gospel and opening new chapters and stamping out sedition as fast as it springs up. The committee has chapters in most of the metropolitan colleges, some high schools, and most neighborhoods across the Commonwealth. Ninety-six chapters by last count, which was 1977. They sprung up like toadstools in the Boston neighborhoods when busing was hot. There's chapters in south Boston, Dorchester, Hyde Park, all over.

Lawrence Junior was right there on the barricades when the buses rolled into South Boston High. He got arrested once for obstructing traffic and once for failing to obey the lawful order of a policeman. Both times his mom had someone down to post bond by the time the wagon got to the jail. Second time he filed suit alleging police brutality on the part of a big statie from Fitchburg named Thomas J. Fogarty, who apparently helped him into the wagon with the front end of his right boot. Case was dismissed.'

'And that's what English does? Runs the Vigilance Committee.'

'I only know what I read in the papers,' I said. 'If they are right, that seems to be the case. A real patriot. Keeping his fifteen million safe from the reds.'

'And the daughter isn't involved?'

'There's nothing about her. Last entry was about her marriage to some guy from Philadelphia in 1968. She was twenty.'

'What's she do now?' Susan said. She was making her circles on the back of my hand again.

'I don't know. Why do you care?'

'I don't – I was just curious. Trying to be interested in your work, cookie.'

'It's a woman's role,' I said.

She said, 'I spent the day talking to the parents of learning-disabled children.'

'Is that educatorese for dummies?'

'Oh, you sensitive devil. No, it isn't. It's kids with dyslexia, for instance – that sort of thing.'

'How were the parents?'

'Well, the first one wanted to know if this had to go on his record. The kid is in the eleventh grade and can't really read.

'I said that I wasn't sure what she meant about the record. And she said if it were on his record that the kid was dyslexic, wouldn't that adversely affect his chances of going to a good college.'

'Least she's got her priorities straight,' I said.

'And the next mother – the fathers don't usually come – the next mother said it was our job to teach the kid, and she was sick of hearing excuses.'

I said, 'I think I might have had a better time in the library.'

She said, 'The coals look pretty good. Would you like to handle the steaks?'

'Where does it say that cooking steaks is man's work?' I said.

Her eyes crinkled and her face brightened. 'Right above the section on what sexual activity one can look forward to after steak and mushrooms.'

'I'll get right on the steaks,' I said.

20

Susan went to work in the bright, new-snow suburban morning just before eight. I stayed and cleaned up last night's dishes and made the bed and took a shower. There was no point banging heads with commuter traffic.

At eleven minutes after ten I walked into the arcade of the Park Square Building to talk with Manfred Roy. He wasn't there. The head man at the barber shop told me that Manfred had called in sick and was probably home in bed.

I said, 'He still living down on Commonwealth Avenue?'

The barber said, 'I don't know where he lives.'

I said, 'Probably does. I'll stop by and see how he is.'

The barber shrugged and went back to trimming a neat semi-circle around some guy's ear. I went out and strolled down Berkeley Street two blocks to Commonwealth. When we had first put the arm on Manfred, he was living on the river side, near the corner of Dartmouth Street. I walked up the mall toward the address. The snow on the mall was still clean and fresh from the recent fall. The mall walkway had been cleared and people were walking their dogs along it. Three kids were playing Frisbee and drinking Miller's beer out of clear glass bottles. A woman with a bull terrier walked by. The terrier had on a plaid doggie sweater and was straining at his leash. I thought his little piggie eyes looked very embarrassed, but that was probably anthropomorphism.

At the corner of Dartmouth Street I stopped and waited for the light. Across the street in front of Manfred's apartment four men were sitting in a two-tone blue Pontiac Bonneville. One of them rolled down the window and yelled across the street, 'Your name Spenser?'

'Yeah,' I said, 'S-p-e-n-s-e-r, like the English poet.'

'We want to talk with you,' he said.

'Jesus,' I said, 'I wish I'd thought of saying that.'

They piled out of the car. The guy that talked was tall and full of sharp corners, like he'd been assembled from Lego blocks. He had on a navy watch cap and a plaid lumberman's jacket and brown pants that didn't get to the tops of his black shoes. His coat sleeves were too short and his knobby wrists stuck out. His hands were very large with angular knuckles. His jaw moved steadily on something, and as he crossed the street he spat tobacco juice.

The other three were all heavy and looked like men who'd done heavy labor for a long time. The shortest of them had slightly bowed legs, and there was scar tissue thick around his eyes. His nose was thicker than it should have been. I had some of those symptoms myself, and I knew where he got them. Either he hadn't quit as soon as I had or he'd lost more fights. His face looked like a catcher's mitt.

The four of them gathered in front of me on the mall. 'What are you doing around here?' the tall one said.

'I'm taking a species count on maggots,' I said. 'With you four and Manfred I got five right off.'

The bow-legged pug said, 'He's a smart guy, George. Lemme straighten him out.'

George shook his head. He said to me, 'You're looking for trouble, you're going to get it. We don't want you bothering Manfred.'

'You in the Klan, too?' I said.

'We ain't here to talk, pal,' George said.

'You must be in the Klan,' I said. 'You're a smooth talker and a slick dresser. Where's Manfred – his mom won't let him come out?'

The pug put his right hand flat on my chest and shoved me about two steps backwards. 'Get out of here or we'll stomp the shit out of you,' he said. He was slow. I hit him two left jabs and a right hook before he even got his hands up. He sat down in the snow.

'No wonder your face got marked up so bad,' I said to him. 'You got no reflexes.'

There was a small smear of blood at the base of the pug's nostrils. He wiped the back of his hand across and climbed to his feet.

'You gonna get it now,' he said.

George made a grab at me, and I hit him in the throat. He rocked back. The other two jumped, and the three of us went down in the snow. Someone hit me on the side of the head. I got the heel of my hand under someone's

nose and rammed upward. The owner of the nose cried
out in pain. George kicked me in the ribs with his steel-
toed work shoes. I rolled away, stuck my fingers in
someone's eyes, and rolled up onto my feet. The pug hit
me a good combination as I was moving past. If I'd been
moving toward him, it would have put me down. One of
them jumped on my back. I reached up, got hold of his
hair, doubled over, and pulled with his momentum. He
went over my shoulder and landed on his back on a park
bench. The pug hit me on the side of the jaw and I stumbled. He hit me again, and I rolled away from it and lunged
against George. He wrapped his arms around me and tried
to hold me. I brought both fists up to the level of his ears
and pounded them together with his head in between.
He grunted and his grip relaxed. I broke free of him and
someone hit me with something larger than a fist and
the inside of my head got loud and red and I went down.

When I opened my eyes there were granules of snow
on the lashes; they looked like magnified salt crystals.
There was no sound and no movement. Then there was
a snuffing sound. I rolled my eyes to the left, and over
the small rim of snow I could see a black nose with slight
pink outlinings. It snuffed at me. I shifted my head slightly
and said, 'Uff.' The nose pulled back. It was on one end
of a dog, an apprehensive young Dalmatian that stood
with its front legs stiffened and its hindquarters raised
and its tail making uncertain wags.

Lifting my head was too hard. I put it back in the snow.
The dog moved closer and snuffed at me again. I heard

someone yell, 'Digger!' The dog shuffled his feet uncertainly.

Someone yelled, 'Digger!' again, and the dog moved away. I took a deep breath. It hurt my ribcage. I exhaled, inhaled again, inched my arms under me, and pushed myself up onto my hands and knees. My head swam. I felt my stomach tighten, and I threw up, which hurt the ribs some more. I stayed that way for a bit, on my hands and knees with my head hanging, like a winded horse. My eyes focused a little better. I could see the snow and the dog's footprints, beyond them the legs of a park bench. I crawled over, got hold of it, and slowly got myself upright. Everything blurred for a minute, then came back into focus again. I inhaled some more and felt a little steadier. I looked around. The mall was empty. The Dalmatian was a long way down the mall now, walking with a man and woman. The snow where I stood was trampled and churned. There was a lot of blood spattered on the snow. Across the street in front of Manfred's apartment the Pontiac was gone. I felt my mouth with my left hand. It was swollen, but no teeth were loose. My nose seemed okay, too.

I let go of the bench and took a step. My ribs were stiff and sore. My head ached. I had to wait for a moment while dizziness came and went. I touched the back of my head. It was swollen and wet with blood. I took a handful of snow from the bench seat and held it against the swollen part. Then I took another step, and another. I was underway. My apartment was three blocks away – one block to

Marlborough Street, two blocks down toward the Public Garden. I figured I'd make it by sundown.

Actually I made it before sundown. It wasn't quite noon when I let myself in and locked the door behind me. I took two aspirin with a glass of milk, made some black coffee, added a large shot of Irish whiskey and a teaspoon of sugar, and sipped it while I got undressed. I examined myself in the bathroom mirror. One eye was swollen and my lower lip was puffy. There was a seeping lump on the back of my head and a developing bruise that was going to be a lulu on my right side. But the ribs didn't appear to be broken, and in fact there seemed to be nothing but surface damage. I took a long hot shower and put on clean clothes and had some more coffee and whiskey, and cooked myself two lambchops for lunch. I ate the lambchops with black bread, drank some more coffee with whiskey, and cleaned up the kitchen. I felt lousy but alive, and my fourth cup of whiskeyed coffee made me feel less lousy.

I looked into the bedroom at my bed and thought about lying down for a minute and decided not to. I took out my gun and spun the cylinder, made sure everything worked smoothly, put the gun back in my hip holster again, and went back out of my apartment.

I walked the three blocks back to Manfred's place a lot faster than I had walked from Manfred's two hours earlier. I was not sprightly, but I was moving steadily along.

21

When I rang the bell Manfred's mom came to the door. She was thin and small, wearing a straight striped dress and white sneakers with a hole cut in one of them to relieve pressure on a bunion. Her hair was short and looked as if it had been trimmed with a jackknife. Her face was small, and all the features were clustered in the middle of it. She wore no makeup.

I said, 'Good afternoon, ma'am. Is Manfred Roy here, please?'

She looked at my face uneasily. 'He's having his lunch,' she said. Her voice was very deep.

I stepped partway into the apartment and said, 'I'll be glad to wait, ma'am. Tell him I have some good news about Spenser.'

She stood uncertainly in the doorway. I edged a little further into the apartment. She edged back a little.

Manfred called from another room, 'Who is it, Ma?'

'Man says he has good news about Spenser,' she said. I smiled at her benignly. Old Mr Friendly.

Manfred appeared in the archway to my right. He had a napkin tucked in his belt and a small milk mustache on his upper lip. When he saw me, he stopped dead.

'The good news is that I'm not badly hurt, good buddy,' I said. 'Ain't that swell?'

Manfred backed up a step. 'I don't know nothing about that, Spenser.'

'About what?' his mother said. I edged all the way past her.

'About what, Manfred?' I said. His mom still stood with one hand on the doorknob.

'I didn't have nothing to do with you getting beat up.'

'I'll not be able to say the same about you, Manfred.'

Mrs Roy said, 'What do you want here? You said you had good news. You lied to get in here.'

'True,' I said. 'I did lie. But if I hadn't lied, sort of, then you wouldn't have let me in, and I'd have had to kick in your door. I figured the lie was cheaper.'

'Don't you threaten my mother,' Manfred said.

'No, I won't. It's you I came to threaten, Manfred.'

Mrs Roy said, 'Manfred, I'm going for the police,' and started out into the hall.

'No, Ma. Don't do that,' Manfred said. Mrs Roy stopped in the hall and looked back in at him. Her eyes were sick.

'Why shouldn't I go to the police, Manfred?'

'They wouldn't understand,' Manfred said. 'He'd lie to them. They'd believe him. I'd get in trouble.'

'Are you from the niggers?' she said to me.

'I represent a woman named Rachel Wallace, Mrs Roy. She was kidnaped. I think your son knows something about it. I spoke to him about it yesterday and said I'd come visit him today. This morning four men who knew my name and recognized me on sight were parked in a car outside your apartment. When I arrived, they beat me up.'

Mrs Roy's eyes looked sicker – a sickness that must have gone back a long way. A lifetime of hearing hints that her son wasn't right. That he didn't get along. That he was in trouble or around it. A lifetime of odd people coming to the door and Manfred hustling in and out and not saying exactly what was up. A lifetime sickness of repressing the almost-sure knowledge that your firstborn was very wrong.

'I didn't have nothing to do with that, Ma. I don't know nothing about a kidnaping. Spenser just likes to come and push me around. He knows I don't like his nigger friends. Well, some of my friends don't like him pushing me around.'

'My boy had nothing to do with any of that,' Mrs Roy said. Her voice was guttural with tension.

'Then you ought to call the cops, Mrs Roy. I'm trespassing. And I won't leave.'

Mrs Roy didn't move. She stood with one foot in the hall and one foot in the apartment.

Manfred turned suddenly and ran back through the archway. I went after him. To the left was the kitchen, to the right a short corridor with two doors off it. Manfred went through the nearest one, and when I reached him, he had a short automatic pistol halfway out of the drawer of a bedside table. With the heel of my right fist I banged the drawer shut on his hand. He cried out once. I took the back of his shirt with my left hand and yanked him back toward me and into the hall, spinning him across my body and slamming him against the wall opposite the bedroom door. Then I took the gun out of the drawer. It was a Mauser HSc, a 7.65mm pistol that German pilots used to carry in World War II.

I took the clip out, ran the action back to make sure there was nothing in the chamber, and slipped the pistol in my hip pocket.

Manfred stood against the wall sucking on the bruised fingers of his right hand. His mother had come down the hall and stood beside him, her hands at her side. 'What did he take from you?' she said to Manfred.

I took the pistol out. 'This, Mrs Roy. It was in a drawer beside the bed.'

'It's for protection, Ma.'

'You got a license for this, Manfred?'

'Course I do.'

'Lemme see it.'

'I don't have to show you. You're not on the cops no more.'

'You don't have a permit do you, Manfred?' I smiled a big smile. 'You know what the Massachusetts handgun law says?'

'I got a license.'

'The Massachusetts handgun law provides that anyone convicted of the possession of an unlicensed handgun gets a mandatory one-year jail sentence. Sentence may not be suspended nor parole granted. That's a year in the joint, Manfred.'

'Manfred, do you have a license?' his mother said.

He shook his head. All four fingers of his bruised right hand were in his mouth and he sucked at them.

Mrs Roy looked at me. 'Don't tell,' she said.

'Ever been in the joint, Manfred?'

With his fingers still in his mouth Manfred shook his head.

'They do a lot of bad stuff up there, Manfred. Lot of homosexuality. Lot of hatred. Small blond guys tend to be in demand.'

'Don't tell,' his mother said. She had moved between me and Manfred. Manfred's eyes were squeezed nearly shut. There were tears in the corners.

I smiled my nice big smile at his mother. Old Mr Friendly. Here's how your kid's going to get raped in the slammer, ma'am.

'Maybe we can work something out,' I said. 'See, I'm looking for Rachel Wallace. If you gave me any help on that, I'd give you back your Mauser and speak no ill of you to the fuzz.'

I was looking at Manfred, but I was talking for his mother, too.

'I don't know nothing about it,' Manfred mumbled around his fingers. He seemed to have shrunk in on himself, as if his stomach hurt.

I shook my head sadly. 'Talk to him, Mrs Roy. I don't want to have to put him away. I'm sure you need him here to look after you.'

Mrs Roy's face was chalky, and the lines around her

mouth and eyes were slightly reddened. She was beginning to breathe hard, as if she'd been running. Her mouth was open a bit, and I noticed that her front teeth were gone.

'You do what he says, Manfred. You help this man like he says.' She didn't look at Manfred as she talked. She stood between him and me and looked at me.

I didn't say anything. None of us did. We stood nearly still in the small hallway. Manfred snuffed a little. Some pipes knocked.

Still looking at me, with Manfred behind her, Mrs Roy said, 'God damn you to hell, you little bastard, you do what this man says. You're in trouble. You've always been in trouble. Thirty years old and you still live with your mother and never go out of the house except to those crazy meetings. Whyn't you leave the niggers alone? Whyn't you let the government take care of them? Whyn't you get a good job or get an education or get a woman or get the hell out the house once in awhile, and not get in trouble? Now this man's going to put you in jail unless you do what he says, and you better the hell damn well goddamned do it.' She was crying by the time she got halfway through, and her ugly little face looked a lot worse.

And Manfred was crying. 'Ma,' he said.

I smiled as hard as I could, my big friendly smile. The Yuletide spirit. 'Tis the season to be jolly.

'All my life,' she said. Now she was sobbing, and she turned and put her arms around him. 'All my rotten goddamn life I've been saddled with you and you've been queer and awful and I've worried all about you by myself and no man in the house.'

'Ma,' Manfred said, and they both cried full out.

I felt awful.

'I'm looking for Rachel Wallace,' I said. 'I'm going to find her. Anything that I need to do, I'll do.'

'Ma,' Manfred said. 'Don't, Ma. I'll do what he says. Ma, don't.'

I crossed my arms and leaned on the doorjamb and looked at Manfred. It was not easy to do. I wanted to cry, too.

'What do you want me to do, Spenser?'

'I want to sit down and have you tell me anything you've heard or can guess or have imagined about who might have taken Rachel Wallace.'

'I'll try to help, but I don't know nothing.'

'We'll work on that. Get it together, and we'll sit down and talk. Mrs Roy, maybe you could make us some coffee.'

She nodded. The three of us walked back down the hall. Me last. Mrs Roy went to the kitchen. Manfred and I went to the living room. The furniture was brightly colored imitation velvet with a lot of antimacassars on the arms. The antimacassars were the kind you buy in Woolworths, not the kind anyone ever made at home. There was a big new color TV set in one corner of the room.

I sat in one of the bright fuzzy chairs. It was the color of a Santa Claus suit. Manfred stood in the archway. He still had his napkin tucked into his belt.

'What you want to know?' he said.

'Who do you think took Rachel Wallace?' I said. 'And where do you think she is?'

'Honest to God, Spenser, I got no idea.'

'What is the most anti-feminist group you know of?'

'Anti-feminist?'

'Yeah. Who hates women's lib the most?'

'I don't know about any group like that.'

'What do you know about RAM, which stands for Restore American Morality?' I said. I could hear Manfred's mom in the kitchen messing with cookware.

'I never heard of it.'

'How about the Belmont Vigilance Committee?'

'Oh, sure, that's Mr English's group. We coordinated some of the forced-busing tactics with them.'

'You know English?'

'Oh, yes. Very wealthy, very important man. He worked closely with us.'

'How tough is he?'

'He will not retreat in the face of moral decay and godless Communism.'

'Manfred, don't make a speech at me – I'm too old to listen to horseshit. I want to know if he's got the balls to kidnap someone, or if he's crazy enough. Or if he's got the contacts to have someone do it.'

'Mr English wouldn't hesitate to do the right thing,' Manfred said.

'Would he know how to arrange a kidnaping?' I said. 'And don't give me all that canned tripe in the answer.'

Manfred nodded.

'Who would do it for him?' I said.

Manfred shook his head. 'I don't know any names, I promise I don't. I just see him with people, and, you know, they're the kind that would know about that kind of stuff.'

Mrs Roy brought in some instant coffee in white mugs that had pictures of vegetables on them. She'd put some Oreo cookies on a plate and she put the two cups and the plate down on a yellow plastic molded coffee table with a translucent plastic top that had been finished to imitate frosted glass.

I said, 'Thank you, Mrs Roy.'

Manfred didn't look at her. She didn't look at him, either. She nodded her head at me to acknowledge the thanks and went back to the kitchen. She didn't want to hear what Manfred was saying.

'I heard he could get anything done and that he was a good man if you needed anything hard done, or you needed to hire anyone for special stuff.'

'Like what?' I sipped at the coffee. The water had been added to the coffee before it was hot enough, and the coffee wasn't entirely dissolved. I swallowed and put the cup down.

'You know.'

'No, I don't, Manfred. Like what?'

'Well, if you needed people for, like, you know, like fighting and getting things done.'

'Like the baboons that pounded on me this morning?'

'I didn't hire them, Spenser. They're from the organization. They wanted to make sure I wasn't bothered.'

'Because you are a Klan mucky-muck?' I said. 'Second Assistant Lizard?'

'I'm an official. And they were looking out for me. We stick together.'

Manfred's voice tried for dignity, but he kept staring at the floor, and dignity is hard, while you're looking at the floor.

'Ever meet his mother or his sister?'

'No.'

'Know anything about them?'

'No.'

'Manfred, you are not being a help.'

'I'm trying, Spenser. I just don't know nothing. I never heard of Rachel Whosis.'

'Wallace,' I said. 'Rachel Wallace.'

22

Manfred and I chatted for another hour with no better results. Hardly seemed worth getting beat up for. When I left, Mrs Roy didn't come to say goodbye, and Manfred didn't offer to shake hands. I got even – I didn't wish them Merry Christmas.

It was a little after three when I got back out onto Commonwealth. The whiskey and aspirin had worn off, and I hurt. A three-block walk and I could be in bed, but that wouldn't be looking for Rachel Wallace. That would be taking a nap. Instead I walked down to Berkeley and up three blocks to Police Headquarters to talk with Quirk.

He was there and so was Belson. Quirk had his coat off and his sleeves rolled up. He was squeezing one of those little red rubber grip-strengtheners with indentations for the fingers. He did ten in one hand and switched it to the other and did ten more.

'Trying to keep your weight down, Marty?' I said.

Quirk switched the grip-strengthener back to his right hand. 'Your face looks good,' he said.

'I bumped into a door,' I said.

'About fifteen times,' Belson said. 'You come in to make a complaint?'

I shook my head. It made my face hurt. 'I came by to see how you guys are making out looking for Rachel Wallace.'

'We got shit,' Quirk said.

'Anything on those license-tag numbers I gave you?'

Quirk nodded. 'The Buick belongs to a guy named Swisher Cody. Used to be a big basketball star at Hyde Park High in the fifties, where he got the nickname. Dodge belongs to a broad named Mary Stevenson. Says she lets her boyfriend use it all the time. Boyfriend's name is Michael Mulready. He's a pal of Swisher's. They both tell us that they were together the night you say they tried to run you off the road and that they were playing cards with Mulready's cousin Mingo at his place in Watertown. Mingo says that's right. Cody's done time for loansharking. Mingo, too.'

'So you let them go,' I said.

Quirk shrugged. 'Even if we didn't believe them and we believe you, what have we got them for? Careless driving? We let 'em go and we put a tail on them.'

'And?'

'And nothing. They both go to work in the Sears warehouse in Dorchester. They stop on the way home for a few beers. They go to bed. Sometimes they drive out to Watertown and play cards with Cousin Mingo.'

I nodded. 'How about English?'

Quirk nodded at Belson.

Belson said, 'Pretty much what you heard. He's chairman of the Vigilance Committee.'

'Eternal vigilance is the price of liberty,' Quirk said, and squeezed his grip-exerciser hard so that the muscles in his forearm looked like suspension cables.

Belson said, 'Spenser been lending you books again, Marty?'

Quirk shook his head. 'Naw, my kid's taking US History. He's almost as smart as Spenser.'

'Maybe he'll straighten out,' I said. 'What else you got on English?'

Belson shrugged. 'Nothing you don't know. He's got money – he thinks it makes him important, and he's probably right. He's got the IQ of a fieldmouse. And he's got an alibi to cover any time Rachel Wallace might have been kidnaped. Did you meet his mother?'

'No. I've seen her picture.'

'Ain't she a looker?' He looked at Quirk. 'We ever have to bust her, Marty, I want you to send some hard-ass kids from the tac squad. You and me'd get hurt.'

'She as nice as she looks?' I said.

'Nowhere near that nice,' Belson said. 'She sat in while we questioned sonny and tended to answer whatever we asked him. I told her finally, why didn't she hold him on her knee and he could move his lips? She told me she'd see to it that I never worked for any police department in this state.'

'You scared?' I said.

'Hell, no,' Belson said. 'I'm relieved. I thought she was going to kill me.'

'She active in the committee?' I said.

'She didn't say,' Belson said, 'but I'd guess yes. I have the feeling she's active in anything sonny is active in. He doesn't get a hard-on without checking with her.'

'You run any check on the family? There's a sister.'

Quirk said, 'What the hell do you think we do in here – make up Dick Tracy Crimestoppers? Of course we ran a check on the family. Sister's name is Geraldine.'

'I know that, for crissake – Geraldine Julia English, Goucher College class of '68.'

Quirk went on as if I hadn't said anything. 'Geraldine Julia English. Married a guy named Walton Wells in June, 1968, divorced 1972. Works as a model in Boston.'

'Wells,' I said.

'Yeah, Walton Wells – slick name, huh?'

'Geraldine Julia Wells would be her married name.'

Belson said, 'You were wrong, Marty. Your kid couldn't be nearly as smart as Spenser.'

'What model agency she with?'

Belson said, 'Carol Cobb.'

'She use her married name?'

'Yeah.'

'And her middle name instead of her first, I bet?'

Quirk said, 'Nobody could be nearly as smart as Spenser.'

'She bills herself as Julie Wells, doesn't she?'

Belson nodded.

'Gentlemen,' I said, 'what we have here is your basic clue. Julie Wells, who is Lawrence Turnbull English, Junior's, sister, was intimate with Rachel Wallace.'

'Intimate intimate or just friendly intimate?' Quirk said.

'Intimate intimate,' I said.

'How do you know this?' Quirk said.

I told him.

'Nice you told us first thing,' Quirk said. 'Nice you mentioned her name at the beginning of the investigation so we could follow up every possible lead. Very nice.' There was no amusement in Quirk's voice now.

'I should have told you,' I said. 'I was wrong.'

'You bet your ass you were wrong,' Quirk said. 'Being wrong like that tends to put your balls in the fire, too – you know that?'

'You're not the Holy Ghost, Quirk. None of you guys are. I don't have to run in and report everything I know to you every day. I made a guess that this broad was okay, and I didn't want to smell up her rose garden by dragging her into this. Can't you see the *Herald American* headline: "LESBIAN LOVER SUSPECT IN KIDNAPING"?'

'And maybe you guessed wrong, hot shot, and maybe your girlfriend Rachel is dead and gone because you didn't tell us something.'

'Or maybe it doesn't mean a goddamned thing,' I said. 'Maybe you're making a big goddamned event out of nothing.' I was leaning back in my chair, one foot propped against the edge of Quirk's desk. He leaned over and slapped the foot away.

'And get your goddamned foot off my desk,' he said.

I stood up and so did Quirk.

'Dynamite,' Belson said. 'You guys fight to the death, and the winner gets to look for Rachel Wallace.' He scratched a wooden match on the sole of his shoe and lit a new cigar.

Still standing, Quirk said, 'How much do you pay for those goddamned weeds anyway?'

Between puffs to get the cigar going Belson said, 'Fifteen cents apiece.'

Quirk sat down. 'You get screwed,' he said.

'They're cheap,' Belson said, 'but they smell bad.'

I sat down.

Quirk said, 'Okay. Julie Wells is a member of the English family.' He was leaning back now in his swivel chair, his head tipped, staring up at the ceiling, his hands resting on the arms. The rubber grip-squeezer lay on the nearly empty desk in front of him. 'She is also an intimate of Rachel Wallace. Which means she's gay or at least bisexual.' I put one foot up on Quirk's desk again. 'Her brother on the other hand is out picketing Rachel Wallace and calling her a dyke and telling her she's immoral and must be stopped,' Quirk said.

'We have here a family conflict,' Belson said. 'And at least an odd coincidence.'

'It could be only that,' I said.

Quirk's eyes came down from the ceiling and he let the swivel chair come forward until his feet touched the floor.

'It could be,' he said. 'But it don't do us a lot of good to assume that it is.'

'We better get together on how we're going to handle this,' I said. 'We don't want to charge in and hit her with it, do we?'

'You had your chance to get together with us on this, hot shot, and you didn't take it. We'll decide how to handle it.'

'You want to teach me a lesson, Quirk,' I said, 'or you want to find Rachel Wallace?'

'Both,' he said. 'Take a walk.'

'How about an address for Cody and Mulready?'

'Blow,' Quirk said.

I toyed with saying, 'I shall return.' Figured it was not appropriate and left without a word. As I left Belson blew a smoke ring at me.

23

I went home feeling lousy. My face hurt, so did my ribs. I'd been making people mad at me all day. I needed someone to tell me I was swell. I called Susan. She wasn't home. I had a bottle of Molson's ale, took two aspirin, made a meatloaf sandwich with lettuce, ate it, drank two more ales with it, and went to bed. I dreamed I was locked in a castle room and Susan kept walking by and smiling when I yelled for help. I woke up mad at her, at five minutes of seven in the morning.

When I got up, I forgot about being mad at Susan. I was mad at my body. I could barely walk. I clanked over to the bathroom, and got under the hot water in the shower, and stretched a little while the hot water ran over me. I was in there for maybe half an hour, and when I got out I had cornbread and country sausage and broiled tomato for breakfast and read the *Globe*. Then I put on my gun and went looking for Mulready and Cody.

It was snowing again as I drove on the Southeast Expressway to Dorchester, and the wind was blowing hard so that the snow swirled and eddied in the air. I was going against the commuter rush, but still the traffic was slow, cautious in the snowfall. I slithered off the exit ramp at the big Sears warehouse, stopped at the guard shack, got directions to the main pick-up point, and drove to it.

Quirk had been childish not to give me the addresses. He'd already mentioned that they worked at the Sears warehouse, and he knew I'd go out and find them that way. Immature. Churlish.

I turned up the fleece collar of my jacket before I got out of the car. I put on a blue navy watch cap and a pair of sunglasses. I checked myself in the rearview mirror. Unrecognizable. One of my cleverest disguises. I was impersonating a man dressed for winter. I got out and walked to the warehouse pick-up office.

'Swisher or Michael around?' I said to the young woman behind the call desk.

'Cody and Mulready?'

I nodded.

'They're out back. I can call them on the horn here.'

'Yeah, would ya? Tell them Mingo's out here.'

She said into the microphone, 'Swisher Cody, Michael Mulready, please report to the call desk. A Mr Mingo is here.'

There were three other people in the call office, two of them men. I stood behind the others as we waited. In less than two minutes two men came through the swinging doors behind the desk and glanced around the room. One of them was tall with a big red broken-veined nose and long sideburns. His short hair was reddish with a sprinkling of gray. The other man was much younger. He had blow-dried black hair, a thick black mustache, and a seashell necklace tight around his throat. Contemporary.

I said, 'Hey, Swisher.'

The tall one with the red hair turned first, then they both looked at me.

'I got a message for you guys from Mingo,' I said. 'Can you come around?'

Mustache started toward the hinged end of the counter and Red Hair stopped him. He said something I couldn't hear, then they both looked at me again. Then Mustache said something I couldn't hear, then they both bolted through the swinging doors back into the warehouse. So much for my disguise wizardry.

I said, 'Excuse me,' to the woman waiting for her pick-up and vaulted the counter.

The young lady behind the counter said, 'Sir, you can't . . .'

I was through the swinging doors and into the warehouse. There were vast aisles of merchandise and down the center aisle Cody and Mulready were hot-footing it to the rear. The one with the mustache, Mulready, was a step or two behind Cody. I only needed one. I caught them as they were fumbling with a door that said Emergency Only. Cody had it open when I took Mulready from behind. Cody went on out into the snow. I dragged Mulready back.

He turned and tried to knee me in the groin. I turned my hip into his body and blocked him. I got a good grip of shirt front with both hands and pressed him up and backwards until his feet were off the ground and his back was against the wall beside the door. The door had a pneumatic closer and swung slowly shut. I put my face close up to Mulready's and said, 'You really got a cousin named Mingo Mulready?'

'What the fuck's wrong with you?' he said. 'Lemme the fuck down. What are you, crazy?'

'You know what I'm doing, Michael baby,' I said. 'You know 'cause you ran when you recognized me.'

'I don't know you. Lemme the fuck down.'

I banged him once, hard, against the wall.

'You tried to run me and Rachel Wallace off the road a while ago in Lynn. I'm looking for Rachel Wallace, and I'm going to find her, and I don't mind if I have to break things to do it.'

Behind me I could hear footsteps coming at a trot. Someone yelled, 'Hey, you!'

I pulled Mulready away from the wall and banged him against the safety bar on the emergency door. It opened, and I shoved him through, sprawling into the snow. I followed him outside. The door swung shut behind me. Mulready tried to scramble to his feet. I kicked him in the stomach. I was wearing my Herman survivor boots, double-insulated with a heavy sole. He gasped. The kick rolled him over onto his back in the snow. He tried to keep rolling. I landed on his chest with both knees. He made a croaking noise.

I said, 'I will beat you into whipped cream, Michael, if you don't do just what I say.' Then I stood up, yanked him to his feet, got a hold on the back of his collar, and ran him toward my car. He was doubled over with pain, and the wind was knocked out of him and he was easy to move. I shoved him into the front seat, driver's side, put my foot on his backside, and shoved him across to the passenger's side, got in after him, and skidded into reverse. In the rearview mirror I could see three, then four men and the girl from the call counter coming out the emergency exit. I shifted into third and pulled out of the parking lot and past the gate house; the guard gestured at us. I turned right through the parking lot at the Howard Johnson's motel and out onto the Southeast Expressway.

In the rearview mirror all was serene. The snow slanted in across the road steadily. Beside me Mulready was getting his breath back.

'Where you going with me?' he said. His voice was husky with strain.

'Just riding,' I said. 'I'm going to ask you questions, and when you've answered them all, and I'm happy with what you've said, I'll drop you off somewhere convenient.'

'I don't know anything about anything.'

'In that case,' I said, 'I will pull in somewhere and maybe kill you.'

'For what, man? We didn't do you no harm. We didn't plan to do you in. We were supposed to scare you and the broad.'

'You mean Ms Wallace, scumbag.'

'Huh?'

'Call her Ms Wallace. Don't call her "the broad".'

'Okay, sure, Ms Wallace. Okay by me. We weren't trying to hurt Ms Wallace or you, man.'

'Who told you to do that?'

'Whaddya mean?'

I shook my head. 'You are going to get yourself in very bad trouble,' I said. I reached under my coat and brought out my gun and showed it to him. 'Smith and Wesson,' I said, 'thirty-eight caliber, four-inch barrel. Not good for long range, but perfect for shooting a guy sitting next to you.'

'Jesus, man, put the piece down. I just didn't understand the question, you know? I mean, What is it you're asking, man? I'll try. You don't need the fucking piece, you know?'

I put the gun back. We were in Milton now; traffic was very thin in the snow. 'I said, Who told you to scare us up on the Lynnway that night?'

'My cousin, man – Mingo. He told us about doing it. Said there was a deuce in it for us. Said we could split a deuce for doing it. Mingo, man. You know him?'

'Why did Mingo want you to scare me and Ms Wallace?'

'I don't know, man, it was just an easy two bills. Swisher says it's a tit. Says he knows how to work it easy. He done time, Swisher. Mingo don't say why, man. He just lays the deuce on us – we ain't asking no questions. A couple hours' drive for that kind of bread, man, we don't even know who you are.'

'Then how'd you pick us up?'

'Mingo gave us a picture of the bro— Ms Wallace. We

followed her when you took her out to Marblehead. We hung around till you took her home, and there wasn't much traffic. You know? Then we made our move like he said – Mingo.'

'What's Mingo do?'

'You mean for a living?'

'Yeah.'

'He works for some rich broad in Belmont.'

'Doing what?'

'I don't know. Everything. Drives her around. Carry stuff when she shops. Errands. That shit. He's got it made, man.'

'What's her name?'

'The rich broad?' Mulready shrugged. His breath was back. I had put the gun away. He was talking, which was something he obviously had practiced at. He was beginning to relax a little. 'I don't know,' he said. 'I don't think Mingo ever said.'

At Furnace Brook Parkway I went off the expressway, reversed directions, and came back on heading north.

'Where we going now?' Mulready said.

'We're going to go visit Cousin Mingo,' I said. 'You're going to show me where he lives.'

'Oh, fuck me, man. I can't do that. Mingo will fucking kill me.'

'But that will be later,' I said. 'If you don't show me I'll kill you now.'

'No, man, you don't know Mingo. He is a bad-ass son of a bitch. I'm telling you now, man, you don't want to fuck with Mingo.'

'I told you, Michael. I'm looking for Rachel Wallace. I told you back in the warehouse that I'd break things if I had to. You're one of the things I'll break.'

'Well, shit, man, lemme tell you, and then drop me off. Man, I don't want Mingo to know it was me. You don't know what he's fucking like, man.'

'What's his real name?' I said.

'Eugene, Eugene Ignatius Mulready.'

'We'll check a phonebook,' I said.

In Milton I pulled off the expressway and we checked the listing in an outdoor phonebooth. It didn't list Watertown.

'That's in the West Suburban book,' Michael said. 'They only got Boston and South Suburban here.'

'Observant,' I said. 'We'll try Information.'

'Christ, you think I'm lying? Hey, man, no way. You know? No way I'm going to bullshit you, man, with the piece you're carrying. I mean my old lady didn't raise no stupid kids, you know?'

I put in a dime and dialed Information. 'In Watertown,' I said. 'The number for Eugene I. Mulready – what's the address, Michael?'

He told me. I told the operator.

'The number is eight-nine-nine,' she said, 'seven-three-seven-oh.'

I said thank you and hung up. The dime came back.

'Okay, Michael, you're on your way.'

'From here?'

'Yep.'

'Man, I got no coat – I'll freeze my ass.'

'Call a cab.'

'A cab? From here? I ain't got that kind of bread, man.' I took the dime out of the return slot. 'Here,' I said. 'Call your buddy Swisher. Have him come get you.'

'What if he ain't home?'

'You're a grown-up person, Michael. You'll figure something out. But I'll tell you one thing – you call and warn Mingo, and you won't grow up any more.'

'I ain't going to call Mingo, man. I'd have to tell him I tipped you.'

'That's what I figure,' I said. I got in my car. Michael Mulready was standing shivering in his shirt sleeves, his hands in his pants pocket, his shoulders hunched.

'I give you one tip though, pal,' he said. 'You got a big surprise coming, you think you can fuck around with Mingo like you done with me. Mingo will fucking destroy you.'

'Watch,' I said and let the clutch out and left him on the sidewalk.

24

Watertown was next to Belmont, but only in location. It was mostly working-class and the houses were shabby, often two-family, and packed close together on streets that weren't plowed well. It was slow going now, the snow coming hard and the traffic overcautious and crawling.

Mingo Mulready's house was square, two stories, with a wide front porch. The cedar shingle siding was painted blue. The asbestos shingles on the roof were multi-colored. I parked on the street and walked across.

There were two front entrance doors. The one on the left said Mulready. I rang the bell. Nothing. I waited a minute, rang it again. Then I leaned on it for about two minutes. Mingo wasn't home. I went back to my car. Mingo was probably off working at his soft job, driving the rich woman around Belmont. I turned on the radio and listened to the news at noon. Two things occurred to me. One was that nothing that ever got reported in the news seemed to have anything to do with me, and the other was that it was lunchtime. I drove about ten blocks to the Eastern Lamjun Bakery on Belmont Street and bought a package of fresh Syrian bread, a pound of feta cheese, and a pound of Calamata olives.

The bread was still warm. Then I went across the street to the package store and bought a six-pack of Beck's beer, then I drove back and parked in front of Mingo's house and had lunch, and listened to a small suburban station that played jazz and big-band music. At three I drove down the block to a gas station and filled my gas tank and used the men's room and drove back up to Mingo's and sat some more.

I remembered this kind of work as less boring fifteen years ago when I used to smoke. Probably not so. Probably just seemed that way. At four fifteen Mingo showed up. He was driving a tan Thunderbird with a vinyl roof. He pulled into the driveway beside the house and got out. I got out and walked across the street. We met at the front steps of his home.

I said, 'Are you Mingo Mulready?'

He said, 'Who wants to know?'

I said, 'I say, "I do," then you say, "Who are you?" then I say—'

He said, 'What the fuck are you talking about, Jack?'

He was big enough to talk that way, and he must have been used to getting away with it. He was about my height, which made him just under six two, and he was probably twenty-five or thirty pounds heavier, which would have made him 230. He had one of the few honest-to-God boot-camp crew cuts I'd seen in the last eight or ten years. He also had small eyes and a button nose in a doughy face, so that he looked like a mean, palefaced gingerbread man. He was wearing a dark suit and a white shirt and black gloves. He wore no coat.

I said, 'Are you Mingo Mulready?'

'I want to know who's asking,' he said. 'And I want to know pretty quick, or I might stomp your ass.'

I was holding my right hand in my left at about belt level. While I was talking I strained the right against the left, so that when I let go with the left, the right snapped up, and the edge of my hand caught Mingo under the nose the way a cocked hammer snaps when you squeeze the trigger. I accelerated it a little on the way up, and the blood spurted from Mingo's nose, and he staggered back about two steps. It was a good shot.

'That's why I wanted to know if you were Mingo,' I said. I drove a left hook into the side of his jaw. 'Because I didn't want to beat the hell out of some innocent bystander.' I put a straight right onto Mingo's nose. He fell down. 'But you're such a pain in the ass that you need to get the hell beat out of you even if you aren't Mingo Mulready.'

He was not a bunny. I'd sucker-punched him and put two more good shots in his face, and he didn't stay down. He came lunging up at me and knocked me back into the snow and scrambled on top of me. I put the heels of both hands under his chin and drove his head back and half-lifted him off me and rolled away. He came after me again, but that extra thirty pounds wasn't helping him. It was mostly fat, and he was already rasping for breath. I moved in, hit him hard twice in the gut, moved out, and hit him twice on that bloody nose. He sagged. I hit him on each side of the jaw. Left jab, right cross, left jab, right cross. He sagged more. His breath wheezed; his arms dropped. He was arm-weary in the first round.

I said, 'Are you Mingo Mulready?'

He nodded.

'You sure?' I said. 'I heard you were a bad ass.'

He nodded again, wheezing for oxygen.

'I guess I heard wrong,' I said. 'You work for a rich woman in Belmont?'

He stared at me.

'If you want to keep getting your breath back, you answer what I ask. You don't answer, and you'll think what we did before was dancing.'

He nodded.

'You do. What's her name?'

'English,' he said.

'She tell you to hire your cousin and his pal Swisher to run me off the road in Lynn?'

He said, 'You?'

'Yeah, me. Me and Rachel Wallace. Who told you to harass us?'

He looked toward the street. It was empty. The snow was thin and steady, and darkness had come on. He looked toward the house. It was dark.

He said, 'I dunno what you mean.'

I hit him a good left hook in the throat. He gasped and clutched at his neck.

I said, 'Who told you to run Rachel Wallace off the road? Who told you to hire your cousin and his pal? Who gave you the two bills?'

He was having trouble speaking. 'English,' he croaked.

'The old lady or the son?'

'The son.'

'Why?'

He shook his head. I moved my left fist. He backed up. 'Swear on my mother,' he said. 'I don't ask them questions. They pay me good. They treat me decent.' He stopped and coughed and spat some blood. 'I don't ask no questions. I do what they say, they're important people.'

'Okay,' I said. 'Remember, I know where you live. I may come back and talk with you again. If I have to look for you, it will make me mad.'

He didn't say anything. I turned and walked across the street to my car. It was very dark now, and in the snow I couldn't even see the car till I was halfway across the street. I opened the door. The inside light went on. Frank Belson was sitting in the front seat. I got in and closed the door.

'For crissake turn the motor on and get the heater going,' he said. 'I'm freezing my nuts off.'

25

'You want a beer?' I said. 'There's four left on the back-seat.'

'I don't drink on duty,' he said. He took two bottles of Beck's out of the carton. 'For crissake, what kind of beer is this? It doesn't even have a twist-off cap.'

'There's an opener in the glove compartment,' I said.

Belson opened the two beers, gave one to me and took a long pull on the other bottle.

'What you get from Mingo?'

'I thought I was ostracized,' I said.

'You know Marty,' Belson said. 'He gets mad quick, he cools down quick. What you get from Mingo?'

'Haven't you talked to him?'

'We figured you could talk with him harder than we could. We were right. But I thought he'd give you more trouble than he did.'

'I suckered him,' I said. 'That got him off to a bad start.'

'Still,' Belson said, 'he used to be goddamned good.'

'Me, too,' I said.

'I know that. What'd you get?'

'English set up the hit-and-run on the Lynnway.'

'Mingo do it through his cousin?'

'Yeah.'

'Cousin tell you that?'

'Yeah. Him and Cody did the work. Mingo gave them a deuce. He got the money from English. I braced Cousin Michael this morning.'

'I know,' Belson said.

'What the hell is this – practice teaching? You follow me around and observe?'

'I told you we had Cody and Mulready staked out,' Belson said. 'When you showed up, the detail called in. I told them to let you go. I figured you'd get more than we would because you don't have to sweat brutality charges. They lost you heading out of Sears, but I figured you'd end up here and I came over. Got here about one thirty and been sitting in the next block since. You get anything else?'

'No. But English is looking better and better. You look into those pie-throwers in Cambridge?'

Belson finished the beer and opened another bottle. 'Yeah,' he said. 'There's nothing there. Just a couple of right-wing fruitcakes. They never been in jail. They don't show any connection with English or Mingo Mulready or the Vigilance Committee or anybody else. They go to MIT, for crissake.'

'Okay. How about Julie Wells? You talk to her yet?'

Belson held the beer between his knees while he got a half-smoked cigar out of his shirt pocket and lit it and puffed at it. Then he took the cigar out of his mouth, sipped some beer, put the cigar back in, and said around it, 'Can't find her. She doesn't seem to have moved or anything, but she's not at her apartment whenever we show up. We're sort of looking for her.'

'Good. You think you might sort of find her in a while?'

'If we'd known some things earlier, buddy, we'd have been more likely to have kept an eye on her.'

'Know anything about Mingo? You sound like you've known him before.'

'Oh, yeah, old Mingo. He's got a good-sized file. Used to work for Joe Broz once. Used to be a bouncer, did some pro wrestling, some loansharking. Been busted for assault, for armed robbery, been picked up on suspicion of murder and released when we couldn't turn a witness that would talk. English employs some sweetheart to drive the old babe around.'

I said, 'You people going to keep English under surveil-lance?'

'Surveillance? Christ, you been watching *Police Woman* again? *Surveillance*. Christ.'

I said, 'You gonna watch him?'

'Yeah. We'll try to keep someone on him. We ain't got all that many bodies, you know?'

'And he's got money and maybe knows a couple city councilmen and a state senator.'

'Maybe. It happens. You know Marty. You know me. But you also know how it works. Pressure comes down, we gotta bend. Or get other work, you know?'

'Felt any pressure yet?'

Belson shook his head. 'Nope,' he said, 'not yet.' He finished the bottle of beer.

'Belmont cops?'

'They said they could help out a little.'

'You got anybody at Julie Wells's apartment?'

'Yeah. And we check in at the agency regular. She ain't there.'

I said, 'You want a ride to your car?'

He nodded, and I went around the block and dropped him off on the street behind Mingo's house. 'You stumble across anything, you might want to give us a buzz,' Belson said as he got out.

'Yeah,' I said. 'I might.'

He said, 'Thanks for the beer,' and closed my door, and I pulled away. It was almost an hour and a half in the snow and the near-motionless rush hour until I got to my apartment. Susan was there.

'I had an Adolescent Development Workshop at BU this afternoon, and when I got out it was too bad to drive home, so I left my car in the lot and walked down,' she said.

'You missed a golden opportunity,' I said.

'For what?'

'To take off all your clothes and make a martini and surprise me at the door.'

'I thought of that,' Susan said, 'but you don't like martinis.'

'Oh,' I said.

'But I made a fire,' she said. 'And we could have a drink in front of it.'

'Or something,' I said. I picked her up and hugged her.

She shook her head. 'They were talking about you all day today,' she said.

'At the workshop on adolescent development?'

She nodded and smiled her fallen-seraph smile at me. 'You exhibit every symptom,' she said.

I put her down and we went to the kitchen. 'Let us see what there is to eat,' I said. 'Maybe pulverized rhino horn with a dash of Spanish fly.'

'You whip up something, snooks,' she said. 'I'm going to take a bath. And maybe rinse out the pantyhose in your sink.'

'A man's work is never done,' I said. I looked in the refrigerator. There was Molson Golden Ale on the bottom shelf. If we were snowbound, at least I had staples on hand. In the vegetable keeper there were some fresh basil leaves and a bunch of parsley I'd bought in Quincy Market. It was a little limp but still serviceable. I opened a Molson. I could hear the water running in the bathroom. I raised the bottle of ale, and said, 'Here's looking at you, kid,' in a loud voice.

Susan yelled back, 'Why don't you make me a gimlet, blue eyes, and I'll drink it when I get out. Ten minutes.'

'Okay.'

In the freezer was chopped broccoli in a twenty-ounce bag. I took it out. I got out a large blue pot and boiled four quarts of water, and a smaller saucepan with a steamer rack and boiled about a cup of water. While it was coming to a boil I put two garlic cloves in my Cuisinart along with a handful of parsley and a handful of basil and some kosher salt and some oil and a handful of shelled pistachios and I blended them smooth. Susan had given me the Cuisinart for my birthday, and I used it whenever I could. I thought it was kind of a silly toy, but she'd loved giving it to me and I'd never tell. When the water boiled, I shut off both pots. I could hear Susan sloshing around in the tub. The door was ajar, and I went over and stuck my head in. She lay on her back with her hair pinned up and her naked body glistening in the water.

'Not bad,' I said, 'for a broad your age.'

'I knew you'd peek,' she said. 'Voyeurism, a typical stage in adolescent development.'

'Not bad, actually, for a broad of anyone's age,' I said.

'Go make the gimlet now,' she said. 'I'm getting out.'

'Gin or vodka?' I said.

'Gin.'

'Animal,' I said.

I went back to the kitchen and mixed five parts gin to one part Rose's lime juice in a pitcher and stirred it with ice and poured it into a glass with two ice cubes. Susan came into the kitchen as I finished, wearing the half-sleeved silk shaving robe she'd given me last Christmas, which I never wore, but which she did when she came and stayed. It was maroon with black piping and a black belt. When I tried it on, I looked like Bruce Lee. She didn't.

She sat on one of my kitchen stools and sipped her gimlet. Her hair was up and she had no makeup and her face was shiny. She looked fifteen, except for the marks of age and character around her eyes and mouth. They added.

I had another Molson and brought my two pots to a boil again. In the big one I put a pound of spaghetti. In the small one with the steamer rack I put the frozen broccoli. I set the timer for nine minutes.

'Shall we dine before the fire?' I said.

'Certainly.'

'Okay,' I said. 'Put down the booze and take one end of the dining-room table.'

We moved it in front of the fire and brought two chairs and set the table while the spaghetti boiled and the broccoli steamed. The bell on the timer rang. I went to the kitchen and drained the broccoli and tried the spaghetti. It needed another minute. While it boiled I ran the Cuisinart another whirl and reblended my oil and spices. Then I tried the pasta. It was done. I drained it, put it back in the pot and tossed it with the spiced oil and broccoli. I put out the pot, the leftover loaves of Syrian bread that I bought for lunch, and a cold bottle of Soave Bolla. Then I held Susan's chair. She sat down. I put another log on the fire, poured a dash of wine in her glass. She sipped it thoughtfully, then nodded at me. I filled her glass and then mine.

'Perhaps madam would permit me to join her,' I said.

'Perhaps,' she said.

I sipped a little wine.

'And perhaps later on,' she said, 'we might screw.'

I laughed halfway through a swallow of wine and choked

and gasped and splattered the wine all over my shirt front.

'Or perhaps not,' she said.

'Don't toy with me while I'm drinking,' I said, when I was breathing again. 'Later on I may take you by force.'

'Woo-woo,' she said.

I served her some pasta with broccoli and some to myself. Outside it was snowing steadily. There was only one light on in the room; most of the light came from the fire, which was made of applewood and smelled sweet. The glow of the embers behind the steady low flame made the room faintly rosy. We were quiet. The flame hissed softly as it forced the last traces of sap from the logs. I wasn't nearly as sore as I had been. The pasta tasted wonderful. The wine was cold. And Susan made my throat ache. If I could find Rachel Wallace, I might believe in God.

26

The sun that brief December day rose cheerlessly and invisibly over one hell of a lot of snow in the city of Boston. I looked at the alarm clock. Six a.m. It was very still outside, the noise of a normal morning muffled by the snow. I was lying on my right side, my left arm over Susan's bare shoulder. Her hair had come unpinned in the night and was in a wide tangle on the pillow. Her face was toward me and her eyes were closed. She slept with her mouth open slightly, and the smell of wine on her breath fluttered faintly across the pillow. I pushed up on one elbow and looked out the window. The snow was still coming – steadily and at a slant so I knew the wind was driving it. Without opening her eyes, Susan pulled me back down against her and shrugged the covers back up over us. She made a snuggling motion with her body and lay still.

I said, 'Would you like an early breakfast, or did you have another plan?'

She pressed her face into the hollow of my shoulder. 'My nose is cold,' she said in a muffled voice.

'I'm your man,' I said. I ran my hand down the line of her body and patted her on the backside. She put her right hand in the small of my back and pressed a little harder against me.

'I had always thought,' she said, her face still pressed in my shoulder, 'that men of your years had problems of sexual dysfunction.'

'Oh, we do,' I said. 'I used to be twice as randy twenty years ago.'

'They must have kept you in a cage,' she said. She walked her fingers up my backbone, one vertebra at a time.

'Yeah,' I said, 'but I could reach through the bars.'

'I bet you could,' she said, and with her eyes still closed she raised her head and kissed me with her mouth open.

It was nearly eight when I got up and took a shower.

Susan took hers while I made breakfast and built another fire. Then we sat in front of the fire and ate cornbread made with buttermilk, and wild-strawberry jam and drank coffee.

At nine fifteen, with the cornbread gone and the strawberry jam depleted and the *Globe* read and the *Today Show* finished, I called my answering service. Someone had left a telephone number for me to call.

I dialed it, and a woman answered on the first ring. I said, 'This is Spenser. I have a message to call this number.'

She said, 'Spenser, this is Julie Wells.'

I said, 'Where are you?'

She said, 'It doesn't matter. I've got to see you.'

I said, 'We're in an old Mark Stevens movie.'

'I beg your pardon?'

'I want to see you, too,' I said. 'Where can I meet you?'

'There's a snow emergency, you know.'

They never said that in the old Mark Stevens movies. 'Name a place,' I said. 'I'll get there.'

'The coffee shop at the Parker House.'

'When?'

'Ten thirty.'

'See you then.'

'I don't want anyone else to know I'm there, Spenser.'

'Then you say, "Make sure you're not followed." And I say, "Don't worry. I'll be careful."'

'Well, I don't. I meant it.'

'Okay, kid. I'll be there.'

We hung up. Susan was in the bathroom doing makeup. I stuck my head in and said, 'I have to go out and work for a while.' She was doing something with a long thin pencilish-looking item to the corner of her mouth. She said, 'Unh-huh,' and kept on doing it.

When Susan concentrates, she concentrates. I put on my white wide-wale corduroy pants, my dark-blue all-wool Pendleton shirt, and my Herman survivors. I put my gun in its hip holster on my belt; I got into my jacket, turned up the fleece collar, pulled on my watch cap, slipped on my gloves, and went forth into the storm.

Except for the snow, which still fell hard, the city was nearly motionless. There was no traffic. The streets were snow-covered, maybe two feet deep, and the snow had drifted in places high enough to bury a parked car. Arlington Street had been partially plowed, and the walking was easier. I turned right on Beacon and headed up the hill, leaning now into the wind and the snow. I pulled my watch cap down over my ears and forehead. It didn't look rakish, but one must compromise occasionally with nature. An enormous yellow bulldozer with an enclosed cab and a plow blade approximately the size of Rhode Island came churning slowly down Beacon Street. There were no people and no dogs, just me and the bulldozer and the snow. When the bulldozer passed, I had to climb over a snowbank to get out of the way of the plow spill, but after it had passed, the walking was much better. I walked up the middle of Beacon Street with the old elegant brick houses on my left and the empty Common on my right. I could see the houses okay, but ten feet past the iron fence the Common disappeared into the haze of snow and strong wind.

At the top of the hill I could see the State House but not the gold dome. Nothing was open. It was downhill from there and a little easier. By the time I got to the Parker House, where Beacon ends at Tremont, I was cold and a little strange with the empty swirling silence in the middle of the city.

There were people hanging around in the lobby of the Parker House and the coffee shop on the Tremont Street side was nearly full. I spotted Julie Wells alone at a table for two by the window looking out at the snow.

She had on a silver ski parka which she'd unzipped but not removed; the hood was thrown back, and the fur trim tangled with the edges of her hair. Underneath the parka she wore a white turtleneck sweater, and with her big gold earrings and her long eyelashes she looked like maybe 1.8 million. Susan was a two million.

I rolled my watch cap back up to rakish and then walked over and sat down across from her. The Parker House used to be Old Boston and kind of an institution. It had fallen on hard times and was now making a comeback, but the coffee shop with the window on Tremont Street was a good place. I unzipped my coat.

'Good morning,' I said.

She smiled without much pleasure and said, 'I am glad to see you. I really didn't know who else to call.'

'I hope you didn't have to walk far,' I said. 'Even an Olympic walker like myself experienced some moments of discomfort.'

Julie said, 'There's someone after me.'

I said, 'I don't blame him.'

She said, 'There really is. I've seen him outside my apartment. He's followed me to and from work.'

'You know the cops have been looking for you.'

'About Rachel?'

I nodded. The waitress came, and I ordered coffee and whole wheat toast. There was a plate with most of an omelet still left on it in front of Julie Wells. The waitress went away.

'I know about the police,' she said. 'I called the agency, and they said the police had been there, too. But they wouldn't follow me around like that.'

I shrugged. 'Why not tell the cops about this guy that's

following you. If it's one of them, they'll know. If it's not, they can look into it.'

She shook her head.

'No cops?'

She shook her head again.

'Why not?'

She poked at the omelet with the tines of her fork, moving a scrap of egg around to the other side of the plate.

'You're not just hiding out from the guy that's following you?' I said.

'No.'

'You don't want to talk with the cops either.'

She started to cry. Her shoulders shook a little, and her lower lip trembled a little, and some tears formed in her eyes. It was discreet crying though – nothing the other customers would notice.

'I don't know what to do,' she said. 'I don't want to be involved in all of this. I want people to leave me alone.'

'You got any thoughts on where Rachel might be?' I said.

She blew her nose in a pink Kleenex and inhaled shakily.

'What shall I do?' she said to me. 'I don't know anyone else to ask.'

'You know where Rachel is?'

'No, of course not. How would I? We were friends, lovers if you'd rather, but we weren't in love or anything. And if people—'

'You don't want people to know that you're a lesbian.'

She made a little shiver. 'God, I hate the word. It's so ... clinical, like classifying an odd plant.'

'But you still don't want it known?'

'Well, I'm not ashamed. You put it so baldly. I have made a life choice that's not like yours, or some others, and I have no reason to be ashamed. It's as natural as anyone else.'

'So why not talk with the cops? Don't you want to find Rachel Wallace?'

She clasped her hands together and pressed the knuckles against her mouth. Tears formed again. 'Oh, God, poor Rachel. Do you think she's alive?'

The waitress brought my toast and coffee.

When she left, I said, 'I don't have any way to know. I have to assume she is, because to assume she isn't leaves me nothing to do.'

'And you're looking for her?'

'I'm looking for her.'

'If I knew anything that would help, I'd say so. But what good will it do Rachel to have my name smeared in the papers? To have the people at the model agency—'

'I don't know what good,' I said. 'I don't know what you know. I don't know why someone is following you, or was – I assume you've lost him.'

She nodded. 'I got away from him on the subway.'

'So who would he be? Why would he follow you? It's an awful big coincidence that Rachel is taken and then someone follows you.'

'I don't know, I don't know anything. What if they want

to kidnap me? I don't know what to do.' She stared out the window at the empty snow-covered street.

'Why not stay with your mother and brother?' I said.

She looked back at me slowly. I ate a triangle of toast.

'What do you know about my mother and brother?'

'I know their names and I know their politics and I know their attitude toward Rachel Wallace, and I can guess their attitude toward you if they knew that you and Rachel were lovers.'

'Have you been . . . did you . . . you don't have the right to . . .'

'I haven't mentioned you to them. I did mention you to the cops, but only when I had to, quite recently.'

'Why did you have to?'

'Because I'm looking for Rachel, and I'll do anything I have to to find her. When I figured out that you were Lawrence English's sister, I thought it might be a clue. It might help them find her. They're looking, too.'

'You think my brother—'

'I think he's in this somewhere. His chauffeur hired two guys to run me and Rachel off the road one night in Lynn. Your brother organized a picket line when she spoke in Belmont. Your brother has said she's an ungodly corruption or some such. And he's the head of an organization of Ritz crackers that would be capable of such things.'

'I didn't used to know I was gay,' she said. 'I just thought I was not very affectionate. I got married. I felt guilty about being cold. I even did therapy. It didn't work. I was not a loving person. We were divorced. He said I was like a wax apple. I looked wonderful, but there was nothing inside – no nourishment. I went to a support group meeting for people recently divorced, and I met a woman and cared for her, and we developed a relationship, and I found out I wasn't empty. I could love. I could feel passion. It was maybe the moment in my life. We made love and I felt. I' – she looked out the window again, and I ate another piece of toast – 'I reached orgasm. It was as if, as if . . . I don't know what it was as if.'

'As if a guilty verdict had been overturned?'

She nodded. 'Yes. Yes. I wasn't bad. I wasn't cold. I had been trying to love the wrong things.'

'But Mom and brother?'

'You've met them?'

'Brother,' I said. 'Not yet Momma.'

'They could never understand. They could never accept it. It would be just the worst thing that could be for them. I wish for them – maybe for me, too – I wish it could have been different, but it can't, and it's better to be what I am than to be failing at what I am not. But they mustn't ever know. That's why I can't go to the police. I can't let them know. I don't mind the rest of the world. It's them. They can't know. I don't know what they would do.'

'Maybe they'd kidnap Rachel,' I said.

27

The waitress said, 'May I get you anything else?'

I shook my head, so did Julie. The waitress put the check down, near me, and I put a ten down on top of it.

Julie said, 'They wouldn't. They couldn't do that. They wouldn't know what to do.'

'They could hire a consultant. Their chauffeur has done time. Name's Mingo Mulready, believe it or not, and he would know what to do.'

'But they don't know.'

'Maybe they don't. Or maybe the guy that was following you around was your brother's. You haven't been living at home.'

'Spenser, I'm thirty years old.'

'Get along with the family?'

'No. They didn't approve of my marriage. They didn't approve of my divorce. They hated me going to Goucher. They hate me being a model. I couldn't live with them.'

'They worry about you?'

She shrugged. Now that she was thinking, she wasn't crying, and her face looked more coherent. 'I suppose they did,' she said. 'Lawrence likes to play father and man of the house, and Mother lets him. I guess they think I'm dissolute and weak and uncommitted – that kind of thing.'

. 'Why would they have a thug like Mulready driving them around?'

Julie shrugged her shoulders. 'Lawrence is all caught up in his Vigilance Committee. He gets into situations, I guess, where he feels he needs a bodyguard. I assume this Mulready is someone who would do that.'

'Not as well as he used to,' I said.

The waitress picked up my ten and brought back some change on a saucer.

'If they did take Rachel,' I said, 'where would they keep her?'

'I don't know.'

'Sure you do. If you were your brother and you had kidnaped Rachel Wallace, where would you keep her?'

'Oh, for God's sake, Spenser . . .'

'Think,' I said. 'Think about it. Humor me.'

'This is ridiculous.'

'I walked a half-mile through a blizzard because you asked me to,' I said. 'I didn't say it was ridiculous.'

She nodded. 'The house,' she said.

The waitress came back and said, 'Can I get you anything else?'

I shook my head. 'We better vacate,' I said to Julie, 'before she gets ugly.'

Julie nodded. We left the coffee shop and found an overstuffed loveseat in the lobby.

'Where in the house?' I said.

'Have you seen it?'

'Yeah. I was out there a few days ago.'

'Well, you know how big it is. There's probably twenty rooms. There's a great big cellar. There's the chauffeur's quarters over the garage and extra rooms in the attic.'

'Wouldn't the servants notice?'

'They wouldn't have to. The cook never leaves the kitchen, and the maid would have no reason to go into some parts of the house. We had only the cook and the maid when I was there.'

'And of course old Mingo.'

'They hired him after I left. I don't know him.'

'Tell you what,' I said. 'We'll go back to my place. It's just over on Marlborough Street, and we'll draw a map of your brother's house.'

'It's my mother's,' Julie said.

'Whoever,' I said. 'We'll make a map, and later on I'll go take a look.'

'How will you do that?'

'First the map. Then the B-and-E plans. Come on.'

'I don't know if I can make a map.'

'Sure you can. I'll help and we'll talk. You'll remember.'

'And we're going to your apartment?'

'Yes. It's quite safe. I have a woman staying with me who'll see that I don't molest you. And on the walk down we'll be too bundled up.'

'I didn't mean that.'

'Okay, let's go.'

We pushed out into the snow again. It seemed to be

lessening, but the wind was whipping it around so much, it was hard to tell. A half-block up Beacon Street Julie took my arm, and she hung on all the way up over the hill and down to Marlborough. Other than two huge yellow pieces of snow equipment that clunked and waddled through the snow, we were all that moved.

When we got to my apartment, Susan was on the couch by the fire reading a book by Robert Coles. She wore a pair of jeans she'd left there two weeks ago and one of my gray T-shirts with the size, XL, printed in red letters on the front. It hung almost to her knees.

I introduced them and took Julie's coat and hung it in the hall closet. As I went by the bathroom, I noticed Susan's lingerie hanging on the shower rod to dry. It made me speculate about what was under the jeans, but I put it from me. I was working. I got a pad of lined yellow paper, legal size, from a drawer in the kitchen next to the phone and a small translucent plastic artist's triangle and a black ballpoint pen, and Julie and I sat at the counter in my kitchen for three hours and diagrammed her mother's house – not only the rooms, but what was in them.

'I haven't been there in a year,' she said at one point.

'I know, but people don't usually rearrange the big pieces. The beds and sofas and stuff are usually where they've always been.'

We made an overall diagram of the house and then did each room on a separate sheet. I numbered all the rooms and keyed them to the separate sheets.

'Why do you want to know all this? Furniture and every-thing?'

'It's good to know what you can. I'm not sure even what I'm up to. I'm just gathering information. There's so much that I can't know, and so many things I can't predict, that I like to get everything I can in order so when the unpredictable stuff comes along I can concentrate on that.'

Susan made a large plate of ham sandwiches while we finished up our maps, and we had them with coffee in front of the fire.

'You make a good fire for a broad,' I said to Susan.

'It's easy,' Susan said, 'I rubbed two dry sexists together.'

'This is a wonderful sandwich,' Julie said to Susan.

'Yes. Mr Macho here gets the ham from someplace out in eastern New York State.'

'Millerton,' I said. 'Cured with salt and molasses. Hickory-smoked, no nitrates.'

Julie looked at Susan. 'Ah, what about that other matter?'

'The shadow?' I said.

She nodded.

'You can go home and let him spot you, and then I'll take him off your back.'

'Home?'

'Sure. Once he lost you, if he's really intent on staying with you, he'll go and wait outside your home until you show up. What else can he do?'

'I guess nothing. He wouldn't be there today, I wouldn't think.'

442

'Unless he was there yesterday,' Susan said. 'The governor's been on TV. No cars allowed on the highway. No buses are running. No trains. Nothing coming into the city.'

'I don't want to go home,' Julie said.

'Or you can stay hiding out for a while, but I'd like to know where to get you.'

She shook her head.

'Look, Julie,' I said. 'You got choices, but they are not limitless. You are part of whatever happened to Rachel Wallace. I don't know what part, but I'm not going to let go of you. I don't have that much else. I need to be able to find you.'

She looked at me and at Susan, who was sipping her coffee from a big brown mug, holding it in both hands with her nose half-buried in the cup and her eyes on the fire. Julie nodded her head three times.

'Okay,' she said. 'I'm in an apartment at 164 Tremont. One of the girls at the agency is in Chicago, and she let me stay while she's away. Fifth floor.'

'I'll walk you over,' I said.

28

The day after the big blizzard was beautiful, the way it always is. The sun is shining its ass off, and the snow is still white, and no traffic is out, and people and dogs are walking everywhere and being friendly during shared duress.

Susan and I walked out to Boylston and up toward Mass. Ave. She had bought a funky-looking old raccoon coat with padded shoulders when we'd gone antiquing in New Hampshire in November, and she was wearing it with big furry boots and a woolen hat with a big pom-pom. She looked like a cross between Annette Funicello and Joan Crawford.

We'd been living together for two and a half days, and if I had known where Rachel Wallace was, I would have been having a very nice time. But I didn't know where Rachel Wallace was, and what was worse, I had a suspicion where she might be, and I couldn't get there. I had called Quirk and told him what I knew. He couldn't move against a man of English's clout without some probable cause, and we agreed I had none. I told him I didn't know where Julie Wells was staying. He didn't believe me, but the pressure of the snow emergency was distracting the whole department, and no one came over with a thumb-screw to interrogate me.

So Susan and I walked up Boylston Street to see if there was a store open where she could buy some underclothes and maybe a shirt or two, and I walked with her in a profound funk. All traffic was banned from all highways. No trains were moving.

Susan bought some very flossy-looking lingerie at Saks, and a pair of Levi's jeans and two blouses. We were back out on Boylston when she said, 'Want to go home and model the undies?'

'I don't think they'd fit me,' I said.

'I didn't mean you,' she said.

I said, 'God damn it, I'll walk out there.'

'Where?'

'I'll walk out to Belmont.'

'Just to avoid modeling the undies?'

I shook my head. 'It's what? Twelve, fifteen miles? Walk about three miles an hour. I'll be there in four or five hours.'

'You're sure she's there?'

'No. But she might be, and if she is, it's partly my fault. I have to look.'

'It's a lot of other people's fault much more than yours. Especially the people who took her.'

'I know, but if I'd been with her, they wouldn't have taken her.'

Susan nodded.

'Why not call the Belmont Police?' she said.

'Same as with Quirk. They can't just charge in there. They have to have a warrant. And there has to be some reasonable suspicion, and I don't have anything to give them. And . . . I don't know. They might screw it up.'

'Which means that you want to do it yourself.'

'Maybe.'

'Even if it endangers her?'

'I don't want to endanger her. I trust me more than I trust anyone else. Her life is on the line here. I want me to be the one who's in charge.'

'And because you have to even up with the people that took her,' Susan said, 'you're willing to go after her alone and risk the whole thing, including both your lives, because your honor has been tarnished, or you think it has.'

I shook my head. 'I don't want some Belmont cop in charge of this whose last bust was two ninth-graders with an ounce of Acapulco gold.'

'And Quirk or Frank Belson can't go because they don't have jurisdiction, and they don't have a warrant and all of the above?'

I nodded.

We turned the corner onto Arlington and walked along in the middle of the bright street, like a scene from Currier and Ives.

'Why don't you find Hawk and have him go with you?'

I shook my head.

'Why not?'

'I'm going alone.'

'I thought you would. What if something happens to you?'

'Like what?'

'Like suppose you sneak in there and someone shoots you. If you're right, you are dealing with people capable of that.'

'Then you tell Quirk everything you know. And tell Hawk to find Rachel Wallace for me.'

'I don't even know how to get in touch with Hawk. Do I call that health club on the waterfront?'

'If something happens to me, Hawk will show up and see if you need anything.'

We were on the corner of Marlborough Street. Susan stopped and looked at me. 'You know that so certainly?'

'Yes.'

She shook her head and kept shaking it. 'You people are like members of a religion or a cult. You have little rituals and patterns you observe that nobody else understands.'

'What people?'

'People like you. Hawk, Quirk, that state policeman you met when the boy was kidnaped.'

'Healy.'

'Yes, Healy. The little trainer at the Harbor Health Club. All of you. You're as complexly programmed as male wildebeests, and you have no common sense at all.'

'Wildebeests?' I said.

'Or Siamese fighting fish.'

'I prefer to think *lion, panther* maybe.'

We walked to my apartment. 'I suppose,' Susan said, 'we could settle for ox. Not as strong but nearly as smart.'

Susan went to the apartment. I went to the basement and got some more firewood from the storage area and carried an armful up the back stairs. It was early afternoon. We had lunch. We watched the news. The travel ban was still with us.

'At least wait until morning,' Susan said. 'Get an early start.'

'And until then?'

'We can read by the fire.'

'When that gets boring, I was thinking we could make shadow pictures on the wall. Ever see my rooster?'

Susan said, 'I've never heard it called that.' I put my arm around her shoulder and squeezed her against me and we began to giggle. We spent the rest of the day before the fire on the couch. Mostly we read.

29

By seven thirty the next morning I was on the road. I had a flashlight in my hip pocket, a short prying tool stuck in my belt, my packet of floor plans in my shirt pocket, and my usual jackknife and gun. Susan kissed me goodbye without getting up, and I left without hearing any more wildebeest remarks. I walked up Marlborough to the Mass. Ave. Bridge along a quiet and narrow lane, one plow-blade wide, with the snow head-high on either side of me. Below the bridge the Charles was frozen and solid white. No sign of the river. Memorial Drive had one lane cleared in either direction, and I turned west. I had learned to walk some years ago at government expense when I had walked from Pusan to the Yalu River and then back. I moved right along. After the first mile or so I had a nice rhythm and even felt just a trickle of sweat along the line of my backbone.

It was shorter than I thought. I was on Trapelo Road in Belmont by ten forty-five. By eleven I was standing two houses away from the English place, across the street. Now if I found Rachel Wallace, I wouldn't have to walk back. The cops would drive me. Maybe.

The house was three stories high. Across the front was

a wide veranda. A long wing came off the back, and at the end of the wing there was a carriage house with a little pointed cupola on top. Mingo probably parked the family Caddies in the carriage house. There was a back door, which led through a back hall into the kitchen, according to Julie. Off the back hall there were back stairs. The veranda turned one corner and ran back along the short side of the house, the one without the wing. Big french doors opened out onto the library, where I'd talked with English before. The yard wasn't as big as you'd expect with a house like that. Last century when they'd built the house there was plenty of land, so no one had wanted it. Now there wasn't and they did. The neighbor's house was maybe fifty feet away on one side, a street was ten feet away on the other, and the backyard was maybe a hundred feet deep. A chainlink fence surrounded the property, except in front, where there was a stone wall, broken by the driveway. There was no sign of the driveway now and very little of the fence in the high snow. It took me nearly two and a half hours of clambering about through snowbanks and side streets to get all of the layout of the grounds and to look at the house from all sides. When I got through, I was sweaty underneath my jacket, and the shoulder rig I was wearing chafed under my left arm. I figured it was better than walking ten miles with the gun jiggling in a hip holster.

There were people out now, shoveling and walking to the store for supplies, and a lot of laughter and neighborly hellos and a kind of siege mentality that made everyone your buddy. I studied the house. The shutters on the top-floor windows were closed, all of them, on the left side and in front. I strolled around the corner and up the side street to the right of the house. The top-floor shutters were closed there, too. I went on down the road till I could see the back shutters.

I knew where I'd look first if I ever got in there. That was the only detail to work out. Julie had told me there was a burglar alarm, and that her mother had always set it before she went to bed. Going in before Mom went to bed would seem to be the answer to that. It would help if I knew who was in there. Mingo, probably. I saw what looked like his tan Thunderbird barely showing through a snowdrift back by the carriage house. There'd be a maid or two probably, and Momma and Lawrence. Whoever was in there when the storm came would be in there now. There were no tracks, no sign of shoveling, just the smooth white sea of snow out of which the old Victorian house rose like a nineteenth-century ship.

I thought about getting in. Trying the old I'm-from-the-power-company trick. But the odds were bad. English knew me, Mingo knew me. At least one of the maids knew me. If I got caught and they got wise, things would be worse. They might kill Rachel. They might kill me, if they could. And that would leave Rachel with no one looking for her the way I was looking for her. Hawk would find her eventually, but he wouldn't have my motivation. Hawk's way would be prompt though. Maybe he'd find her quicker. He'd hold English out a twenty-storey window till English said where Rachel was.

I thought about that. It wasn't a bad way. The question was, how many people would I have to go through to hang English out the window? There were probably at least five people in there – Mingo, English, Momma, and two maids – but the whole Vigilance Committee could be in there sharpening their pikes for all I knew.

It was two o'clock. Nothing was happening. People like English wouldn't have to come out till April. They'd have food in the pantry and booze in the cellar and fuel in the tank and nothing to make winter inconvenient. Did they have a hostage in the attic? Why hadn't there been some kind of communication? Why no more ransom notes or threats about canceling the books or anything? Had they been snowed out? I didn't know any of the answers to any of the questions, and I could only think of one way to find out.

At two fifteen I waded through the snow, sometimes waist-deep, and floundered up to the front door and rang the bell. If they knew me, they knew me. I'd deal with that if it happened. A maid answered.

I said, 'Mr English, please.'

She said, 'Who may I say is calling?'

I said, 'Joseph E. McCarthy.'

She said, 'Just a moment, please,' and started to close the door.

I said, 'Wait a minute. It's cold, and we've had a blizzard. Couldn't I wait in the front hall?'

And she hesitated and I smiled at her disarmingly but

a bit superior, and she nodded and said, 'Of course, sir. I'm sorry. Come in.'

I went in. She closed the door behind me and went off down the corridor and through a door and closed it behind her. I went up the front stairs as quietly as I could. There was a landing and then a short left turn, then three steps to the upstairs hall. Actually there were two upstairs halls. One ran from front to back and the other, like the cross of a capital T, ran the width of the house and led into the wing hall.

I had the general layout in my head. I'd spent most of my time in front of yesterday's fire looking at Julie's diagrams. The stairway to the attic was down the hall in a small back bedroom. The house was quiet. Faintly somewhere I could hear television. There was a smell of violet sachet and mothballs in the small bedroom. The door to the stairs was where it should have been. It was a green wooden door made of narrow vertical boards with a small bead along one edge. It was closed. There was a padlock on it.

Behind me I heard no hue and cry. The maid would be returning now to say that Mr English didn't know a Joseph E. McCarthy, or that the one he knew wasn't likely to be calling here. I took my small pry bar from my belt. The padlock hasp wasn't very new, and neither was the door. The maid would look and not see me and be puzzled and would look outside and perhaps around downstairs a little before she reported to English that Mr McCarthy had left. I wedged the blade of the pry bar under the hasp and pulled the whole thing out of the wood, screws and all. It probably wasn't much louder than the clap of Creation. It just seemed so because I was tense. The door opened in, and the stairs went up at a right angle, very steep, very narrow treads and high risers. I closed the door and went up the stairs with hand and feet touching like a hungry monkey. Upstairs the attic was pitch-black. I got out my flashlight and snapped it on and held it in my teeth to keep my hands free. I had the pry bar in my right hand.

The attic was rough and unfinished except for what appeared to be two rooms, one at each gabled end. All the windows had plywood over them. I took one quick look and noticed the plywood was screwed in, not nailed. Someone had wanted it to be hard to remove. I tried one door at the near end of the attic. It was locked. I went and tried the other. It opened, and I went in holding the pry bar like a weapon. Except for an old metal-frame bed and a big steamer trunk and three cardboard boxes it was empty. The windows were covered with plywood.

If Rachel was up here, she was back in the other room at the gable end. And she was here – I could feel her. I could feel my insides clench with the certainty that she was behind that other door. I went back to it. There was a padlock, this one new, with a new hasp. I listened. No sound from the room. Downstairs I could hear footsteps. I rammed the pry bar in under the hasp and wrenched the thing loose. The adrenaline was pumping, and I popped the whole thing off and ten feet across the attic floor with one lunge. There was saliva on my chin from holding the flashlight.

I took the light in my hand and shoved into the room. It stunk. I swept the flashlight around. On an ironframe bed with a gray blanket around her, half-raised, was Rachel Wallace, and she looked just awful. Her hair was a mess, and she had no makeup, and her eyes were swollen. I reversed the flashlight and shone it on my face.

'It's Spenser,' I said.

'Oh, my God,' she said. Her voice was hoarse.

The lights went on suddenly. There must have been a downstairs switch, and I'd missed it. The whole attic was bright. I snicked off the flashlight and put it in my pocket and took out my gun and said, 'Get under the bed.'

Rachel rolled onto the floor and under the bed. Her feet were bare. I heard footsteps coming up the stairs, and then they stopped. They'd spotted the ruptured door. It sounded like three sets of footsteps. I looked up. The light in this room came from a bare bulb that hung from a zinc fixture in the ceiling. I reached up with the pry bar and smashed the bulb. The room was dark except for the light from beyond the door.

Outside, a woman's voice said, 'Who is in there?' It was an old voice but not quavery and not weak. I didn't say anything. Rachel made no sound.

The voice said, 'You are in trespass in there. I want you out. There are two armed men out here. You have no chance.'

I got down on the floor and snaked along toward the door.

In the light at the head of the stairs was Mingo with a double-barreled shotgun and English with an automatic pistol. Between them and slightly forward was a woman who looked like a man, and an ugly, mean man at that. She was maybe five eight and heavy, with a square massive face and short gray hair. Her eyebrows came straight across with almost no arch and met over the bridge of her nose. They were black.

'Give yourself up,' she said. There was no uncertainty in her voice and certainly no fear. She was used to people doing what she said.

From the dark I said, 'It's over, Momma. People know I'm here. They know I was looking for Rachel Wallace. And I found her. Throw down the weapons, and I'll bring her out and take her home. Then I'll call the cops. You'll have that much time to run.'

'Run?' Momma said. 'We want you out of there and we'll have you out now. You and that atrocious queer.' Mingo had brought the shotgun to the ready and was looking into the room.

I said 'Last chance,' and rolled right, over once, and came up with my gun raised and steadied with my left hand. Mingo fired one barrel toward where I had been, and I shot him under the right eye. He fell backwards down the stairs. English began to shoot into the room – vaguely, I guess in the direction of my muzzle flash, but panicky and without much time to aim. He squeezed off four rounds into the dark room and I shot him, twice, carefully. One bullet caught him in the forehead and the second in the throat. He made no sound and fell forward. He was probably dead before he landed. I saw Momma start to bend, and I thought she

456

might keel over, but then I realized she was going for the gun, and I lunged to my feet and jumped three jumps and kicked it away from her, and yanked her to her feet by the back of her collar. There was a little bubble of saliva at the corner of her mouth, and she began to gouge at my eyes with her fingers. I held her at arm's length – my arms were longer than hers – and looked down at Mingo in a tangle at the foot of the stairs. He was dead. He had the look. You see it enough, you know.

I said, 'Mrs English, they're dead. Both of them. Your son is dead.'

She spat at me and dug her fingernails into my wrist and tried to bite my arm. I said, 'Mrs English, I'm going to hit you.'

She bit my arm. It didn't hurt, because she was trying to bite through my coat, but it made me mad. I put my gun away, and I slapped her hard across the face. She began to scream at me. No words, just scream and claw and bite and I hit her with my right fist, hard. She fell down and began to snivel, her face buried in her son's dead back. I picked up English's gun and stuck it in my pocket and went down the stairs and got Mingo's shotgun and jacked the remaining shell out and put that in my pocket and went back up the stairs.

Rachel was standing in the doorway of the room, looking at the carnage and squinting in the light. She had the gray blanket wrapped around her and held with both hands closed at the neck.

I walked over to her and said, 'Okay, Jane Eyre, I got you.'

Tears began to run down her face, and I put my arms around her, and she cried. And I cried. In between crying I said, 'I got you. I got you.'

She didn't say anything.

30

The first cops to show were cruiser people – three cars'-worth despite the snow emergency – and one of them was Foley, the young cop with the ribbons and the wise-guy face. They came up the attic stairs with guns drawn, directed by the frightened maid who'd called them. He was first. He knew who Rachel was the first look he took.

'Son of a bitch,' he said. 'You found her.'

His partner with the belly squatted down beside English and felt his neck. Then he and another prowlie half-lifted, half-helped Momma English off her son's body. While the prowlie held her, the pot-bellied cop got down on his hands and knees and listened to English's chest. He looked at the young cop and shook his head.

'Gonzo,' he said. 'So's the horse at the bottom.' He nodded at Mingo, still sprawled at the foot of the attic stairs. They must have had to climb over him. 'Two in the head,' he said. He stood up and looked at me. I still had my arms around Rachel. 'What the hell you crying for?' he said. 'Think how these guys feel.'

Foley spun around. 'Shut up,' he said. 'I know why he's crying. You don't. Close your fucking mouth up.'

The older cop shook his head and didn't say anything.

Foley said to me, 'You ace these two guys?'

I nodded.

Foley said, 'Chief will want to talk with you about all this. Her, too.'

'Not now,' I said, 'now I'm taking her home.'

Foley looked at me for maybe thirty seconds. 'Yeah,' he said. 'Take her out of here.'

The cop with the belly said, 'For crissake, the chief will fry our ass. This clown blasts two guys, one of them Lawrence English, and he walks while we stand around. Foley, we got two stiffs here.'

I said to Foley, 'I need a ride.'

He nodded. 'Come on.'

His partner said, 'Foley, are you fucking crazy?'

Foley put his face close to the older cop's face. 'Benny,' he said, 'you're okay. You're not a bad cop. But you don't know how to act, and you're too old to learn.'

'Chief will have your badge for this and mine for letting you do it.'

Foley said, 'Ain't your fault, Benny. You couldn't stop me.'

Mom English said, 'If you let that murderer escape and allow that corrupt degenerate to go with him, I'll have every one of your badges.'

There were four other cops besides Foley and Benny. One of them had gone downstairs to call in. One was supporting Mrs English. The other two stood uncertainly. One of them had his gun out, although it hung at his side and he'd probably forgotten he had it in his hand.

'They murdered my son,' she said. Her voice was flat

460

and heavy. 'She has vomited filth and corruption long enough. She has to be stopped. We would have stopped her if he hadn't interfered. And you must. She is a putrefaction, a cancerous foul sore.' The voice stayed flat but a trickle of saliva came from the left corner of her mouth. She breathed heavily through her nose. 'She has debauched and destroyed innocent women and lured them into unspeakable acts.' Her nose began to run a little.

I said, 'Foley, we're going.'

He nodded and pushed past Benny. We followed. Rachel still had the blanket around her.

Momma shrieked at us, 'She stole my daughter.'

One of the other cops said, 'Jesus Christ, Fole.'

Foley looked at him, and his eyes were hot. Then he went down the attic stairs, and Rachel and I went with him. In the front hall on the first floor the two maids stood, silent and fidgety. The cop on the phone was talking to someone at headquarters and as we went past he glanced up and widened his eyes.

'Where the hell you going?' he said.

Foley shook his head.

'Chief says he's on his way, Fole.'

We kept going. On the porch I picked Rachel up – she was still in her bare feet – and carried her through the floundering waist-deep snow. The cruisers were there in front with the blue lights rotating.

Foley said, 'First one.'

We got in – Foley in front, me and Rachel in back. He hit the siren, and we pulled out.

'Where?' Foley said.

'Boston,' I said. 'Marlborough Street, Arlington Street end.'

Foley left the siren wailing all the way, and with no traffic but cops and plows we made it in fifteen minutes. He pulled into Marlborough Street from Arlington and went up it the wrong way two doors to my apartment.

'You ain't here when we want you,' Foley said, 'and I'll be working next week in a carwash.'

I got out with Rachel. I had been holding her all the way. I looked at Foley and nodded once.

'Yeah,' he said.

He spun the wheels pulling away, slammed the car into snowbanks on both sides of the street making a U-turn, and spun the wheels some more as he skidded out into Arlington.

I carried Rachel up to my front door and leaned on my bell till Susan said, 'Who is it?' over the intercom.

I said, 'Me,' never at a loss for repartee.

She buzzed and I pushed and in we went. I called the elevator with my elbow and punched my floor with the same elbow and banged on my door with the toe of my boot. Susan opened it. She saw Rachel.

'Oh,' she said. 'Isn't that good!'

We went in and I put Rachel down on the couch.

I said, 'Would you like a drink?'

She said, 'Yes, very much.'

'Bourbon, okay?'

'Yes, on the rocks, please.'

She still had her gray blanket tightly wrapped around

her. I went out in the kitchen and got a bottle of Wild Turkey and three glasses and a bucket of ice and came back out. I poured each of us a drink. Susan had kept the fire going and it went well with the Wild Turkey. Each of us drank.

'You need a doctor?' I said.

'No,' she said. 'I don't think so. I was not abused in that sense.'

'Would you like to talk about it?' Susan said.

'Yes,' Rachel said, 'I think I would. I shall talk about it and probably write about it. But right now I should very much like to bathe and put on clean clothes, and then perhaps eat something.' She drank some bourbon. 'I've not,' she said, 'been eating particularly well lately.' She smiled slightly.

'Sure,' I said. 'Spenser's the name, cooking's the game.'

I started to get up. 'No,' she said. 'Stay here a minute, both of you, while I finish this drink.'

And so we sat – me and Rachel on the couch, Susan in the wing chair – and sipped the bourbon and looked at the fire. There was no traffic noise and it was quiet except for the hiss of the fire and the tick of the old steeple clock with wooden works that my father had given me years ago.

Rachel finished her drink. 'I would like another,' she said, 'to take into the bath with me.'

I mixed it for her.

She said, 'Thank you.'

Susan said, 'If you want to give me your old clothes, I

463

can put them through the wash for you. Lancelot here has all the latest conveniences.'

Rachel shook her head. 'No,' she said. 'I haven't any clothes. They took them. I have only the blanket.'

Susan said, 'Well, I've got some things you can wear.'

Rachel smiled. 'Thank you,' she said.

Susan showed Rachel to the bathroom door. 'There are clean towels,' Susan said. 'While he was out I was being domestic.'

Rachel went in and closed the door. I heard the water begin to run in the tub. Susan walked over to me on the couch.

'How are you?' she said.

'Okay,' I said.

'Was it bad?'

'Yeah,' I said.

'Was it English?'

I nodded. She rubbed my head – the way you tousle a dog.

'What was that old song?' she said. '"Joltin' Joe DiMaggio, we want you on our side."'

'Yeah, except around here we used to sing, "Who's better than his brother Joe? Dominic DiMaggio."'

She rubbed my head again, 'Well, anyway,' she said. 'I want *you* on my side, cutie.'

'You're just saying that,' I said, 'because DiMaggio's not around.'

'That's true,' she said.

31

While Rachel was in the bath I made red beans and rice. Susan put out the rest of the cornbread and I chopped green peppers and scallions. When Rachel finally came to dinner, she had put on some of Susan's makeup and a pair of Susan's jeans and a sweat shirt of mine that was considerably big. The sleeves were rolled up and made a bulky ring around her arms above the elbow. Her hair had been washed and blown dry and looked very straight.

I said, 'You want some more bourbon?'

She said yes.

I gave her some more, with ice, and she sat at the table in the dining area and sipped it. I served the beans and rice with the chopped vegetables and some canned chopped tomato on top and put out a dish of grated cheddar cheese. Susan and I drank beer with the meal. Rachel stayed with the bourbon. Like the martinis she'd been drinking when we met first, the bourbon seemed to have no effect.

There was very little talk for the first few minutes. Rachel ate rapidly. When she had nearly finished, she said, 'Julie is that woman's daughter, did you know that?'

'Yes,' I said.

'They took me because of her, you know.'

'I thought they might have.'

'They wanted to punish me for corrupting their girl child. They wanted to separate us. They wanted to be sure no one would ever see Julie with me. The idea that her daughter could be a lesbian was more than she could think. I think she thought that if I weren't there, Julie would revert to her normal self.'

She said *normal* with a lot of bite in it.

'It wasn't anything to do with your books?' Susan said.

'Maybe it was, too,' Rachel said. 'Especially the man. I think he was more comfortable with the kidnaping if it was for a cause. He called it a political act.'

'And what did they plan to do with you?' I said.

'I don't know. I don't think they knew. I think the one that actually took me, the big one that works for them . . .'

'Mingo,' I said. 'Mingo Mulready.'

'I think he wanted to kill me.'

'Sure,' I said. 'You'd make a damaging witness if you survived.'

Rachel nodded. 'And they didn't conceal their identities. I saw them all, and they told me they were Julie's people.'

'Did they treat you badly?' Susan said.

Rachel looked down at her plate. It was empty.

I said, 'Would you like more?'

She shook her head. 'No. It's very good, but I'm full, thank you.'

'More bourbon?' I said.

'You know, that's the thing you've said to me most, since I got here. You must have great faith in its restorative powers.'

'It's a way of being solicitous,' I said.

'I know,' Rachel said. 'And yes, I'll have another. I, too, have great faith in its restorative powers.'

I got her the bourbon.

'I wonder why they didn't kill me,' she said. 'I was afraid they would. I'd lie up there in the dark, and each time they came I'd wonder if they had come to kill me.'

'Probably didn't have the balls,' I said. 'Probably would have had to find a way to maneuver themselves into having Mingo do it.'

'Like what?' Rachel said.

'Oh, get up some kind of ultimatum and present it to the cops. An ultimatum that couldn't be met. Then they could say it wasn't their fault. They'd been left no choice, and they'd had to do it to stop your poison because the officials were duped by the Antichrist, or the commies, or Gore Vidal, or whoever.'

'The mother would have wanted to most,' Rachel said. She looked at Susan. 'They didn't mistreat me in the sense of torture or anything. I wasn't tied up or beaten. But the mother wanted to humiliate me. And the son. Julie's brother.'

'Lawrence,' I said.

'Yes, Lawrence.' She shivered.

'What did Lawrence do?' Susan said. Her voice was quite soft.

'He used to come up with my food and sit beside me on the bed and ask me about my relations with Julie. He wanted explicit detail. And he would touch me.'

I said, 'Jesus Christ.'

'I think he got excited by the talk of my lovemaking with Julie. And he would say in his position he rarely had the opportunity to be with a woman, how he had to be careful, that he was in an exposed position and couldn't risk being compromised by a woman. And then he would touch me.' She stopped.

Susan said, very quietly, 'Did he rape you?'

'Not in the traditional sense,' Rachel said. 'He—' She paused, looking for the right way to say it. 'He couldn't in the traditional sense. He seemed unable to erect.'

'His mom probably told him not to,' I said.

Susan frowned at me a little.

'And,' Rachel went on, looking into the glass half-full of bourbon, 'I would try not to talk about Julie and love-making because I knew how he would get. But if I didn't tell him, he would threaten me. "You are entirely under my control," he would say. "I can do anything to you I want to, so you better do what I say." And he was right. I was. I had to do what he said. It was kind of a paradigm of the situation of men and women – the situation which I have so long opposed and tried to change.'

'Not only Lawrence but his mother,' Susan said.

'Yes. She, too. The matriarch. Trying to prevent the world from changing and making what she had always been seem unimportant, or even worse, silly.'

'I wonder how conscious they were of that,' I said.

Susan shrugged.

Rachel said, 'Not conscious, I think. But subconscious. It was a kind of dramatization of the way they wanted the world to be.'

'Who took your clothes?' Susan said.

'The mother. I assume she wanted to demean me. She had Lawrence and the other one that worked for them strip me when they took me to that room.'

'I wonder if that might have been for Lawrence, too,' Susan said.

Rachel drank some more bourbon. She held some in her mouth while she looked at Susan. 'Perhaps. I hadn't thought of that. But perhaps she had some sense that he was not sexually ordinary. Maybe she thought the chance for a nice uncomplicated rape would help him along.' She finished the bourbon. I poured her some more without asking.

Susan said, 'You haven't said anything very much about how you felt about all this. You've told us what happened. But maybe it would be good to get some feelings out.'

'I don't know,' Rachel said. 'I have learned to keep my feelings under very strong control. Maybe not so different from himself here.' She nodded at me. 'I have had to, doing what I do. I'll write about the feelings. I write better than I speak. I do know that being a captive is a humiliating, a debasing experience. To be in someone else's hands. To be without control of yourself is terribly destructive of personality and terribly frightening and terribly . . . I don't know quite what I want to say. Terribly . . .'

'It ruins your self-respect,' Susan said.

'Yes,' Rachel said. 'You feel worthless. That's just right. You feel contemptible, almost as if you deserve the mistreatment. As if you're somehow at fault for being where you are.'

'And the sexual mistreatment merely intensifies the feeling, I should think.'

Rachel nodded. I opened another beer and drank most of it. I had little to offer in this conversation. I gestured the beer bottle at Susan. She shook her head.

Rachel turned and looked at me. She sipped some bourbon and held the glass toward me. 'And you,' she said. For the first time there was just a faint blurring in her speech. 'There are things I need to say to you. And they are not easy to say. While I lay back in your bathtub and tried to soak some of the filthiness of this all away, I thought about what I should say to you and how.' She looked at Susan. 'You are invited,' Rachel said to Susan, 'to help me with this. Maybe you have some sense of where my problems lie.'

Susan smiled. 'I'll pitch in as needed,' she said. 'I suspect you won't need me.'

'There are a lot of things that don't need to be said,' I said.

'But these things do,' Rachel said. 'I always knew that if someone found me, it would be you. Somehow whenever I fantasized being rescued, it was never the police, it was always you.'

'I had more reason,' I said.

'Yes, or you would see yourself as having more reason, because you would perceive yourself as responsible for me.'

I didn't say anything. The beer was gone. I got up and got another bottle and opened it and came back and sat down.

'And you did it the way I expected you would. You bashed in the door and shot two people and picked me up and took me away. Tarzan of the Apes,' she said.

'My brain is small. I have to compensate,' I said.

'No. Your brain is not small. If it were, you wouldn't have found me. And having found me, you probably had to do what you did. And it's what you could do. You couldn't remain passive when they wanted to eject me from the insurance company. Because it compromised your sense of maleness. I found that, and I do find that, unfortunate and limiting. But you couldn't let these people kidnap me. That, too, compromised your sense of maleness. So what I disapproved of, and do disapprove of, is responsible in this instance for my safety. Perhaps my life.'

She stopped. I didn't say anything. Susan was sitting with her heels caught over the bottom rung of the chair, her knees together, leaning forward, her chin on her left fist, looking at Rachel. Her interest in people was emanant. One could almost feel it.

Rachel drank some more bourbon. 'What I am trying to do,' she said, 'is to thank you. And to say it as genuinely as I can. I do thank you. I will remember as long as I live when you came into the room and got me, and I will always remember when you killed them, and I was glad, and you came and we put our arms around each other. And I will always remember that you cried.'

'What'll you charge not to tell?' I said. 'Makes a mess of my image.'

She went on without pausing. 'And I shall in a way always love you for those moments.' Her glass was empty. I filled it. 'But I am a lesbian and a feminist. You still embody much that I must continue to disparage.' She had trouble with *disparage*. 'I still disapprove of you.'

'Rachel,' I said, 'how could I respect anyone who didn't disapprove of me?'

She got up from the dinner table and walked softly and carefully around to my side and kissed me, holding my face in her hands. Then she turned and went to my bedroom and went to sleep on my bed.

We just got the table cleared when the cops came.

32

They were with us a long time: the chief of the Belmont force and two other Belmont cops; a man from the Middlesex DA's office; Cronin, the twerp from the Suffolk DA's office; Quirk and Belson.

Cronin wanted to roust Rachel out of bed, and I told him if he did, I would put him in the hospital. He told Quirk to arrest me, and Quirk told him if he couldn't be quiet, he'd have to wait in the car. Cronin's face turned the color of a Christmas poinsettia, and he started to say something, and Quirk looked at him for a minute, and he shut up.

We agreed that I could give them a statement and that they would wait until morning to take a statement from Rachel Wallace. It was late when they left. Cronin gave me a hard look and said he'd remember me. I suggested that his mind wasn't that good. Susan said she was very pleased to have met everyone and hoped they'd have a Merry Christmas. Quirk gave her hand a small squeeze, Belson blew smoke at me, and everyone left.

In the living room Susan and I sat on the couch. The fire was barely alive, a few coals glowing in the gray ash.

'We've spent a lot of time here the last few days,' Susan said.

'There are worse places,' I said.

'In fact,' Susan said, 'there aren't too many better.'

'We may spend a lot more time here, because she's in our bed.'

'The final sacrifice,' Susan said.

'We could think of ways to make the best of it,' I said.

'You had to kill two people today,' Susan said.

'Yeah.'

'Bother you?'

'Yeah.'

'Want to talk about it?'

'No.'

'Sometimes people need to get feelings out,' Susan said.

'Perhaps I could express them sexually,' I said.

'Well, since it's for therapy,' Susan said. 'But you'll have to be very quiet. We don't want to wake Rachel up.'

'With half a quart of bourbon in her?' I said.

'Well, it would be embarrassing.'

'Okay, you'll have to control your tendency to break out with cries of *atta boy*, then.'

'I'll do my best,' she said. 'Merry Christmas.'

Much later we heard Rachel cry out in her sleep, and I got off the couch and went in and sat on the bed beside her, and she took my hand and held it until nearly dawn.